EVERYTHING HAS HAPPENED

Also available by T. Greenwood

The Still Point
Such a Pretty Girl
Keeping Lucy
Rust & Stardust
The Golden Hour
Where I Lost Her
The Forever Bridge
Bodies of Water
Grace
The Glittering World
The Hungry Season
Two Rivers
Undressing the Moon
Nearer Than the Sky
Breathing Water

EVERYTHING HAS HAPPENED

A NOVEL

T. GREENWOOD

NEW YORK

Books should be disposed of and recycled according to local requirements.
All paper materials used are FSC compliant.

This is a work of fiction. All of the names, characters, organizations, places, and events portrayed in this novel are either products of the author's imagination or are used fictitiously. Any resemblance to real or actual events, locales, or persons, living or dead, is entirely coincidental.

Published in the United States by Crooked Lane Books, an imprint of The Quick Brown Fox & Company LLC.

Crooked Lane Books and its logo are trademarks of The Quick Brown Fox & Company LLC.

Library of Congress Catalog-in-Publication data available upon request.

ISBN (hardcover): 979-8-89242-528-5
ISBN (paperback): 979-8-89242-529-2
ISBN (ebook): 979-8-89242-530-8

Cover design by Meghan Deist

Printed in the United States.

www.crookedlanebooks.com

Crooked Lane Books
34 West 27th St., 10th Floor
New York, NY 10001

First Edition: April 2026

The authorized representative in the EU for product safety and compliance is eucomply OÜPärnu mnt 139b-14, 11317 Tallinn, Estonia, hello@eucompliancepartner.com, +33757690241

10 9 8 7 6 5 4 3 2 1

For my teachers,
and in especially fond remembrance
of Burt Porter (1937–2020).

July 2023

It feels violent, this storm. I'm restless as the rain batters the roof and windows, thunder rumbling, ominous. It's been raining for weeks: one deluge after another. Earlier this month, half the state awoke submerged in floodwaters. We're high on a hill, safe, but lately, I dream of the house becoming unmoored from its foundation, powerless to the angry waters as it's swept away.

My watch says it's only nine p.m., but I'm on my mother's schedule now: early to bed and up at the first glimmers of light. My daughter Ariel is awake, though; I can hear her moving around in her room across the hall. She made me a cup of tea before I went to bed: magnolia, lavender, and chamomile. She drinks it for her own insomnia and promised it would help me sleep, too, but I'm still wide awake.

It's dark in my childhood bedroom, a black hole where time has collapsed, past and present conflated. I am fifty-five, but in this room, I am also six, twelve, seventeen. I am lingering in this nebulous place when thunder cracks and lightning severs the sky.

I grip the covers, squeeze my eyes shut. Then a nerve-rattling ring sounds out, an ancient but familiar cry, and I bolt up, heart pounding.

The tip line?

When it rings again, I leap from my bed and rush down the stairs. Daisy, our old tabby, follows me through the kitchen and into the family room, where I lunge for the phone.

"Hello?"

But it's too late; on the other end is only momentary silence followed by the deep buzz of the dial tone, muted by the thunderous pounding of blood in my ears.

I reach to turn on the desk lamp but am met with nothing but a hollow click and darkness; the power must have gone out.

"Edie?" My mother's voice swims to me, shivery, from her room down the hall.

"It's okay, Mom," I insist, but my heart aches; this phone has never rung with good news.

Nearly forty years ago, after my little brother, Charlie, disappeared, my father installed this phone in the family room: black and heavy with a rotary dial, long cord curling umbilical-like between the handset and base. It's a dedicated line, with its own number: the one that was printed on the "Missing" posters and in the paper, broadcast on radio stations and TV news, painted on billboards all over New England. Billboards were not permitted in Vermont, where we lived; otherwise, they would have posted that number in every open field, at the edge of every road, along with Charlie's third-grade class picture: all big brown eyes and sweet, wild grin.

"Hope is the thing with feathers," Emily Dickinson once wrote. A bird whose song never ceased. In our house, hope was this black, featherless beast, whose clamorous warbling kept us going. It rang day and night back then: each call a possibility, a promise.

I saw him with a man over at the Cumberland Farms. Had a truck with Florida plates.

There's a family down the street that's got an extra kid now; little boy like yours. Said he's a cousin up from Boston for the summer but seems fishy to me.

I had a dream last night, about Charlie. I have visions, you see. And this one was of your boy. I sense he's in danger.

My father answered the phone in those days, though each time it sounded, my mother and I also convened in the family room, bleary-eyed soldiers roused by reveille. Together, we would watch my father's cheeks flush, his chest expand, as he inhaled whatever information was being offered. We heard the tremble in his voice as he patiently asked questions, reaching to the cup filled with the flat-sided carpenter pencils he brought home from work. He diligently took notes as my mother and I anxiously listened, both of us perched on the old plaid sofa, waiting for the call that would bring my brother back to us and undo the tangled knot our lives had become. But in the end, the yellow legal pad became little more than a documentation of so much heartache.

Sighting at the park.

Boy looking out the window of a trailer near the river.

A sneaker found in the woods. Same size as Charlie's?

Eventually, the phone stopped ringing. The world moved on. The posters came down, the radio announcements ended, the billboards were replaced with ads for motels or restaurants or other lost boys. Regardless, my mother refused to cancel the service, dutifully writing a check to the phone company month after month for decades.

For the last thirty-seven years, the phone has sat on the writing desk where my father paid bills and my mother wrote letters, and where I now keep my laptop. A hulking relic in our museum of sorrow.

Until tonight, it hasn't rung in years.

When my father passed away four years ago, Ariel went off to college, and I moved back home to take care of my mother, I had wanted to remove it: this memorial to all we'd lost. But my mother had only shaken her head. "What if someone calls?" she said. "Someone who's seen Charlie."

"Edie?" my mother cries out now. At least she knows who I am tonight. She's been calling me *Nora*, her sister's name, off and on for a month.

I press my hand against my pounding chest and walk down the dark hallway, poke my head into my parents' room; she is only a shadow sitting upright in her bed.

"Who was that?" Without her teeth in, the words tumble loose like marbles in her mouth.

"Nobody, Mom."

"Did they find Charlie?"

I pause, my throat thick. "Not yet, Mom. Let's just go back to sleep."

Though I know I won't be able to sleep now. I feel unnerved, anxious, my hands trembling as I cling to her doorknob.

Just a wrong number, I think. *A telemarketer. A prank.*

"Can you help me to the bathroom?" she asks.

"Of course," I say, releasing the knob. "But the power's out, so I need to use my phone for you to see, okay? Be careful."

I guide her into the pitch-black bathroom, set the glowing flashlight of my phone on the counter, and turn away as she pees, grateful she doesn't need my assistance for this yet. But she does need help returning to the high, queen-sized bed she shared with my father. I give her a boost before tucking her in, then kiss her cheek.

Lately, I've found myself offering her the sort of maternal tenderness I'd reserved for Ariel for the last twenty-two years. My mother is the one in the early days of dementia, but sometimes I also forget who *I* am, and where I am in time. I become my mother's mother in these moments, and I can't help but wonder if one day Ariel, too, will politely turn away as I lower myself to the toilet then kiss my own hollow cheek before tucking me in. An endless chain of mothering and daughtering.

Part of my disorientation comes from this house, which is a virtual time capsule. Little has changed between these walls since my parents purchased it as newlyweds. The modest cape, built in the early '60s, is—Ariel insists—*retro cool* now with its wall-to-wall carpeting, wood paneling, gold-flecked countertops, and pink-tiled bathroom. My mother worked full-time as a pediatric nurse for twenty years; redecorating was low on her list of priorities. And after Charlie disappeared, preservation became a willful choice.

"What if he comes home?" she always said. So, his room remains the same: an elegy in plaid wallpaper and olive-green shag. Poor Ariel has been forced to sleep among her lost boy-uncle's things since the pandemic sent her home from college three years ago. Of course, we'd thought her return was temporary; we never expected she'd stay.

"Goodnight, Mom," I say. "Sweet dreams."

"They need to look for the birthmark. Did you remind them about his birthmark? It's shaped like a heart, right where his heart is." She presses her hand to her breast. How, when most of her memories have faded, do the ones of Charlie remain so clear and fresh?

My friend Amanda, who teaches English with me at the high school, told me that her own mother believes that Amanda's father is still alive, and she doesn't have the heart to tell her otherwise. Whenever her mom asks where he is, she makes up an excuse for his absence: *Gone fishin'. Business trip. Atlantic City!* How wonderful it would be to create a world for my mother where my dad was still living. Where Charlie was simply playing outside.

But I promised myself nearly forty years ago that I would never lie to my mother again.

In the kitchen, Daisy weaves in and out of my legs, meowing. I fumble in the dark fridge for the open can of cat food and indulge her. The memory of the phone ringing is now just a distant ache in my chest, but as soon as Daisy and I start back up the stairs, it jangles again, and I dash back down the hall to the family room, trip on the threshold, and grab the receiver.

"*Hello*," I demand this time, breathless, the phone cold and heavy in my hand.

No dial tone. Nothing except a tinkling sound—wind chimes? I huff in frustration. Maybe it *is* just some kids making prank calls. My friend Lisa and I made those all the time in junior high.

"Hello?" a soft-spoken man asks at last. "Is this the Marshall residence?"

"It is," I say, heart thrumming.

"I'm sorry to call so late. I tried a few minutes ago, but I've been having trouble with cell service during the storm."

"Who is this?" I ask and sit down on the hard desk chair, sweat running cold down my sides. Reflexively, I reach for a pencil, eyes scanning futilely for my father's legal pad. Not a wrong number or prank. A *tip*.

"Is this Mrs. Marshall? Bonnie Marshall?"

"No, this is her daughter. Can I help you?"

"Oh," he says, sounding alarmed then somewhat wistful. "*Edie*? I didn't realize you were still . . . I haven't seen you since you used to come by The Farm with Trill." He pauses. "That summer. I'm sorry. This is Jericho."

Thunder rumbles followed by a flare of lightning, and for a moment, I feel myself splitting. A violent and certain cleaving.

Girl, woman. Past, present. Before, after. *Right, wrong.*

"Jericho?" I say, my voice also riven.

There's a long pause. "I'm calling because . . . well, I was clearing up some debris that was blocking the footbridge over the river earlier today. From the flood? Trees and such. I'm sorry I didn't call right away. This was the only number I could find for your family. I wasn't sure it would even work anymore. Anyway, I found something out there . . ."

I have dreamed of bones, imagined them unearthed. It would begin with this, I thought, when someone says, "I found something" when they really mean, "I found *him*."

"Oh my God, did you . . ." I ask. "Is it Charlie?"

"Oh. No! I'm so sorry. I didn't mean . . . but I do, um, I do think it belonged to him." His voice cracks. "It could be evidence."

My fingers ache from gripping the handset so tightly. I want to hang up. To pretend the phone never rang.

"Listen, Edie? Obviously, I'm worried that if I call the police, they're going to think . . ." He pauses again. "To be honest, I thought about throwing it away, never telling anybody. But keeping a secret like that when it might help your family would be wrong. I feel awful that I even considered it."

My knees weaken; it feels like an accusation. But I need to remind myself: he doesn't know what I did. No one does.

"What is it?" I ask. "What did you find?"

There is silence on the other end of the line. Then he says, "Would you be willing to come out to The Farm? I'd rather you see it in person."

I press the receiver against my ear: wind chimes tinkling.

"Maybe if you're free in the morning?" he asks.

"Nora?" my mother's voice calls from the other room.

I cover the mouthpiece. "It's okay, Mom! Go back to sleep." But when I return the phone to my ear, the line is dead.

"Mom?" Ariel stands in the doorway to the family room wearing an oversized UVM T-shirt, holding Daisy. "Is Grammy okay? I heard her yelling for Auntie Nora." She sits down with Daisy in her lap.

"She's fine. Just confused."

I hang up the phone and sit down next to her on the old sofa, the one where my father religiously watched the nightly news, where I used to lie under an afghan, eating Chicken & Stars soup when I was home sick, where Charlie used to sit with his coloring books and crayons on a TV tray in front of him. *Oh, Charlie.*

I press my hand to my mouth, as if to keep my thoughts from escaping.

"Are *you* okay, Mom?" Ariel asks. "Was that about Uncle Charlie?"

Hope is the thing with feathers.

My hope is that she can't see the tears forming in my eyes. Or feel the way my body has begun to quake. That she can't sense the scissure, the fissure, of my broken heart widening into the deepest crevasse.

My hope is that she didn't hear the tinkling windchimes singing, *Trillium*.

When I finally sleep, I dream of Trill. Of The Farm. Of the summer my brother disappeared. And so, in the morning, the phone call feels like a dream as well, Jericho Jenkins's voice only a visit from a ghost. Also, Daisy is meowing desperately at my door, starving, as if I didn't give her a half a can of cat food at nine o'clock last night. Perhaps it *was* just a dream.

But no. I remember the windchimes. Jericho's saying he found something he believes belonged to Charlie. Though I can't begin to count the number of times we received calls to the tip line, the caller convinced they'd found Charlie's baseball cap, his sneaker, his briefs. Every call renewed both our hope and our terror, and when the objects inevitably weren't Charlie's, we felt both crushing disappointment and relief. But why didn't Jericho just come out and tell me what it was? He could have snapped a photo with his cell phone, sent me a picture. Then again, maybe he didn't find anything at all; maybe he's trying to get me to come out there for some other reason. Maybe to ask the questions whose answers still feel like fresh bruises even after all these years. Is it possible he found out somehow?

I shudder, suddenly chilled. Maybe I should call him back, demand to know what he found, but how? The tip line doesn't have caller ID.

"Hold on, Daze," I say and stretch, my body a symphony of aches and pains. I need to run; I think best when my body is moving. Maybe if I go for a run, I can figure out what to do about Jericho.

The power is back on, and, miraculously, it's stopped raining. By my count, we haven't had a truly sunny day in nearly three weeks.

I let Daisy into the room then pull on a pair of running shorts and a T-shirt.

"Come on, Crazy-Daze," I say, and Daisy responds with another meow.

I walk down the hall, stopping at the closed door to Charlie's old room, Ariel's now. Back when she first came home, we set her up in this room, the bins and boxes from her dorm stacked in the corner, ready to be loaded into the car as soon as the lockdown ended. I cleared a space for her to work at Charlie's desk, putting most of his stuff in the basement, though my mother pleaded with me to leave things as they were. I didn't remind her that Charlie would be forty-six years old. If he were to walk through the front door now, I highly doubt he'd care that we moved his Muppets notebooks and Matchbox cars, his Legos and Lincoln Logs. He would be a grown man, not a boy anymore, but I'd held my tongue.

I must walk past this doorway a dozen times a day without much thought, but now, I touch my finger to the pencil marks tracking his growth on the woodwork: Charlie, Age 9, 4'5". My eyes fill, and I furiously blink away the tears. The last time I checked this wall was when I helped my mother make the flyer, the one she mimeographed at work, the one that hung in every storefront and on every lamppost and telephone pole in town for nearly a year:

MISSING (Below this, my brother's sweet, pixelated face.)

Name: Charles "Charlie" Marshall
Age: 9
Height: 4'5"
Weight: 65 lbs.
Hair Color: Dk Brown
Eye Color: Brown (glasses)
Wearing: red T-shirt, blue gym shorts with white piping, Superman Underoos, blue Nike sneakers, and a red canvas backpack (inside: one pair of wet swim trunks in a bread bag, Stretch Armstrong toy, Rubik's cube, and a small sketch pad)

Last seen: leaving Quimby Public Pool and Park on foot at 10:00 AM Friday, July 18, 1986.
Any information, please call: 555-4151

The tip line number.

Downstairs, I confirm that I did, indeed, feed Daisy last night—the empty can in the trash evidence.

I hear the shower running in my mother's bathroom, and I hope she's using the shower seat we got her after she fell last fall. Thankfully, she didn't hit her head, but she broke her wrist, which was enough to scare her into compliance. Most of the time.

She comes into the kitchen, looking remarkably bright-eyed and alert as I'm making a pot of coffee.

"Good morning," she says, and I feel the knot in my gut loosen. Maybe the clouds in her brain, like the ones outside, have cleared.

"Hey, Mom. It's so nice out this morning, I thought I'd go for a run," I say. "You okay for a little bit? I'll wake Ariel up before I go."

She waves her hand at me dismissively. "Don't wake her up. I'm fine. I'm just going to do the Wordle and listen to my podcast."

I bought my mother a tablet during the pandemic, thinking she might get on Facebook to connect with old and far-flung friends. But she wound up using it mostly for playing games and listening to true crime podcasts, a steady stream of stories of lost boys and murdered women. She seems to find a strange solace in the fact that there is so much injustice in the world; maybe it brings her comfort to know she isn't alone in her anguish.

"I wish someone would do one of these about Charlie," she keeps saying. "They didn't have all that DNA stuff back then. Everything has changed. They even found that boy in Minnesota." My mother had been consumed by that poor family's story—back when the little boy first disappeared in 1989, only three years after Charlie, and again in 2016 when his remains were found, and a local man was arrested. Recently, she's been obsessed with a podcast about the case, as if the answers to Charlie's disappearance could be found there.

"I heard the phone ring again last night," she says as she reaches with shaky hands for a coffee mug in the cupboard.

I hold my breath as I wait for further questions.

"Maybe someone has a new tip. Maybe someone has seen him," she says, as if she somehow knows that Jericho called. But then again, she has always seemed to know the things I thought were secret.

"Maybe, Mom," I say, and grab the creamer from the fridge for her. I pour a little bit into her cup, my hand trembling. "I'm sure if that's true they'll call back."

I can't tell her that Jericho called, or what he said. If it had been anyone else, there would be no hesitation. No question.

What if I don't go? Maybe he'd actually be relieved? He said himself that his first instinct was to keep quiet, but he felt compelled to help us. But what if I refuse his help? Tell him that after all this time, the wounds have healed?

No. There is nothing further from the truth.

My nerves feel ragged.

I search for my running shoes but can't find them. I've been running on the treadmill in our basement most days lately because of the rain; I must have left my shoes down there. I descend into the fusty, musty rec room my parents once thought would be a place for teenaged Charlie to gather with friends. Now, a forlorn ping-pong table sits dead center, with a couple cast-off chairs up against one wall. The bulky console TV that used to be in our family room rests in the corner. On the far side of the room is the treadmill and a stack of boxes.

At the bottom of the stairs, I click on the light and spy my shoes, but when I step onto the floor, I catch my breath. The carpet is completely saturated. *Crap.* I walk gingerly across the soggy floor; there must be three inches of water in here. I'll need to call someone to take care of this. As much as I hate to ask him for help, maybe Nathan can recommend somebody. Nathan and I grew up together; his family lived next door, and he was my first boyfriend.

He owns a contracting company and has been telling me we need to get the basement sealed for a while now.

I slog across the wet carpet to the stack of boxes. Thankfully, the ones on top are okay. But the boxes at the bottom of the pile are destroyed, the cardboard bottoms drenched. The first holds my father's work files, a box we should have discarded long ago. But as I rifle through the next one, my eyes well up. Inside is all the artwork Ariel made in elementary school; the construction paper collages and tempura paintings disintegrate in my hands. And then, as I move to the third box, I stifle a sob.

The cardboard flap is labeled in blurred Sharpie: *Charlie's.*

I open the lid, and inside, carefully folded, are his little T-shirts and blue jeans, his collection of *Choose Your Own Adventure* paperbacks, and his catcher's mitt. Everything sodden and filthy from the water. I pick up one of the T-shirts with a peeling decal of Papa Smurf and press it to my face, letting the tears come. It smells musty, rotten.

What could Jericho have possibly found? It's probably nothing. Just another bit of false hope. But as deeply as I do not want to, I know I should at least go and see.

Upstairs, my mother has moved into the family room with her iPad, so I pull on my running shoes, which are—thankfully—dry, and call Nathan, cradling the phone between my shoulder and my ear as I tie my shoes.

"Hey," I say. "I'm sorry to bug you on a Saturday."

"No worries," he says. "What's up?"

"We've got some flooding in the basement. It's bad."

"*Edie.*"

I ignore his scolding tone. "Would you have time to come by on Monday?"

"We shouldn't wait. Mold can start growing as quick as twenty-four hours after a flood. I'll swing by this morning, bring my Shop-Vac and some fans to help dry things out. What time is good?"

I pause. I should have waited to call him until after I saw Jericho.

"Mold is bad," he says. "Like really bad. You need to think about Ariel's asthma. About your mom's health, too."

I sigh. "I have an errand to run, but I can be back by noon. Could you come by then?"

"Is that Nathan?" my mother asks from the other room. Always with that Spidey-sense. Nothing gets past her, even now.

"Yes, Mom. He's coming by to clean up some water in the basement."

I remember my father's papers, Ariel's art. Charlie's things. Nathan is right: I should have been on top of this.

"Oh, good," my mother says. "Nathan is such a godsend."

She's always treated Nathan like a son. And after both of his parents were gone, I know she and my dad were like parents to him as well. He's also been super helpful to her since my dad passed.

I take a deep breath and look out the window, squint at the sun. It's nine-thirty; I have two and a half hours to get out to The Farm, talk to Jericho, and get back before Nathan comes.

Upstairs, I knock on Ariel's door and hear her grumble inside. I gently push the door open and am met with the heady smell of incense and weed. Of course, it's legal now, and she's of legal age to smoke it, and she swears it helps her with both her anxiety and insomnia. But I worry it's not helping with her motivation.

"Hey, Air," I say. "It finally stopped raining, so I'm gonna go for a run. You don't have to get up, but keep an ear out in case Grammy needs you."

She rolls over, squinting at the unexpected sunlight coming through the windows. Daisy yawns and stretches at the foot of her bed.

"Are you going to the library today?" I ask.

"Not until one thirty."

She works a few nights each week at Carmello's, the pizza place in town, but on the weekends, she volunteers at the library. My friend Effie is a librarian there, and her daughter Paige convinced Ariel to join her volunteering for the summer, reading to the kids for story hour and helping them check out books. Since the flood destroyed the children's room and archives last month, she's been helping repair the salvaged books on Sundays when the library is closed.

"Is Grammy doing better today?" she asks. "I was worried last night."

"She seems pretty good, but just in case. I'll be back by noon."

She sits up and rubs her eyes, and for a moment, she could be a little girl again. Black hair in two low pigtails. Cheeks flushed pink. I see Charlie in her big brown eyes.

In the kitchen, I grab a protein bar and put it in my pocket then go to the family room.

"I'll be back before Nathan comes," I say to my mother.

"Oh! Are you two going to a matinee?" she asks.

Nathan and I haven't seen a movie together since 1986.

"No, Mom. Remember? He's coming to check the basement."

"I know that," she snaps. "I was just kidding."

Despite the bright sun, the lawn is riddled with puddles. The zinnias and marigolds I planted this spring look forlorn. Next door, at Nathan's old house, lilies hang their heads. The Nichols haven't lived there for decades. The current owners are a young couple with four boys. The backyard, which I can see from my bedroom window, looks like the set of *American Gladiators* with a trampoline, zipline, elaborate monkey bars, and an above-ground pool. When Nathan was growing up, he and his brother Mickey only had a playset back there. The metal slide would get so hot in the sun I once got second-degree burns on the back of my legs.

As if this is any other day, I put my foot up on the porch railing to stretch my hamstrings and use the steps to loosen my tight Achilles'. Then, like every other day, I select my go-to playlist and set off.

My knees complain as I begin the descent from our neighborhood to the high school and onto the main road that, if I *were* simply going for my normal run, would loop me around town. People call it *Charlie's Loop* now, because it was the route he was taking when he vanished. My chest aches as I imagine Charlie, the sound of his little feet scuffing against the pavement, heavy backpack filled with treasures weighing him down.

Charlie. Charlie lives in my mind as a nine-year-old boy. Only once did I dream him into the future. I must have been in my thirties then, and in the dream, I was at a wedding. And suddenly, there he was. But instead of being the grass-stained boy with scabby knees I remembered, he was in his twenties. Doe-eyed still, but a man. "You grew up," I said to him. "How did you grow up?" But he didn't answer me. Instead, he lifted the glass of champagne he was holding as if in cheers, and I realized it was *his* wedding.

Sometimes I allow myself to imagine how different our lives would have been if Charlie hadn't disappeared, though it's a terrible game to play: an exercise in futility, torturous and pointless. Every bit of sadness in our lives is a direct offshoot of that single afternoon: my parents' marriage, which didn't break but certainly brittled; my own life, which became progressively smaller and smaller until I could barely remember who I once was, never mind who I once wanted to be; and Charlie. What sort of extraordinary things might he have done?

As the ground levels out, I quicken my pace and ignore the pain in my knees. At the bottom of the hill, I turn left, onto the loop, passing the school then running toward the covered bridge. The old bridge is rickety and narrow. Remarkably, there's only been one fatal accident here, about ten years ago when a car went over the edge. Ariel hates the bridge, and so did Charlie.

The sun is warm, and as I pass under the structure's wooden beams, I appreciate the delicious coolness of the dark enclosure. I look down as I run, watching the river rushing between the weathered floorboards. Fortunately, they withstood the latest floods.

The first notes of the Talking Heads' "Same as It Ever Was" begin to play—the playlist song that always starts as I emerge from the bridge. I check my pulse, close my eyes, and for a moment, I am in the front seat Trill's car, *Stop Making Sense* in the cassette deck. *Same as it ever was.*

When you never leave a place, the past and present are braided together, separate strands but intertwined. Every location has a memory associated with it, a hundred memories. Open fields become drive-in theaters. A vacant storefront is where your best friend worked, renting out videos and selling stale popcorn. A lonely road is where your brother vanished. This town breaks my heart every day.

Despite my resolve to go see Jericho, I still hesitate at the juncture beyond the bridge. If I were to turn right, I could simply continue clockwise on Charlie's Loop, through town, along the long rural stretch of road where Charlie disappeared, then back home. But if I turn left, I will find myself headed west on Route 42, which leads to Lost River Road. To Jericho.

He doesn't know, I remind myself. *Assure* myself.

It's only about a mile from the covered bridge to the turnoff. The river meandering alongside Route 42 is high, frothing as it rushes loudly over the rocky bed beneath. Fog hovers above the water. On the opposite side of the road are rolling fields, a palette of brilliant greens dotted with black-and-white Holsteins in the distance (*Ben & Jerry's cows*, Ariel calls them), groves of evergreens, the occasional farmhouse, and several trailers with toys in the yards and broken-down cars. It isn't raining, but it is humid; my lungs feel full.

The bent metal sign is nearly overtaken by a cedar tree. You could miss it, if you didn't know it was there. But I remember. How many times have I slowed at this exact spot, my heart swelling with the thrill of what turning here meant?

The road is narrow, rarely traveled. You don't take it unless you're going to The Farm, or up to the defunct Lost River Playhouse, an old summer stock theater owned by Ryan Flannigan, that actress from the '70s. Her daughter Sasha went to school with Ariel. It's a dead end. Turning onto it is a lot like entering the covered bridge, though the tunnel here is made of leaves rather than wooden beams. Treetops bow to each other overhead, obscuring the sky, filtering the sun, making lacy shadows across the ground.

On either side are black-eyed Susans and bright orange day lilies. It's a bit of a climb, the incline steady. I'm breathless by the time I get to the old purple mailbox that still reads in white painted script: "505 Lost River Road."

Next to the mailbox is a sign nailed to an oak, also hand-painted: PRIVATE DRIVE. KEEP OUT. A shiver runs through me. I know Jericho has kept to himself after everything that happened—remarkably I have only ever seen him around town once or twice in all these years—but signs like this are usually posted in response to some sort of trespass. Had someone come onto his property? And was it morbid curiosity or ill-intent that brought them here?

I check my smartwatch. I've stopped running, but my pulse is still racing. It isn't too late to turn around. But I'm an adult now, I remind myself, not that terrified teenaged girl I was the last time I was here, and so I take a deep breath, trying to still my heart, and make my way up the gravel drive.

The farmhouse is exactly as I remember it. I smile at the sight of two faded turquoise chairs on the sagging porch, at the silverware windchimes still hanging from the eaves. *Trillium.*

I climb the steps but wait a moment, again considering simply running back home, but then the gingham curtains in the window part, and a man peers at me through the glass, offers a small smile, and opens the door.

Jericho.

Jericho Jenkins. Person of interest in the disappearance of my little brother. The only suspect in all these years.

But also: my best friend Trill's brother.

January 1986

TRILLIUM POPPED UP in AP English that last week of January like her namesake flower: an early bloom amid the tiresome gray of another Vermont winter. The holidays were over, but the snow and bitter cold had just begun. With Christmas behind us, there was nothing to look forward to besides months of gray skies and frigid temperatures followed by mud and rain and black flies before summer arrived. She had felt like sunshine, like *hope*, the moment she walked into Mr. Howard's classroom that frigid Tuesday morning.

She was tall and thin, wearing a long, purple Indian print skirt with a pair of worn leather work boots underneath. She also wore a fuzzy Icelandic sweater, olive green with a snowflake-patterned yoke. Wavy, strawberry-blond hair fell halfway down her back.

Mr. Howard peered up over his reading glasses at the new girl and gestured with his chin to a seat front and center, the one right next to me, and gave us both a soft smile. I adored Mr. Howard, with his suspenders and pot belly, tweed jackets and classroom library, a curated collection shelved behind glass. He had a steno notebook, pages bisected by a pale pink line. On one side, you wrote your name. On the other, the borrowed book's title. Mine would often be the only name for pages and pages, my literary obsessions documented in my messy handwriting: *Edie Marshall | Sexton, Dickinson, Plath.* I loved the reverence Mr. Howard had for language, the way he cradled the books he read aloud to us. I loved the way he walked between the rows of desks and gently knocked his knuckles on the ones where boys dozed on folded arms, without pausing his recitations of Whitman or Williams, Bishop or Rich.

I wanted to be a poet back then. I didn't know much at seventeen, but I did know this. I collected words, studied rhythms, and I loved the luminous way it felt when I pressed my pencil against the soft flesh of my notebook. I cherished the notes Mr. Howard scribbled in the margins of the poems I offered him like tender slices of my own heart.

By January of my senior year, I had already been awarded a scholarship to the state college in my hometown, but Mr. Howard had encouraged me in the eleventh hour to apply to at least one dream school. "Take a chance, Edie," he'd said. "Fortune favors the bold!" And so, I had chosen Smith College, the alma mater of my favorite poet, Sylvia Plath. I'd read each of her poems a thousand times and felt a kinship with her I couldn't quite articulate. Everyone had heard about her tragic demise, but that was only part of her story. I'd read *The Bell Jar*, but I had also devoured her journals and letters, and I identified with the girl in those pages: her ambition and yearning. Her hunger. I was so hungry back then: a five-foot-tall bundle of raw *want*, though I didn't know yet exactly what it was that I wanted, only that whatever it was likely wasn't to be found in Quimby, Vermont.

My parents had no idea I'd applied to Smith. I'd even paid the application fee myself. The plan had always been that I would go to State, live at home to save money, and get my teaching degree or become a nurse like my mom. A private girls' college in

Massachusetts was nothing they would have ever envisioned for me, though I was near the top of my class.

Still, I'd studied the brochure I got from Mrs. Fulwiler, the guidance counselor. I bookmarked Smith in my copy of *The College Handbook*, memorizing the stats as if they were a magic formula for happiness. But mostly, I dreamed myself onto the campus where Sylvia had studied and written. I envisioned walking through the ornate, iron Grécourt Gates onto campus. I imagined reading under one of the lovely heritage trees, autumn leaves scattered around me. I pictured myself, a *Smithie*, skating across the frozen surface of Paradise Pond in the winter, cheeks flushed pink.

It was just a dream, of course; my parents would never let me go. Couldn't afford to let me go. But after I sent the application off, it felt like maybe my future wasn't *entirely* set in stone. Until I heard back from Smith, anyway. And it was in this liminal place that Trillium Jenkins found me that January morning and changed everything.

"Hi," she said. "I'm Trill." She thrust her hand into the air between us, the stack of silver bracelets on her wrists making a kind of music as I awkwardly shook it. "Trilli*um*."

"I'm Edie," I said. Ed*ith*, I thought.

"I know who you are," Trill said, shrugging her backpack off her shoulders. It landed with a thud on the linoleum floor. She pulled off her sweater, and her hair was staticky, crackling. "I remember you from sixth grade."

I searched my memory for her face, which—now that I thought about it—did seem remotely familiar, like an actress you might recognize on TV but not remember where from. Pretty. Green eyes. Freckles. But the *name*. Shouldn't I remember a name as unusual as Trillium?

"I used to live out at The Farm," she said. "I've been in New York with my dad, but he got a job overseas, so I came back to live with my mom and my brother."

The Farm was a commune, or a former one anyway, an old dairy farm a bunch of New York hippies bought at a foreclosure auction back in the '60s. "Four generations of Whittakers worked that land. And just like *that*," my mother said, snapping her fingers, "sold out from under them to the highest bidder." She had been friends with the Whittaker girls in high school, had practically grown up there herself, riding horses and milking cows alongside them. And not only were the new residents interlopers but *activists*, too, and their antiwar sentiments didn't go over well with a small town that had lost six of its young men in the Vietnam War. My own dad had served in the navy, doing mostly humanitarian work in Vietnam. My mother called the men on The Farm "draft dodgers," but my father—despite having lost his best friend in the war—was more forgiving. "Bonnie, they just want peace. What's so terrible about that?"

I knew a few kids who had grown up on The Farm, kids—like Trill—who were homeschooled until they joined us at junior high. They'd seemed like feral creatures to me: some wild and unruly, always in trouble, while others were cripplingly shy. They stuck together, never mingling with us townie kids. And by the '80s, most of The Farm families had given up on their utopian dreams and moved back to the cities they came from. The only people who still lived out at The Farm anymore were, as far as I knew, the elementary school art teacher, Mr. Jenkins, and his mother, Phyllis, who sold herbal remedies and bread at the farmers' market.

Jenkins. Trillium *Jenkins*. Now I remembered! Everyone had called her *T.J.* in sixth grade, and she was only at our school for a year before she moved away. I flashed on a memory of junior high recess, the races held in the field behind the playground. I remembered running until my legs were burning, my sneakers covered in dust, but always coming in behind that one girl that nobody in sixth grade could outrun. The one who kicked off her shoes and ran barefoot.

"I remember!" I said. "No shoes! You were wicked fast."

Trill reached down to unzip her bag, but instead of a spiral notebook or colorful Trapper Keeper, she pulled out a worn leather-covered notebook tied shut with a suede cord. A delicate silver pen.

I glanced at my own ratty notebook and Number 2 pencil, pocked with teeth marks.

"Do you still run?" I asked. "Like cross-country? Or track?"

"We didn't have a team at my old school," she said, sweeping her hair up and twisting it into a knot on her head, using the silver pen to secure it. "But I might do tryouts. I could probably run the hundred-yard dash. I'm fast but have *zero* endurance."

I was the opposite. I wasn't very fast, but I could run forever.

"You should totally go out for track," I said. "We need sprinters."

"Deal," she said and outstretched her hand again. Her nails were cut straight across, with slivers of moon at the tips, but her fingers were long, each with at least one silver ring. Some with large colored stones, one a swirly mood ring.

I shook her hand again, aware of my own nails, bitten to the quick, cuticles ragged and embarrassing. When she let go, I shoved both my hands under my thighs.

Trill smelled herbal, earthy. Whenever she moved, that spiced wood scent wafted over to me. Mr. Howard's classroom usually smelled of dust, old books, and the faint scent of his pipe tobacco. The new combo was heady.

Mr. Howard was at the front of the class, his *ahem* a gentle call for our attention.

"My plan was to walk you through Frost's 'Out, Out—,' today," he said. I'd been looking forward to his guidance in navigating the grisly poem about a boy who dies after a farming accident. "But Principal Gilman has suggested we all watch the launch instead."

The space shuttle was being sent up so they could study Halley's Comet. It was a big deal because there was a female teacher on the crew. *Two* women aboard.

Mr. Howard went to retrieve the AV cart with the TV, and rolled it to the front of the room, trying to locate the power cord. He never showed movies in class, except for Olivier's *Hamlet,* and only then, he said, because plays were meant to be watched, not read.

"Oh my God, I wish I could go into space," Trill said. "Can you imagine?"

"Totally," I said, though while I liked to think I'd jump at such a chance, space terrified me. Charlie was obsessed with black holes. He'd taken a half dozen books about them out of the library, gleefully rattling off facts at supper, but the concept of bottomless space-pits filled me with dread. Infinity was petrifying.

"So, apologies, no Frost today," Mr. Howard said as he turned the TV on and clicked around until he found the station that would be airing the launch.

We paid attention as the crew boarded but chatted during the lengthy commentary and commercials. When it was time for liftoff, we all silently, respectfully, watched the *Challenger* shoot up into the air. A few people clapped weakly. Mark Rainier, sitting to my left, yawned. But Trill and I both studied the rocket, rapt, as it lifted off, exhaust billowing behind it. I thought about those people inside, on a trajectory into the great abyss.

People had started talking again, but when a ball of fire burst beneath the rocket and the smoky trail split in two like two antennae on the body of a long skinny bug, we all gawked at the screen. After several terrible, uncertain moments, the announcer said, "Flight controllers here are looking into the situation . . . obviously, a major malfunction." But this pronouncement was followed by nothing but silence as the disaster unfolded. Finally, he said, "We have a report from the flight dynamics officer that the vehicle has exploded."

"Holy shit," Mark Rainier said, alert now.

Mr. Howard rushed to click the TV off then stood at the front of the class. His face was red, and he was gripping the edge of his desk. "Okay, everybody, this is clearly not what we planned for today. I think it's best if you watch this on the news with your parents this evening." His face slowly turned from crimson to ashen; his hands shook as he rearranged his papers.

"I'm sorry," he said. "I'm sorry you all had to see that. Why don't we skip 'Out Out—' today and take a peek at 'Birches' instead."

I felt Trill's hand in mine for the third time that morning then. But now, she was gripping it as though she and I were on that rocket instead of witnessing it on an ancient RCA, and for a brief, horrible moment, I felt—inexplicably—like I'd gotten a glimpse into my future.

After the last bell, Nathan was waiting for me by my locker, holding a battered paperback of *On the Road* in one hand, the other shoved into his pocket. He wasn't a big reader, but he'd said he wanted to start reading more, and so I'd recommended Kerouac. Boys our age always loved Kerouac.

"Hey," he said, cheeks dimpling, and I leaned into him, his arm encircling my neck the same way the football players embraced their cheerleader girlfriends, though we were neither. But after only a moment, I pulled away, reaching for the lock on my locker. I'd felt out of sorts all day after the explosion.

"Are you running the bleachers today?" he asked.

"Yeah."

"Bummer," he said. "My tapes finally came." I'd helped him pick out the half dozen cassettes from the Columbia House flier, selecting music we didn't get on the local radio station. "I thought we could hang out in my room and listen to music."

"Hanging out" was Nathan-speak for *making* out. When we first started dating, "hanging out" with Nathan was fun. He was cute and sweet, but lately instead of feeling butterflies, I'd been feeling kind of bored. I'd read that when Sylvia Plath first met her future husband, Ted Hughes, she'd been so overwhelmed with passion, she'd bitten his cheek. Drew blood! I wanted *that* kind of love, the kind that made you mad with it. Of course, to be fair to Nathan, it's hard to get too crazy over someone you've known your whole life.

Nathan and I had known each other since we were born; our mothers were best friends, and they'd been pregnant with us at the same time. Mr. Nichols's contracting company subcontracted my father, who was a carpenter. Our little brothers were joined at the hip too. We'd been teased about being *boyfriend and girlfriend* since we were five, but we didn't start dating until sophomore year. Nathan was like an old pair of slippers. Comfy and familiar. Plus, he was a nice guy—a good Catholic boy, a literal altar boy at our church—and so he never went too far. He was waiting for marriage; he didn't have to say that he meant marriage *to me.*

Despite my daydreams about Smith, I knew I would most likely be going to State. Nathan would also stay in Quimby, and in June he'd start working full-time for his dad. He planned to live at home until he and his father finished the house they were building up near Lake Gormlaith. They owned twenty acres and would first build a house for him and eventually one for his younger brother, Mickey. A family compound. When their dad retired, the boys would take over the business: *Nichols Contracting* becoming *Nichols & Sons.* Nathan's future was clear: he wanted to run his dad's business, get married, and have a family. I should have considered myself lucky; so many girls would have. But how could you know this was what you really wanted if you hadn't experienced anything else? Neither of us had ever lived anywhere but here in Quimby, population holding pretty steady at about 3,500 people. His dreams were so modest, so humble, it almost made me feel bad for wanting more.

I hadn't told him I'd applied to Smith. It would hurt him to know I'd gone behind his back. And what was the point unless they said yes, anyway?

"You okay?" he asked, brow furrowed. He was a full head taller than me, and I had to look up unless I wanted to stare at his knobby Adam's apple. "Maybe you can come over for supper tonight. Mom's making Shake-n-Bake. I'm sure she can make an extra drumstick."

"Sorry, I'm just feeling kind of weird about the whole *Challenger* thing," I said.

"Oh yeah, me too. It's a major bummer."

I unlocked my locker, 10-27-32 (Sylvia's birthday), offloaded the books I didn't need, and shut it again. The halls were crowded.

Nathan's cousin Jake came up behind him and smacked the back of his head. "Hey dude," Jake said.

"*Dude*," Nathan protested, rubbing the back of his skull.

"Oh, hey, *Dolly*," Jake said to my chest. He had been calling me *Dolly Parton* since fifth grade when my boobs first arrived.

At this, Nathan's face reddened, and he huffed as Jake took off down the hall.

"Sorry he's such a jerk," he said as if it was his fault that Jake was so rude.

"It's fine," I said. "I'll call you later, okay?"

"Yeah. Have a good run," he said.

January in Vermont is a prison for anyone who needs to move. It's too cold to exercise outside, the air like blades, slicing at your lungs. The ground is inhospitable as well; if it isn't a frozen slab, it's slushy and wet. Quimby High had one treadmill, which—in January—was usually occupied by one of the baseball players gearing up for the spring season. This left no other option but to run the bleachers in the gymnasium. Up and down, the metal rattling my teeth and jarring my knees.

I kept my running gear in the girls' locker room, which was cold and empty today. The boys' and girls' basketball teams both had away games. I pulled off my sweater, wriggled out of my jeans, and leaned into my locker to search for my running shorts and T-shirt.

"False advertising," a voice said.

I whipped around, clutching my T-shirt to my nearly naked torso.

Trillium was sitting on the bench, having again bloomed out of thin air.

"What?" I asked.

"It's Tuesday," she said, motioning to me. "Your underpants say Wednesday."

Mortified, I twisted around to confirm. Indeed, sprawled across my butt was *Wednesday* alongside a peeling strawberry decal. I'd had these panties since eighth grade.

"I like to keep people on their toes," I volleyed.

"Touché," she said. "What are you doing?"

"Running the bleachers."

"Can I join you?"

"Okay." Running was an activity I usually did alone. The only "team" sports I participated in were those where I didn't really have to answer to anyone but myself.

"I don't have any running clothes," she said. "Do you have extras?"

"Sorry," I said. "Maybe check the Lost and Found?"

"It's cool," she said, pulling off her sweater and bending down to unlace her boots.

She reminded me, in demeanor and dress anyway, of the weird girl in *The Breakfast Club*. Nathan and I had gone to see it three times last year. Nathan was more of the nerdy, nice guy type, but after we saw the movie, he'd found a Judd Nelson-style denim jacket at a yard sale and wore it until it got too cold and he had to swap it out for his old blue parka.

"What about shoes?" I asked, pointing to her mismatched wool socks.

"I'm still faster barefoot." She peeled off her socks, stuffing them into her boots.

Trill took the visitors' bleachers overlooking the basketball court, while I claimed the home side. Up and down, we pounded the steps. After several minutes, the cacophonous clamor gave way to a certain percussive rhythm, though I couldn't tell if she was matching my strides, or if I was matching hers. All I knew was that I was pushing myself harder than I would have had I been alone. Sweat stung my eyes, and my curly hair frizzed around my face.

As I was descending the bleachers for the fourth or fifth time, I glanced across the basketball court, meeting eyes with Trill, who had hiked her skirt up and tied it into a knot at her hip. Her hair was in a high ponytail. Barefoot. She looked ridiculous, and I found myself smiling.

We reconvened in the locker room, both our faces flushed with heat.

"I stepped in something," she said, lifting her foot to examine the bottom.

I cringed. I was intimately familiar with the bleachers and their various delights: spilled soda, gum, and once a glob of chewing tobacco I'd barely managed to sidestep.

"I think it's Pop Rocks," she said, mystified but also weirdly delighted. "Or maybe Nerds?" She stretched her foot out to me, and embedded in the dirty ball of her foot were hot-pink granules. "I need a shower," she said, sniffing her underarm. "Do you have a towel?"

I reached into my locker for the beach towel I kept in there. It was one of Charlie's: Garfield sitting on a beach chair under a palm tree, *Let's Party* written across the top.

"Thanks," she said, before yanking down her skirt and panties (ones without any day of the week on them, I noted), and pulling off her tank top. She wasn't wearing a bra, because—unlike me—she didn't need one. When she turned to take the towel from me, I looked away, embarrassed. I never understood how some girls could be so cavalier about changing in front of each other. I'd always been so self-conscious. Even as a little kid, I'd refused to change unless the door was locked. My breasts were large, like my mother's. When they first showed up, my mom had special ordered JogBras for sports, but big breasts got in the way of more than my athletics, so I wore that contraption under my regular clothes as well. To boys, especially boys like Jake, I went from being invisible to an oddity to be gawked at. Luckily, after I started dating Nathan, most guys left me alone, but the shame I felt lingered. On the other side of puberty, I still couldn't imagine casually disrobing in front of anyone. My own mother hadn't seen my naked body since I was five or six. And while Nathan and I had fooled around, a *lot*, he'd never seen me without my JogBra.

I quickly changed back into my school clothes while Trill was occupied in the shower. When she emerged, using the Garfield towel to dry off then bending over, naked, to wrap her wet hair in a turban with it, I studied my Pumas.

"Do you need a ride home?" she asked.

"You have a car? I thought people in New York didn't know how to drive."

"My brother taught me at The Farm a couple summers ago," she said.

I had also gotten my license at sixteen, but our family had one vehicle, a woody station wagon, which my parents shared. Each morning, my dad dropped my mom off at the pediatrician's office where she worked then picked her up at five. I was only allowed to use the car on the weekends and then only when neither of my parents had errands to run. So basically never. During the week, my mom relied on Nathan's mom to shuttle Charlie around. Nathan's little brother, Mickey, was a year older than Charlie, but he had leukemia when he was in first grade, so he'd had to repeat. Luckily, he was in remission now, and he and Charlie were in the same class. But the elementary school started and ended earlier than the high school, so Nathan gave me a ride in the morning in his dad's beat-up old work truck. After school and extracurriculars, I walked the half mile home, which was fine in the fall and spring, but winter was a different story.

"I would totally love a ride," I said.

Trill's car was a rust-dappled, yellow Chevy Vega. The front seats were covered with scratchy motheaten Patagonia blankets, and the rearview mirror was necklaced with a swinging heart-shaped prism, which cast rainbows across Trill's face and hands as she gripped the wheel. The car had that same herby scent I'd noticed in class.

"Her name is Nico," she said, lovingly patting the dash. "After the singer. The Velvet Underground?"

I didn't tell her I'd never heard of that band.

She drove so fast that my stomach bottomed out as we flew over the final hill before our neighborhood. I couldn't help but think about the passengers in the *Challenger*. How they'd gotten into that rocket thinking they were about to make history of one kind only to make history of another. Did they know they were going to die? Or did it take them by surprise?

"Thanks," I said as I got out and hoisted my backpack onto my shoulders.

"Anytime!" Trill said, smiling. "Hey! You should come out to The Farm sometime!"

"That would be awesome," I said, though I wondered how my mother would feel about that, and waved as she backed out of our driveway, the engine backfiring when she peeled out onto the road.

It was four thirty already. Inside, I dialed the Nicholses' number and asked Mrs. Nichols to send Charlie home. Less than a minute later, the door flew open, and Charlie was in the mudroom handing me the mail he'd grabbed on his way in, all the while babbling about his day. I helped him offload his red backpack with the *Ninja Turtles* patch I'd sewn on for him, then his coat and boots, as he told me about a game of dodgeball at recess, someone getting sent home for having lice, Melanie Belville barfing up the Fig Newtons they'd had for snack.

"It got all over Jessica Harvey's desk! It was *brown*."

Charlie was eight but small for his age, skinny and concave chested. He had a tangle of dark curly hair like mine and the same wide brown eyes, only he had thick black eyelashes like Bambi. He'd finally lost his front teeth, and the scalloped edges of the new ones poked out from the pink flesh of his gums.

My mother had set out what I'd need to make American Chop Suey, including the sauce-splattered, handwritten recipe card, though I'd made it a hundred times before.

"Can I help?" Charlie asked.

Charlie's "help" made everything take twice as long, but he liked to cook, so I had him fill the pot with water and let him light the burner. I told him to tell me the second it started to boil, and as he watched the pot, I chopped up green peppers and onions, browned the ground beef, and smacked the bottom of the Ragu to loosen the lid. I let Charlie dump the box of elbow macaroni into the boiling water and had him keep an eye on that as well. As expected, his patience quickly ran out, and he asked if he could go watch TV instead.

"Sounds good," I said. "But I might need you, so keep an ear out."

I heard the TV come on, and his clicking through the three channels we were able to pick up without cable. At five on a Tuesday night, this meant news, news, or news.

I was dumping the macaroni into our biggest stainless-steel bowl, the one we used for popcorn and (once a year or so) for the stomach flu, when I remembered the *Challenger* explosion. I was pretty sure Charlie hadn't heard about the disaster at school. Otherwise, it would have been all he could talk about.

"Hey!" I hollered. "Come help me set the table."

Charlie's face was pale when he came into the kitchen.

"You okay?" I asked.

He was trying not to cry. "Did they *know*?"

"Did they know what?" I asked, though I knew exactly what he meant.

"Did they know they were going to die?"

I shook my head. The tragedy, once again, felt oddly and deeply personal.

"I don't think so," I said, mustering a certainty I didn't have.

"Because I wouldn't want to know," he said, his eyes glossy. "If I was about to die."

I thought about those poor people, stomachs flip-flopping as they hurtled into the sky. I thought about flying up the hill with Trill and truly hoped they'd only felt the delicious expectation of it all.

March 1986

In March, the Soviets were the ones who managed to fly close enough to Halley's Comet to take photos, though the image captured was just a white blur against black. It made my heart ache that the *Challenger* passengers had given their lives for not much more than a cosmic smudge. By March, NASA had also found the remains of those aboard the *Challenger*. We'd all been shaken by the disaster, but both the novelty and the horror of it had worn off by then, like the snow that had blanketed the football field at school for months that was beginning to melt under the spring sun.

"That looks like prison food," Trill said, looking at my tray, as I dumped my half-eaten lunch in the cafeteria trash bin right as the bell rang.

"Fitting," I said. Though even as I complained, Trill's arrival in Quimby had changed everything. I was still restless, yes, but now I had a friend to be restless with. We had almost all our classes together, and lunch period too. After school, when I wasn't with Nathan, we ran the bleachers, prepping for track tryouts.

We hung out every day, but she hadn't asked me to come out to The Farm again, and as curious as I was to see where she lived, I was glad not to have to try to explain that to my mother. I hadn't even told her about my new friend yet.

"You should just pack a lunch," Trill said. She brought veggie and cheese sandwiches made on thickly sliced homemade bread. Blood oranges and fruit leather. I'd love to have lunches like that, but all we had at home was Wonder Bread and bologna. Foil-wrapped Ding Dongs and Devil Dogs. My mother also firmly believed that a "hot lunch" was inherently better for you than a "cold lunch," regardless of what that lunch was.

"Tryouts are at two thirty, right?" Trill asked.

"Yep," I said. "Did you get some cleats, or are you going full Zola Budd?"

"Zola Budd is a *goddess*," she said and clomped down the hall toward her French class.

I was so excited for track to start. I missed running outside, and it would keep me occupied after school. Lately, the basketball teams had been using the gym most afternoons, so I'd had no excuses to offer Nathan when he wanted to hang out. While our brothers played downstairs, Nathan got handsy with me in his room. He felt even needier that winter, as though he somehow knew I was pulling away.

"I love you so much," he'd say, kissing my neck, rough fingertips climbing up under my sweater. "You too," I said. But I didn't really love him. Not in the way he wanted me to, anyway. He left me notes, shoved into the vents of my locker. *Hi cutie! Thinking of you. Love you, Nathan.* These messages made me feel like the worst, because while Nathan was thinking of me, all I could think about lately was Smith.

Mr. Howard had told me that if I went to Smith, I'd be allowed to study at any of the schools in the Five College Consortium, which meant that being accepted to Smith was really like being accepted to five different amazing colleges. Some afternoons, I sat in the guidance office and pored over the course offerings like menu items at a fancy restaurant: *American Women Poets* at Smith or the *Joyce Seminar* at Mount Holyoke. A *Poetry Writing Workshop* at Hampshire or the *Harlem Renaissance Poets* at Amherst. The course offerings at State couldn't compare. When I looked at State's meager selection, my heart sank.

I was supposed to hear any day now; acceptance letters went out in late March. Despite my slim chances, I was a bundle of raw nerves as I waited for the letter. It might have been because of this that my skin felt prickly each time Nathan's fingers crept under my shirt, playing with the band of my JogBra. When it was too much, I'd pull away, citing cramps. Fortunately, Nathan was clueless about cycles and period durations.

Then on the day of track tryouts, I woke up (of course) with the worst cramps I'd ever had. I took an 800 mg ibuprofen leftover from getting my wisdom teeth removed over the holidays, but by last period, study hall with Mr. Howard, I was in agony again.

I sat in the front row with my friends Effie and Tess. We were Mr. Howard's groupies, his pets, all of us avid readers and aspiring writers. During study hall, we usually worked on his assignments. Today he'd asked us to pick a poem about spring to analyze.

"Have you chosen your poem?" he asked me.

"Yes! 'Prologue to Spring,'" I said.

"Ms. Plath, of course," he said.

I had selected this poem because it captured exactly how I felt lately. Trapped. Imprisoned. Waiting! Sylvia always had the words I needed.

"Speaking of Sylvia, have we heard from Smith yet?"

"You'll be the first to know," I promised, which was probably true. If I somehow managed to get in, I'd need some time to formulate how to break this news to my parents, as well as do some research about financial aid. Though I knew it was more than money that would make Smith seem nonsensical to them. My parents both grew up in Quimby. My dad had traveled when he was in the navy, but my mom had gone to school here and had been at the same job for the past two decades. I knew they wouldn't understand my urgent longing to leave a place that had always been my home. But just because a place is your home doesn't mean you are bound to it forever. Why couldn't I make a *new* home in Northampton, Massachusetts? What about England? What about *Greece*?

By the time study hall ended, I was doubled over in pain. Tryouts were going to be a nightmare. I would just have to power through. I popped my last ibuprofen and hoped for the best.

Trill was, as I remembered, *wicked fast.* Her stride had to be twice the length of mine. She'd definitely make varsity.

"You should do hurdles," I said. "You're like a freaking giraffe."

Sweaty and exhausted after only an hour of timed laps and sprints, a few of us headed to the pole vault pit, the gigantic square cushion where the pole vaulters landed. It was soft and the vinyl cover warm from the sun. We lay down on our backs and squinted up at the sky.

"This reminds me of a poem Sylvia wrote about Gulliver."

"That giant guy?" Trill asked and rolled over on her side to face me, but I kept staring at the diaphanous clouds, the rare bluebird sky, reciting the poem that had always spoken to me. Poor Gulliver tied down, while the clouds above him are free. No strings. *All cool, all blue.*

I could feel the heat from the vinyl burning the backs of my arms and neck. The air was muggy, the sun bright. Happiness radiated through me.

"*All cool, all blue,*" she repeated dreamily, then sat up. "I'm roasting. Let's go for a drive."

"That dude is such a creeper," Trill said as we drove past the football field.

The red van was parked in the lot shared by the high school and the elementary school; it was often parked there when school got out, though I'd seen it on the roads, too, tinted windows and missing hubcaps. I'd assumed it belonged to a local. Probably one of the guys in my class. The people who did have cars at school had beaters, and this was a beater.

"I bet he was jacking off to us at tryouts," she said.

"Ew."

"There was a guy on the bus I took to school back in the city who did that. We called him Chester the Molester."

"Oh my God," I said.

I knew guys did this. Obviously. Because Nathan and I weren't having sex, I was pretty sure he must do it as well. But I didn't like to think about it. I certainly didn't like to think that some weird guy was doing it while he watched us at track practice.

Windows down, we pulled out onto the road. It was only three thirty. Charlie would be with Mickey at Nathan's house until I got there. My mother had bought a Stouffer's lasagna, Charlie's favorite, and put it in the fridge to defrost that morning. As long as I was home in an hour, it would have time to cook before my parents got home.

A wave of pain rolled through my lower belly, and I leaned back, moaning. I had no more ibuprofen.

"What's the matter?" she asked.

"Wicked cramps," I said as we drove past the field where Jake and a couple other guys had stuck around and were lobbing javelins and hurling discuses.

"Well, you're in luck," she said. "Because my mom makes a special tea for that. It's freaking magic," she said as we slipped into the covered bridge's cool, dark shadows. "That cool?"

I hesitated. My mother would be livid if she knew I was going to The Farm. She was also a nurse; she'd balk at the idea of treating pain with anything that didn't come from a pharmacy.

Trill's eyebrow was raised, expectant.

"Yeah," I said and gave a stupid thumbs-up. "All cool, all blue."

After turning onto Lost River Road, Trill drove about a quarter mile then stopped the car next to a bright purple mailbox with daisies painted on it, rolled down the window and reached over to open the lid. She pulled out a handful of mail, which she sifted through quickly before tossing it into the back seat.

"Anything?" I asked

She shook her head. "This is torture."

She was also waiting to hear from colleges, though she'd cast a wider net: The New School, Hampshire, and Sarah Lawrence on the East Coast. UC Santa Cruz, Evergreen, and Humboldt out west. Bennington and Goddard in Vermont. She'd been accepted at Humboldt and rejected by Sarah Lawrence but was waiting on the rest.

We drove up a long drive, gravel crushing under Nico's tires. The Talking Heads tape she'd been playing had come to its end, but she didn't flip it over.

While I knew about The Farm, I'd never been out here. When I was little, my mom would take me with her to the weekly farmers' market, but she refused to patronize The Farm's booth. The women from the commune had seemed like exotic creatures to me: silky hair and ruddy cheeks, wearing crocheted halter tops and bell bottoms. There was one who always let me choose a strawberry from the pints that brimmed with wild red fruit. "Go ahead. Have two, Sunshine," she'd say, winking.

"Say *thank you*," my mother would nudge bitterly. My mother, like many locals, felt vaguely threatened by these "flatlanders" who came to Vermont, settling into our town like unwelcome houseguests. My parents were both fourth-generation Vermonters; they had little patience for these "back to the land" kids playing at being farmers. But their strawberries were so much better than the pale, plump ones we got at the grocery store, somehow both sweet and tart. I'd hold the strawberry under my tongue, savoring it, as my mother wandered among the other farmstands.

I remembered Trill's mother, Phyllis, as well. She made tinctures and teas, herbal remedies. She had wild black hair and a sharp nose, older than the other women who worked the stand. Her appearance called to mind the Wicked Witch from *The Wizard of Oz*, though she was smiling and friendly.

"Will your mom be home?" I asked Trill now.

I didn't know many people whose mothers were home during the day. Most of my friends' moms worked. Even Nathan's mom worked part-time at the bank. Most of us in Quimby were latchkey kids, nobody waiting at home for us the way mothers on TV were.

"She's probably out foraging. Fiddlehead season," she said. "We might see her later."

"So, this must be a lot different from New York," I said as we parked in front of an old farmhouse with a large barn behind it.

"Little bit," Trill said, pinching her forefinger and thumb together. I noted she was wearing her mood ring again today, which swirled blue. Trill was always "calm and peaceful." She'd let me try it on once, and it immediately turned a deep mustard color. "What does that mean?" I'd asked. "It means you're anxious," she'd said. "Like *bunny rabbit* anxious."

"So did you guys live anywhere near Times Square?" I asked. My only familiarity with New York was Dick Clark's *New Year's Rockin' Eve*.

She laughed. "No. My dad lives on the Upper East Side. Totally boring high rise."

New York was only a seven-hour drive from Quimby, but I'd never been. My dad had wanted to go see the Red Sox play the Yankees at Yankee Stadium a couple years ago, told my mom that maybe we could go to a Broadway show. *The Bell Jar* was based on Sylvia's summer in New York City working for *Mademoiselle*. I was dying to see if I could locate some of the famous sites in the book: the "Amazon" (based on the Barbizon Hotel), the UN, and Bloomingdale's. But after my mother researched what tickets would cost and how much a hotel would be, she suggested we go camping for a week instead. We'd borrowed an RV and parked it at the edge of a lake. My dad fly-fished while my mom suntanned. I'd been bored and disappointed. Charlie and I played Uno and swam. But the bottom of the lake was mucky and the second day a leech attached itself to my ankle, and my mother had to use a spatula to slide the dreadful creature off me. I refused to go into the water after that, staying in the camper to sulk and read and eat stale marshmallows intended for s'mores. "We'll go someday," my dad promised, but we still hadn't.

"*Come*," Trill said, swinging the driver's side door open.

I followed her up the path to the house. She moved as if there were music running through her head, swinging her hips and wiggling her arms. We were still in the clothes we'd worn for tryouts. Trill had on her CBGB T-shirt, from some punk club in New York, and baggy gray sweats that rode low on her narrow hips. My fingers flew to my own hips, which swelled outward even when I was in my best shape.

Inside the little kitchen, Trill boiled water and then filled a dented Thermos with her mom's special tea. She handed me a blue ceramic honey pot, and I dripped a dollop of honey in it then took a sip; it was fragrant and still sort of bitter but seemed to instantly settle me.

"Bring it with you," she said and motioned for me to follow her outside again.

"What's that?" I asked. Behind the house and the barn, an old school bus sat at the top of a hill and was painted the same purple as the mailbox with giant white and yellow daisies. Near the back end of the bus, a chimney stuck up through the roof, and a trail of smoke spiraled out. The air smelled yeasty.

"That's The Bakery," she said.

I thought about the loaves of bread sealed in crinkly cellophane sold alongside Trill's mother's herbs and those sweet strawberries.

"My brother only teaches at the elementary school part-time," she said. "When he's home, he bakes. Do you want some? It's *otherworldly*."

"Sure," I said.

We walked up a worn path past the house and barn to the bus. Now that we were closer, I could see that what had, at first, looked like part of the landscape, were actually sculptures of people—their limbs and torsos formed from living trees, hair made of leaves and twigs and moss. I stopped in front of one, a pregnant woman, the tree trunk belly bulging out. Her hair was a cascade of branches intertwined with ivy.

"I call her Gaia," Trill said, patting the tree lady's belly.

"These are amazing," I said.

The yeasty smell intensified as we approached the bus. Through its windows, I could see someone moving around inside. Trill motioned for me to follow her. The accordioned door was open, and we stepped in.

It was humid inside, the air heavy and heady, the windows foggy with condensation. The bus had been stripped of all its seats, and along each side were rough butcher-block counters. There was a deep sink set into one counter, and the other was littered with colorful ceramic bowls. Loaves of freshly baked bread steamed on wire racks. In the back, Trill's brother was leaning over to pull a tray from a wood-burning cookstove.

He must not have heard us when we boarded the bus, because he turned, startled, and his free hand flew to his chest. "Trill!" he said. "You scared me."

His voice was more like a boy's than that of a large man. He had to have been over six feet tall, his head nearly touching the bus's ceiling. He was thin though, like Trill, with long limbs, and he wore a pair of white carpenter's overalls with a worn blue T-shirt underneath. He had a scruffy red beard, floppy hair, and a pair of bright green eyes like his sister's.

"This is my new best friend, Edie," she said matter-of-factly. "Edie, this is Jericho."

He set the tray down, brushed flour off on his pants, and reached out to shake my hand. His skin was soft and warm.

"Edie's a poet," Trill said, and I felt myself blush.

"The world needs more poets," he said kindly.

"Can we have some?" Trill asked, gesturing to the steaming loaves.

"Of course," he said. "It's sourdough. I hope that's okay?"

I'd never had sourdough bread before.

"I made some garlic-herb spread. Goat cheese. Do you eat cheese?" he asked.

I thought about the bright orange slices in their plastic envelopes in our fridge that I ate as snacks, folding the squares like origami paper before popping them into my mouth. I nodded.

He pulled a serrated knife from a magnetic strip hanging above the counter, sawed at a crusty loaf, then reached for a small blue bowl. Using the same knife, he smeared the spread across the slices. He handed the first one to me, and Trill grabbed the second.

"Thanks, J," she said, and motioned for me to follow her back outside.

"Thank you," I said to him, and he smiled at me before returning to the oven.

Back at the house, we sat in a couple of turquoise metal chairs on the porch where windchimes made from antique spoons and forks tinkled in the spring breeze. In the distance was the sculpture of a man holding his arms out, as if waiting for a hug.

The first bite flooded my mouth with the sharp tang of goat cheese and earthy herbs. The bread was warm and delicious.

"Oh my God," I said. "This is so good."

"Told you," she said and stood up. "How are you feeling?"

And I realized the cramps were completely gone.

"Awesome!" I said.

"Let's go to the barn."

The doors to the barn were open, but it was dark inside. Trill clicked a switch by the door, filling the room with light, bare bulbs hanging from above.

"What is this?" I asked as my eyes tried to make sense of what I was seeing.

"It's Jericho's studio," she said.

Inside the cavernous barn were dozens of sculptures. The heads were gigantic, made of papier-mâché with hand-painted expressive eyes and mouths. Their bodies were draped in faded calico fabric, patchworked and threadbare. They appeared to be watching us as we walked toward the back of the building, where a set of stairs led up to a loft with a wooden railing overlooking the gallery below.

"And this," she said, climbing the stairs, "is The Library."

The space was large. Three lumpy couches made a circle around a low round wooden table at the center of the room. Each of the three unfinished walls had been converted into floor to ceiling bookshelves, which were stuffed with books. There were stacks of books on the floor and piles of books on the table. Standing lamps, the kind in old movies with fringed shades, illuminated the reading area. The floor was covered in layers of worn Persian rugs.

I thought about the single bookcase in our house that held my mother's nursing school textbooks. Our family's Bible. The outdated encyclopedia set that had belonged to my father as a kid, his name, *Burt Marshall*, written inside each volume. He told me once that he had wanted to be a teacher when he was young, but that instead he had joined the navy, where he learned his trade. Charlie and I both loved to read. He had a small collection of books from the Scholastic Book Fairs at school. But the only books I had of my own were those I borrowed from the Quimby Athenaeum or from Mr. Howard's makeshift library at school. It had never occurred to me that someone could *own* so many books.

"Whose books are these?" I asked.

"They belonged to The Farm. But when everyone moved away, they left them here."

I walked from shelf to shelf, gobsmacked.

"I'm not a huge reader, but I like to come here anyway. It's peaceful." Trill had said she preferred movies to books. She wanted to be a filmmaker one day.

"When it rains, it sounds like music up here," she said, gesturing to the high ceiling above us, the wooden trusses like the ones inside the covered bridge.

I didn't have words for what I was feeling. I wanted to stay here, to *live* here. I wanted this to be my home. My library. I wanted to eat that delicious bread every day and drink herbal tea that took my pain away and curl up on one of these sofas and read and listen to the rain on the roof. The fact that this place had been here all this time was so strange. Like those dreams where you discover a room you didn't know existed in your house. It felt like . . . everything.

"Ugh," I said. "I wish I could stay, but it's almost four thirty." I didn't want to go home, but I needed to get the lasagna in the oven. To help Charlie with his homework and do my own.

"No problemo," Trill said. "Mi casa es su casa. You can come back anytime."

As we backed down the driveway, Jericho was coming out of The Bakery. He looked like a red-headed scarecrow, tall and reedy. He waved at us from the top of the hill, and I waved back, grinning, through the open car window.

July 2023

JERICHO OPENS THE door, his eyes bright with recognition.

"*Edie*," he says.

His beard is now long and white; he is still tall, but stoop-shouldered. He was only twenty-eight when Charlie disappeared, but he is an old man now, ten years older than me. A senior citizen.

"I'm sorry. I would have called, but I didn't have your number . . ." I say.

He smiles, and my heart plummets. "Please, come in."

I enter tentatively.

"Have a seat," he says, gesturing to the wooden kitchen table.

I comply, sitting down and studying the red-and-white gingham tablecloth, the bright yellow bowl in the center. It looks like a painting.

"Can I get you some coffee?" he asks. "Tea?"

"Tea would be nice," I say.

He shuffles over to the sink and fills a kettle with water, turns the burner on.

"I always loved this little kitchen," I say.

"Thank you," he says and glances around the room, as if trying to see it through my eyes.

We are both quiet a moment. A fat housefly hovers sluggishly in the air between us.

"So, you said that you, um, found something?" I ask, feeling a strange tug, remembering that I don't have long until I need to be home. "May I see what it is?"

"Of course," he says.

He reaches across the counter to the top of the microwave where there is a box of disposable latex gloves, the kind we kept around early in the pandemic. He sets the box in front of me and says, "To protect any DNA on it."

"Oh," I say and obediently pluck two flimsy gloves from the box.

"I'll be right back," he says. "It's in my room."

As I wait for him, I look around at the kitchen. Like our home, it, too, is a time capsule: stained-glass moon in the window above the sink, scuffed butcher-block counters, pale blue woodwork. I hear him in the bedroom: a shuffling, a squeaky door. And then he returns, placing the bundle in his arms on the table.

I don't know what I was expecting, but it certainly wasn't this.

Charlie's backpack.

His *backpack*, which—like Charlie—has been missing for nearly forty years. It feels impossible. But even though it is tattered, crusted with mud and faded to a terra-cotta pink, I know it is his. The *Ninja Turtles* patch. The straps tightened to the size of his small shoulders.

I look at Jericho, horrified. "You found this in the river?"

When Charlie disappeared, rescue workers dragged miles and miles of Lost River. Was it possible this could have surfaced from those roiling waters after all this time?

He sits down in a chair across from me, wrings his hands.

"Yesterday I was clearing some downed trees. They'd created a jam by the footbridge during the flood. After I managed to haul them out, I found this stuffed into the hollow trunk of an old elm."

Not floating in the river. *Hidden.*

"I pulled it out it and realized what it was right away. I remember the description from the fliers. I haven't opened it. I thought I should wait for you."

The kettle starts to whistle, and he stands. He turns off the flame and retrieves two mugs from an open shelf next to the sink.

"Here," he says, setting the mug of hot tea in front of me. "There's the honey." He gestures to a sticky crock, that familiar blue honey pot, and I am overwhelmed by the scent, that heady smell of chamomile, of lavender, of Trill.

"Please, take your time with it," he says and gently touches my shoulder, his fingers long and bony like his sister's. "I'll be outside."

After the screen door has shut behind him, I turn the backpack over tenderly and slowly unzip the front outside pocket. Eyes on fire, I look inside.

Of course, the content list is as familiar to me as a memorized poem: *One pair of swim trunks (wet) in a bread bag, Stretch Armstrong toy, Rubik's cube, and a small sketch pad*. Indeed, inside that front pocket is the Rubik's cube he'd gotten for his birthday in June, the stickers on each cube curling at the corners. Never solved. The sketch pad is also in the front pocket, swollen to twice its thickness. The pages are adhered together, his drawings captured inside. I set the two items on the table and unzip the main body, pulling out the plastic bag I presume holds his trunks. But the bag is black with mold, and I recall Nathan's warning, *Mold is bad*, and so I simply set it on the table. I check to confirm the last item on the list. But Stretch Armstrong, that weird rubbery doll he adored, is not here.

For the first time, I realize that list of objects must have come from somewhere, and that somewhere was my mother's memory. Or speculation. How did she get this wrong? And if she got this wrong, what other errors might she have made? She was constantly berating my father for his lack of attention to detail, but had she also made mistakes?

I feel queasy, anxious, as I search again. Then I feel something in one of the open outer pockets. Stuck to the inside. A piece of paper? No. An envelope. Or half an envelope, anyway. I carefully peel it away from the fabric.

It's torn down the middle, a letter trapped inside. It's the right half, bearing the postmark and the stamp. I don't have my reading glasses, besides which, the ink is smudged and faded. The only part I can make out—holding the envelope at arm's length—is half of a typewritten address:

arshall
ley Drive
Y, VT 05899

It appears to have been sent to our house, but by whom? The postmark is blurred beyond recognition. I try to separate the envelope from the letter inside, but the gloves make this impossible. Charlie liked to get the mail from the mailbox for us. It must be a letter he grabbed on his way out then shoved into his backpack. But why, or how, had it been torn? And where is the other half?

When Jericho taps at the door, I panic and stuff the envelope into my shorts' pocket.

"Come in," I say, my heart hammering.

"It's his?" Jericho asks, and I nod.

He sits down, rests his elbows on the table and puts his head in his hands. I want to comfort him, to tell him it will be okay. But the words are stuck in my throat. When he looks up from his hands, his eyes are rheumy and red.

"I really don't know if I can do this again," he says. His voice reminds me of a fire gently crackling. He is an old man. A gentle old man who has never harmed a soul in his entire life. I *know* this.

I stare at Charlie's backpack, sitting on the table in front of me.

"I hope it's okay, but I just need a little more time. Before I go to the police with this, I mean," Jericho says.

"But if you come forward, they'll know you didn't do it," I say. "Right?"

Jericho looks at me with pity. I'm being naive.

"I'll call Monday."

"Of course," I say. "Monday."

For a little while, nearly everyone in town was convinced he had taken Charlie. He'd stopped being a person of interest only because there was no physical evidence connecting him to my brother. Everything was circumstantial, but now, my brother's backpack has been unearthed on his property, hidden for decades in the deep hollow of a tree, where it might have stayed forever if not for the deluge.

Charlie's backpack. *My god.*

"So, you said you haven't touched it—other than to retrieve it from the tree, right?" I ask, thinking of the envelope. "You didn't handle anything inside?"

"Nothing," he says firmly. "It's evidence."

I feel lightheaded. My stomach is empty. I remember the PowerBar I stuffed into my pocket earlier. When I pull it out, I feel the edge of the torn envelope, and my heart skitters.

Maybe I should show him the envelope. See if he can make any sense of it. But how will I explain pilfering it? Why *did* I take it? I didn't even know what it was. *Everything* inside that backpack is evidence.

No. It's probably just junk mail that Charlie tossed into his backpack rather than into the trash. Charlie was a boy whose pockets were filled with rocks and snail shells and candy wrappers. He was a little boy, a collector of butterfly wings and fossil-stamped stones.

"Sorry," I say as I tear open the bar. "Low blood sugar."

"No, please go ahead," he says, and I chew a small bite, hoping it will steady me.

"Does your mother know you're here?" he asks.

His question takes me aback. As if I am seventeen again, as if I need her permission.

He sees my confusion. "I mean, have you told her I called?"

"My mom," I start. "She has dementia. I mean, it's the early stages. She has lucid days. But she's easily confused. I'm not sure if I should say anything to her yet. Maybe not until you've gone to the police? Right now, it's probably best to wait."

Jericho frowns sympathetically. He doesn't know the things she has said about him. What she thinks he did to Charlie. He'd called fully expecting she'd be the one to answer the phone.

"She still thinks he'll walk in the door one day," I say, recalling my mother's reaction to his call last night. *Did they find Charlie?*

His mouth twitches, and his eyes became glossy.

"But I know he's never coming home," I say.

He nods. He knows this too.

"Would you have time for me to show you something else?" he asks.

"Of course," I say. Though I'm not sure I can take much more. Charlie's backpack sitting on the table as if he simply dropped it there after school is already too much.

Still, I follow him outside, the screen door slamming shut behind us, and we walk through the overgrown grass toward the barn behind the house. It doesn't look much different from how it did all those years ago, though the roof sags a bit now and the barn boards are even more weathered. Forget-me-nots still grow in the damp trough along the barn's exterior walls, the tiny petals an impossible pale blue. I remember weaving them through Trill's hair.

Above the open barn doors is a new sign—or new to me, anyway. It is painted on a battered piece of wood: white paint. Block letters:

THE MUSEUM OF INNOCENTS

Jericho gestures for me to go inside.

My skin prickles, and I feel a rush of nostalgia as the familiar smells of hay and wood hit me. My eyes sting, and I blink as they adjust to the dimness.

The papier-mâché sculptures stored here nearly four decades ago are gone. The barn is cavernous and empty. Or it seems to be, until Jericho clicks on the lights, and I can see that the space has, indeed, been transformed into a gallery of sorts. The walls are all hung with several portraits in antique gold frames. I walk along the first wall slowly, as though I'm at the Louvre instead of inside a crumbling barn, reading the handwritten placards below each frame.

Scottsboro Boys, says the first. I study the somber, sweet faces of the nine young Black men. *Falsely accused of raping two white women in 1931*, the placard says. *5 convicted and sentenced to death. A collective 130 years served in prison before release. 3 posthumous pardons.* I look closely at what had first appeared, from a distance, to be a painting. But up close, I realize the portrait is made of bits of newsprint, collaged news articles detailing their so-called crimes.

On the opposite wall hangs a triptych: *Kimberly Long*, *Freda Susie Mowbray*, and *Jane Dorotik*. I study the bits of newsprint and gather that all three of these women were accused of murdering their husbands or partners. All three, later exonerated.

I walk to the next image: *Henry McCollum and Leon Brown*, two young Black boys accused of the murder of a little girl. *Exonerated after 31 years in prison.*

Marsha Colbey stares stoically at me from behind another frame. *Accused of the murder of her newborn, exonerated when it was determined the baby was stillborn.*

Several more faces, names I don't know. I presume, from the text that make up their faces, they were all wrongfully accused.

At the far end of the barn is the largest piece, illuminated by floor lights. Five boys. *The Central Park Five*, the placard says. Behind the young men, in wallpaper repetition, is Trump's 1989 ad in the *New York Times* calling for the reinstatement of the death penalty. It is breathtaking. Sickening. *Convictions vacated in 2002.*

I look to Jericho, whose eyes are pleading with me.

And then I see, in the shadows behind him, another portrait, this one framed in rough-hewn wood.

In the picture, Jericho stands, staring straight ahead, hands at his sides. Painter's coveralls. A dirt-smeared T-shirt. Bare feet. Red-bearded and green-eyed. His image looks straight at me, but as I get closer, the clear picture of this man begins to fragment: the way an Impressionist painting makes sense from a distance, but up close becomes a blur of brushstrokes. This portrait of Jericho consists of stories about my brother's disappearance: accusations, speculations, facts, and opinions. Pictures of Charlie's smiling face, those missing teeth. His bright eyes behind glasses. Yellowed *MISSING* flyers, with that tip line phone number repeated a thousand times.

I back up, forcing the chaos to come to order again, until I am no longer staring at the story of my brother's disappearance but at the man everyone once assumed was responsible for it. It strikes me, like a cold dull hammer to the temple, what the portrait is really saying: that the man standing here is nothing more, anymore, than the crime he was accused of.

I shake my head. He was a person of interest, yes. But he'd never been arrested. Never gone to prison. How many times had I comforted myself with these facts?

"I need you and your mother to know I never hurt Charlie." His voice rises, pleading. "I never hurt *anyone*."

I turn to face him. It feels important to look him in the eyes.

"I know," I say.

He cocks his head at me, as if trying to gauge my sincerity.

"I *know*," I repeat firmly and gaze upward toward The Library, dreaming myself back into that loft, into that afternoon. When I made the mistake that—it now appears—destroyed this man's life.

He walks me back to the driveway. Overhead, clouds have begun to fill the sky again, obscuring the sun and darkening the world, the woods around us. The sky feels ominous, the air electric. Thunder rumbles in the distance.

"My sister is coming," he says.

"What?" I ask, and my smartwatch buzzes at my heartrate's sudden surge.

"I'm going to need a lawyer."

Trillium is not a lawyer. Not unless she's gone to law school since I last Googled her. The last time I'd checked, she was working for an independent production company that makes documentaries shining light on social justice issues.

"I thought she was a filmmaker," I say.

"Oh," he says. "No. I'm sorry. Her wife is the lawyer."

"Her wife?"

Trill is not on social media. I didn't know she was married. Where she lives. If she has children.

"Paloma's a defense attorney. She works with a lot of people who are falsely accused." There is no malice in his voice. No blame. But the fact that Trill is married to someone dedicated to exonerating defamed innocents feels sharp, and it pierces my old, broken heart.

"They're driving up from the city this afternoon. They should be here tonight."

Stupidly, I picture Trill not as an adult, but as a seventeen-year-old girl, flying along the highway in Nico. Windows down. The Talking Heads blasting from the speakers. I imagine her mischievous grin and the way she used to look at me—expectant—as if *I* were the one with something to offer.

"Trill is coming home?" I ask.

March 1986

When Trill dropped me off at my house following that first visit to The Farm, I felt like I'd been pulled from a dream, like Dorothy waking up back in Kansas after her adventures in Oz. My own house was unfamiliar now. Small. Sad. The aluminum pan of lasagna made me ashamed. The plates my mother had bought one by one from the Shop-N-Save embarrassed me. The loaf of frozen garlic bread, which I usually loved, now seemed cheap. I'd glimpsed the technicolor of Oz, but unlike Dorothy, I found no comfort in home.

"Charlie? Did you get the mail?" I asked.

"Take that, GI Joe!" I heard him growl in Stretch Armstrong's voice in the family room.

As the lasagna baked, I went out to the porch to check the mailbox. It was stuffed with bills and junk. Publishers Clearing House. My mother's *Good Housekeeping*, my *Seventeen* with a ponytailed Jennifer Connelly on the cover.

Nothing from Smith.

I tossed it all into a pile on the counter that my father would sort through before supper, separating the bills from the junk mail, which he would later roll into tight "logs" he used to start fires in the woodstove. When I was little, we would do this together, and he'd pay me a nickel for each one I made.

We ate together as a family that night, as we did most nights, my father asking Charlie and me about school. My mother reminded me that I'd promised to help with the rummage sale at St. Paul's that Sunday after church.

"You had track tryouts today, right?" my dad asked then teased, "Think you'll make the team?" My parents rarely went to my meets, but he knew my dresser was covered with trophies, medals hanging in a tidy row over my bed.

"Maybe JV?" I grinned. "If not, I can probably ask to be assistant manager or something."

"Where were you after tryouts?" my mother asked, loading Charlie's plate with lasagna. "Judy said you weren't next door when I called to check on Charlie. Nathan didn't know where you were either."

"I got a ride home with a friend," I said, my chest tight. "We drove around for a little bit first, grabbed a snack. It was a nice day."

My mother's thick, dark eyebrow lifted. "Lisa?"

Lisa was my best friend from kindergarten until freshman year when she got a boyfriend, though we'd outgrown each other long before that. In high school, I was on the college prep track, and Lisa didn't plan to go to college, so we didn't even have classes together. Our friendship was little more anymore than saying *hi* in the halls at school.

"No, a new girl," I said. "She just moved here."

"To Quimby?" my father said, laughing. "I didn't think anyone moved *to* Quimby."

My mother scowled at him. "Right before graduation?" she asked me.

"Yeah," I said but didn't elaborate.

I'd never hung out with any of The Farm kids before. She knew all the local families' children because she worked at the pediatrician's office. I had no idea if the kids from The Farm had even gone to the doctor or if they'd just gone to Trill's mom when they got sick.

"Charlie," my dad said, saving the day as always, "have you heard about this new movie called *Flight of the Navigator*? It's about a boy and a UFO. Sounds right up your alley. And the *best* part is your Grammy in Florida said they were filming just down the street from her. We might even see her house in the movie! Can you imagine?"

"Can we go see it?" Charlie asked, delighted.

"It won't be out until August," he said.

"Oh." Charlie frowned, as though he'd said it wouldn't be out for ten more years.

But August was only five months away. So soon. If Smith said yes, my August might look totally different from how I'd planned.

"My mom reads tea leaves," Trill said that Friday as we lay on the pole vault pit again. It was overcast today though, and without the sun, the vinyl was cold. "Maybe she can figure out your future."

I shook my head. It seemed dangerous to mess around with things we weren't supposed to know. I felt the same way about Ouija boards and the séances Lisa had always wanted to do at sleepovers.

"It's in *God's* hands now," my mother would have said if she had any idea I'd applied. I was born and raised Catholic, but I wasn't so sure about God; still, I said a short prayer after Communion at Mass every Sunday. It couldn't hurt.

"Do you want to come over and watch a movie this weekend?" Trill asked. "I'm working tonight, but maybe tomorrow?" Trill had gotten a job at Video-Q. She only made $3.35 an hour, but she got to rent as many movies as she wanted for free.

"I told Nathan I'd go see *Pretty in Pink* with him tomorrow night," I said.

"Didn't you guys already see that?" she asked. "And ugh. I know you love John Hughes, and no offense, but he is so . . . *middle America*."

"I know," I said, though I did love the movie. I totally identified with the main character, Andie: the way she couldn't make herself love Duckie Dale back, even though he was adorable and adoring, the one person who would never judge her or let her down. I didn't know if Nathan saw himself in Duckie or maybe he aspired to be like the rich boy, Blane. I did notice that after the first time we saw it, he started wearing crisp khakis and white button-down shirts. Pastel polo shirts with the collars flipped up. Nathan was like Silly Putty, everything imprinting on him, though fainter than the original. Imperfect and smudged.

"You guys have a TV, right?" Trill asked.

Of course, we had a TV. We had *three* TVs. One in the family room, one in my parents' bedroom, and I even had a small black-and-white one. We weren't rich, but we had TVs.

"You don't have a TV?" I asked.

"Just for the VCR. No reception at The Farm. My mom also says TV rots your brain."

How funny. I wanted to be a writer, but my family didn't have books. Trill wanted to make movies, but her mom didn't have a TV.

"The Oscars are on Monday night. Maybe I could come over to watch?" she asked.

The idea of Trill coming to my house made me feel queasy. I thought about Andie—the way she hadn't wanted Blane to pick her up at home, ashamed of how different their lives were. Though Trill certainly wasn't a rich snob, her home was magical. Beautiful. Art-full. While mine was—not.

She thought *John Hughes* was *middle America*, I tried to imagine Trill sitting on our ugly plaid couch, eating popcorn from the stainless-steel barf bowl. Wondered what she would make of our matted shag carpeting and popcorn ceilings. Or my own room, which hadn't been updated since I was six, the Pepto Bismol-colored walls nauseating to me now. Then I felt guilty for being ashamed of the house my parents had worked so hard for. And in the end, the idea of Trill wanting to come hang out at my house trumped all that.

"I'll check with my mom. I don't usually have friends over during the week, but she might be okay with it."

I tried to remember the last time anyone besides Nathan had been over and couldn't. In middle school Lisa came over all the time: sleepovers, *double* sleepovers in the summer. At school, I was friends with Tess and Effie, but they were more of a duo, and despite my having a lot in common with them, they didn't really ask me to hang out with them on the weekends. They probably assumed I was with Nathan. Which I usually was.

"I'll tell her we're studying for AP Chem. I have a TV in my room. It's black-and-white, though."

"Awesome!" she said.

My parents had no real idea what I was doing in school. I brought home report cards with straight As but rarely talked much about my classes or upcoming tests or grades, and so my mom had looked confused when I started babbling about the AP Chem exam on enthalpy (a real test, but one that wasn't for two more weeks).

"Okay," she said. "Who is this girl again?"

"Her name's Trillium," I said.

"That's unusual."

"Like the flower." Again, I didn't mention that she was one of The Farm kids. "She might need to stay kind of late. The test is a practice test for the AP exam."

"Who will pick her up?" my mother asked.

"She has her own car. Remember—I told you we went for a drive the other day?"

"Oh," she said. "That's right. Is she coming for supper? I can pick up a couple frozen pizzas."

Trill had come home with me after track practice, so she was already at my house when my parents got home from work. My mom had caught a stomach bug from one of her patients, so she handed over the frozen pizzas, told me to preheat the oven, and looked over her shoulder as she raced down the hall to the bathroom and said, "It's nice to meet you, Trillium!" I cringed when I heard her turn on the faucet to mask any noises she might be making, but Trill didn't seem to notice or was too polite to react.

Dad told Charlie they could have their pizza in front of the TV since Mom was feeling sick. He told him he'd play Connect Four with him before Charlie's bath.

"Can I eat with Edie and her friend?" Charlie asked hopefully.

"They're doing homework. Come with me, buddy," he said and winked at me and Trill. "We've got some maple walnut ice cream for dessert too."

In my room, Trill and I sat on the floor with paper plates and frozen pizza. I thought about the delicious homemade bread Jericho had given us out at The Farm, grimacing as she picked up the anemic slice of Tombstone she had loaded with hot pepper flakes. But she devoured it, nodding and making happy sounds.

"Sorry it's frozen. I bet you're used to amazing pizza in New York."

"Oh, no, I totally love frozen pizza. But New York pizza is definitely in a class of its own. There's a place in the Village my dad and I go that has the best pizza on the planet. I'll take you there sometime. It's unbelievable."

What was unbelievable was the idea of Trill and me going to New York City together. The way she so casually suggested it. It felt like she'd suggested we go get pizza on Mars.

We got out our AP Chem books on the off chance that my parents checked on us, though after I disappeared into my room each night, my parents rarely, if ever bothered me. Besides, my mom was sick. I had heard the downstairs toilet flush a half dozen times already. My mom almost never got sick and, despite being a nurse, had little patience for complaints.

"I can ask my mom to make a tea to help with her nausea," Trill said.

"That's okay. She'll be fine."

There was no way my mother would drink Trill's mom's tea.

Robin Williams and Jane Fonda were the hosts of the Oscars. I used to love *Mork and Mindy*, and my mom would do the Jane Fonda workout video in the basement, though I was pretty sure I'd seen the tapes for sale at our last garage sale.

"Have you seen any of these movies?" I asked. I hadn't even heard of most of the Best Picture nominees. The only one that had come to our local theater was *Witness*. Nathan and I had seen it together, but he preferred Harrison Ford in *Star Wars* and *Raiders of the Lost Ark*, which we'd seen four times.

"Yeah. I've seen almost all of them," she said. "I'm rooting for *Kiss of the Spider Woman*, but it probably won't win because the main character's gay, and the Academy is filled with homophobes. But it's also Will Hurt. He was *amazing* in *The Big Chill*."

I didn't know who he was, and I hadn't seen that movie either.

"*Brazil* is up for screenplay and art direction. You've seen it, right?"

I shook my head. I felt as though I had been living under a rock. A giant rock in the shape of my town.

"Oh my God. It's so wild. It's set in this dystopian world, a total takedown of capitalism. But it's like super funny too. Satire."

I nodded, but she knew I wasn't getting it.

"It's like if Kafka made a movie," she said.

Now she was speaking my language. We'd read *The Metamorphosis* in Mr. Howard's freshman English class, and he'd lent me *The Trial* and *The Penal Colony*.

"We should rent it when it comes out on VHS."

"Totally," I agreed.

When the pizza was gone, we sat on my bed. Trill was glued to the screen. "I'm going to be invited there one day," she said, jaw set. "To the red carpet. Wear a fancy-ass dress. Halston maybe? Or no! Versace! But barefoot, of course." She wriggled her feet, which were bare, long toes with bright blue polish on her nails.

Her certainty was inspiring; it was nice to be around someone who knew exactly what she wanted and seemed to have no doubt that she would get it.

"Have you heard from any more schools?" I asked.

"What?" she asked, without turning her gaze from Sally Field, who was announcing the nominees for Best Actor.

"Any more letters from colleges?"

"Oh my God, *yes*!" she said, turning to me. "I totally forgot to tell you. I got into Hampshire."

"You *did*?"

"I know! I'm so excited. Now you just need to get into Smith. Then we'll be neighbors!" We'd figured out that Hampshire was exactly seven miles from Smith.

For the first time, I wondered what I would do if Smith said no. I hadn't meant to get my hopes up, but now here they were. Just about as high as they could be.

"And the winner is William Hurt in *Kiss of the Spider Woman*," Sally said.

"Holy shit!" Trill said, reaching out and grabbing my wrist.

"So awesome!" I said, delighted because she was delighted.

"Wow," she said, her mouth open as William Hurt made his way to the stage, giving Sally a big hug.

"Wow," I echoed.

"Like Bobby Dylan said, 'The times they are a changin','" Trill said sagely.

We sat there for a moment, Trill still clutching my arm. My skin felt buzzy; I had to look at my arm to confirm it wasn't being tickled by a thousand tiny butterflies.

"Edie, where's my Stretch Armstrong?" Charlie asked. He had opened the door and was standing in the doorway in nothing but his Superman Underoos. The birthmark on his chest was bright red. It was always bright red after a bath.

I almost snapped at him for interrupting us. The Oscars. Why wasn't he wearing any clothes? And why was he so obsessed with that weird doll? But then I reminded myself, he was just being Charlie; he couldn't know that my arm had gone from humming to feeling like still, warm water under Trill's touch. That all of me felt oddly *liquid*.

"Did you check the kitchen? You had him when we were getting pizza."

"Oh yeah," Charlie said. But he didn't make a move to leave. He was studying Trill.

"You have pretty eyes," he said, and I was mildly mortified. Charlie didn't think before he spoke; he just said exactly what was on his mind. Though to be fair, she did have pretty eyes. Like two mossy pebbles underwater.

"Thanks," Trill said. "You have pretty eyes too."

For some reason Charlie thought this was hysterical and clutched his belly, laughing. Charlie had a belly laugh that was super contagious. Like chicken pox contagious. Soon the three of us were laughing so hard I was worried I might pee my pants. Trill flopped backward on the bed, trying to catch her breath.

"So, what's Smith?" Charlie asked when we'd recovered.

My chest felt heavy. "Why?" I asked.

"No reason." But his face was red, a tell-tale sign he'd been spying.

"It's a college," I said. "In Massachusetts."

"But I thought you were going to college here."

Trill looked at me. She knew I hadn't told anyone in my family about Smith.

"Hey Charlie, Edie told me that you're like really into space stuff?" Trill said.

He nodded warily.

"So, did you know that if two pieces of the same kind of metal touch each other in space, they immediately bond together?"

Charlie's eyes widened. "How?"

"Well, on Earth, there's either air or water separating everything all the time. But in space, there's no oxide layer to keep like metals apart." She grabbed the forks we'd been using for our pizza and gave me a wink as she clinked them together, their tines intertwined. "Bonded forever," she said.

July 2023

TRILL IS COMING home.

When I walk back into the house after running all the way home from Jericho's, the world feels tilted. As I unlace my sneakers and peel off my sweaty socks, Daisy winding in and out of my legs, I recall that haunting self-portrait, think about how many lives were destroyed that summer. I also think of Trill, coming home to Quimby after so many years. Despite the scab being torn off this old wound, I feel a nervous sort of anticipation. Excitement. It isn't the appropriate emotion, but that old swell of expectancy is there, nevertheless.

My mother is sitting at the kitchen table now, listening to a podcast. The podcaster's voice is oddly soothing.

"Is Ariel up yet?" I ask.

"Not yet."

I'm not surprised. I told her not to get up, after all. She's a night owl now, her days flip-flopped. It started when she came home at the beginning of the pandemic, when schedules became obsolete for so many of us, but she still hasn't managed to get back on track. She was finishing her second semester at the University of Vermont when the world shut down. She finished her freshman year online, barely, but she didn't go back to school in the fall. She decided to take a year off, return when classes were all in person again—online art classes were awful, she said—but what would have been her sophomore year soon passed, then her junior year.

She's turning twenty-two soon; she should have graduated this spring. She should be out in the world, not living with her mom and elderly grandmother. I know better than to push, but my hope is that she'll return to school this fall—if only to the state college in town. Baby steps.

The pandemic is over. Classes are all in person now, and the art department at State is really great. But when I sent her a link to the course catalog, she left my text on Read. Her best friend, Tyler, is at Tulane, starting grad school this fall. I offered to fly her there for a visit—hoping that might inspire her—but she just said, "I'm fine here, Mom." When I was her age, I wanted nothing more than to spread my wings. The world is hers for the taking. How can she not want it?

I think of how Trill and I couldn't wait to get out on our own, to be free of this place. It's been nearly forty years, but my ragged heart still feels raw when I think of her. Of how things between us ended.

Hands trembling, I pour the last bit of coffee into a mug and lean into the fridge. "You hungry for some lunch yet, Mom? How does tuna salad sound?"

"Make sure you put those sweet pickles in that I like," she says.

"Have you heard anything from Nathan?" I ask as I pull the pickle jar and mayo out of the fridge.

"Nathan?"

"Yes, remember I said he's coming by to look at the basement? We've got a little water down there. From the flooding last week."

Then, like he was only waiting for his cue, Nathan knocks on the door before pushing it open. "Knock, knock!" His timing is disarming.

He removes his baseball cap at the sight of my mother.

"Hi, Mrs. Marshall," he says.

She looks at him, a bit lost, then presses her hand to her heart. "Nathan," she coos, standing up and hobbling over to him for a hug. "Are you here to take Edie to the movies?" Again, with the movies.

"Not today," he says, smiling at me sympathetically.

The last time Nathan came over was when the old sugar maple in our backyard fell over and crushed the garage roof. I hadn't known who else to contact. Nathan hooked us up with a tree guy who turned the fallen tree into firewood and a roof guy who repaired the broken gutter and replaced the damaged shingles. We really are lucky to have him; I should be more grateful.

"Hey," he says to me.

"Hey. You want a sandwich?" I ask, motioning to the spread on the counter. "Tuna salad."

"I'm good."

Nathan has aged. Without his cap on, I can see that his hair has gotten even grayer and thinner. He works with his hands, but he is soft around the middle. A few too many fried fish dinners at the Miss Quimby Diner, I assume.

"Did you get any flooding up at your place?" I ask.

"No, thank God," he says then reaches quickly to knock on the wooden table.

We stand there, awkwardly silent, for a moment.

"So, speaking of which," I say, and motion to the basement door.

Nathan is as familiar with our house as his own, so I just send him down and say, "Holler if you need me. I'll be up here having lunch with Mom."

I make the tuna salad, pour two glasses of lemonade, and sit down across from my mother, who plucks the crusts from her sandwich like a toddler might, then looks between the slices of bread to make sure I put the pickles in there. I reach across the table and touch her hand. The veins are deep blue under her papery flesh. She is so frail. How can I possibly tell her about Charlie's backpack without breaking her? How can I tell her that the man she's been convinced took Charlie has somehow found all his things (save that Stretch Armstrong doll)? How can I convince her this isn't proof of Jericho's guilt but rather of his innocence?

I look at my mother, peering at the screen of her tablet again, only a single bite taken from her sandwich, and I know that the discovery of the backpack, hidden on Jericho's property, will function for her as evidence that she was right all along. My mother had wanted so desperately to know what happened to Charlie that when the police offered up their half-baked theory about Jericho, she'd clung to it as truth. But my father had never bought it.

"It doesn't make sense," he had said, as my mother regurgitated the postulations.

Jericho Jenkins was close to thirty in 1986, but unmarried, no girlfriend, living with his mother. He was an artist, soft-spoken and shy. He had been known to offer kids rides home when their parents forgot or when it was too cold to walk. Of course, this alone wasn't unusual in 1986. Teachers and parents often gave kids rides home. We were a tightknit community; everyone knew everyone, and we looked out for each other. Jericho had even given Charlie a ride home once when I had a cross-country meet after school and couldn't get him. My mother hadn't said a word about it then except to tell Charlie to make sure to thank him. But the cumulative collage of innocuous details created a different picture. A single, unmarried man, a man who worked with children, quickly became a monster who took her only son.

This news will do nothing but send her on the same kind of spiral she went on about all those missing people, all those crimes that have gone unpunished, and all those shattered mothers describing their lost sons and daughters.

Then I wonder, ludicrously, what would happen if I just told her what *really* happened that day. What if I just offered up the truth, like a tuna sandwich on a clean platter? But the thought sends a chill through me, the same full-body shiver that has overwhelmed me hundreds of times over the last several decades. Like being caught up in the violent current of a river.

"Mind if I take a quick shower?" I ask.

"I'm fine," she mutters, distracted by her tablet. "Nathan's here if I need him."

She pushes her sandwich aside and turns up the volume on her iPad.

"In 1975, seven-year-old Jimmy Cummins vanished while on a camping trip in northern Arizona. Documentarian Ann Simmerman goes back to the town she grew up in to look for answers."

April 1986

The Saturday before Easter, my mother had solicited my help in hiding eggs for Charlie. After an early supper, she sent him upstairs to take his bath then told him that he could play as much Nintendo as he wanted since it was a holiday weekend.

It was supposed to be a beautiful day on Sunday—with highs in the mid-70s, so we decided to hide the eggs outside. Charlie was eight, but he still believed in the Easter Bunny, or wanted to, anyway. She'd retrieved the Easter bin from the basement, filling the multicolored plastic eggs with jellybeans, the speckled malted milk balls Charlie loved, and the foil-wrapped Rolos I favored. She filled each of two large golden eggs with a crisp five-dollar bill she'd had Mrs. Nichols bring home from the bank.

"Make sure to hide them well. Charlie's older now," she said. It wasn't even six o'clock yet, but the sun was setting, so she'd clicked on the floodlights so we could see what we were doing. Our backyard was big enough for a swing set and an old sand box that, to my mother's chagrin, had become the neighborhood litterbox. She had been on my father to remove it for over a year now. "Not in the sandbox," she said, sidestepping it to place a pink egg in the bird bath.

My mother was short, like me. Just over five feet, so none of the eggs would wind up in high places. I used camouflage as a tactic instead; I filled the lilac bushes with purple eggs and put white ones next to the house. Pink in the azaleas and yellow in the forsythia.

"How's Nathan?" she asked as we walked along the fence line that separated our yard from the Nicholses'.

"Fine," I said. I never knew what to do when my mother tried to tease out what was going on in my personal life.

My mother knew Nathan was my boyfriend, of course. But she and I didn't have the kind of relationship where I confided in her about boy stuff. I often wished I had a mom I could talk to like a girlfriend, and I don't know why I kept my distance from her. But we weren't close the way Lisa and her mom were. Mrs. Campbell had been super involved in Lisa's life from the time we were in kindergarten. She was the room parent every year of elementary school, the Brownie leader, chaperone at the junior high dances. She was always the one to host sleepovers, lingering to get the latest gossip, plying us with pizza rolls and Hot Pockets and Crunch 'n Munch. I learned about periods from Lisa's mom; she gave me a pad when it came the first time during a sleepover at her house. Lisa's mom was a housewife, home every day after school, making sure Lisa did her homework and checking in to see which boys she liked. When Lisa started dating Bobby, Lisa told her everything. Mrs. Campbell even took her to Planned Parenthood to get birth control. My mother would have been appalled had she known. But I told her nothing.

I had read the letters between Sylvia Plath and her mother alongside Sylvia's journals. And the dichotomy between the Sylvia of her diary and her mother's beloved *Sivvy* was exactly like the one I felt—as if I had two lives: the one I was living for my mother, and the other one, which was private and secret. And real.

"I can't believe you'll be eighteen so soon," my mother said. "All grown up and going to college. I feel like I was just starting nursing school myself."

She was looking at me with baffled curiosity, like she was realizing for the first time that I wouldn't be a kid forever.

God, how I wanted to tell her about Smith. How Mrs. Fulwiler had told me that 25 percent of the students went abroad their junior year. That their travel program gave Smithies a chance to study in Paris, in Geneva, in *Cairo*. That my life in Quimby felt like one of these plastic eggs, about to crack wide open with delicious surprises inside. Maybe she'd see what an opportunity this would be. Maybe she'd understand how much I longed for something Quimby couldn't offer. Maybe she'd be excited for me. Proud. Sylvia's mother had, at least, been proud of her daughter.

"So, listen," she said, standing on her tiptoes to reach the bird feeder, where she hid a yellow egg. "I want to spend some time this summer teaching you basic finance stuff. Balancing your checking account, paying bills, that kind of thing," she said. "You didn't take Home Economics, but these skills are important. And if Nathan is anything like your father, you'll want to be the one in charge of the budget and finances. I mean, if you two . . ."

She trailed off, and noting my slumped shoulders, frowned.

"You sure everything is okay with Nathan?"

"It's fine, Mom," I said. "He's *fine*."

"Good," she said, holding the coveted gold eggs in her hands. "So where should we put these?"

Back inside, I went to my room and picked up Sylvia's journals. It made me angry that Ted Hughes had been the one to edit not only her poems but her private words as well. I tried to imagine Nathan going through my journals after I was dead, deciding which passages were worthy or salacious or too cruel. I longed for those lost pages, the ones her husband had destroyed or hidden. Forbidden.

I had bookmarked all the pages about her time at Smith with sticky notes and read them like my mother read her favorite psalms. But my prayers were about rage and passion and desire and loneliness and ambition. And *words*. How could words manage to make me feel so alive in a way that nearly nothing else did?

An hour or so later, when the phone rang, I realized I'd fallen asleep. My pillow damp with drool, my eyes crusty. I'd been deep asleep and dreaming in poetry. I struggled to remember the words, scratching them down in the notebook I kept next to my bed. "I am at the edge of tomorrow . . ." Were these my words or hers?

"Edie!" my mom hollered up the stairs. "It's for you."

Nathan. I was sure of it. He'd probably heard us outside earlier and would want me to come over.

"I'm in the shower!" I said, then, as an afterthought. "Who is it?"

"It's Trillium," my mother said.

Oh. Thank God. Not Nathan.

I had a phone in my room. I'd bought it myself when I got sick of stretching the cord for the kitchen phone down the hall for privacy.

"Got it, Mom," I said, and I heard my mother hang up. "Hi!" I said to Trill.

"Hey, do you want to go to a movie tonight?"

"It's Easter tomorrow," I said dumbly, as if there were some unwritten rule about socializing with friends on the night before a religious holiday.

"Oh, that's right," she said glumly. "Do you have to like, go to church tonight?"

Trill had no religion and no idea what it meant to have one. She said her mom was a pagan and her dad was an atheist. She, herself, was firmly agnostic.

"Not until tomorrow morning," I said. "I can ask my mom. What's the movie?"

"*A Room with a View*," she said. "At the Savoy. The show's at nine, but I think we can make it if we leave ASAP."

The closest theater only showed blockbusters, but if we were willing to drive to Montpelier, we could catch the more obscure films Trill loved.

"I need to ask my parents. Can I call you right back?"

My mom was half-asleep in front of *The Ten Commandments* in the family room, so I went looking for my dad, who I thought might be a better bet anyway. I found him sitting outside on our back porch, staring into the dark backyard, smoking a cigarette.

"Hi," I said.

"You did not see that," he said and hurriedly snubbed the cigarette out in a planter.

"See what?" I offered.

It felt like days since Mom and I had been back here hiding eggs rather than just a couple of hours. Time felt strange lately. Some days stretched like Stretch Armstrong's rubbery limbs. Others felt compressed, weeks (even months) cartwheeling ahead. I was turning eighteen in June, a milestone that had once been so far away, but now here it was, here *I* was, standing at the *edge of tomorrow*, wondering how I got here. Yes! My words for sure.

"Trill invited me to go see a movie tonight," I said. "In Montpelier."

"Trill's the new girl, right?"

"Yeah," I said.

"Where did you say she moved here from?" he asked.

I hesitated. "New York City. She lives out at The Farm."

"Aha," he said. "I wondered if she might have something to do with those folks. Hanging out with flatlanders now, are we?"

"*Dad*."

He chucked my arm. "I'm just teasing. I never really understood why the locals feel compelled to give them so much grief. Seems like they're just trying to make a quiet little life for themselves here. Same as the rest of us. Live and let live, is what I always say."

"So, I can go?" I asked hopefully.

"What did your mother say?"

"She's watching Charlton Heston," I said.

"Well, then I guess it's up to me! Can you be back before midnight?"

"I can."

"And can you keep this a secret?" he asked, pulling another cigarette from the pack he had hidden in his pocket.

I made a motion to zip my lips then tossed the imaginary key.

The movie theater was in downtown Montpelier, with brick walls and old seats, scuffed floors. Trill had made popcorn and stashed it in a brown paper lunch sack, and I had grabbed some leftover Easter candy on my way out. We sat a few rows from the back. There was no one else in the theater, probably because of the holiday.

It had been such a sunny day, and it was still sixty degrees, warm for late March. I was wearing a pair of Levi's 501s and a white V-neck T-shirt I stole from my dad's drawer. I had brought a men's tweed suit jacket in case it got chilly later, the inside a pale blue silk. My personal style was somewhere between preppy and jock with the occasional thrift store ensemble thrown in. Of course, my dad had noticed Trill wasn't like my other friends; she didn't dress like anybody else in Quimby. She looked like she was on her way to Woodstock most of the time: long skirts and gauzy blouses. Tonight, she was wearing a bright yellow sundress with a navy bandanna tied kerchief-style on her head, with braids and dangly earrings and her ubiquitous work boots, which she propped up on the seat in front of us.

As the trailers played, we waited for other people to show up, but the seats remained empty. It was so peculiar being the only members of the audience: like the film was made just for us. Without the distractions of people coughing or fidgeting or whispering, it felt like I was being swallowed whole by the story. I was with Lucy Honeychurch, the main character, as she played the piano, the pent-up passion coming out in her attack on the keys. I was with her in that field when she and her forbidden love, George, embraced. Reckless and dangerous. I was so lost in the story, I startled when Trill nudged me and said, "Wow, you look exactly like her."

Helena Bonham Carter, the actress playing Lucy was, like me, short with long curly brown hair. Her dark eyes and fair skin might have resembled mine as well. Her small mouth. But she looked like a porcelain doll to me, achingly beautiful, and I did not consider myself beautiful. I knew my boobs were attractive to guys; I'd heard the jokes and comments since junior high. Even Nathan didn't seem to have any opinions about my face, but he was always saying how nice my body was. I'd been called "cute" once or twice as a little girl. But once puberty hit, I'd often felt headless, as if my body and head (including my brain) were two separate entities, joined simply by chance

I studied Lucy. Because of Trill, I felt—oddly—as though she *was* me. Or I was her? So, when Lucy unceremoniously ditched Cecil, the guy she was supposed to be with, it felt like *I* was the one breaking off the engagement. And when Lucy's *true* love, George, and she sat in the window, gazing out at the view before them, overwhelmed by love and passion and possibility, a tremendous gut-wrenching sob overwhelmed me. Mortified, I tried to suck it back in, but this only made it worse, and soon the tears were rolling, and Trill was looking at me wide-eyed. Thank God we were the only ones in the theater.

"Hey," she said. "You okay?"

I laughed, embarrassed at my absurd display. It was a *happy* ending. Lucy was free!

"I'm going to call you Lucy Honeychurch from now on," Trill said definitively as we stood up. She draped one of her long arms across my shoulder and we bumped hips up the aisle to the exit. "*Lucy Honeychurch*," she repeated in a thick British accent this time.

"I think I'm going to break up with Nathan," I blurted out in the car.

"Wow," she said. "That's big."

"I know."

Trill dropped me off moments before my curfew. I walked to the house, still feeling tangled up in the dream of the beautiful film.

The next morning at Mass, I sat in the back of the church with my parents and Charlie, who was swinging his legs, causing the entire pew to move. It was Easter. Spring! A time for new beginnings. To be reborn. But I was already feeling antsy, trying to figure out the best way to let Nathan down. While it had seemed so easy, so obvious, last night, now I was racked with guilt. I wished I could simply blame it on Smith, but I still hadn't heard from them. I had no excuse. This would hurt him, and I was not a person who liked hurting other people.

Charlie accidentally kicked the pew in front of us. A few people turned to see what was causing the commotion.

"*Charlie*," I reprimanded.

He was hopped up on sugar, having eaten half of the foil-wrapped hollow chocolate bunny as well as his weight in jellybeans.

When Mass started, I leaned over and said, "If you hold still, I'll give you my Rolos."

He stiffened like a board, shoulders back and hands clasped in his lap. The last thing he needed was more chocolate, but at least it would keep everyone from staring at us.

Nathan was the thurifer, the one who carried the incense during the procession at the beginning of Mass. He took his role seriously, despite having a super sensitivity to the incense.

"Why don't you ask Father Tavares to give you another job?" I'd asked him once, and he'd looked at me like I'd suggested he show up to Mass naked.

"Being the thurifer is an honor, Edie."

And truthfully, I was hardly one to criticize somebody doing something out of a misguided sense of duty.

I could see he was trying not to sneeze the whole way down the aisle. When he passed, I noted his eyes were red and watery, as if he'd been crying. I wondered if he would cry when I broke up with him. I *hated* when Nathan cried.

After Mass was over, my parents lingered outside on the steps, talking to Nathan's parents, who were waiting for him to finish up inside. Our mothers were complimenting each other's dresses, and our dads were talking about some new building project. Charlie and Mickey wrestled on the grassy area next to the parking lot.

"Yes!" my mother said. "Join us for Easter dinner. It's so beautiful out, we thought we'd do hotdogs and hamburgers on the grill."

My stomach pitched.

"Okay," Mrs. Nichols said. "I was just going to put a ham I got from Schwan's in the oven, anyway. But I have a potato salad I can bring over. Ambrosia salad?"

"*Perfect.* Come on, Charlie!" my mother said, as the boys tussled in the grass. Their best Sunday clothes would be grass-stained, maybe even torn, but for some reason, my mother never bemoaned this. Boys will be boys.

"Come on, Mickey!" Mrs. Nichols echoed.

Charlie and Mickey untangled themselves and came running toward us, and we all looked at them in horror.

The boys were both wearing white button-down shirts, and both their shirts were now soaked in blood. There was blood on their hands and blood all over Mickey's face.

"Oh my God!" my mother said, rushing to Charlie. "What happened?"

After much confusion and questioning, the mothers figured out it was a nosebleed. Mickey's nose had opened like a faucet and drenched them both.

Mrs. Nichols's face blanched. This was exactly how it had started when he was diagnosed with leukemia two years ago: a bloody nose and mysterious bruises she had initially attributed to Mickey being a rough and tumble kid.

My mother seemed to know exactly what was running through her mind, and she became Nurse Marshall, the calm, cool, collected medical professional. She got Mickey to sit down on the ground and pulled a hanky from her purse. She had him tip his head back, pinching his nostrils together with the handkerchief.

"I'm sure it's just a bloody nose, Judy. The boys always play so rough."

Just a bloody nose. Mrs. Nichols was clearly clinging to my mother's assurances, but I was overwhelmed with worry. What if she was wrong? What if the cancer had come back? My mind spooled out the awful possibilities for the months ahead. Mickey in the hospital, Mickey going through chemo, maybe a bone marrow transplant. I thought about how awful it had all been for Nathan and his family the first time. How much Nathan had needed me back then. Then, terribly, I thought, *I'll never be able to break up with him now.*

The Nichols didn't come over for Easter dinner. My father also realized he was out of charcoal, so the backyard barbeque was a bust anyway. Charlie crashed and burned after the sugar rush, passing out on the couch. After we ate our hotdogs (boiled instead of grilled), my dad disappeared into his workshop, and my mom decided to organize her spice rack.

I took a shower and put on my pajamas. When I came downstairs, the kitchen table was covered with spice containers, and my mother was sitting at the table staring at the mess. The air smelled like cinnamon and oregano. She looked like she was emerging from a dream when she finally noticed me. My mom was usually level-headed and stoic; her vulnerability filled me with dread.

"You okay, Mom?"

She offered a sad smile that failed to reassure me. "Just thinking about Mickey."

"I'm sure he'll be fine," I said. Though I wasn't sure at all.

"I don't know what I'd do if anything like that happened to you or Charlie," she said.

"Nothing bad will happen to me or Charlie," I said, as if I had any control over our respective fates. "Are they going to the doctor?"

"Judy took him to the ER. They're waiting on the bloodwork. She'll call when they get the results."

"Is Nathan at home or at the hospital?" I asked.

"He's at home," she said. "You might want to check on him."

I opted to call rather than go over. In my room, I shut the door and curled up under the covers with the phone.

"Hey," I said when he picked up after one ring.

"Hi," he said. I could tell that he'd been crying; his voice sounded like it was traveling through a tunnel to reach me.

"My mom said that Charlie's at the ER?"

"Yeah," he said. I could hear how much he needed me to be there, to sit on his bed and hold his hand while he cried and talked about how worried he was about his brother. About how guilty he felt for every mean thing he ever said or did to him. We'd been through this before. But I couldn't do it. The last place on earth I wanted to be was sitting on his twin bed, clutching a pillow while his heart broke open. I was a terrible girlfriend. I was Lucy, and he was poor Cecil.

"I'm sure he's fine," I repeated. "Probably just a bloody nose."

"Yeah," he said, unconvinced.

Then, though I had no intentions of doing this now, I blurted, "So, I've been thinking about next year . . ."

There was silence on the other end of the line. But then his voice swam to me—a flailing, struggling voice: "What *about* next year?"

What was I doing? It was Easter Sunday, and his brother was in the emergency room. Mickey might have *cancer* again. Now was not the time.

"Oh nothing," I said, trying to sound upbeat, but my heart was ramming against my chest. "I was just thinking how crazy it is that we're graduating already. That we're like practically grownups."

"Yeah. Crazy," he said. "Hey, I'm sorry, but I really have to go. I don't want to tie the phone up in case my mom calls from the hospital. See you tomorrow morning."

After we hung up, I lay on my bed and stared up at the popcorn ceiling, tears running down the sides of my face. But they weren't for Mickey. And they weren't for Nathan.

When I called Trill, Jericho answered.

"Hi, Edie!" he said brightly. "Hold on." In the background I could hear the windchimes that hung on their front porch. This was where Trill took their kitchen phone whenever we talked. I could picture her sitting in one of those turquoise chairs, long legs tucked up under her. A bug bite on her knee, a mug of steaming tea. I wished I was there too.

"So did you break that poor kid's heart?" she asked.

"Not yet," I said.

"*Lucy*," she reprimanded in her haughtiest British accent. "That sounds *noncommittal*."

"I know," I said, and threw myself back on the bed.

"You okay?" she asked.

"I think so?" I said then told her everything that had happened with Mickey.

"Shit. That really, really sucks," she said. "Hey, listen. I'm watching *My Beautiful Laundrette*. It's really funny. And romantic. Daniel Day Lewis. You want to listen along? I'll bring you inside with me."

The windchimes trembled in the breeze and I pictured her going back into the house, heard her slippers scuffing the floor, the screen door slamming behind her.

"Okay. Ready?" she asked, and the MGM lion roared.

It wasn't quite the same as being there watching with her, but it was close.

July 2023

In the bathroom, I study my face in the mirror and wonder what Trill will see when she looks at me now. The days of Lucy Honeychurch with her milky skin and bee-sting lips are gone. I still wear my hair long, up in a sloppy bun most days, but the dark chestnut of my youth is threaded with silver now. I am fifty-five years old. An athlete still, and so my body is strong. But my neck gives me away, and no amount of concealer can hide the circles under my eyes. My eyes. Have they always been downturned like this? I struggle to remember what I used to see in the mirror. Of course, I recall the acne along my chin and the ongoing battle with my curly hair. I remember thinking, as I do now, of my body and my head as two separate and unrelated things.

I lift my shirt over my head and unhook my bra. Then I pull down my shorts, the torn envelope falling to the floor. I pick it up, set it on the counter and run my finger across the place where it has been ripped.

Then I get an idea.

By the time I get out of the shower, my mother has disappeared into her room for her afternoon nap. Ariel is up finally and doing yoga in the living room. Nathan's truck is still in the driveway, and I can hear the whir of the fans and the roar of the Shop-Vac below.

Ariel has pushed the coffee table against the sofa to clear a space in the center of the room. She is in child's pose, on her knees, forehead tipped to the floor.

"Hey, Air?" I venture, sitting on the couch. "What time are you heading to the library again?"

She sits up on her knees and stretches her neck.

"I told Paige I'd be there by one thirty."

Ariel grew up in the children's room at the Quimby Atheneum. Many of the books that were destroyed in the flood had cards inside with her name and the dates borrowed. She said it had broken her heart to discover the sodden copy of *Elves and Fairies*, her favorite.

"What do you know about saving documents that have been water damaged? Like letters and such?"

"Well, the archives room was totally flooded. We've been salvaging a lot of stuff like that. Why?"

My body tenses, and I try to focus on my breathing, as if I'm the one doing yoga.

"I have a letter. Actually, it's just half a letter. It's probably nothing important, but I don't want to toss it if it is. Do you know what the best method to dry it out is? I thought maybe a blow dryer would work, but not sure if heat is the best thing?"

"Oh no! Is it something from the flood in the basement?"

"Yeah," I say, thinking about all her ruined childhood art projects, wondering if they can be salvaged as well. "I just wanted to make sure I'm not throwing out anything important."

"Let me take it in with me," she says, popping up from the floor.

"Where?"

"To the library," she says. "We have a whole room set up. I can get Henry to look at it. He's been working on the special collections stuff that got damaged. He's got all the tools."

"Oh, no, that's okay," I say, feeling panicky. "I just wanted to know if you had any tips. I can do it at home. I don't want to waste his time. The special collections are much more important than this."

"It's totally no big deal. Give it to me, and I'll have him take a peek as soon as he can. It might take a couple days, but I'm sure he'd be happy to help."

I should never have brought it up with her. I should have just Googled it. What an idiot. But then again, what harm will it do? It's likely junk. But junk that has been in my missing brother's missing backpack. *Evidence.*

"Seriously," she says and starts to roll up her yoga mat. "I can take it in with me today."

Trapped, I nod. Really, it's probably nothing more than a bill or a bank statement or a report card. Oh, maybe *that's* what it is. A bad report card? Or a letter from the school? Maybe Charlie had been in trouble at school and hadn't wanted our parents to see it. Something he shoved in his backpack at the end of the school year and forgot. Was that possible?

Maybe. Though it seems unlikely. Charlie was a great kid. He never got in trouble, and certainly not the kind of trouble that would warrant a letter home. Then again, maybe Charlie also had secrets we didn't know about.

After Ariel leaves for the library, torn envelope in hand, I am overwhelmed with regret. How careless that was—first to steal it, then to hand it off to my daughter as though it wasn't a potential key to solving the mystery of Charlie's disappearance. Hopefully she'll return it intact, but what then? Do I return it to Jericho? Take it to the police?

My phone buzzes on the kitchen table, and I hold my breath. Could it be Trill already? No. Jericho said that she and her wife were driving up from the city this afternoon. I highly doubt that reaching out to me will be the first thing she'll do. We haven't spoken in almost thirty-seven years.

I flip my phone over and see it's my friend Amanda. We haven't seen each other at all this summer despite our promises to hang out when school wasn't looming over our heads. During the school year, we're thick as thieves, our classrooms sharing a wall. She teaches Freshman Comp, and I teach the honors and AP classes in Mr. Howard's old room. We work together, eat lunch together, and even coach track together. But when school lets out, we tend to retreat to our respective homes and obligations.

"Hi!" I say, immediately regretting the decision to pick up. Amanda is perceptive; she'll know the second I start talking that something's awry. But maybe I can tell her what's going on. Amanda is clear-headed and wise; she can also keep a secret.

"*Hey*," she says somberly, and I feel guilty.

"I'm so sorry I haven't checked in," I start. "Our basement flooded. And my mom, well, she's been kind of a handful lately . . . also—"

"My mom passed," she says.

"What? When?"

"Two nights ago," she says. "In her sleep, thank God. And it's okay. I mean, I'm okay."

I feel terrible. Amanda and her mom were close. Unlike me, Amanda never complained about taking care of her mother; she took her shopping, to doctors' visits, out for lunch. They went to the gym together, where they did yoga or water aerobics. Amanda read to her, washed her hair. They went to the movies. Not long after her dementia diagnosis, they had even gone on an Alaskan cruise together. I had looked at the photos she took and felt a stab of jealousy at the way her mother beamed at her. I don't think my mom has ever looked at me like that. But then again, what have I done to earn that kind of love?

"What can I do?" I ask. "For you, I mean?"

Amanda has no children, no partner. Her mom was her entire world.

"Nothing, really," she says. "She didn't want a funeral, but we'll do a celebration later. If it ever stops raining."

"I'll help you. Whatever you need. I can do the food. I can help you find a venue."

"Thanks, Edie. I might just need to call you and cry sometimes. Would that be okay?"

"Of course," I say. "Amanda, I really am so sorry."

"Well, listen. I have a lot of stuff to get rid of now. Maybe your mom could use some if it? I've got an adjustable bed and a wheelchair. I mean, I know she doesn't need it yet. But . . ."

"I'll come over and help you go through stuff. Just call me when you're ready."

When I hang up, I hear my own mother snoring in the other room and know I should feel thankful that I still have her. But gratitude eludes me.

The rain is coming down again, battering the windows that overlook our drenched yard. I think about the basement, the cement walls weeping. Water pooling. I imagine Nathan assessing the damage, shaking his head.

In the kitchen, I clear away my mother's lunch, the sandwich barely touched. I wrap it in plastic and put it in the fridge, knowing I'll be the one to finish it later. I load up the dishwasher and am wiping down the counter when I hear Nathan climbing up the basement stairs.

The industrial fans whir loudly below when he opens the door.

"How bad is it?" I ask.

"It's bad, Edie. We need to get it dried out, and then we need to remediate the mold."

"There's *mold*?"

"Well, definitely in the unfinished part of the basement. But we need to get behind the drywall in the rec room to make sure it hasn't started there too."

"Okay," I say, feeling like a terrible caretaker of this house.

"After that, I think the smartest thing to do is to get a sump pump in. I honestly can't believe you don't have one."

"How much will that be?" I ask.

"I can get it at a discount and do the install myself. But the mold remediation is another story. It's pretty bad, Edie."

"You said that," I say, feeling the irritation I felt when we were kids and he'd repeat himself for emphasis. Here he is offering his help, and I am being a pill.

"Okay," I say. "If it needs to be done."

"It does. We also need to tear up the carpet. I've got a dumpster up at the Masons' I can use to dispose of the damaged stuff. If you can move anything you want to keep into the garage and leave the stuff you don't want in the basement, I'll load it up in my truck."

I think about all those rotten boxes of my father's papers, Ariel's art, Charlie's wet books and clothes.

"Thanks, Nathan."

I show him to the door, as if he doesn't know the way out. As if he hasn't walked out of our kitchen a million times before.

I step onto the porch with him and close the door behind me to keep Daisy from escaping.

"I appreciate you coming," I say, apologetic.

"No problem," he says, but he doesn't move toward his truck.

"What?" I say.

"You really shouldn't let things like this go," he said. "Ignoring things doesn't make them go away."

April 1986

IT WASN'T JUST a bloody nose. Mickey's cancer had returned. Acute lymphoblastic leukemia. And after last period that Easter Monday, Nathan met me at my locker, looking distracted and dejected, and I felt even worse than when I'd tried—and failed—to break up with him. I'd been swept up in *A Room with a View*, but I was no Lucy Honeychurch. I was Edith Marshall, spineless and meek.

"So, what happens next?" I asked Nathan as he walked me down to the locker rooms before track practice. "Will he have to go to Boston this time? For treatments?"

Poor Mickey had been so little the last time he went through this. He'd gotten sick in September when Nathan and I were freshmen, and Mrs. Nichols had taken a leave from the bank and spent three months at Boston Children's Hospital, living at the Ronald McDonald House. Nathan and his dad had stayed behind for school and work, going to the hospital on the weekends, delivering the bags of letters Mickey received from classmates and teachers and even strangers who'd heard about his illness. Charlie made cards every week, sent toys of his own with Nathan and Mr. Nichols. He'd even wanted to send his Stretch Armstrong doll until our dad talked him out of it. "He's your favorite, buddy," he'd said and convinced Charlie to give him one of his Transformers instead.

"They're sending him home today," Nathan said. "He'll start chemo next week. Unless there are complications, like last time, they said he can do all his treatments here."

I didn't know what to say, and when he put his arm across my shoulders and pulled me in, I let him.

At least I still had Smith. Or the possibility of Smith, anyway. If I went away for school, then maybe things would just fizzle between us, slowly and painlessly. Long-distance relationships were hard. He'd get tired of talking on the phone, of mailing letters, of driving down to visit. Maybe he'd even meet somebody in town. And if it happened this way, I wouldn't have to be the bad guy. If I got into Smith, I would just need to make it through the summer. Hopefully by then Mickey would be in remission and I would be moving into my dorm room. It was a cowardly plan, but it was a plan, nevertheless.

But then I got the letter.

I wouldn't have seen it at all, if the *Ladies' Home Journal* on the counter hadn't dropped to the floor when I was making supper that night. Somehow, the envelope had gotten stuck between the pages.

As I picked it up, all the blood in my body rushed to my extremities. My hands tingled. My heart felt white hot. I studied the envelope, experienced a sinking feeling as I recalled what people had said about thin envelopes: they usually meant rejections. State's envelope had been thick, filled with info and forms to fill out.

Trembling, I grabbed a butter knife sitting on the counter. I never used a letter opener, but it felt important to open this properly.

I pulled the single sheet of paper from the envelope and carefully unfolded it, squinting, intentionally blurring my vision to keep the message unknown for a bit longer. I took a deep breath and began to read.

Dear Edith,

We are writing to inform you that the College Admissions Committee is unable to make a final decision on your acceptance at this time.

Trembling, I shook my head. What?

We received a record number of applications this year. And while we cannot currently offer you a spot in the freshman class, we were impressed by your outstanding achievements and promise. We have placed your name on the waiting list in the event that a spot opens.

I shook my head. No, no, no. The *waiting list*? This was the purgatory of the college admissions process.

If you would like to remain on the waiting list, we ask that you send a letter of continued interest, where you may include any additional information which might be relevant to your application.

I took a deep breath, swiped at the tears that were falling freely now.

It wasn't a *no*. But it wasn't a *yes* either. It was a *maybe*. My whole future was riding on a single letter of continued interest, never mind somebody else turning down their spot at Smith.

At track practice that week, I pushed Mickey and Nathan and Smith out of my mind, focusing on running as fast and as hard as I could. When my legs had turned to jelly, I would move to the javelin area to practice throwing. Last, I'd make my way to the long jump pit, where I ran and jumped, ran and jumped. My shoes and shorts and hair filled with sand, but at least my mind was calm.

On Friday, when the coach released us, I jogged on wobbly legs to the pole vault pit and climbed up, collapsing onto the sun-warmed vinyl. Trill came jogging over from the track where she had been practicing hurdles and plopped down next to me, kicking off the cleats she was forced to wear. Trill had a bouncy way about her, even when she was trying to be still, and the pit bounced like the inside of a jumpy house.

We both lay on our backs and looked up at the sky, at the cold blue. Clouds like afterthoughts.

"*My father says there's only one perfect view, the view of the sky,*" Trill said dreamily in that over-the-top British accent.

"Your dad?" Trill almost never talked about her father. I got the sense that she'd been hurt when he took the job overseas, basically exiling her from her life in the city.

"*No,*" she said. "It's what George said to Lucy. Or something like that anyway. Remember?"

Oh, the movie. I was trying not to think about Lucy Honeychurch.

Trill's shoulder was touching mine. I could hear her breathing.

"So have you started the letter yet?" she asked. "For Smith?"

I'd tried. I'd started it about a hundred times, but everything I wrote sounded so cheesy. I'd already written an essay as part of my application, arguing my case for why I belonged at Smith. I really had zero left to add; there was literally nothing that differentiated me from the thousands of other applicants. I had excellent grades, high SAT scores, loads of extracurriculars. I loved poetry, and Mr. Howard said I had promise as a writer. But other than having a way with words, I had no special talents. I also had not faced any major challenges or obstacles. I had a mother and a father, a little brother. My parents were gainfully employed. We had food on the table each night. We were 100 percent typical, and Smith wanted *extraordinary*.

"I have no idea how to convince them I belong there. And honestly, I'm not sure I do."

"Of course you belong there," she said, propping herself up on one elbow.

I groaned. I had tried to imagine myself at State. Living at home, next door to Nathan. Hanging out with Trill only when she came home for breaks. Why hadn't I applied to any other out of state schools?

"I have an idea," Trill said. She popped up and started re-braiding her hair, which was always springing loose from braids and ponytails.

"For my letter?" I asked.

"Sort of," she said. "When is it due?"

"The end of April. People who got in have until May first to accept their spots. Then they start pulling people off the waitlist."

"Perfect. What are you doing for spring break?" she asked.

Spring break was the third week of April. This year, like every year, I had no plans at all. We were not a family that went on vacations. The doctor's office was busy with kids getting their physicals during the break, so my mother could never get time off. Most of the families that could afford to travel went to Disney World, with one or two families making trips to places more exotic, like the Bahamas. Lisa's family had gone to St. Bart's last year, and she came back golden brown with Bo Derek braids. Nathan's parents had a timeshare in Myrtle Beach.

"Nothing. Watching Charlie, probably." My mother hadn't asked me to babysit, but I knew that with Mickey sick, she'd expect me to be at home to watch him.

"Do you think you could get away for the weekend? Just like Friday to Sunday?"

I felt a quiver excitement. What was she suggesting? And what did it have to do with my Smith essay?

I sighed. "I doubt it. Who will watch Charlie when they're at work on Friday?"

"You're not their nanny, you know," she snapped, then softened when I looked at her, eyebrow raised. "I'm sorry. I just mean they shouldn't take advantage of you like that."

I hadn't thought about it like this before. Taking care of Charlie was one of my jobs. Like making supper. And doing the laundry.

"I can ask my mom, I guess," I said. "Where do you want to go?"

"To *Smith*," she said.

My vision of Smith was based exclusively on the brochure I had and what I had read in Sylvia's journals. It was my dream school, but it was literally just a dream—I had never been, though it was only three hours away.

"We *have* to go," Trill said. "To both Smith and Hampshire. How can we make our decision unless we've seen the campuses? We'll make a weekend of it. My aunt lives in Northampton. We can stay with her. We could even go over to Boston, it's not that far."

The way Trill talked so casually about travel made me feel inexperienced and sheltered. It had never dawned on me that I could just get in a car and drive to a major city.

"We'll visit and then we'll decide," she said.

Again, I felt that electric bolt inside me. The idea that Trill would base her college decision on where I wound up made me feel special. That was exactly why I loved spending time with her. She made me feel like I *was* extraordinary. It was different from being with Nathan. Nathan loved me, but his affection made me feel like he wanted something from me. With Trill, she just *liked* me. She thought I was smart and cool and fun to be around. And unlike Nathan, she never demanded anything. Until now.

"We *have* to go," she said, squeezing my hand. "I'll help you write a letter they won't be able to refuse."

"I don't like this idea," my mother said.

The only thing more difficult than convincing my parents to go somewhere turned out to be convincing them to let *me* go on a road trip with Trill in her beat-up Chevy Vega.

"It's *spring break*," I said, trying not to whine.

"Why on earth would you go to Massachusetts for spring break? It's not like it's any sunnier down there."

It was Friday night, and she had set the ironing board up in the family room and was ironing her uniforms; the air smelled like starch. The iron hissed in her hands. My father was on his second scotch, watching *The Twilight Zone*.

"Can Nathan go with you two? Help drive?" my mother asked. "It would be nice for him to get away. It's been so hard with Mickey being sick again."

"Nathan?" I said, making a face I quickly regretted. "I mean, why would Nathan come? He's not even going to college."

My mother scowled.

"Oh, we're going down so Trill can look at colleges," I said, realizing my error. "She's been accepted to Hampshire."

"Never heard of it," my mother said as though this was reason enough for her to say no.

"Nathan's going to be working with his dad that week," I argued. Now that the snow was gone, construction work had begun.

"That's a long drive," my mother said.

"Trill's had her license for almost two years," I said. "She's a good driver, she's never had an accident, and it's less than three hours away. We'll go straight to her aunt's, and I'll call you from there. We won't leave until Friday morning, and we'll be back by Sunday night."

"What am I supposed to do with Charlie on Friday?" my mother asked. "He can't go to the Nicholses' with Mickey sick."

You're not their nanny.

"It's just one day," I said. "Lisa babysits. She'll be on spring break too. I can ask her."

"I do miss having Lisa around," my mother said, considering. "She's always been sweet to Charlie."

"So, I can go?" I asked.

My mother looked to my father, and he shrugged. "If we let you go, you need to be home in time for supper on Sunday," she said.

I couldn't wait to tell Trill. She'd already planned out our whole trip, from where and what we'd eat to the music we'd bring to listen to in the car. But when I picked up the phone to call her, there was already somebody on the line.

"Hello?" I said.

"Edie? It didn't even ring," Nathan said. "Great minds . . ."

"Oh, hi," I said. "What's up?"

"Nothing, I just haven't seen you much lately."

"Yeah," I said. "I know. I've just been like super busy with school and track and stuff."

He didn't speak.

"How's Mickey?" I asked.

"Listen, Edie? I really need you right now, and I feel like you're . . . like . . ."

The call waiting started to beep. I wasn't used to it. My dad loved technology, though, and had signed us up for it as soon as it was available.

"I'm sorry, Nathan, there's somebody calling in," I said. "It might be important." That was, after all, my father's reasoning in getting call waiting; it ensured the line wouldn't be tied up while I was on the phone with Nathan for hours on end. "Hold on a sec."

I clicked over, and Trill's voice chirped, "Hey! Can you sleep over tonight?"

"Tonight?" I asked, though thrilling at the prospect of staying over at The Farm. "We have a meet tomorrow."

"Bring your cleats! I'll pick you up in twenty," she said. "Also, does Charlie have a telescope, by any chance?"

"A telescope? He got one for Christmas."

"Bring it," she said.

I remembered Nathan waiting on the other line, but when I clicked back over, he was gone.

I got my duffle out from under my bed, found my cleats and uniform, my socks. I grabbed my toothbrush from the bathroom and some clean underwear and pajamas from my drawer, all while trying to figure out what I could tell my mom that would convince her to approve a last-minute sleepover when I'd just used all my persuasive powers to convince her to agree to spring break. And out at The Farm, no less.

The phone rang, and I worried it was Nathan, so I waited for somebody else to pick it up.

I raced down the stairs into the kitchen, where my mother was sitting at the table, phone pressed against her ear. She was frowning. "What's his white blood cell count?"

Mrs. Nichols.

I motioned to my mother that I needed her attention. "Hold on a second, Judy," she said and covered the mouthpiece with her hand. "Where are you going?"

"Trill's house. We're lab partners in Chem. Lab report. She's picking me up, and she'll take me to the track meet tomorrow. I'll come home right after."

She offered a curt *okay* and went back to her call.

I opened the door to the garage, eager to make my escape before she could change her mind or wonder why we were doing homework on a Friday night. Charlie's telescope was in the corner by our bikes. He was so excited for summer to come to use it. I felt kind of bad borrowing it without his permission, but going back inside would mean risking my mom changing her mind.

Outside, the air was cold. More like winter than April. The light was on in Nathan's room next door. At least the Nicholses' phone was tied up, a good excuse for not calling him back.

I leaned the telescope against the porch, sat down on the steps, and took a deep breath.

Nathan was going to be mad about me going away for the weekend of spring break, especially if he felt like I wasn't spending enough time with him already. He would be working during the week but probably off for the weekend, and he'd been wanting me to come with him to order his tux for prom to make sure he got the right color cummerbund and tie. I hadn't gotten my dress yet, though my mother kept bringing it up. She'd even gone through my latest *Seventeen* and marked some pages with sticky notes. Fluffy Gunne Sax dresses in Easter egg colors. Ballet pink and buttery yellow. Colors that were not a part of my wardrobe. "You need to decide soon," she told me. "We'll have to order it in time to get it tailored."

When Trill pulled into the driveway, the Vega's muffler rattling loudly, I saw the curtains in Nathan's room part. I clumsily carried the telescope down the walkway to Trill's car. "Put it in the back!" she said, and I did, carefully laying it across the back seat before throwing open the passenger door and getting in.

"Let's go," I said, like I'd robbed a bank and she was my getaway.

We drove past school and across the covered bridge, Nico's funny little honk announcing us to any oncoming traffic, and turned onto Route 42. But instead of turning off at Lost River Road, we kept driving. "Where are we going?" I asked. Though honestly, she could have said we were going anywhere, and I would have been fine with it.

"Have you ever been up the fire tower on Franklin Mountain?" she asked.

I had not. I didn't ski, so my only knowledge of Franklin Mountain was as a landmark when I started driving and needed orientation so I wouldn't get lost.

"It's kind of dark out," I said, as she turned onto the old toll road that zig-zagged its way up the mountain.

"We're going to try to see Halley's Comet!" she said.

"Oh wow! Really?" I remembered that the *Challenger* had been heading into space for this same purpose.

"Charlie to the rescue!" she said, motioning to the telescope.

"We're carrying that thing to the top of a mountain?"

To be fair, Franklin Mountain was hardly Mount Everest. The diehard skiers in town often hiked to the top before the mountain officially opened for the season, lugging their skis on their shoulders. The toll road would take us almost to the top.

"I've seen your triceps," she said. "Major brawn."

I snorted. Though I did have some pretty serious arm strength from hurling javelins.

Trill grinned, and I took a moment to study her attire. Tonight, she was wearing her ubiquitous long skirt with a puffy down jacket. A handknit hat with a pom-pom and earflaps, the yarn ties hanging like colorful braids on either side of her head.

At least I had jeans on, but it would probably be cold up on the mountain, and my windbreaker wouldn't cut it.

"My bomber jacket's back there too," she said.

She had a leather flight jacket that I had coveted from the first time she wore it to school. On the inside was a silky map of Europe. She said she'd bought it at a thrift store in the Village. The best secondhand find I had was my dad's old navy peacoat, but it smelled like mothballs and was missing buttons.

I reached into the back and slipped on her jacket, maneuvering the seatbelt to get my arms through the sleeves. The silky lining was cool, but I warmed up quickly. It smelled like her.

We slowly drove up the toll road, reaching the upper lodge parking lot, where we parked and unloaded the telescope. Trill reached into the glove box and pulled out a headlamp—the kind miners wore in movies—and affixed it over her hat.

We must have looked ridiculous, carrying the telescope up the muddy trail to the fire tower, which perched like an odd skeletal bird at the top of the mountain. The old fire warden's quarters, a small shack, was at the base, but the real view, she said, was to be seen from the top.

I liked to consider myself a pretty brave person when it came to physical challenges. I was not afraid of jumping off the high dive at the pool or going on the scarier rides at the county fair. But it was pitch-black, save the weak glow coming from Trill's headlamp, and the telescope was cumbersome. If I had been with anyone else—Nathan, for example—I would have rationalized why this was absolutely not a good idea. But it was Trill. She made me want to be braver. To live bigger. Here was another moment when I felt like we were playing an unspoken game of Truth or Dare, with Dare being the only real option.

I got on the ladder and had her hoist the telescope up until I had a decent hold on the top of it. She started up behind me, and slowly, we were climbing and maneuvering the instrument, which weighed nearly as much as Charlie.

It dawned on me then that I had forgotten to say goodbye to Charlie. Not a big deal, except that he was kind of weird about goodbyes. It didn't matter if I was fast asleep or in the shower; if he was leaving, he'd bang on the door and holler, "Bye!" Anytime I forgot to do the same, he'd melt down. Since he was a toddler, Charlie liked to know where everybody was at all times, and if somebody just took off, he freaked out that they were gone. Maybe I could call him when we got back to The Farm, though by then, he would probably be asleep.

We made our way to the top of the fire tower, and bracing myself, I used my *brawn* to pull the telescope up onto the platform. Out of breath, I sat down as Trill made her way up the last few rungs.

It was like being at the top of the Ferris wheel times a hundred. Below lay our sleepy village, pitch-black save the warm specks of light coming from the various neighborhoods.

"Which way is The Farm?" I asked, and Trill pointed. I squinted but saw nothing to indicate she was right.

"And school?" I asked.

"Seriously? This is your town! I'm just a tourist here." She laughed. "Over there's your neighborhood. And Main Street."

"I'll take your word for it," I said and laughed.

Trill worked on getting the telescope set up while I tried and failed to orient myself.

"I'd have made a terrible pirate," I said. "My navigational skills suck."

"Aye, matey, follow the stars," Trill said. She was good with directions. She'd told me that she'd started taking the subway by herself when she was only twelve. This was completely unfathomable to me. Though heights and speed didn't faze me, the idea of having to get myself around a city felt impossible.

"You're a country mouse," she'd said. "It's not a *bad* thing. It's just a thing."

I felt—as I often felt around Trill—like she had a wisdom and confidence I might never have. Though she never made me feel that way.

When Lisa and I were best friends, she had been the one who knew more about everything: about boys, about bodies, about sex. Though she patiently explained, *imparted*, that knowledge, her tone was condescending, like an adult talking to a child. "The S on the tampon box means *super* not *small*," she'd patronized. "You can't get pregnant on your period," she'd proselytized. (I'd bought this hook, line, and sinker until our gym teacher debunked that theory.)

The sky was a deep indigo blue, heavy clouds obscuring much of it.

"Do you think we'll be able to see it?" I asked skeptically. "The comet?"

"I hope so. It's supposed to be passing over Vermont now."

She sat next to me and rifled through her parka pocket, pulling out a cigarette. I had never seen her smoke before. My parents quit when I was ten (other than my dad's occasionally stolen butt).

"Ew. I hate cigarettes," I said. I found that I could be honest with Trill. It was another refreshing thing about her. Because she didn't judge, I could be exactly who I was.

"Me too," she said and danced it in front of my face playfully. "It's a joint."

"Oh," I said.

Lisa and I got into her parents' liquor cabinet once when we were fourteen, got sick on peach schnapps. Nathan and I sometimes snuck his father's beers up into his room or into his old tree fort in the small patch of woods behind his house. I'd gotten tipsy at some parties, including my aunt's wedding on pilfered champagne. But I'd never gotten stoned.

"It's medicinal," she said. "Seriously. My mom smokes it for her arthritis."

The word *medicinal* made me think of Mickey, and I got the same guilty pang that kept ringing in my brain like a struck gong lately.

"I've never smoked pot," I confessed. "I don't even know how to do it."

"No biggie. I'll show you."

An hour later, or maybe only minutes—who knew, time felt as liquid and pitchy as the sky—Halley's Comet passed overhead. I only knew because Trill was looking through the telescope and squealed. It was a girly, high-pitched squeal that startled me. I had been studying my own hand, baffled by the fact that it was so dark I couldn't even see *myself.*

"Come look!" she said and motioned for me to join her. I scrambled to my feet, feeling rather formless, and peered into the telescope.

It was just a puff of white, like smoke from that joint we'd shared—but it was moving.

"That's it!" Trill said. "And we'll probably never get a chance to see it again unless we live to be ninety-three."

"Also, I doubt we'll be climbing fire towers at ninety-three," I said.

"Speak for yourself."

I don't know whether it was the weed or the thrill of being on the top of a fire tower on top of a mountain in the middle of the night or the idea that we were witnessing something we would probably never ever witness again, but I was completely overwhelmed by emotion. It was like the feeling I'd had in that empty theater when my heart blew open. The universe felt suddenly enormous. Though, oddly, not with the vast uncertainty of a black hole, but the brilliant illumination of the comet making itself known to us. The thing that the poor *Challenger* passengers had died pursuing was *right here*, a private spectacle before our very eyes.

"My heart feels swollen," I said.

"Mine too," Trill said, reaching for my hand and holding on. I waited for her to release it, but she didn't. Her thumb stroked the side of my thumb, and I felt shivery.

We watched together, taking turns looking into the glass that magnified this miracle.

"We should probably head back to my house," she said after a few minutes, and we both returned to Earth.

"I love this jacket," I said as we made our way down the fire tower.

"Keep it," Trill said.

"*Really*?"

"Totally. I have like a hundred other jackets."

"Thanks. Also, I want a cheeseburger," I said. "Like a really big cheeseburger. With pickles."

"Your wish is my command," Trill said.

In Trill's kitchen, she cooked up two giant burgers, which she covered in extra sharp Cabot cheddar and put between thick slices of toasted bread brushed with homemade dill pickle juice. We devoured the burgers, trying not to make too much noise; both Jericho and Phyllis had already gone to bed.

I remembered again that I hadn't said goodbye to Charlie. And, in my impaired state, it felt urgent.

Trill motioned to the phone.

My mother answered on the first ring. "Hello?" Her voice was froggy.

This was a bad idea.

"Hi, Mom," I said, and my words felt elastic and rubbery. "I just realized I didn't say goodbye to Charlie before I left. Can you tell him I called in the morning?"

"Okay," she said, but she sounded distant. I'd probably woken her up. "And Edie, just so you know what's going on, they're sending Mickey down to Boston Children's tomorrow. He may need a bone marrow transplant."

Trill looked at me, quizzical.

"So, if you could just be *kind* to Nathan . . ." here she trailed off. "He's having a really rough time right now."

July 2023

On Sunday morning, I wait for my mother to get ready for church and log on to the local news, half-expecting that Jericho's discovery will be splashed across the headlines. I know it's premature; he hasn't even gone to the police yet, but I'm on edge, waiting. Before I left The Farm yesterday, I gave him my cell number so he wouldn't call the tip line again, but he still hasn't reached out. I assume Trill and her wife arrived last night. I try to picture them sitting at that kitchen table, Charlie's backpack a strange centerpiece. I imagine Trill's tear-filled eyes.

I wonder what the discovery of the backpack will mean for an investigation that has been bitter cold for decades. The local detectives originally assigned to the case are long gone. They had both called my mother and father to announce their respective retirements, though they assured them that if anything new were to come up, then someone else would be assigned to follow up. The backpack is a new discovery, but what, if anything does it prove?

On July 18, 1986, my brother, walking home alone from day camp, backpack on his back, had disappeared into thin air. At first, we assumed (hoped) he'd simply gotten distracted and followed a critter into the woods (a bunny, a frog?) and gotten lost. But the next morning, a man walking the loop saw something sparkle in the grassy field alongside the road and curious, he'd walked into the tall grass where the items had appeared one after another: a damp Garfield beach towel, a wooden popsicle stick stained cherry red, a Walkman with a tape curling through the grass, and the shattered glass that had first sparked his curiosity: Charlie's broken eyeglasses. Something had happened to Charlie in that field.

Still, we prayed he'd only fallen, bumped his head maybe and wandered into the woods, injured and disoriented. For weeks, the police combed the forest surrounding the field, slowly extending their search wider and wider, like circles emanating from a stone tossed into water. But they found nothing.

Then, in early August, an anonymous caller on the tip line told my father he'd seen Jericho Jenkins's truck racing away from the site of the items not fifteen minutes after Charlie left the pool. Law enforcement paid a visit to The Farm, where they found Jericho, who recognized the photo they'd brought of Charlie, who said, yes, yes, of course he knew Charlie Marshall—he'd been his art teacher last year. Who said he'd been so sad to hear what happened.

Jericho had no idea the police had a theory taking shape: that he had seen Charlie walking home. That maybe he'd tried to offer him a ride, and when Charlie declined there had been some sort of struggle. That he'd snatched Charlie and fled. Jericho didn't know that every question they asked was meant to implicate him.

Where were you between 11:45 and 12:30 that day? they had asked, and he had answered without hesitation. But his story—that he had been at The Farm, replacing a broken oven in The Bakery—had no one to corroborate it. His mother had been out of town, and his sister had been home, but sick with a summer flu and asleep, knocked out on cough medicine. They'd questioned Trill for three hours—she'd said of course he was home, but when pressed, she admitted that the last time she had actually seen her brother was the night before when he brought her some soup and then not again until the next day. No, she hadn't seen his truck in the driveway. There was no one who could confirm his alibi.

And so, less than a month after Charlie disappeared, the police believed they had their guy. With just a bit more evidence—something concrete—to connect him to Charlie, they could take him into custody. But they hadn't been able to locate that string, that golden thread that tethered him to my brother. There was nothing in his house (which he opened up to them), in his barn (except for *thousands of disturbing "art" pieces*), or on his land. No evidence that Charlie had ever been inside his truck or at The Farm. And so, they'd had to let him go.

Until now. Charlie's backpack. Of course, there is no way of knowing at what point it was hidden inside that tree. It could have been immediately following his disappearance. Or it could have been weeks, or months, or even years later. Or maybe this is the kind of thing that forensics could determine? It sounded like one of my mother's podcasts. But here is the real question: Was the backpack put there *before* Jericho was a suspect, or *because* he was a suspect? If the former, then someone had been trying to frame him. If the latter, they were an opportunist capitalizing on his already being under suspicion. This feels a lot more likely. It would also explain why the dogs that had been set loose, with the scent of my brother their goal, had found nothing.

But what would the police think now? Would it be enough that Jericho had come forward with the new evidence? Or would they speculate that he had reached out to me as some sort of apology or confession?

"Okay, let's go," my mother says. She is ready for church, but she is dressed as if it is a hot summer day: a pink linen sleeveless shift. Sandals. Outside, it is cold and raining again.

"You look pretty, Mom. But it's raining out, so let me get your coat."

At Mass, we sit near the back, as we always do. Ariel opted out. I didn't raise her in the church, and until my father passed, I hadn't set foot in St. Paul's myself in decades. But my mother isn't able to get herself to Mass alone anymore, and so when in-person services resumed after the pandemic, I acquiesced. At church she sees friends who take the time to say hello and catch her up on whatever is going on in their lives. She seems buoyed by these encounters, and anything that might lift her up feels worth the effort.

After church, she likes to go to the Miss Quimby Diner, where I get the Greek omelet and she usually orders coffee and a slice of chocolate cream pie, Charlie's favorite. But today, she has an appointment for her shingles vaccine, so we swing by the Walgreens first. She's fidgety and nervous, which is odd given the number of shots she herself has administered over the years. She clutches my hand so tightly my bones ache, a bit of terror in her eyes as she insists on watching the syringe plunge into her arm. Afterward, she spends nearly an hour searching for a birthday card for Ariel. I wait patiently at first, browsing the cards alongside her, weighing in on which one Ariel might like. But after about ten minutes of her poo-pooing my suggestions only to pick up a card I showed her just moments ago, I excuse myself and take a seat by the blood pressure kiosk, though I know better than to use it.

By the time we get to the diner, I am irritable and starving, but thankfully, the after-church rush is over. A couple of men sit at the counter with newspapers and coffee. Two of my female students are giggling in a booth near the windows, a shared plate of fries between them. But the rest of the booths and tables are empty.

"Hi, Ms. M!" the dark-haired girl, Kelsey, says. She was in my Honors American Lit class last year, a good student and writer. The rest of the tables are empty, the waitresses wiping down the tops and replacing the paper placemats and napkin-swaddled flatware.

"Hi, ladies," our waitress says. "Slice of chocolate pie, Mrs. Marshall?"

My mother orders the pie, but when it arrives, she doesn't eat it. She never does. She's been on a diet my entire life. She was a nurse but ate terribly. She tried every fad diet imaginable when I was a kid: the Scarsdale Diet, the Grapefruit Diet, and the Beverly Hills Diet. Later it was Atkins, South Beach, Jenny Craig. She even tried Weight Watchers, but they said she was too thin to attend the meetings. It had always felt ridiculous to me, given that my father hardly noticed when she went up or down a dress size. You'd think that as a carpenter he would be attentive to details. At work, I suppose, he was. But when it came to my mother, haircuts, new clothes, and weight loss simply didn't register. This blindness drove my mother crazy. But when Charlie disappeared, what had been low-grade annoyance became a simmering rage.

When the police came that night after he vanished, I remember my mother yelling at my father, "No! He was wearing *blue* sneakers. He's four feet *five.* His backpack is *red.*" My father's oversights became egregious instead of simply irritating. My brother was missing, and my father could not recall any of the most important details.

It was probably because of this that every single day from kindergarten through Ariel's senior year, I would do a thorough scan as she walked out the door. From head to toe, I would take note of her clothes, her jewelry, her footwear: the catalog of details imprinted on my brain, in case she too vanished. I would not make the same mistake my father had made, the one that haunted our family and created a rift between my parents that remained until my father died.

I wonder what my father would make of Jericho's discovery.

"Can I have a bite?" I ask, motioning to the pie.

She pushes it toward me, and I dig my fork in. I close my eyes and chew the pie slowly. It is so delicious. I wonder if Charlie were here if he'd still enjoy it. It was his favorite at nine, but he also loved Cheese Whiz on apples back then. He liked to sprinkle sugar on his french fries. He was just a little boy.

My mother is staring out the window. She is definitely out of sorts today. The pharmacist warned that the shingles vaccine could make her feel a bit under the weather, but I can't help but attribute her behavior to her intuition that I'm withholding something from her. I've kept secrets from my mother before, but she is sharp, and I've often had the sense that she knows exactly what I'm not saying. Now, she fidgets with her napkin, clearly agitated, that pie sitting between us, and I worry she knows, somehow, that I have news about Charlie.

"I need to use the restroom," she says, scowling.

"I'll take you," I say and start to stand.

"I can do it," she snaps. Accepting help at home is one thing; having your daughter go to the bathroom with you in public is another.

"Okay," I say. "But take your phone. Text me if you need me."

She navigates the labyrinth of tables, tottering to the restroom near the entrance to the diner. After she closes the bathroom door, the bells on the diner's door jingle. I expect to see another one of my students or a colleague or one of my parents' friends. It's rare to see someone I don't know at the diner, but I don't recognize these women.

The one in front is petite, with a jet-black pixie cut. Brown skin, flushed cheeks. One bare arm is sleeved in brightly colored floral tattoos, the other circled with silver and turquoise bracelets. The woman trailing behind her is a head taller and wearing a bright yellow raincoat, hood up. Once inside the restaurant, she pulls the hood down. Pale skin and strawberry hair, pushed back by a paisley scarf that trails down one shoulder. Dangly chandelier earrings, green eyes.

Trill?

Of course, I have imagined seeing her again, rehearsed what I would say. I have anticipated the way my throat might constrict, the way my hands might tremble, the nausea that might overwhelm me at the sight of her face. But I have not envisioned this paralysis. This numbness. I am not prepared. I glance down at my hands because I can no longer feel them.

The waitress motions for the two women to take a seat anywhere they like, and the dark-haired one—*Paloma,* I presume—looks around then straight at me. She stops and studies my face, furrowing her brow as she tries to place me. We have never met, of course, but she has clearly seen me before, in a photo maybe? Then, the knock of recognition seems to hit.

"What?" Trill asks her, and Paloma motions with her chin toward me.

The terrifying stillness that has overtaken me is replaced by the more predictable trembling. I watch as Trill's curiosity turns to disbelief then stunned despair. A thousand emotions cross her face, and I feel the same kaleidoscopic swirl playing out on my own.

When Trill approaches, Paloma close behind, the chocolate cream pie turns to cement in my throat. I feel myself standing up, the habitual, appropriate, *expected* response to seeing an old friend at a restaurant. But my ears burn, and my mouth twitches furiously as I smile.

Trill appears afflicted by the same stunned paralysis. Paloma, thankfully, reaches out her hand and says, "You must be Edie. I'm Paloma."

I shake her hand but keep looking at Trill, whose eyes are watery. Cheeks red.

When Paloma releases my hand, I step toward Trill. The chocolate cement shifts, and I manage to speak.

"You're here?" A question you might ask a ghost. "I thought . . ."

Trill reaches for both of my hands and leans close to me, studying my face.

"*Lucy,*" she says, her voice breaking.

"There's a booth down this way," Paloma says firmly, and Trill comes back from wherever she's been. "*Trillium*–"

"I'm sorry," I say, my heart pounding in my temples. "Can I get your number? Or—Jericho has mine. I was waiting to hear from him. Will you call me? I'll be home later today."

"Of course," she says, but Paloma jerks her head sharply. *No.*

I scowl. Is she suggesting that Trill isn't *allowed* to call me? Seriously? I start to protest, but then my phone buzzes on the table.

"Oh shoot," I say. "It's my mom. She needs help in the restroom."

"We'll be in touch," Paloma says, forcing a smile, as though this is some sort of business transaction, and steers Trill away from the table to the back of the diner. Trill looks over her shoulder back and me and mouths, "Sorry."

I put cash down for the bill, grab my purse, and walk quickly to the restroom door.

"Mom?" I say. "It's me."

The rain starts again in earnest the moment I get my mother settled back in at home. She is, indeed, not feeling well after her shot. She says her head is aching and she feels feverish, though I still can't help wondering if something else is going on. She was in the bathroom during the whole exchange with Trill, but it feels like she knows things are amiss. I feel prickly as well. The way Paloma so quickly and decisively shut down our reunion irked me. But then again, she has come here not only as Trill's wife, but as Jericho's legal counsel. Jericho was the accused, and my family the accusers. Of course, she wouldn't want Trill speaking to me.

I help my mother into her bed, bring her Tylenol and water, then leave her to try to get some sleep.

"Did they call back yet?" she mumbles. Her dentures float in one of my father's old whiskey tumblers on her nightstand.

"Who's that, Mom?"

"The person with the tip about Charlie."

April 1986

Trill came to pick me up Friday morning of spring break just as the sun was coming up. It had been a long and exhausting week; the only thing keeping me going was this trip to Smith.

Per my mother's request, I had been *kind* to Nathan. I'd had to watch Charlie all day since Mrs. Nichols had taken Mickey to Boston, and he had no one to play with, but after my parents got home from work each night, I would go over and help Nathan and his dad make supper. Neither of them had any idea how to cook, so they were grateful, even though my repertoire consisted mostly of different versions of pasta. After tuna noodle casserole or spaghetti or mac and cheese, Nathan and I would watch TV or hang out in his room listening to music. He was having a rough time. He didn't even really want to make out that much.

"I'm really worried," he said, hands clasped between his knees as we sat together on his bed, listening to an old Phil Collins album.

"He'll be okay," I said, though I was worried too.

I'd heard my mother talking softly on the phone with Mrs. Nichols almost every night, assuring her with statistics and science, telling her about a clinical trial she'd read about. But sometimes, I could tell that Mrs. Nichols was crying, because my mother would grow quiet, just nodding her head and listening.

It felt like the longest spring break in history. On top of it all, the weather had been awful, cold and dreary, and so keeping Charlie entertained had meant endless TV and games of Operation and Chutes and Ladders. On the one nice day we'd had, I'd taken him down to the high school football field and we'd run lap after lap on the track and bounced around on the pole vault pit until he got bored, then we'd ridden our bikes to the diner for chocolate cream pie and fries. By the time Friday rolled around, he was sick of me and looking forward to a day with Lisa, who had promised him she'd take him to the planetarium in St. Johnsbury then to the video arcade after. Nathan had the weekend off, and as expected, he'd been disappointed that I was going away.

"We were supposed to order my tux. I don't even know what color cummerbund to get," he'd said.

"Just go ahead and get black. I hate the colored ones anyway."

He'd looked at me sad-eyed, probably hoping I would change my mind.

I could have let him know about Smith then. I could have been honest and told him that I wanted more than State had to offer, than Quimby had to offer, than *he* had to offer. But that would have killed him, and I didn't want to hurt him any more than he was already hurting.

So instead, I said, "Maybe I can get you a new Sox cap. We might go to Boston too."

Trill's plan was to get to her aunt's house in Northampton early enough to get settled in and then have the whole afternoon to visit Smith and Hampshire, on a school day while students were on campus.

"What about the rest of the weekend?" I had asked Trill. "Are we going to Boston too?"

"We'll see," she'd said playfully.

"Awesome," I said. I usually needed to know exactly what to expect. I was somebody who liked itineraries. Schedules. My Day Runner was my lifeline. But when I was with Trill, I let myself be easygoing. Spontaneous. I liked who I was around her, which was unusual, because when I was with Nathan lately, I didn't care for myself much at all.

My parents were both up, my dad in the shower and my mom packing their lunches, but Charlie was sleeping in. Now that he was almost nine, when he didn't have school, he wasn't up with the sun the way he used to be. I sort of missed the way he'd tumble into my room, peeling my eyelids open and yelling, "Wake up!"

I knocked on his door, and when he didn't answer, I let myself in. "Bye, Charlie! See you Sunday." He rolled over sleepily and gave me a thumbs-up.

"Bye, Mom," I said, hoisting my duffle bag onto my shoulder.

I had written Trill's aunt's phone number down and put it on the fridge under a smiley face magnet. Her name was Maude. She was an orthodontist, which surprised me given Trill's mom's less than traditional career.

"Tell Trillium to drive safely. Call us collect tonight to let us know you got there."

"Okay. Bye, Dad!" I hollered down the hall. He poked his wet head out of the bedroom and gave me a funny salute.

Outside, Trill idled in the car.

"Hi," I said as I tossed my bag into the back and climbed into the passenger's side. A paper bag balanced between the seats.

"Muffins," she said. "Jericho made them this morning. They're still hot."

"Ooh," I said, peeking into the bag, where two steaming muffins were nestled. They were heavy and tasted like Raisin Bran. Pads of sweet butter melting inside.

She reached into the back seat for her zippered cassette holder and pulled out a tape.

"What's the soundtrack?" I asked. It was an expression Trill used and I'd adopted. It made me feel like everything we did together was part of a movie. Having the right music, the *soundtrack*, made it even more cinematic.

"I made a road trip mixtape," she said and tossed me the cassette holder. Trill had the best handwriting. Mine was loopy, messy, but hers was artful. Careful. She'd made a mini collage that lay behind the plastic case: the silhouette of two girls, heads tilted toward each other, in front of them a sea of constellations. I thought about those forks bonded together in space.

The song list was eclectic. The Grateful Dead and The Doors. One Prince song, and a whole lot of Bob Marley. The Cure and The Clash and, of course, The Talking Heads. It was random and yet not random at all.

Trill seemed to know the way without any maps. *Aye, matey, follow the stars!* I still wasn't even sure how to navigate between Quimby and some of the small towns around us. I'd never paid attention when my parents were driving, my nose firmly inside a book during any trip longer than a couple of miles.

"How's Nathan doing?" she asked as we got on the interstate.

"Fine," I said and sighed. "He's upset I won't be home this weekend."

"I meant how's he doing with his brother sick?"

"Oh," I said, feeling like a jerk. "Not great. Mickey is down at Boston Children's now."

"Oh! Do you want to go visit him?" she asked, her expression filled with concern.

I honestly hadn't made the connection that Trill and I would be anywhere near Mickey's hospital.

"I doubt they'd let us in since we're not family, and like minors." The excuses were weak, I knew. But this was spring break. It was the first trip I had ever taken without my parents. Going to a hospital was not at all what I had envisioned.

"Well, if it's any consolation, my mom has had cancer twice, and she's totally fine now," Trill said.

"Oh wow," I said.

"That's part of the reason I went and lived with my dad," she said. "Breast cancer."

"Oh my God," I said. "I didn't know."

"The second time, they did a mastectomy. So far, so good."

I looked out the window. We had crossed the border into Massachusetts, and I noticed immediately how the mountains flattened out: bright and green still, but not a hill in sight.

"It's actually been super hard on Nathan," I said, finally answering her question.

"That's why you can't break up with him?"

I was stunned that she'd read my mind.

"No offense, to either him or you, and I know he's a nice guy, but you deserve more."

Not *better*. More. In Trill's mind, Nathan wasn't a bad person but not enough. Weirdly, this was exactly how I felt. I just wanted *more*. I wanted to feel the excitement I felt around Trill. I wanted that sense of adventure, to feel like anything was possible.

"You really think that?" I asked.

"I *know* it," she said.

We both reached to flip the tape over, our hands bumping into each other. My face grew hot. "Sorry," I said and retracted my hand, busied myself with the last crumbs of my muffin.

The first song on the second side of the tape was "Road to Nowhere," as if she'd personally and perfectly scored the soundtrack.

Trill's Aunt Maude lived on the first floor of a Victorian house in downtown Northampton. She rented the upstairs apartment to two Smith graduate students. She was at work, so she'd left us a key hidden in the eaves of the porch. Inside, the kitchen was warm and bright, painted yellow with calico curtains, and a vase of red tulips on the kitchen table.

One of my favorite Sylvia Plath poems was about tulips; it was like she was welcoming us herself.

Maude had left a note on the table telling us to make ourselves at home, that our room was the one at the end of the hall. She said to help ourselves to anything we wanted in the fridge and cupboards, that she'd see us this evening and she hoped Italian would be okay.

We brought our bags down the hall to the bedroom, where a king-sized bed was centered against a curved wall of windows.

"You cool to share?" Trill asked, spreading out across the pale pink comforter.

"*All cool, all blue,*" I said. The times I'd slept over at her house, we slept on the couches in The Library under heavy handmade quilts.

"If I talk in my sleep, you promise you won't tell anybody if I divulge my darkest secrets?" she said.

"Cross my heart," I said.

"Okay. Let's go pretend to be college girls."

The Smith campus looked exactly the way college campuses were supposed to look. Stately brick buildings, impeccably manicured lawns. I felt like I'd walked onto a Hollywood movie set.

We wandered past College Hall which, Trill told me, had been overtaken earlier in the semester by antiapartheid student activists demanding that the college divest the millions of dollars in stocks they held in companies that did business with South Africa. I thought of these brave young women fighting against state-sanctioned racism, and I started to worry about the letter of continued interest I'd finally settled on. I'd written five or six versions, and Trill had listened as I read each of them. *Boring. Pretentious. Really boring.* Finally, she had said, "Why don't you use that poem you've been working on?"

I'd written a poem for Mr. Howard's class, and he told me it was the best poem I'd written so far. It was about being young and wanting. About need. It was honest and hard to write, but when it was done, and the words were on the page, I felt proud of it, especially the final lines: "I am at the edge of tomorrow. At the beginning of now. At the precipice of forever. Holding my impatient breath."

Trill had teared up when I read it to her, which made me blush.

"Just submit this, Edie. It's so good! It's *you*. Like your guts are splattered on the page."

"That's disgusting."

"It's *perfect*."

Trill's idea was that I turn it in in person; she thought that my showing up on campus, letter in hand, would speak volumes about my "continued interest" in Smith. "Also, how can they say no to this face?" she had teased, squeezing my cheeks with her fingers.

"You ready?" she asked now, gesturing to the large wooden doors of the castle-like administration building.

But the idea of entering with my silly poem in hand now felt foolish.

"I'll do it on our way back," I promised.

We walked across the sprawling lawns, the air redolent with the scent of the lilacs that hung heavy from their branches. And everywhere, more crimson tulips.

"Wait. This is Haven House," I said, dumbfounded, staring at the sunny yellow building where Sylvia had once studied and slept. I was too overwhelmed to move; I just stood, looking at the yellow clapboards, white columns and balconies. The porch swing.

"Which room?" Trill asked.

"Huh?"

"Which room was she in?"

"Room six," I said. "Second floor. She lived there her sophomore year with her best friend, Marcia." I was a bottomless well of Sylvia trivia.

"Okay then," she said. "Let's go in."

"Seriously?"

"Why not?"

Then, as if we belonged here, as though we were just a couple of Smithies, we walked into the dormitory, scooted quickly past the reception area, and went up the stairs. As I climbed, I thought of Sylvia, *became* Sylvia. But at the door to Room 6, that dream slipped away. I was Edie again. Edith Marshall. Waitlisted at Smith.

"Well?" Trill said. "Aren't you going to knock?"

"Knock? Like on the door?"

But before I could turn to scurry back down the hall, Trill reach out and banged on the door. Mortified, I stood frozen.

The door swung open, and a girl in glasses and overalls stood there.

"Hi," Trill said when my voice didn't work. "This is my friend Edie, and she's like totally obsessed with Sylvia Plath, and we heard this was Sylvia's room during college. Can she look around? We promise we'll be quick."

The girl looked startled but said, "Sure."

The room was small and tidy with a bay window filled with the green of spring leaves. There was a poster of The Smiths hanging over one bed and a *Repo Man* poster over the other.

"Oh my God, I love that movie!" Trill said and moved across the room to study the poster with Emilio Estevez, giving him a boop on the nose with her finger and then turning to the girl. "So, does she ever visit?" Trill asked.

"Who?" the girl asked.

"*Sylvia*," Trill said.

"I don't really believe in ghosts," the girl said. "My roommate said once she heard typewriter keys. But I'm pretty sure it was the radiator."

I thought of all the girls that had lived in this room. What would my world be like if I wound up here? At Smith. In Room 6 at Haven House. If I could somehow join this lineage. This wasn't fair. I *needed* this.

Trill sat down on the absent resident's bed. The girl looked uncomfortable.

"We should go," I said. "Thanks for letting us take a peek."

Trill popped up from the bed and lunged to shake the girl's hand. "Yeah, thanks a bunch. And if you see Sylvia, tell her Edie Marshall says it's *all cool, all blue*!"

I smiled. The idea of this poor college student sending her regards to Sylvia Plath's ghost made me giddy.

"So?" Trill said when we stepped off the porch.

"So what?"

"Do you like it here?" she asked.

"Yeah," I said. "I *love* it here."

"Well, then, let's do this."

At Trill's urging, I walked into the administration building and hand-delivered my letter. The woman at the reception desk looked at me with baffled compassion. But she took my envelope and winked. "I'll make sure it gets to the Admissions committee," she said. And as I let out my breath, she whispered, "Good luck."

Mission accomplished, we left Smith and drove to Hampshire, which was just across the Connecticut River. The campus was rural, wooded, with a large red barn and rolling pastures between the academic buildings. The students wandering around campus all looked like Trill: hippie kids with jangly jewelry and tie-dyed shirts, ankle-grazing skirts and blue suede clogs. Tattered jeans and Birkenstocks.

"Oh my God, I'm *home*," Trill said, pulling me past a group of boys playing hacky sack.

On the sprawling green lawn, we ate the lunch we'd packed back at Maude's house.

"So, Nico and I can totally come get you at Smith. You can visit me, and I can visit you. We can go back to Quimby together for breaks. And we can road trip wherever we want! Down to see my dad in the city. We could even do a cross-country trip!"

For two hours, I forgot about everything else. I forgot about Quimby. About Nathan. About Mickey. I didn't think about my mother or father or high school or Charlie. Instead, I imagined myself in Haven House writing poetry at a small wooden desk, and thought about coming here to visit Trill, where we would go on one adventure after another.

That night, I called home and told my mom we'd gotten there safely and that I'd give a call before we left to come back on Sunday. Trill's Aunt Maude brought home lasagna with cannoli for dessert. Maude was quiet and reserved, but she was also kind and welcoming. I did catch her studying my slightly crooked teeth; I felt a little embarrassed by them, but my parents didn't have the money for braces. My father had insisted they gave me character. After we finished cleaning up, Maude excused herself, yawning, and said she'd see us in the morning.

I was exhilarated after seeing Sylvia's room and handing off my letter, my body buzzing as I lay on the big bed in Maude's guest room. Trill was also restless, and neither of us could stop talking about how we envisioned our futures.

Trill fell asleep first, practically midsentence, curled up like a pill bug, facing me.

Moonlight shone through the curved windows behind the bed, illuminating us in a soft beam of light. I studied Trill's sleeping face, the freckles scattered across her nose. Trill was the only person I knew who smiled in her sleep. What must it be like to be so untroubled? To be so certain in the world? A piece of hair had come loose and covered one of her closed eyes. Instinctively, I brushed it away from her face, tucking it over one of her ears.

"Mmmm," she mumbled.

Sometime later, in the middle of the night I awoke, heart racing. I was lying on my side, and Trill's body was spooned against mine, her knees touching the back of my knees, her belly and breasts pressed against my back. Her arm was thrown over my ribs. Holding my breath, I slowly found her hand and squeezed it and then held it against my flittering heart. I lay awake like this, too afraid to move, until the sun crept through the curtains.

When I felt Trill waking, I released her hand and rolled onto my stomach, realizing my entire right side was numb. Trill flopped onto her back, stretching her arms over her head, yawning. I feigned sleep, waiting until I could hear the shower running before I let out my breath and tried to lift my dead arm.

After a breakfast of leftover cannoli and bacon, Trill loaded up the trunk with a Styrofoam cooler. "What's in there?" I asked.

"It's a surprise," she said.

"Oh. I thought we were going to Boston today," I said.

"Change of plans."

"I promised I'd get Nathan a Sox cap," I said, unsure why I was being so contrary.

"I thought you said his mom was in Boston?"

"Oh, true. But she's at the hospital. I doubt she'll be going to any baseball games."

Trill looked mildly irritated. "They sell Red Sox shit everywhere. Gas stations, even."

"You're the one who suggested we go visit Mickey at the hospital," I said, my voice breaking. What was wrong with me?

She gently reached for my wrist. "I'm sorry. That was bitchy. We'll find one."

Despite my best efforts, I had been feeling guilty about Nathan all morning. About leaving him alone this weekend. About Mickey. And the prickly numbness in my shoulder lingered, a reminder that I had spent half the night curled up with Trill. Though that was just Trill; she was what my mother called "a hugger." She was the kind of person who threw her arms around you when she was happy, leaned into you when she wanted comforting. She punched shoulders and patted heads and played with other people's hair. Mine was not a house where people casually showed affection. I could count the times my mother had embraced me on two hands. My father, too, was reserved, though slightly more inclined to give me a shoulder squeeze or pat on the head. I never saw my parents show physical affection for each other either; they never kissed in front of us and were not the kind of couple who held hands.

Because I had not grown up being touched, I never touched other people. It felt taboo. Invasive. But with Trill I had been given permission: to touch, to hug. That's all it was, just a long hug, and she hadn't even been awake, anyway. Still, I felt a strange tug of *something.*

I climbed into the passenger seat, and Trill loaded up the back before getting into the driver's seat.

"So where *are* we going, then?" I asked, rolling my shoulder. The pins and needles had been replaced with a soreness, as if I'd been hurling javelins all night.

"We're going on a pilgrimage."

"Like *The Canterbury Tales*?" I asked.

"What?"

"*The Canterbury Tales*—remember? AP English. They were all pilgrims going to the shrine of Saint Thomas Becket?"

"Um, yeah, not that."

"So where?" I asked.

She groaned. "Why don't you just let me surprise you?"

I was dying to know where we were going, but she wouldn't even let me help navigate. She had her map on her lap and kept glancing down every time we came to an intersection, putting it away only when we got on the on-ramp to I-90 East.

I looked at her for a clue.

"Oh my God, just pick the soundtrack," she said and motioned to the zippered cassette case in the console.

I rifled through the tapes, searching for something adventurous and fun, and knew that because this was her collection, I probably couldn't go wrong.

Simon and Garfunkel. *The Concert in Central Park.* Trill had introduced me to this record, and it had felt like the musical equivalent of a warm bath on a cold day. I loved every song on the album, but my favorite was "American Tune." Without fail, it made my throat swell and my eyes water every time it played. I couldn't tell you why, except that it felt so hopeful.

"American Tune" came on as we exited the interstate. Trill was singing at the top of her lungs, and I was trying, despite that lump in my throat.

As soon as we were on secondary roads, she turned down the volume and studied the map again.

"Where are we?" I asked.

"Wellesley," she said. "I think."

Wellesley was where Sylvia Plath had moved after her father died. It was where she had been living in the summer of 1953 when she tried to commit suicide for the first time and her brother, Warren, found her, nearly dead, in the crawlspace beneath the breezeway in their home.

"Oh my God," I said. "Are we going on a *Plath* Pilgrimage?"

"A Syl-grimage!" she sang, gripping the wheel and turning onto the road that would take us to Sylvia's house.

In the quiet neighborhood, we pulled up and parked on the street across from the house, pretending to read the map. I gawked at the modest, white two-story home, at that breezeway, at the car in the driveway. I was practically shaking. I was worried that Trill was going to make me go knock on the door like she had at Haven House, but she just waited as I snapped some photos with the camera she'd insisted I bring along.

"Ready for the next stop?" she asked.

Next, we went to Lookout Farm in Dover where Sylvia had spent a summer. "Bitter Strawberries" was about her time there, but it was too early for berries at the farmstand, so we drove on to Winthrop, the coastal town where Sylvia had lived as a baby, stopping at the cemetery where Sylvia's father was buried. We parked the car and wandered up and down the rows of crumbling gravestones until we found Otto's marker. She'd written a poem about this: "Electra on Azalea Path." I tried desperately to remember the words. At the gravesite, I made the sign of the cross and clumsily genuflected. I had no idea how to behave at my literary idol's father's grave. After, we drove to her childhood home, then to her grandparents', which was right on the beach.

"How did you know where to go?" I asked as we got out of the car and started to walk along the sea wall.

"I have my ways," she said.

"No, seriously," I said. "I know everything about Sylvia, and I wouldn't have been able to find these spots."

Trill grinned. "Maude's ex-boyfriend, David, is on the faculty at Smith. He knows all these Sylvia scholars there, and so he helped me."

I felt my chin quiver. Nobody had ever done anything like this for me before. Gone to such trouble. I was pretty sure my own parents didn't even know who Sylvia Plath was.

"He told the lady in charge of the special collections what I was doing, and she came up with all these ideas."

We were headed north now, the sea to our right. I rolled the window down, and Simon and Garfunkel crooned, "Old Friends," another gut-puncher of a song. The air was brisk and salty. Soon we were passing through Swampscott, where Sylvia and her college roommate, Marcia Brown, had been nannies for a summer. It was the place Sylvia had written about in her poem "The Babysitters." I knew exactly where we were headed.

Children's Island.

In Marblehead, we kept driving north until we reached a park at the edge of the sea, and Trill grinned.

"You know the poem?" I asked.

"I do. I mean, I do now. I asked Mr. Howard which one was your favorite."

In "The Babysitters," Sylvia wrote about the time she and Marcia paddled out from Marblehead to Children's Island in a rented boat. They'd pilfered a ham and pineapple from their employers and while Sylvia rowed, Marcia read a novel.

I knew immediately what was in the cooler.

"Did you bring a freaking *ham*?" I asked as she unloaded the Styrofoam cooler.

"And pineapples!" she said. "They're canned. Hope that's okay."

Together we carried the cooler down from the parking lot to a grassy area at the shore, where we looked out toward Children's Island.

"Holy shit," she said, looking out at the island. "Were they insane?"

It was really, really far. There was no way I was getting in a rowboat and paddling out there.

So instead, we stayed ashore, eating slices of ham and rings of pineapple with our fingers, staring out at Children's Island, until the sun began to set. Then we sat for a while longer, just looking at the dark water. When I felt a tickle on the side of my pinkie finger, my first thought was that it was an ant; we'd been picnicking, after all. But when I glanced down, I could see that it was Trill's pinkie finger, barely grazing mine.

I looked at her, a silhouette in the fading light. After a moment, she turned to me, her face a question. Heat rushed to my cheeks. Then her hand covered mine, skin sticky with pineapple juice. My heart quickened, my shoulders trembling as the sun disappeared.

"We should head back," I said but did not move my hand from under hers.

"We should," she said but stayed perfectly still.

When a seagull swooped down, swiping at my wadded napkin, Trill jumped up. "Hey!" she squawked, flapping her arms, and I stood up as well, laughing. We tossed a couple of chunks of ham to the bird and got in the car to drive the three hours back to Maude's.

Trill cranked the heat, and sleepy, I bunched up the bomber jacket and leaned against the glass, closing my eyes.

"The Babysitters" was a poem about friendship. About time. And memory and distance. I loved everything that Sylvia wrote, but this poem seemed to capture exactly what it felt like to be young, and to know that youth is fleeting. That even the closest friendships are ephemeral. That in a blink of an eye, suddenly everything has happened, and all you can do is wave and call out to each other across continents. It made me think about Lisa, about the way we had once been as close as sisters but now barely spoke anymore.

I didn't want this to happen with Trill. I wanted to be near her. I wanted to be *with* her, touching her, bodies nestled together like spoons. Melded like forks in space. It was like I had found the person I'd been looking for my whole life. And if I didn't get into Smith, there was a chance it would all end.

"Thank you," I said as we pulled into Maude's driveway. "For the Syl-grimage."

"The pleasure was all mine, Miss Honeychurch."

It was almost eleven o'clock, but the lights were on. Maude was in the kitchen, and there was coffee brewing on the counter.

"Oh my God, you read my mind—*coffee*," Trill said, moving toward the counter, where she hugged Maude. Maude returned her embrace but pulled gently away and looked toward me.

"Edie, sweetheart?" she said, smiling at me sadly.

I felt my stomach bottom out, and I *knew*. I knew in the same way I knew when my grandfather had died.

"Your mom called earlier. She said to give her a call as soon as you got home. It's about your boyfriend's brother."

Mickey. I thought about Nathan, about the stupid hat he wanted. I hadn't thought about him the entire day.

"What happened?" I asked.

She took a deep breath and nodded curtly. "Give her a call, hon. She'll explain."

Mickey was gone.

The chemo infusions had made him susceptible and weak, and he'd contracted an infection in the hospital that turned to sepsis, and his body simply shut down. It was sudden, unexpected. An unfathomable tragedy.

"You need to come home right away," my mother said. I was sitting on the edge of the bed in the guest room at Maude's house staring at Trill, who was on the window seat looking at me with both misery and pity.

"Where's Nathan?" I asked.

"With his dad. They're on their way to Boston to get Judy. To take care of the logistics. They'll need to bring him home, of course." I could hear the grief in my mother's voice.

My hands felt clammy, and I wiped them one at a time on my pants.

"We weren't planning to be home until tomorrow," I said, as if asserting that the world was unchanged, that the unthinkable hadn't just happened to Mickey, that my insistence could undo it all. I was clinging to a reality in which our plans would continue to play out in the way we had expected them to.

"*Edith*," my father said sternly. I hadn't realized he'd been on the other phone. I pictured him sitting on their bed, head in hand.

"I need to ask Trill. It's really late, and she's the one driving."

Trill nodded and mouthed, "We can go."

Tears welled in my eyes. Mickey was *dead*. Nathan must be reeling. I tried to imagine losing Charlie and couldn't.

It felt like eons instead of hours since Trill and I had sat staring out at Children's Island, eating the sweet slices of ham and pineapple with our fingers. *Everything has happened*, I thought. But oddly, it wasn't grief or shock I felt, but *fear*. Like the world had become unrecognizable. A place where a little boy could close his eyes and never wake up.

We packed our stuff and loaded the car. Maude used the rest of the ham to make sandwiches for the trip, adding two apples, and a couple Cokes. Quietly, we got into Trill's car, and she started the engine. The stereo volume was still on high. But rather than clicking it off, I turned it up and allowed myself to cry as Simon and Garfunkel harmonized. *But it's all right, it's all right . . .* Trill held my hand the whole way home, steering with the other.

July 2023

As my mother sleeps off her shingles shot, I am trying, and failing, to distract myself by reading one of the books I plan to teach in the fall, when my cell phone rings. *Trill*, I think, I *hope*, but it's only Nathan.

"Hey," I say.

"So, I've got a remediation crew who can come tomorrow morning," Nathan says. "Everyone is crazy busy right now after the flood, but the owner owes me a favor. I'll come by to help get them set up. Around eight AM if that works?"

Tomorrow morning. Monday. Jericho plans to reach out to the police tomorrow morning.

I start to protest but then stop. "That would be great."

"I'll get the carpet pulled up tomorrow too and haul the damaged stuff up to the Masons' dumpster. I also ordered the sump pump, but it won't be here for a few days. Hopefully the rain will hold off for a bit. But I swear, the forecasts are only right about half the time."

"Thanks, Nathan. Just let me know what we owe you."

"Don't worry about it for now. Also, how's your mom doing? She seemed a little off yesterday. That whole thing about me taking you to the movies," he says, chuckling awkwardly.

"Wishful thinking. I mean on her part," I say and feel like a mean teenager, so I add, "She still adores you."

My mother, of course, does still adore Nathan. I know she's convinced that if we'd stuck it out back when we were kids, then the disaster that was my romantic life might never have happened.

When I married Michael, Ariel's father, my mother had made sure to enumerate all the ways that he was nothing like Nathan, though honestly it was these differences that drew me to him. Michael was an intellectual, for one. While Nathan had not gone to college, Michael had a PhD. He was brilliant and educated and articulate. He was also ten years older than me, and my English professor, totally taboo, which I'll admit was part of the attraction.

Unlike Nathan, Michael wasn't handy, didn't believe in God, and was not the nicest guy. We snuck around when I was in college and still living at home. I moved into an apartment in town as soon as I started working at the high school after graduation, and we were on again and off again for years. We decided to get married on a whim when I was thirty, but the night before our civil ceremony, my mother pleaded with me not to marry him, which of course made me even more determined to do exactly that. But two years later, when I got pregnant with Ariel, Michael made it clear he had no interest in having a baby and took off with one of his grad assistants, ditching us as well as his position at State, and my mother offered little except for *I told you so* head shaking.

"Nathan would never have left you," she said, "to be a single mom."

She was right. He wouldn't have. He would never have left me at all if not for everything that happened that spring of our senior year.

"See you tomorrow morning, then," Nathan says. "I'll swing by Dunkin's and get your mom some of those crullers she likes. Can I get you anything? Apple fritter? Maple bar?"

"I'm good," I say. "Thanks, though."

I hear a car pull up and look out the window at the driveway and see a silver SUV. On Sundays, Ariel usually gets a ride home from Effie and Paige, but this isn't their car.

Then I see the New York plates.

My phone buzzes with a text from a number I don't recognize. Can u come outside?

My mother stirs in the other room. "Nora?" she says.

I walk quickly to her room, heart racing. "No, Mom. It's me, Edie. Listen. I have to run out for a bit. Ariel will be home soon. You okay alone until she gets here?"

I know I shouldn't leave, but Ariel will, indeed, be here any minute.

"Where are you going?" she asks. Was that a tinge of suspicion?

"I have a quick errand to run. I'll be back in time for supper." On Sundays, I usually bring her supper to her, and she eats in bed while she watches *60 Minutes*. Sometimes Ariel will give her a manicure or set her hair on Sunday nights.

"Ariel is coming home?" she says hopefully.

One perk of Ariel living here is that she brings out the best in my mom, whose moods have become erratic. Some days, she is placid and kind. Other days, bitterness bubbles at her lips, her body simmering with old rage. With Ariel, though, she is even-tempered and sweet.

"Yes. She'll be here soon, okay?"

Still, I have the same gut-wrenching feeling I used to get whenever I had to leave Ariel alone when she was young. This was one of the hardest parts of being a single mother—the calculated risks I had to make because there was simply no backup. Leave the sleeping child in the car for the thirty seconds it takes to pay for gas inside when the machine is broken? Take a shower while the toddler plays alone? Run to the store for medicine when the ten-year-old is too sick to go out in the cold? Now, here I am again, playing this game of chance. *She'll be fine*, I tell myself. *She'll probably just fall back asleep.*

In the mudroom, I pull on my rain boots and jacket and then go outside. Daisy looks up at me, as though she wants to know where I am going. She has always been more dog than cat.

In the driveway, Trill idles. Alone. Thank God. Through the window, she motions for me to get in the passenger side.

The car is pristine. It smells like leather and floral perfume, nothing like the heady, herbal scent of Nico. I assume it's the scent of Paloma.

I turn to Trill, feeling that same surge of emotions I'd felt at the diner. *She's really here?*

"I can't believe you're here," I say.

"Me either," she says, blinking rapidly.

Trill motions for me to hug her. It stuns me, to feel her arms around me, to smell that same earthy scent of her. It transports me, and I feel my knees weakening.

"Just so you know," she says, pulling away gently. "Paloma says I'm not supposed to talk to you."

I frown, though I have been here before. Forbidden from seeing or speaking to Trill. The ache of this is like my bad knee, a pain that has been there so long, I can barely remember a time without it.

"She's upset that Jericho reached out to you at all. She says neither of us should have contact with your family. She's wearing her lawyer hat."

"Maybe she's right," I say. "I mean, I don't want to make things worse for him."

I think of the No Trespassing sign, the self-portrait.

"I also think she's a little jealous," she says, and I flush with heat.

She presses the back of her hand to my reddened cheek, startling me, but I lean into it before she lowers her hand again and I sit back, embarrassed.

"Where did you tell her you were going?" I ask.

"Jericho has nothing to eat at the house. I told them I'd pick up Chinese food," Trill says. "I figure we can talk while we wait for it."

She fumbles with the key fob then the shifter, confirming this is definitely not her vehicle.

"I never drive anymore. I seriously don't remember the last time I was behind the wheel. I'm pretty sure it was a stick. What are you supposed to do with your left foot?" she says. "God, I miss Nico."

"Me too," I say.

The Good Luck, the only Chinese restaurant in town, is across the street from the library. My heart clunks when I spot Effie's car parked out front. They haven't left yet.

I quickly shoot off a text to Ariel: Grammy's alone. U home soon?

Nothing, and I start to panic. I shouldn't have come.

About to leave, she responds.

Thank goodness. It will only take a few minutes for her to get back to the house.

Trill pulls into the parking lot on the side of the restaurant and turns off the engine.

"I have a daughter," I blurt.

"You *do*?" Trill turns to me, her eyes wide.

"Her name is Ariel. She's turning twenty-two next week."

"*Ariel*," she says, pressing her palm to her chest.

I had named Ariel after the collection of poetry Sylvia wrote mere months before her suicide. The titular poem captured the rage and striving toward independence I was feeling in those last months of pregnancy—knowing that Michael had one foot out the door. That I would be tasked with raising this beautiful child all alone. The poem was scary and fierce. About death and rebirth.

I look across the street to the library. I wish she would emerge from the heavy front doors so I could show her off to Trill. Trill and I have not seen each other in almost forty years. There is so much to catch up on, but in many ways, it feels like Ariel is the only thing I have to show for those decades. My perfect, amazing daughter. I want desperately for Trill to see her.

"I bet you are an incredible mother," she says. Her eyes are wet but smiling.

"She's the best thing I ever made," I say, feeling overwhelmed. "Here," I say, scrolling through my phone for a recent picture of her.

Trill studies the photo. I took it one afternoon when I walked in on Ariel sitting with my mother, holding her hand and listening intently to whatever my mother was saying.

"She looks exactly like you," Trill says without taking her eyes off the screen. "Like when I knew you."

What a strange thing to say. But it's true. Trill did know me once. But she doesn't know me anymore, not really. And Ariel does look like me back then. She looks so much like me that it truly feels like Michael had nothing to do with her. He has been absent from her life, and he is absent from her face, her body, her personality. She is mine alone.

"Your mom," she says, her smile fading. "She's so *old*."

"Eighty this year," I say. "I read that your mom passed. I'm sorry."

"Me too. She had a difficult life."

Her words are true, but they still sting. I know she means many things: divorce, single motherhood, cancer. But could she also mean what happened to Jericho? I had never considered this before. How the accusations against Jericho would have affected *her*.

"Should we go in?" she asks. "To order? Or maybe I should go by myself . . ."

"Sure," I say. "Let's go in." I sound bold, as if ready to challenge anyone who might be in there to say something. To speculate. But the truth is, I know the restaurant will be empty. It's Sunday night at five o'clock. Since the pandemic nearly shuttered the restaurant, it's a wonder they've survived. The Chens, who own the restaurant, are lovely people; I have taught all five of their children.

The tables are set with goblets and cloth napkins and flickering red cut-glass candle holders. A fish tank near the hostess stand bubbles and glows an eerie blue.

Trill reads the order from her phone to Angela, the youngest of the kids, who is manning the hostess counter. She was this year's valedictorian. She'll be heading to Dartmouth this fall. Pre-med. But she's also a brilliant writer. She fell in love with Ocean Vuong this spring, taking *Night Sky with Exit Wounds* out of my classroom library so many times, I told her to keep it.

"Are you still writing?" I ask her.

"A little," she says shyly.

"Well, if you ever decide to trade your scalpel in for a pen, you let me know," I say.

"Thanks, Ms. M.," she says, and Trill and I make our way to the bar at the back.

I order a glass of wine, and Trill asks for a whiskey sour with extra cherries.

"I don't really drink anymore," she says. "But I like cherries."

It dawns on me that we were only eighteen the last time we saw each other. We'd never gone to a bar, never shared a glass of wine or a beer. We were *kids*. It feels impossible that we do not know each other as adults.

Two Chinese men sit at the bar, both wearing dirty kitchen aprons. They're watching a horse race on the TV mounted in the corner. I gather from their animated conversation that they have money on a horse named Copper Flash. We sit in silence, watching along with them. I had never thought about how barbaric horse racing is until Ariel sent me a link to an article about how many horses die each year during the racing season. I turn back toward Trill.

She looks both the same as the girl I knew and yet different in critical and irrefutable ways. She has deep smile lines at the edges of her eyes now, the corners turned slightly downward. Her skin, which was once golden, is a bit ruddier now too. Her hair, though, unlike mine, which is threaded with silver, remains the same strawberry blond.

"How long have you and Paloma been married?" I ask, emboldened by the wine.

"We met about six years ago," she says, "when I was working on a documentary." At this she blushes a little, and it makes me uneasy. Is she remembering how they met, how they fell in love? Or is she uncomfortable talking about Paloma with me?

"Do you have any kids?" I ask, thinking about how much could have happened in the last thirty-seven years. Paloma may not be her first wife. Trill, like me, could have adult children. Grandchildren. Or, she and Paloma could have a younger child together. It kills me, all I don't know about her when I used to know everything.

She shakes her head. "I mean, none of my own. Paloma has a son. He's twenty. But he's always lived with his other mother. So, technically I'm a stepmom . . . but I guess, now I may not even be that anymore." She trails off.

I cock my head.

"Oh," she says. "We're separated. Or, *separating*. It's complicated. Not sure if Jericho mentioned that."

He had not mentioned this. But why would he have?

"I imagine it would have been hard to be a parent with your work," I say. "You must travel a lot?"

Her eyes light up. "Yes! I've gone all over the world. Just like we talked about."

I remember our plans to study abroad. England for me and Italy for Trill.

"Did you ever make it to Italy?"

"I did, but not during college. I actually dropped out of Hampshire."

"You *did*?" I ask, surprised. "When?"

"Second semester sophomore year. I met someone. We partied too much. And Hampshire wasn't really the best place for me. Lots of rich kids pretending to be poor. *Trustafarians.* That's what we called them," she said and laughed.

It dawns on me that I had never thought much about Trill's family's finances. Her mom and brother lived modestly at The Farm. I'm not even sure I knew what her dad did for a living. I think I always assumed she had money, but maybe she didn't.

"Wow," I say.

"My dad had moved back to New York, so I broke up with my partner and moved in with him. Got a job at a small production company, but I never finished school."

"Is your dad still around?" I ask.

"Yeah. But he's not doing great. Parkinson's. I'd love to get out of the city, but he needs me. I've been staying with him for the last six months. While Paloma and I figure things out."

"I'm sorry," I say. "Nobody prepares you for this part. Of being a grownup, I mean." I think of Amanda losing her mom. My own mother tottering between clarity and confusion.

A loud cheer erupts from the men at the bar.

"You've been here all this time?" she asks softly, stirring her drink.

I take a deep breath, sadness enveloping me like those little pockets of warmth in an old house. Stepping into one is shocking, but you also can't help but linger there. Sorrow is like this. An enticing, enveloping pool.

"I mean, you never left?"

"How could I?" I say, feeling a thousand things, but mostly regret.

Trill studies her drink, twirls the stirrer, and the cherries trail red in the amber liquid.

"I was so terrible," she says suddenly, apropos of nothing, shaking her head.

"What?" I say.

"Pushing you. Making you feel bad about things you shouldn't have felt bad about."

"What do you mean?" I ask.

"Well, turning you against Nathan, for one. Making it seem like Quimby was a place you needed to escape."

"But *I* wanted those things. I wanted them before I knew you. You just gave me the courage to do something about it," I say. I feel strange, the alcohol going straight into my bloodstream. "You made me *brave*."

"I think I wanted you to be something you were not," she says cautiously. "I'm always doing that. I do it with Paloma too."

I don't know what to say to this. How could she possibly think this is true? How do I tell her I was exactly who she thought I was? That what she and I were together was true, while everything that happened before and after us was the lie.

She sucks the last drops of her drink and takes a deep breath.

"Jericho told us you came to the house on Friday. To see what he found," she says. "It's his—Charlie's backpack—I remember it."

I nod.

Trill's eyes fill with tears, and at the sight of that sorrow, of so many sorrows, I feel my own eyes beginning to sting.

"Will Paloma be able to help Jericho?" I ask.

"I hope so," she says. "And maybe this will give you answers too? Maybe this will finally bring you and your family peace?"

She reaches for my hand across the bar, and her fingers interlace with mine, squeezing.

May 1986

MY MOTHER TOLD me to pick out any dress I wanted from the bridal shop catalog for prom. I didn't argue. I just chose the one that looked like it would be the most comfortable—a simple pale pink dress without too many ruffles.

"You're sure?" she said when I pointed at the tea-length strapless dress. The ones my mother was drawn to looked like antebellum monstrosities: more confection than couture.

I shrugged. I didn't want to go to prom. I didn't want to go through any of the expected traditions: prom, Grad Night, even graduation itself. We were all pretending like these things mattered, as if ritual could keep little boys from dying in their sleep.

We were stunned, grieving, but also strangely stoic. That is the only way to describe the mood in our house after Mickey died. My mother and father now spoke in hushed, serious tones. Charlie was confused and heartbroken, but he didn't cry; he simply retreated to his room. He had never known anyone who died before, and now his best friend in the world was gone. My mother assured him that Mickey was in heaven, but that wasn't enough. He wanted to know where heaven *was*. Was it in space? Could you get there in a shuttle?

While the rest of us numbly proceeded, Nathan's mom fell apart, and my mother was the one picking up those pieces, because Mr. Nichols had chosen to escape into his work. When he wasn't on one construction site or another, he was at Lake Gormlaith, building what should have been his sons' compound. But Nichols & Sons had become Nichols & Son overnight, because now there was only Nathan.

Nathan.

I'd gone to his house the morning after he and his dad had retrieved his mom from Boston, and he'd come to the door looking broken. I hadn't known what to say, and so I'd hugged him, and his body shook violently in my embrace. Eventually, I offered my platitudes. *I'm sorry. He's in a better place. There are no words.* This was a cliché, of course, but also the truth; for someone who believed that words were magic, they truly felt inadequate now. Nothing I said would change the fact that Mickey was dead.

Every day, after track practice, Trill dropped me off at home, and I would gather the casseroles that had been left on the Nicholses' front porch and bring them inside, where Nathan would be watching TV and his mom would be locked in her room, his father still at work.

We'd sit in Nathan's room, kissing a little, until Nathan inevitably started crying. It was awful. But then he started talking about prom, lighting up, and I didn't have the heart or the courage to say no. To suggest that maybe limousines and corsages and a stupid DJ and crepe paper-decorated gym were not going to make anyone feel better. So, I'd agreed.

"Come with us," I had pleaded with Trill. "Please. Nathan said Jake will take you. We can double."

It was a Wednesday, and Trill and I were sitting on the grass after gathering up all the javelins after practice. I was dragging my feet, not wanting to go home and deliver another pan of lasagna to Nathan.

"Jake is a prick," she said. This was true. Jake played football. He was popular and big and liked to corner girls in the hallway and lick their necks. Because I was dating Nathan, he usually left me alone, but I knew he'd gone after Trill at least once before. No matter. I was desperate. I told her that just because she went to prom with him, she wouldn't have to *stay* with him.

"Please," I said. "I cannot do this by myself."

Trill plucked a dandelion from the grass and tucked it into my ponytail.

"Are you ever going to break up with him?" she asked.

"Oh my God, how?" I said. "Do you have any idea how much he'd freak out? How bad my mom and dad and his parents would freak out? Even Charlie would freak out."

She laid back on the grass, pulling her knees one at a time to her chest in a half-assed stretch. She lowered them both and sat up, exasperated.

"Do you *love* him?" she asked.

"What?" I asked, feeling weirdly embarrassed. The way I had when my mother told my father I'd started my period for the first time.

"I said do you *love* him?" She was looking at me intently, and her expression was serious. I felt my skin getting hot.

"I don't know what that has to do with anything," I said.

She stood up and started to grab her stuff.

"Hey," I said. "What's the matter?"

I could feel the stem of the dandelion tickling behind my ear and adjusted it.

She stood and faced me. She looked mad.

"You really need to shit or get off the pot," she said.

I felt my jaw drop open. It was the kind of expression I'd heard Nathan's dad use. The kind of crass dictum that seemed wrong coming out of Trill's mouth.

"His brother just *died*," I said, trying to appeal to her sense of humanity. Nathan was grieving. He was completely devastated.

What kind of person kicks someone when they're down? Leaves them when they need you the most?

"You have one life," she said. "One. Do you really want to spend it in Quimby, Vermont, with Nathan Nichols? Popping out a kid or two or three? Going to church on Sundays and eating fucking tuna casserole? Is that what you really want?" She had raised her voice, and the guys over at the long jump pit were clearly eavesdropping. "Is it?"

"Oh my God," I said, embarrassed but also stung. "Stop being so fatalistic. And what do you have against tuna casserole?" I tried to laugh, but instead, a sob bubbled up in my throat.

"One fucking life, Edie, and you'd rather piss it away than hurt some guy's feelings. It doesn't make you a good person. It makes you a coward."

My heart ached, as though she'd speared it with a javelin.

She turned and started to charge up the hill from the track to the school. But, not done yet, she turned back to me with her hands on her hips. "Are you forgetting what happened to your beloved *Sylvia*?"

"What do you mean? Sylvia Plath killed herself."

"No. Being married to *that man* killed her."

Chin trembling, I gathered my stuff, shoving everything into my backpack. Then I picked up the javelins and carried them to the field house. Trembling, I sat down on the back steps. I felt like I might pass out.

"Trouble in paradise?"

I whipped my head around. *Jake.*

Jake dropped discuses one by one into the storage locker, each clang heavy and deafening.

"Shut up," I muttered and looked down at my sneakers. With unsteady fingers, I retied them tightly.

"Sounds like your *girl*friend's jealous of your *boy*friend," he said.

I rose to my feet, my body electric.

"I said, *Shut up.*"

Jake slammed the storage room door shut and held his fingers up to his face, spread them in a V, and stuck his tongue between them lewdly.

My heart was racing, and the heat I'd felt in my face earlier spread through my body.

"You're a prick," I said, and stormed out of the field house and started to run home.

Trill and I didn't speak the rest of the week. In the classes we had together, I feigned laser focus on my notes. I ate my lunch in Mr. Howard's room with Effie and Tess. I even struck up a conversation with Lisa when I spied Trill across the hall. I was angry still, but mostly it was Jake's words that echoed in my head. Did people think that Trill and I . . . my stomach turned. We were best friends. Yes, I adored her. She was everything I wished I was. Strong. Brave. Smart and cool and worldly and *free*. But then I remembered the electricity of her finger grazing mine at the shore on Marblehead, the way it had felt when her whole body pressed against mine in that moonlit bed, the warmth I had felt holding her hand in the car. I thought of the way she smelled and felt a sickening heat envelop me.

Do you love him? she'd asked me.

Of course, I loved Nathan. Nathan was like a brother to me. But that's not what she meant.

"Do you want to go out somewhere?" I asked Nathan on Friday night. Since Mickey died, we hadn't done much but hang out in Nathan's room. It was starting to feel claustrophobic. "A movie maybe? *Police Academy 3* is playing."

I was grateful to have made it through the week at school and happy there was no track meet this weekend, so I wouldn't have to face Trill. I missed her, but I had no idea how to make things better. Maybe I was waiting for her to reach out with an apology, but a prickly burr in my chest told me she didn't really owe me one. She'd only been speaking the truth, right? I wasn't "in love" with Nathan, and yet I was letting him believe I was. Was that compassion or cruelty? She was right. I was a coward. And a liar.

"Let's just rent a movie and stay in," he said, picking up Mickey's stuffed dog that he now slept with. The fur was matted, one button eye loose. I reached out and touched the dog, giving him a sad little pat.

At least Trill didn't work at the video store on Friday nights; the last thing I wanted to do was run into her with Nathan in tow.

We drove into town in Nathan's truck, picked up some Milk Duds and a couple cans of Jolt at the Cumberland Farms, and then parked in front of Video-Q. I followed Nathan inside, stomping mud off my sneakers at the threshold.

"Hey."

I glanced up to see Trill behind the counter, looking as startled as I felt.

"Hey," I said.

"Hey, Trill," Nathan said.

I pretended to be looking through the horror flicks as Nathan asked Trill if she knew when *Top Gun* would be out on video (it was in the theater still—he and I had already seen it twice), and what she'd recommend for someone who really liked *Top Gun*.

She pointed him to *The Right Stuff* and *Risky Business*, probably thinking any Tom Cruise would do.

"Actually, you might like this too," she said, and reached under the counter. "But it's a bootleg, so you can't tell anyone where you got it."

He took it from her, glancing at the door like the FBI might be waiting outside to bust him for piracy.

"What is it?" he asked, nervous.

"It's called *A Room with a View*," she said, handing it to him. "I mean it's no *Top Gun*, but . . ." Trill said.

"I've seen it already," I said to Nathan and took it from him, putting it back on the counter and pushing it toward her, my eyes pleading. *Please don't.*

"Cool," she said. "Whatever."

That night Mrs. Nichols was already in bed, and Mr. Nichols followed silently behind, leaving Nathan and me alone in the family room. After the credits to *The Right Stuff* rolled, we kissed and kissed until my lips felt bruised. I took his hand and guided it up under my sweater, allowing him to touch my breasts, under my JogBra for the first time. I didn't pull my head away when he started to suck on my neck. Instead, I squeezed my eyes shut and thought, *This will show Jake. That prick.*

My parents didn't impose a curfew anymore. Not since Mickey died, and especially not if I was with Nathan. So, it was after midnight when I left his house, chest flushed, a fresh hickey blooming blue on my neck. In the dark kitchen, which smelled like the pork chops my mother had made for dinner, I went to the fridge and pulled out the leftovers, put together a plate, and quietly climbed the stairs to my room.

My parents' light was out, but there was a sliver of light under Charlie's door.

I knocked gently and pushed the door open. Sometimes Charlie fell asleep reading, and I figured I'd tuck him in and turn out the light. But he was sitting up in bed, and it looked like he'd been crying. His glasses were foggy.

"Hey," I said and set my plate down on his nightstand on top of *Space and Beyond*, one of those *Choose Your Own Adventure* books. He read these books over and over again, choosing different options with each read. It thrilled him that changing a single decision could alter the character's whole trajectory, so many possible stories in a single book. "What's up, Chuck?"

Usually, this made him laugh, but tonight he shook his head.

"Hey. What's going on, buddy?"

"What if there's nothing?" he said.

"What do you mean?" I sat down next to him on his bed.

"When you die. What if there isn't God or angels like Mom says," he said. "What if it's like a black hole. Just infinity. Just nothing?"

I bit my lip. I lifted his glasses from his face and dried them on my T-shirt before putting them back on him. "Listen," I said. "Have you ever had a really good sleep?"

He shrugged.

"Like when you fall asleep in the car and Dad has to carry you inside?"

He nodded. "I like that."

"That's what I think it must be like," I said. "Dying, I mean. Like a really, really good sleep."

"But you don't wake up."

For some reason, it felt like Charlie deserved the truth. I couldn't give Nathan the truth, but I could offer it to my brother.

"Yeah. But you don't wake up."

"That would be okay, I guess," he said.

"I think so too," I said.

With that, Charlie shoved all the books off his bed, reached for Stretch Armstrong, and slid down under his comforter. I reached over and pulled it up to his chin. I grabbed my plate and clicked off his light.

"Goodnight, Charlie Brown," I said.

"Goodnight, Edie Gonzalez."

In my room, I tried to eat the pork chop but had lost my appetite. I looked in the mirror at the bruise on my neck and felt repulsion. It was gruesome. Why had I let him do that?

I put on my pajamas and climbed into bed, wanting nothing more than to talk to Trill. My anger had faded the way I hoped this bruise would fade. It felt tender, whatever that argument had been between us, but less raw. Though I also knew that the reason her words had stung was because they were *true*. And unless I was willing to either shit or get off the pot, she'd still be angry with me.

July 2023

I FEEL TIPSY FROM the two glasses of wine I sucked down while waiting with Trill for the Chinese food.

In the car, Trill opens one of the steaming cardboard cartons and offers me a crab rangoon. She balances a little cup of duck sauce on the console, and I dip. The fried wonton is hot, but the cream cheese and crab inside are hotter.

"Ow!" I say, spitting into my napkin. The roof of my mouth blisters.

"Here," she says, handing me a water bottle from the cup holder. The water is warm.

We eat quietly for a minute, the rain enclosing us as it comes down in sheets.

"What do we do now?" I ask.

Trill stops eating and studies me intently, but I can't bring myself to say the words I should say. They're trapped inside the cage I made almost forty years ago.

"I think Jericho told you, his plan is to call the police tomorrow. Paloma says that if there's any DNA on the backpack that's survived, it could help clear him. And help you find out who took Charlie."

Trill's eyes are kind and sad. I note, again, the deep lines etched in the corners. I'd thought they were smile lines, but worry could just as easily have put them there. How strange that both joy and sorrow can take the same toll on our bodies.

"I don't know what's going to happen next," she says. "But Paloma's told him to say nothing. He's going to tell the police he found the backpack, sought legal counsel, and is turning it over."

"Okay," I say. "Is he going to tell them he showed it to me?"

"I don't think so. Paloma says that calling you was a mistake."

My heart aches as I remember Jericho giving me those moments alone with the backpack. Allowing me the space and time to process what it meant. His kindness. God, he'd been so kind.

"But honestly, we both know what will happen next. Once the media hears about this, they'll be all over him. I'm positive the investigation will be reopened. Paloma has asked the police for the old case files, but she's a lawyer, not a detective. And FOIA requests take forever."

I recall the detectives that tried and failed to find Charlie. How they went from assured to wary to resigned in the days then weeks then months that followed his disappearance. I think of the hours we spent talking to them, repeating the same stories again and again. How many times had I relived that day, been forced to revive every moment of that horrific afternoon? The idea of starting over with new detectives, new questions, fills me with dread.

"I know your mom has always believed it was Jericho," Trill says.

Her words cut deeply, but it's true. My mother had wanted so badly to believe that the answer was an easy one: Jericho had seen Charlie walking along the road from the public pool to his house and had taken him. Though she also allowed herself to believe that

Charlie had somehow survived, escaped. That he was still alive somewhere but unable to get home. It was magical thinking, desperate faith.

My mother had clung to this certainty even as my father insisted that none of it made sense. Jericho was a beloved teacher who had no history of violence. He had taught at the elementary school for five years with not a single complaint from either child or parent. He spent his summers working his mother's land: gardening and making bread. But, my mother argued, he had no one to corroborate his alibi—that he had been at home. Someone saw his truck racing away from town at the same time Charlie disappeared, she said. But if that was true, why hadn't the anonymous caller left their name, my father had ventured. Also, Jericho had been questioned for hours and hours and never wavered from his story. He had passed three lie detector tests. There had been nothing in his truck to support the theory that my brother had ever been inside. No blood. No hair. No fingerprints. And when they brought in the dogs to search the acres of The Farm, they had found nothing at all. No backpack. No body.

"He's not dead," my mother had cried out. "He's alive. Don't ever say that."

I had heard my parents arguing, the hushed whispers not meant for my ears, and I'd pressed the heavy feather pillow over my head to muffle my mother's insistence and my father's logical skepticism.

But now, the backpack has been found. My mother, I know, will see this as the missing piece that will make the puzzle of our tragedy whole. My father is gone, no longer able to counter her accusations with his rationalizations.

Her short-term memory, like many with Alzheimer's, is proving to be the primary casualty of her illness. But her memories of the distant past, especially the tragic events of that past, are remarkably clear. She can't remember what medications she's taking, but she can tell you that Charlie had three pieces of bacon and one scrambled egg that morning.

"I told Jericho I don't plan to tell my mother yet," I say. "Not until after he's spoken with the police."

"Actually," Trill says. "I was thinking your mom might be able to help."

"Wait," I say. "I thought Paloma didn't want you talking to us . . . that . . ."

"Listen," she says. "None of the cops involved in this case are still around, and the local police are, honestly, ill-equipped for this sort of investigation."

It's true. My brother is not the only child who's gone missing here, but he's the only one who has *stayed* missing.

"What does that have to do with my mother?"

"Paloma was saying last night that the only chance we have to get the resources we need is if the FBI gets involved."

"The FBI?"

"Local law enforcement doesn't have the resources the FBI does, but they might not want the feds taking credit for solving the case. Paloma says that to get the FBI involved, it really helps to have the victim's family make the request. Especially the parent of the missing child."

But there is no *child* anymore, I want to say. The child that Charlie was would be long gone, even if he had returned to us.

"Also," Trill adds, "if your mom comes forward in defense of Jericho? It will go a long way in terms of the rest of the town. And the media."

I try to imagine in what scenario my mother would let go of this belief she's held onto so tightly for the last four decades.

My phone buzzes with a text from Ariel.

Im home, grammys asleep

My shoulders relax.

"Would you be willing to talk to your mom? About all this?" Trill asks.

Trill had asked me for only a handful of things in all the time I knew her, though I was incapable of giving her any of them. Does she expect my refusal again? Is she resigned that I will always disappoint her? Even now that we're grown?

She says finding the real culprit is the only way to definitively prove Jericho's innocence.

But I know that isn't true.

What would it mean if I went to the local police myself? Told them exactly what happened that day? Would they believe me after all these years? There would be questions I'd have to answer, secrets I would have to reveal. My mother would never forgive me, and neither would Trill. I can't begin to imagine what this would do to Jericho.

And what about the law? Could I go to jail for this?

No. Trill was right. Getting the FBI involved is the only answer. DNA testing. Fancy forensics that will eliminate Jericho once and for all as a suspect. We need a new team who can prove what I already know: that Jericho was exactly where he said he'd been that day. And that someone else hurt Charlie.

May 1986

On prom night, Trill and I were still not speaking. And I was starting to worry she might not speak to me again unless I broke up with Nathan. But until prom was over, there was nothing I could do.

Mrs. Nichols and my mother insisted we have a small get together at Nathan's house before the limo that Nathan and Jake had rented took us (along with Jake and his date) down the hill to the high school. My mother had suggested I invite Lisa and Bobby too, but they had reservations at the steakhouse. Their own limousine.

I got ready alone, blowing my curly hair straight then crimping it into more manageable, corrugated waves. Nathan tried to come over while I was doing my hair, loitering on the porch, waiting, I guess, for someone to let him in. It was only four o'clock, but he was already in his tux. I could see him from the guest bathroom window where I was waiting for the crimper to heat up. I knocked on the glass, mouthed, "Not yet," and shoedd him away. When he turned to leave, he bumped into the mailman who was coming up the steps, which made the carrier drop the mail in his hands. Nathan was so clumsy. I was worried about prom, about how awkward he'd be. Usually, we sat together and watched other people dance, but I was worried that tonight he'd insist on dancing. Nathan was doing an apologetic bowing thing with the mailman, and I sighed, pulling the curtain across the window and returning to the crimper, which was steaming on the counter.

I did my makeup and put on the dress, which now reminded me of cotton candy. I wore nylons and the white pumps I'd gotten for confirmation two years before, which pinched my heels and squeezed my toes. I stared at my reflection and thought about what Trill would say. Would she think I looked pretty or pathetic?

It had been less than a month since Mickey passed away, but it felt like years. Mrs. Nichols had emerged from her bedroom, where she'd been burrowed since Mickey died, just in time for prom, in a manic frenzy. She ordered frozen jumbo shrimp from Schwan's and stuffed mushroom caps with crabmeat. She also made Nathan's favorite sweet and sour mini wieners cooked in a crockpot with grape jelly and barbeque sauce. She told us we were allowed to each have a glass of champagne, Asti Spumante, in plastic flutes. She seemed almost happy.

I couldn't help but think of what Trill would say, probably that prom was bourgeois.

She would have been right; nothing said middle-class like wieners bathing in grape jelly and plastic cups of Martini & Rossi. Then I felt angry. Who was she to judge us? I wouldn't have thought twice about any of this before I met her. Though when I recalled what my life had been like before I met Trill, I couldn't bear the idea of going back.

It was a cold evening, and I wished I'd opted for a full-length gown, instead of this strapless tea-length dress. I also realized now that my boobs looked huge because of the low bodice, and I dug futilely through my mother's closet looking for some sort of wrap.

"You look beautiful," she said. "You shouldn't cover yourself up the way you do."

"What do you mean *the way I do*?"

"I don't know," she said. "You're always wearing baggy sweaters and jeans. You have a nice figure. You should show it off. What I wouldn't give to go back . . ."

I rolled my eyes despite my best efforts not to.

Nathan had picked out a wrist corsage at my request. The idea of him trying to pin flowers so close to my decolletage seemed dangerous. The corsage was pretty at least, pink carnations and baby's breath, with a pink lace-covered elastic band to go around my wrist.

Jake and his date, Serena, showed up in the limo, and we endured about an hour's worth of picture-taking. My father got out his new camcorder to take video footage.

Charlie had been tasked with serving everyone mushroom caps from a tray, and he was taking his job very seriously. He was even dressed up in his Easter suit, though my mother had thrown away the blood-drenched shirt.

"I wish *you* were my prom date," I had whispered to him, teasing.

He approached Mrs. Nichols as she was about to snap her fiftieth photo of us.

"Hors d'oeuvres?" Charlie said in a fancy accent and held out the tray.

Mrs. Nichols lowered the camera, looked down at Charlie, and started to crumble.

My mother swooped in, putting an arm across her shoulders and steering her back to the kitchen under the pretense of needing more ice.

Nathan's mouth twitched, and he dropped my hand. He'd been crabby since I shooed him away from our porch. But seriously. He'd been almost an hour early.

When the mushroom caps were gone and Mrs. Nichols had disappeared into the house, leaving Mr. Nichols to collect the empty champagne glasses and dirty napkins from the table, we all moved outside to where the limo was waiting.

Nathan and I climbed into the limo with Jake and Serena. For the two-minute ride to the school, I ignored Jake, making small talk with Serena, a bubbly cheerleader.

Nathan looked out the window as we drove away from the house. Quiet.

"Hey," I said.

He turned to me, but his expression was unreadable.

"I'm sorry about earlier," I said. "You aren't supposed to see the dress before."

"That's for a wedding," he said.

"Oh," I said. "Right."

He turned back to the window.

I knew he hoped our prom would be like the ones in the movies. He wanted it to be the night of his life. He'd hinted, in the throes of our last make out session, that maybe we could "do *more* stuff" on prom night. But now, he didn't seem to want to touch me.

I remembered what Jake had said to me in the field house, what he'd done with his fingers and tongue. Had he said something to Nathan? I looked at Jake, and he gave me a little disgusted snort, and I quickly turned to look out the window.

The prom theme was "One More Night." *How fitting*, I thought.

The gym had been transformed. Silver and white balloons. Tinsel skirts on the tables. Thankfully, by the time we got our photo taken under an archway made of aluminum foil stars, Nathan's mood had lifted a bit, and he and Jake were even joking around a little.

Nathan, as I'd feared, did want to dance, though thankfully, he only led me to the floor for the slow songs. We sat out "Let's Dance" and "Relax," but Nathan clung to me for all the slow ones: "Open Arms," "Take My Breath Away," and, after the Prom Queen and King were crowned, "One More Night."

Oddly, while I wanted it all to be over, I also wanted the night to last forever, because after the prom glitter had settled, I knew it was time to tell him about Smith, to let him know that if I got off the waitlist, I might be leaving Quimby in just a few months. And that even if I didn't go away to college, I still thought he deserved—*more*. That he was a good guy and that there was a girl out there who would love him the way he should be loved. This would both set me free *and* prove to Trill that I wasn't a coward.

But as Nathan pulled me by the hand to the dance floor and leaned down, touching his forehead to my own, I looked up at him and felt like I might vomit. For one horrifying moment, I thought about the shrimp, the crabmeat, the wieners. Was it possible I'd gotten food poisoning? I quickly looked around, spotting Jake, who was cupping Serena's tiny butt in his big paw, and realized I was apparently the only one feeling sick, and that it likely had nothing to do with the hors d'oeuvres.

As Nathan pulled me close to him, I could smell the familiar scent of his sweat combined with the distinct fragrance of his . . . dad? He must have pilfered and spritzed some of Mr. Nichols's signature English Leather. I felt even queasier.

Phil Collins pleaded for just one more night, and Nathan pressed his body against mine. I could feel his erection hitting my stomach. His chin rested on top of my head. His heart beat against my chest. I imagined it like glass, shattering and splintering.

The song ended, but Nathan held on. His heart was beating so fast I started to wonder if he might be having a heart attack.

I pulled gently away and motioned for him to follow me back to our table, where we sat, watching the dance floor.

"Can we actually go somewhere alone?" Nathan asked, reading my mind. "To talk?"

"Sure," I said, but then I started getting anxious again. What could he want to talk about? What could be important enough to ditch prom? I thought again about Jake, not ready for the questions Nathan might have. The accusations he might make.

In the parking lot, kids congregated, smoking weed in back seats, drinking, and scheming. The limo wouldn't be back to pick us up until after the prom was over, and so we walked back up the hill to our houses.

"Can we maybe go for a drive?" he asked.

"Sure."

"Where are we going?" I asked, as he headed away from town, regretting agreeing to this. I shivered; I'd accidentally left my wrap in the limo.

When he turned onto Route 42, I started to panic. Was he driving to The Farm, taking me to Trill, to confront us both?

No. We passed the turnoff to Lost River Road, and I realized where we were headed.

Sure enough, after about twenty minutes of bumping along a dirt road in the pitch-black created by a starless sky, we reached Lake Gormlaith. I only knew we were at the lake because some of the camps had lights on, reflecting on the black surface of the still water.

The Nicholses' land was not right on the lake but up a steep gravel drive off the road that circled it. Nathan's headlights illuminated the construction site, a backhoe and the wooden skeleton of a house. I hadn't been up to see it yet, though Nathan had invited me several times. It was large—it would one day have four bedrooms, he said. They had originally planned to build another house on the opposite side of the land for Mickey. But now, the woods would remain intact. Nathan would own this land alone.

Nathan got out of the truck. He had loosened his bow tie and unbuttoned his tuxedo shirt. At some point, it appeared, he had also removed his cummerbund. Dumbly, I put my nose to my wrist corsage and inhaled deeply.

He was fiddling around in the back of the truck, but when I turned to look out the rear window, I could only see his silhouette.

Nathan had a flashlight in one hand and something under his arm when he tapped on my window. I got out of the truck, felt my pumps sinking into the muddy ground, and he helped me step across to where the pavement began.

I followed him to the house, or the bones of the house. The air smelled of sawdust.

He illuminated our path with the flashlight, and we walked up the steps to what I assumed would soon be a front door.

"Watch your step," he said.

It wasn't until he stopped and turned to me that I realized it was a sleeping bag under his arm. I felt uneasy.

"This is going to be the family room," he said proudly, shining the light at the space before us. "There'll be a fireplace there, and here's where the couch will go. The TV."

I followed him.

"It'll be hardwood floors downstairs, and wall-to-wall upstairs."

I sniffed the corsage again.

Like a magician, he unfurled the sleeping bag; the nylon made a snapping sound before settling on the unfinished floor.

"Sit," he said, and took my hand as I lowered myself to the ground. "Are you cold?"

He started to take off his jacket for me but patted the breast pocket and seemed to change his mind.

"Oh, wait," he said. "I forgot."

Oh god, he doesn't have a ring, does he? No, no, no!

He got up and disappeared into the darkness. I could hear him fumbling around in the truck. When he came back, he had a bottle of Boone's Farm in his hand. Wild cherry. Not a ring. *Please, not a ring.*

"Where did you get this?" I asked.

"I have my ways," he said, laughing, then handed me his tuxedo jacket.

I pulled the jacket on then took a big swallow of the Boone's Farm. It was terrible, too sweet, but I hoped it would give me courage.

"You and your dad have made some good progress," I said, feeling like I should say something about the house.

"It's been keeping us busy so we don't just mope around."

I chewed on my lip. I had wondered how soon he would bring up Mickey. Every time I started to talk about the future, he started talking about his brother, as if daring me to break some unspoken rule.

"Keeping busy is good," I said.

Nathan took the bottle from me. Other than a few of his dad's beers and communion wine, I'd rarely seen him drink anything. He was mustering his courage for something. I'd been wrong about him having a ring. Maybe, I thought, illogically, hopefully, he planned to break up with me?

"I think I'm ready," he said, nodding solemnly.

I hadn't planned to do this tonight, but did he already know? Maybe? He'd been weird all night.

"Nathan, listen, I've been thinking about . . ."

At this he reached over and pulled me close to him. It nearly knocked the wind out of me. I pulled away from him, and the open bottle of Boone's Farm teetered.

"What are you doing?" I asked.

"No. I am definitely ready. I mean, I know we said we would wait, that it wasn't right since we're just kids still, not married. But, Edie, I've known you my whole life. I plan to know you for the rest of my life. To *be* with you for the rest of my life."

Oh god.

He reached for me and pulled me close to him. I felt my breath leaving me.

"I have, um, protection . . ." he said into my hair.

"Nathan, I can't breathe," I said into his shirt, pushing against him.

"Oh, sorry," he said and loosened his grip.

"No, not literally. I mean I'm *suffocating*," I said. "I care about you, but I don't want this. I don't want to live in the middle of nowhere with a bunch of kids eating tuna casserole every night."

"Who said anything about tuna casserole? I don't even like tuna casserole," he said, befuddled.

I scrambled to my feet.

"What's the matter with you, Edie? I brought you here because I thought it would be cool if we lost our virginity here. In this house I'm building for you. For *us*. I thought it would be romantic." He was sitting on the floor with his head in his hands.

I felt a wave of guilt cresting; I could not allow myself to be consumed.

"Well, did you ever stop to think about what I want?" I hollered. "It's not romantic, it's presumptuous."

He slammed his fist against the floor; I felt the shock of it run through my whole body.

"It's because of her," he said. "*Trill*."

"What are you talking about?" I asked, trembling.

"She thinks she's so cool and smart because she's from New York. But she's a phony. She's also kind of a bitch, and since you've been hanging out with her, you've honestly been kind of a bitch too."

Wait, what?

I had been feeling so guilty, but now I was filled with rage that he would say things like this about Trill. About me.

"How would you know?" I asked. "You don't even know me. You don't care about anything I want to do or be."

"And what are you going to be, Edie? A poet? Fucking Sylvia Plath? Because, for your information, things did not end well for her."

He had the bottle of Boone's Farm and was pulling on it again like he was Judd Freaking Nelson.

"Take me home," I said.

"No."

"What do you mean, *no*?"

"I mean, I'm not taking you home. It's prom night. You're my girlfriend. I planned this whole thing, and honestly? It's the least you can do."

Fury was like fire in my chest now. I yanked off his jacket, my bare shoulders grateful for the crisp spring air. I could feel sweat rivering down my back.

"Fine. I'll walk then," I said, and I made my way to the doorway.

He didn't follow, and I quickly realized how stupid this was. There were no streetlights around the lake. I was dressed like a cone of cotton candy and wearing heels. I could get hit by a car, or worse.

"If you don't drive me home," I said. "I'll tell your mom what you tried to do tonight."

Suddenly, we were six years old again, and I was threatening to tattle on him.

He looked at me, the flashlight that lay on the floor casting ghostly shadows across his face. I chewed the inside of my cheek, sparing my lip from further abuse.

"My little brother is *dead*," he said, and I heard the fury in his voice rising. "My mother is never going to get over it. But yeah—go tell her . . . whatever it is you think I did to you."

Silently, he knelt and rolled the sleeping bag back up into a tight bundle and put it under his arm. He screwed the top back onto the wine bottle and chucked it into the woods. This time, he didn't open the door for me; he simply got into the driver's seat and waited for me to get in.

Just before the main road, we hit a pothole, hard, and the glovebox door flew open. I moved to close it, but he smacked my hand away.

"I've *got* it," he said, stuffing the contents about to spill out back inside, and slammed it shut.

We didn't speak the rest of the way home. Or after we pulled into his parents' driveway, and he cut the engine. We just sat there.

"We can still be friends," I said, stupidly.

"You're not my friend," he said.

I got out of his truck, shut the door, and didn't look back even once as I made my way to the porch and inside the house.

Everyone was asleep, so I took off my shoes and quietly climbed the stairs, feeling the anger simmering still. Like a pot of boiling water pulled from the flame.

In my room, I tore off that pink monstrosity and threw it in my closet. I peeled off my nylons and shoved them in the wastebasket by my desk. I pulled on a pair of sweats and found Trill's CBGB T-shirt in my hamper. I'd borrowed it before our fight. I pulled it over my head, and the scent of her made tears well in my eyes.

We had a system for late-night calls so we wouldn't wake anyone up.

I let Trill's phone ring once then hung up. Then I waited. And waited.

Finally, I clicked off my light and lay back against the pillows and curled into a ball, but with one hand on the phone just in case.

When it rang, I unfurled.

"Trill?" I whispered.

"Lucy?" she said, her voice smoky. "Are you okay? It's super late."

"Yeah," I said. "I mean no. I just wanted to say you were right. About Nathan. About . . . me." Oddly, I felt the way I did in the confessional at church. Confession. Contrition. Shame. I told her everything that happened at prom and later at the lake house.

She was quiet for a long time, so long I worried she was gone.

"Trill?"

"I'm sorry for what I said," she said. "You *are* a good person." Her voice sounded weird. "But I just wish . . ."

"Wish what?"

"That you were *my* person."

I wasn't sure I had heard her right, or what it meant if I had, but either way, I felt a delicious lightness. Things had gone terribly with Nathan, but it was over now. At last.

July 2023

On Monday morning, Nathan arrives with a remediation team and a box of Dunkin Donuts: three maple bars and three crullers. He hands me the box and peels off his wet raincoat, hanging it on the coat tree by the door as if he lives here. His familiarity with the house bugs me. He helped my parents out a lot in the years I was with Michael. Nathan was the one they called when repairs needed to be made, especially when my dad got sick. After I moved back home, he kept coming by, but I rejected his offers of help. I was perfectly capable of raking leaves and stacking wood. When the pandemic hit, I'd felt almost relieved: the world finally conspiring to keep us apart rather than forcing us together. But now, I hate to admit, we really need him.

Through the window, I see the remediation team open the back of a van and gather their equipment, and I flash on early news footage of the pandemic in Wuhan. The three men are outfitted in Hazmat suits with gloves and respirator masks. I imagine black mold growing up the walls, inside the drywall, climbing like ivy, spreading like a virus, until the entire house is consumed by it. I think about the toxins we are breathing. The poison in our lungs.

Ariel is asthmatic. During Covid, I was terrified of infection. Those first few months after she came home, I was obsessed with keeping her safe. I ordered air purifiers, fans. I wiped down the groceries. On the rare occasions that I left the house, I'd change out of my clothes in the mudroom and seal them in a plastic bin before coming inside again. I insisted on KN-95 masks before we knew that the flimsy fabric masks we were all making were useless.

She only had one severe asthma attack as a child, but it had sent me reeling. I was driving a twenty-year-old Volvo back then, and it wouldn't start. I had put her in the back seat and the sounds she was making were otherworldly. The sound of someone not being able to breathe is terrifying; when it's your own child, it feels like listening to the sound of death itself. Luckily, a neighbor had seen me struggling and offered to drive us to the hospital.

Mickey's sudden death, followed so closely by Charlie's disappearance, had changed me. I was only seventeen that year, young enough to be under the misbelief that children do not die or disappear. Almost overnight, I went from naive and confident in the power I had over my own destiny to certain that the trajectory of my life was completely and utterly out of my control. That night, as I carried Ariel in my arms into the emergency room, I had been 100 percent certain that I would leave the hospital without her.

Before Charlie disappeared, my mother, like so many parents of Gen X kids, never seemed to worry about us much. Not until the unimaginable happened. It took her forty-three years to learn that the world is unfair, cruel even. But I have known this since I was seventeen. The pandemic did not surprise me. Impending climate disaster seems simply par for the course. I would not be surprised by a nuclear attack. Unfortunately, this doesn't make me any less anxious or miserable, just oddly resigned. However, preventing black mold from enclosing us, infecting my elderly mother and my asthmatic daughter is something I do have control over. At least there are some disasters I can still prevent.

"I'll go down and let them in through the basement door," he says.

"Thanks," I say. "I really do appreciate this."

"I have to run over to the Masons' place to drop some tools off, but I'll be back in about an hour to get started on the carpet. Have you moved the stuff you want to keep out of the basement?"

"Yeah," I say. "Everything but the treadmill."

After I got home last night, I moved the undamaged boxes to the garage, leaving the ones filled with Charlie's soggy clothes and books, Ariel's art, and my father's papers to be disposed of. The console TV. The ping-pong table. None of it is worth saving.

"I'll have one of the guys help me load the truck," he says.

My mother must have heard Nathan leaving, because she hobbles out of her room wearing her robe, her thinning hair a mess. Daisy trails behind her.

"How are you feeling, Mom?" I ask. The pharmacist assured me that the side effects from the shot would be gone by this morning.

"What's going on out there?" she asks. She hasn't put her teeth in yet. I worry today is going to be a less than lucid day.

"It's just the guys working in the basement," I say as cheerfully as I can.

She looks at me blankly.

"Nathan wants to make sure we don't get any more water down there."

At Nathan's name, she softens, but she still looks confused.

"Why don't you sit, Mom. I'll get you some coffee. Nathan brought those crullers from Dunkin."

She shuffles in her house slippers to the kitchen table and sits down.

I check my phone again; I've been checking it every five minutes since I got up, waiting for Trill to give me an update.

She said that Jericho's plan is to call the police station this morning, to let them know he found Charlie's backpack on his property. Paloma has advised him to say nothing more. I also agreed that once the police reach out, because they are certain to reach out, I will ask, on behalf of the Marshall family, for the FBI to be looped in, that the backpack be sent off for DNA analysis. Trill's other request—that my mother speak out on behalf of Jericho—feels impossible though.

My mother is fiddling with the edge of the tablecloth, the one my grandmother hand embroidered. How on earth will I tell her what is happening?

"Remember, you have a hair appointment today, Mom," I say, but she is fixated on the embroidered roses.

Once a month I take my mother to get her hair cut at a salon downtown. Jean is patient and kind and listens to my mother's stories that she repeats each time she sits in the salon chair. "Mom?"

"You thought I wouldn't find out," she says, without looking up from the tablecloth.

"What?"

"You always *lie* to me." Her eyes are glossy and unfocused.

My heart stutters. What is she talking about? Is it possible she knows about the backpack? Or is it something else?

She's gripping the tablecloth with her fist now, and it is starting to pull across the table, the coffee cup and her plate of toast moving too.

"I'm not sure what you're talking about, Mom," I say.

"Thinking I wouldn't know, when it was right there in front of me." Her voice is pitchy and strained.

I stand up and go to the sink, setting my mug down.

She pulls the tablecloth again. I lunge for her mug before it tips over and spills hot coffee in her lap.

"There's a stain here," she says.

"What are you *talking* about?"

"You thought you could fool me. But you could never fool me."

I still have no idea what she's talking about, and the phantom stain she's referencing could have come from any number of spills. How many thousands of meals have we eaten at this table? Does she think I somehow stained the tablecloth and lied about it?

"Maybe today's not such a good day to go to the salon," I say, trying to coax her back. "I can reschedule with Jean for later this week if you want."

"I know when you're lying!" she says loudly. "I'm not crazy!"

"Hey, everything okay?" Nathan asks, opening the kitchen door. I've never been so grateful to see him in my life; I'm not even angry he didn't knock.

"Mom's having a rough day," I say, trying to slow my racing heart.

She doesn't appear to notice that he's come in; she's so fixated on the troublesome stain.

"Any idea how long it's going to take down there?" I ask, still rattled by my mother's accusations.

Nathan has an odd look on his face. It's not good.

"Oh god," I say. "Is it worse than you thought?" I imagine the walls enveloped in mold, creeping up the drywall to the first floor, the second story.

He motions for me to join him out on the front porch, and I leave my mother, who has grabbed a cruller from the box and is studying it as if it's a foreign object.

"Listen," he says quietly. "I don't know what this is about, or if it has anything to do with . . . um . . . your family?"

"What are you talking about?" I ask.

"I've still got the police scanner in my truck," he said. "From back when I was volunteering at the fire department."

"Yeah?"

"I had it on on my way back over, and it sounded like there's some activity out at The Jenkinses' farm," he says.

"Activity?"

"Yeah," he says. "Police activity of some sort. I passed a cruiser heading west on Route 42 on my way back from the lake."

My heart hammers.

"A couple minutes later, a sheriff's cruiser blew past me," Nathan says.

"The county?" I ask. "Can you find out from Jake what's going on?"

Jake has been at the sheriff's department since the nineties, slowly working his way up the ranks from to Deputy to Undersheriff, second in command, last year. The fact that the sheriff's department is poking its nose in already is not a good sign.

"Jake and I aren't really in touch," Nathan says. It makes sense. Being related to someone doesn't mandate a lifelong friendship, but you'd think Nathan could at least try to find out what's going on.

"Listen," he says. His eyes dart to my mother in the kitchen then back to me. "I'm sure whatever it is will be in the paper tomorrow. Or the news tonight?"

Oh god. The media. This is exactly what Jericho was afraid of.

"And I promise, I'll let you know if I hear anything from Jake," he says.

June 1986

I HADN'T PLANNED ON going to Grad Night, the school-sponsored all-night celebration on campus the weekend before graduation, but Trill, who had been put in charge of the movie room, pleaded with me to come with her. "Pretty please? Be my date," she'd said, and I had started to think it might be fun. Besides, the only alternative was a party at Jake's house, where I was pretty sure Nathan would be.

After prom, I had avoided Nathan almost completely. He wasn't in my classes, and we had different lunch periods. I was worried that if I ran into him, he might somehow pull me back now that I'd managed to break free.

I was *free*. It was such strange feeling, to be unencumbered by another person's expectations and demands. Without Nathan occupying so much of my time and my brain, I felt *lighter*. Of course, I was still on pins and needles about Smith's waitlist, but even if I had to stay in Quimby, at least I wouldn't be tied down. Trill had accepted her spot at Hampshire and promised that if I didn't get off the waitlist, I could still visit her, said she could come home on the weekends too. Maybe I could even transfer to Smith after my first year at State.

Mr. Howard, who was chaperoning Grad Night, had approached Trill about the movies; he knew she was a film buff and had given her free rein over the selections. We were all seventeen, allowed to watch R-rated films, and so he'd worked it into the permission slips that parent signatures granted permission for us to participate in all activities, which might include R-rated movies. Most parents were so grateful their teenagers wouldn't be out on the roads that night, they would have signed onto almost anything.

The basic idea of Grad Night was that instead of going to boozy parties, students would spend the night in the school—with wholesome activities like water balloon fights for the jocks, movies and dancing for couples, and marathon games of Dungeons and Dragons for the nerds. At midnight, we would all convene on the football field for pizza and a celebratory howl.

"It'll be like *The Breakfast Club*," Trill promised, appealing to my John Hughes soft spot. Spending the night at school did seem kind of cool. We were allowed to hang out anywhere in the building except for the administrative offices and the infirmary, which would all be locked. The only other rule was that if we left campus, we would not be allowed to return.

Trill had picked five movies to show over the course of the evening, starting at seven PM and ending at seven AM. Together we had agonized over the list. She had wanted to mess with people's minds with her favorite cult movies: *Eraserhead* and *Harold and Maude* and *This Is Spinal Tap*. I had gently suggested that the student population at Quimby High might not be ready for that kind of cinematic education, and so we came up with a good mix of the movies most kids in the Class of 1986 had loved as kids (*Willy Wonka* and *The Wizard of Oz*), the ones we flocked to in high school (*The Breakfast Club*, *Back to the Future*, and *Indiana Jones*), and then a late-night set (*Rocky Horror*, *Pink Floyd's The Wall*, and *Friday the 13th*).

We were setting up the AV equipment in the auditorium when Trill said, "I thought you said Nathan wasn't coming."

"What?" I asked.

"I saw him outside at the water balloon fight when I got the videotapes out of my car."

Nathan was lost without me. I knew this. The last few weeks at school, he'd looked like a zombie wandering the halls. Because we spent so much time together, he hadn't maintained many close friendships. He had Jake, of course, and a couple other guys he was friendly with: boys he knew from junior high band (he'd played the bassoon), some teammates from cross-country (he'd been JV freshman and sophomore year before he stared working with his dad on the weekends). If he was here, I would have expected him to be playing D&D in the library, not outside with the jocks and squealing cheerleaders.

"You sure?" I asked.

"A hundred percent sure."

I sighed. Now I would have to figure out a way to avoid Nathan all night. When I'd suggested we could still be friends, it had been my effort to mend his broken heart, but it was like sticking one of those stupid pinkie-finger Band-aids on a gaping wound.

I hadn't had to tell my parents about the breakup, because Nathan's mom had relayed the news to my mother before I'd even woken up the morning after prom. She'd stood in my doorway, arms crossed, shaking her head and frowning.

"Great timing," she had said. "Jeez Louise, Edith. He just lost his only brother."

I had groaned and rolled over dramatically, pulling the covers over my head.

"He's a good kid," she said. "A sweet boy. Someday you'll wish you had a good, sweet boy like Nathan in your life. But if you're serious about this, you had better at least be nice."

And I *was* nice. Of course I was. It's not like I had any ill-will toward Nathan.

But now, on the night I'd planned on gorging myself on free snacks and pizza, watching cheesy movies with Trill, and howling into the late spring sky, I was stuck in a locked-room scenario with my ex-boyfriend.

"Which one first?" Trill asked. "*Willy Wonka* or *The Wizard of Oz*?"

"*Wizard of Oz*," I said. "It's a classic."

After Trill got the movie going, she was free to roam in and out of the auditorium. When Dorothy landed in Oz and Glenda gave her the ruby slippers, she motioned for me to follow her.

It wasn't quite dark out yet, but the tall windows facing the football field were filled with the glorious orange and yellow and pink of the setting sun. I felt a swell of sentimentality as Trill ran down the hallway toward the cafeteria where the DJ had started playing.

"Let's go dance!" she said, motioning for me to follow her.

Trill had opted for a hippie-meets-hobo look for the night: oversized men's black suit jacket, bowler cap, and a pair of army pants and high-top Chucks. I was dressed in a pair of State sweatpants, trying to embrace my inevitable matriculation, and the Icelandic sweater she'd given to me when I complimented her on it. I realized I had to be careful about the compliments I gave her, because anything I coveted, she offered to me. At her encouragement, I had started wearing my hair curly lately. Nathan had always said he liked it straight. But letting it be natural was literally saving me hours every day. I'd stopped worrying about getting it wet; I'd stopped worrying about sweat. It was liberating. It was awesome.

"It's like Andie McDowell's in *St. Elmo's Fire*," Trill had said, pulling one spiral and watching it bounce back.

"Thanks," I said, blushing.

In the cafeteria, an earnest DJ, a kid in our AP Chem class, was behind a table laden with equipment. The speakers on either side of him were pounding with the bass of "Let's Go Crazy," but the dance floor was empty. A couple of girls sat at a table in the corner. Effie and Tess, who had been tasked with dance duty, were moving chairs and tables out of the way.

"Hey!" Trill said. Effie waved, and Tess kept maneuvering.

"Where is everybody?" I asked.

"It'll pick up once the water balloon fight is over," Tess said.

Sure enough, the doors to the cafeteria blew open, and everyone who had been out on the field entered the cafeteria and raced to the dance floor properly hooting and squealing and dripping water everywhere.

Trill and I, swept up like *two corks dolls* (thanks, Sylvia) caught in a current, bobbed and dipped and let ourselves be swept away.

We danced until we were sweaty and red-faced. Trill took off her bowler hat and put it on my head, shaking hers like a puppy coming in from the rain. We danced to the fast songs, and we danced to the slow songs, dramatically, sillily, laughing and having the time of our lives. It was like Prom Take 2.

"Oh my God," I said, panting. "I need to sit down for a minute."

Trill followed me to the refreshment table, where I downed a warm can of Mountain Dew and stifled a sweet burp.

We grabbed two more sodas and made out way to a table that had been pushed up against the wall. I sat down, removed Trill's hat and blew air up toward my sweaty forehead.

"Here," Trill said and handed me a Grad Night flyer, and I created a makeshift fan, fanning myself first then Trill.

I felt a tap on my shoulder and jumped. I turned around, and there was Nathan, hands shoved into the pockets of his jeans.

"Hey."

"Hi," I said. "I didn't know you were coming. I figured you'd be at Jake's."

He shrugged.

Trill smiled without showing her teeth.

"Would you want to dance with me?" he asked.

The DJ had started playing "In the Air Tonight." Nathan loved this song. It was on the *Risky Business* soundtrack. Tom Cruise again.

I looked to Trill to save me, but her face was blank. She wouldn't condone or condemn, no matter how much I wanted her to. I pleaded with her to read my mind. *Save me.* Nothing. I thought about what she'd said about wanting me to be *her person*. Was I? And what did that mean?

I sighed. "Sure."

On the dance floor, I rested my wrists on Nathan's shoulders and swayed to the music. He kept about four inches between us. Far enough so we weren't touching, but close enough that we didn't look like a couple of geeky middle-schoolers. I could feel the heat of his body though his shirt. It was so hot in here. I blew air upward from my bottom lip again, trying to cool off my own hot face.

"I like your hair like that," he said.

Slowly, Nathan started to close the gap between us. As if I wouldn't notice. Soon, I could feel his heart pounding, knocking against me. As he tightened his arms around my waist, I felt like I might be sick. Hot and nauseous—Mountain Dew burbling in my belly.

"Hey," I said, pushing his shoulders to get him to back up, but he was holding me tight now, and I could feel his body trembling.

"Nathan," I said firmly and pushed harder, wriggling out of his arms and looking at him in disbelief. "Don't do this to me."

I immediately regretted it. Because he was no longer blubbering but raging.

"You are not a good person," he said. "Something is wrong with you." With this, he looked past me. Toward Trill.

I pushed him away from me, my body electric. "Please leave."

Nathan stormed off then, weaving through the crowd of swaying couples.

Back at the table, Trill gave me an *I told you so* look. Then she looked at her watch, a giant-faced Timex, and said, "Oh shit. Time for *Willy Wonka*."

For the next four hours, I hid out in the back row of the auditorium with Trill watching *Willy Wonka* then *The Breakfast Club*. The auditorium filled for that one, and I worried that Nathan would barge in, conjuring his inner Judd Nelson again. But he didn't. Maybe he'd gotten the message. Still, I couldn't stop thinking about what he'd said to me. *Something is wrong with you.*

At midnight, we paused the movie and everyone booed, but then Trill announced that we were taking a brief break to convene on the football field to eat pizza and howl.

It had gotten cold, and the grass on the football field was already wet with dew. I wished I had grabbed my sweater, because despite having been literally dying of the heat in the cafeteria, I was now shivering. Fortunately, Nathan hadn't joined the throngs outside. Teeth chattering, I managed to scarf down four slices of pepperoni pizza, and then Mr. Howard stood up with a bullhorn and announced that it was time for the annual *Barbaric Yawp*. For those of us who'd read Whitman with Mr. Howard, it felt like an inside joke. For the rest, it was a chance to howl.

"On the count of three," he hollered. "One . . ."

Trill grabbed my hand, and we looked at each other. A flush of heat warmed me.

"Two . . . Three!"

We howled. From our bellies to our breath. From our guts to God's ears. We hollered until our throats were raw and our ears rung. We looked at each other and yawped then yawped again. After, breathless and gutted, we laughed until we were almost peeing our pants.

Mr. Howard then led the group back up the hill, while some kids lingered.

"Look! The stars are out!" Trill said and jogged toward the edge of campus, where the sprawling grounds met the cemetery.

"We're not allowed to go off campus," I said, nervous. They had made it super clear that we were—under no circumstances—to leave school grounds.

"Oh my God, it's *barely* off," she said.

"What about the movie?" I was starting to feel the same prickly anxious feeling I got whenever someone tried to get me to break the rules. I hated it. I hated that I couldn't relax. Seriously. It's not like we were drinking. And the cemetery adjacent to the school hardly counted as off campus. We could probably just play dumb if we got caught.

"Somebody will press Play. *Come,*" she said, and dragged me by the hand toward the cemetery.

I had family buried here. Ancestors. The dates on some of the stones went back to the 1800s. I could never remember where they were exactly, and certainly not in the dark, and so I was surprised when the first stone we came to said *Alasdair Marshall.*

"That's my great-grandfather!"

"You're kidding," she said, wide-eyed.

"Nope. And his wife. And their children," I said, pointing to the little stones next to them. Three in all. One after another, they had all died in 1918 from the Spanish flu. The only surviving child had been my Grampa Marshall, my dad's dad.

I explained this to Trill, who touched the gravestones one by one, as if she were stroking the head of a child.

"It must be cool to have such deep roots. I don't know where any of my family is buried."

I had never really thought about it before. Everyone I knew had relatives in this cemetery.

"This town *belongs* to you," she said. "To your family."

"That's one way of putting it," I said. Instead, I felt like I belonged to this town. Like it owned me.

"I don't want to be buried," Trill said, sitting down and leaning her back against Alasdair's headstone.

"No?"

"Nope. I want to be cremated, and I want somebody to spread my ashes all over the world. Wouldn't that be cool? Like a little bit of me in Alaska and a little bit of me in Antarctica? Alabama and Antigua?"

"Only *A* names? What about Botswana? Bangladesh. *Bolivia!*" I joked, but my uneasiness had returned. I couldn't imagine wanting to be scattered like that, in unfamiliar places. With no place where people who loved you could go to pay their respects. I thought of Mickey's grave somewhere among the labyrinth of headstones.

I sat down next to Trill, and she pointed up at the sky. "You know, they say that we're nothing but stardust. Well, like ninety-seven percent."

"What do you mean?"

"Like every atom in our bodies—iron, calcium, oxygen, carbon—all of it was inside the stars, then after the Big Bang, Earth was created, and everything in it and on it was made of that stardust."

"Like the song!" We had listened to some of her mom's old records up in The Library just the week before. Joni Mitchell's voice had reminded me of crushed leaves and bells.

"Like the song," Trill said and leaned her head on my shoulder.

My heart was beating hard now. I didn't know whether it was being in the cemetery or the idea of Trill's ashes floating all over the world, stardust to stardust, when she was very much a solid, whole human girl breathing next to me now. Or if it was something else. But when she reached for my hand and held it, I felt overwhelmed by it all. The cold air, the Spanish flu, Mickey, and stardust and the way she smelled—inexplicably—like Thanksgiving. *Sage*, I thought, comforting and familiar and good.

When she leaned her head on my shoulder and her lips brushed my neck, that feeling of being swallowed whole was almost too much. I trembled and closed my eyes, felt every part of her that was touching me, every atom, every bit of stardust.

When I opened my eyes, she was looking at me, our faces so close, our noses were almost touching. Our lips.

"Trillium?" The man's voice swam to us in the dark and I swooned, dizzy.

"Shhh," she said, grabbing my leg.

"Are you out there?" the voice said. *Mr. Howard.* "Edie?"

He was usually so calm, but now his voice had a tremulous edge. It was the same way he'd sounded when the *Challenger* exploded.

"We're here!" I said, jumping up.

"Shit," Trill whispered and scrambled to her feet too.

We stumbled through the sparse patch of trees that separated the cemetery from the campus.

"We're here. We're sorry, it's just the stars were so . . ." I rambled.

Mr. Howard was standing on the grassy hill, rubbing his forehead as we emerged.

"We're so sorry," I kept bumbling, stumbling. "We weren't doing anything wrong . . ."

At this, I felt a jolt in my body, like a bee sting. I thought of Trill's lips grazing the skin of my neck. About the whisper of her breath as she leaned toward me.

"Edie," he said. "You need to come with me."

For a moment, I felt like my heart was beating outside my chest. He knew: not only what we had almost done, but how I *felt.*

"It's Nathan, dear," he said.

"What?"

"There's been an incident. He'll be okay, but he's been asking for you."

By the time we made our way back up the hill to the school, I could hear the ambulance coming, see the red lights painting that starry sky.

"Oh my God," I said. Trill was behind us. I couldn't look back at her; I wasn't sure I would ever be able to look at her again.

Inside the school, the paramedics were helping Nathan, who was sitting upright in the hallway, his back against the lockers. His eyes looked glazed over. When he saw me, he hung his head, and for some reason that made me feel worse than if he'd yelled at me.

"What happened?" I asked Mr. Howard. "Is he drunk?"

I thought about the bottle of Boone's Farm he'd brought to prom. Wondered why he'd sneak booze into Grad Night when he could have just gone to the keg party at Jake's.

Mr. Howard leaned over and said softly, "No, no. Valium. He was trying . . ."

And I realized what he meant.

I went to Nathan, who was standing now on wobbly legs, my fear turning into rage.

"How could you?" I yelled. "How could you do this to your mom? What is wrong with you? You're so selfish. You don't think about anybody but yourself!" Then I was hitting him, my hands slapping upward at his chest.

"Hey, hey, now," one of the paramedics said and pulled me away from him. "Come on now, sweetheart."

"We're taking him to the ER to make sure he's okay," the medic said to me. "He your boyfriend?"

"No," I said loudly.

At this, Nathan hung his head and walked out, escorted by the two medics like an old man instead of a seventeen-year-old boy. My body was trembling and buzzing. Dangerous.

Nathan was fine. They didn't even keep him overnight. He hadn't taken enough Valium to kill himself, not even enough to knock him out. And despite the whole point of Grad Night being to *Just*

Say No, he hadn't gotten in trouble for bringing his mother's sleeping pills. Principal Gilman, who knew Nathan had recently lost his brother, gave him a pass. Nathan's dad's company was also one of the school's biggest sponsors, with a full-page ad in the graduation program. They'd laid the foundation for the field house and were regularly called on for major repairs. Rick Nichols was well-respected in town, an alumnus of Quimby High himself. We were a week from graduation. What was the principal going to do? Hold Nathan back another year?

Mrs. Nichols told my mother what had happened, and, of course, my mother blamed me. She didn't come out and say it. She didn't come out and say anything. But she did agonize at how hard poor Nathan was struggling. Losing his brother and now his girlfriend.

All of it was too much. Now I was counting the minutes until graduation, praying I'd hear from Smith soon. I was still—ridiculously—holding out hope; other waitlisted kids were still receiving notifications from the colleges that had put their lives on hold, though I knew most schools had already closed out their waitlists. The idea of staying in Quimby in the fall had been Plan B, but after Grad Night and what happened with Nathan, it truly felt untenable. With every day that passed without word from Smith, my worry increased. *Maybe I should apply somewhere else*, I thought. *Somewhere with rolling admissions.* I was third in my class. Some state college somewhere would take me. Maybe U. Mass, Amherst? That was close to Hampshire. But when I went to the guidance office and the counselor told me what it would cost me as an out of state student to attend, I realized that if Smith didn't say yes and offer up a healthy financial aid package, I would be stuck here.

"Will they, like, send a letter saying I'm *not* getting in?" I asked Mrs. Fulwiler.

"I can call for you," she said. "Inquire on your behalf?"

I hadn't thought about just calling them. Everything I'd read said never to contact school admissions offices directly. Maybe my hand-delivering the letter had been a mistake. I'd broken the etiquette? But this was different. *I* wasn't calling; my guidance counselor was.

I sat down at one of the tables that was littered with military recruitment brochures as she dialed. *Maybe I should enlist in the army,* I thought miserably.

"Hello, this is Frances Fulwiler from the Quimby High School guidance department in Quimby, Vermont. I have a student here who was placed on the waitlist for this fall, and I'm calling for an update on her status. She hasn't received any kind of notification."

While she was on hold, she crossed her fingers hopefully and smiled at me.

"Oh, okay," she said, nodding. "Thank you, yes, if you could resend the letter, that would be wonderful."

I felt my heart dip. For a moment, I'd allowed myself to get my hopes up. But clearly, they had already sent the rejection. It just hadn't made it to my house.

"Thank you," she said.

Trying not to cry, I hoisted my backpack onto my shoulders. The fact that it was over, just like that, felt impossible: wanting something for so long, and now it wasn't even a dream anymore. What was I going to do?

"They sent the acceptance letter three weeks ago," she said.

I stopped.

"What?"

"It went out the first week of May along with a financial aid offer. The deadline to accept your spot is this Friday."

"Oh my God," I said. "Oh my God!"

"They were impressed by your letter, but even more impressed that you took the time to drop it off in person. They said that you are exactly the kind of student they need at Smith."

"But . . ." I said, thinking about the tuition. The money. It would all come down to this now. "How much?"

"You filled out the FAFSA for State, right?" she asked.

"Yeah."

"She said they've offered a significant need-based tuition scholarship. The merit scholarships were given to first-round picks. Room and board would need to be covered by loans. But if you've filled out your FAFSA, I'm certain you'll qualify. And there are private loans to fill in any gaps."

I shook my head. All of this was too much. I thought about my parents. I thought about Charlie, how this would break his heart. I thought about Trill.

We hadn't spoken about what happened on Grad Night in the graveyard. With each day that passed, it felt more and more unreal. Only stardust. But now that Smith wanted me and she had accepted the offer to go to Hampshire, my world, which had felt like it was collapsing in on itself, had begun to expand. I felt *expansive.* My whole future was ahead of me.

I went to Mrs. Fulwiler and embraced her. "Thank you!" I said then flew out the door and down the hall to Mr. Howard's room. School was over for the day, but he was still inside.

"I got in!" I said, breathless in the doorway.

He looked up and his smile bloomed. "To Smith?"

"Yes!"

"Well, I do believe this merits a barbaric yawp!"

Together we yawped. Loud enough that the school secretary poked her head in to make sure everything was okay. Then I floated all the way home.

But. I only had until Friday to convince my parents to let me go. Four days.

July 2023

I NEED TO TALK to Trill about whatever is happening with the cops out at The Farm.

The men are still working downstairs. Through the window I see Nathan lugging the soggy boxes from the basement to his truck, then one of the guys is helping him with a large roll of shag carpeting. Reeling from what he said about the police scanner, about the police, I go to my room, find Trill's number in my phone.

"It's Trillium!" her voicemail sings. "Leave a message. Or don't. I'll still know you called . . .'cause, technology."

"Hey," I say into the void. "Please call me."

I am pacing the length of my bedroom when Ariel lumbers out of her room across the hall. It's nearly noon, but she is just waking up.

"Air," I say. "Are you working today?"

"Not until tonight, why?" she asks, yawning and coming into my room, where she flops down on my bed. Daisy jumps onto the windowsill, peering outside. "Is there coffee?"

"It's *noon*," I say, irritated. "And Grammy's not doing great today."

She grumbles.

"I need you to keep an eye on her," I say. "Like really keep an eye on her. *Awake.*"

"*Okay*," she says and rolls dramatically off the bed. I follow her into the hall and down the stairs. She still acts like a teenager sometimes, but she moves like an old lady. From the back, she could be my mother shuffling down the hall.

I'll just drive out to The Farm. What can Paloma do to stop me? Also, if the cops have come for Jericho, then the damage is already done.

In the kitchen, I search for my purse, trying to remember where I put it. Through the window, I see Nathan's truck backing out of the driveway.

"What time is my hair appointment?" my mother asks, her mood abruptly shifting from crabby to chipper.

"Oh. Shoot. It's at one o'clock. But I have an errand to run. I should be back in time. If not, I'll have Air take you in a Lyft, okay?"

"I need some Tums while you're out," she says.

My mother eats Tums like candy. She would *never* eat real candy, so, I suppose, this is the next best thing.

"Sure, Mom," I say.

After she disappears down the hall to her bedroom, Ariel sits at the kitchen table staring sleepily into her mug of coffee.

"Have you seen my purse?" I ask.

"It's next to mine on the coat rack."

I have no recollection of hanging it on the coat rack.

"Oh! Wait!" she says, as if the caffeine has rushed to her brain, firing all her synapses at once. "Grab my bag?"

I pull mine off the rack and take down her canvas tote, too, which she reaches into.

"So, Henry was able to dry the envelope at the library yesterday. The letter inside too. It's a little hard to read because the other half is gone, but it looks like it's some sort of letter from a school."

I knew it. It must be exactly what I thought—a report card of Charlie's. Or a letter from a teacher, or the elementary school principal. It's nothing important.

She hands me the half of the envelope, which is stiff now. I shake it, and the letter inside comes out into my palm.

I carefully unfold it. It's the right half of a piece of stationary.

> on behalf of the Committee on
> it gives us great pleasure to inform you
> We were so impressed by your dedication
> hievements. We believe you will be an asset
> ith College Class of 1990. We look forward to
> ion.

No signature. But there, at the top of the page, embossed in a red as faded as Charlie's backpack, is the round seal. Only half of the Greek motto shows—Ἐν τῇ ἀρετῇ τὴν γνῶσιν—but I know it by heart. *To virtue, knowledge.*

Smith College.

It's my acceptance off the waitlist. It wasn't lost in the mail; Charlie had *taken* it. He'd wanted me to stay home. To never leave. When all I had wanted to do was to go. But how had he known what it was? Then I remembered Oscar night, when he'd asked me about Smith.

I try to recall Charlie's behavior that night at dinner when I told my parents I had been accepted. On scholarship. That I would only be three hours away. That I wanted this more than I had ever wanted anything, and that I had never asked for anything from them ever, how could they say no? When my mother began to shake her head, I had felt anger bubbling up inside me and I'd yelled that I was suffocating here, that I couldn't live under this roof for another minute. That if they refused me this, after how hard I had worked, I would never speak to them again. And that what they said didn't matter anyway. Because I would be eighteen years old soon. Old enough to do this on my own. Just like everything else.

My memory is focused on my parents, on my dad's befuddlement and my mother's dismissal, but I'm also able to conjure Charlie, staring at his plate, loading the tines of his fork with peas. He'd flinched when I smashed my fist on the table, milk sloshing in his tumbler. His chin had trembled when I stood up and said I needed to go for a walk. When I'd slammed the door shut, I could hear him on the other side yell, "You have to say *goodbye*!"

But I hadn't cared about upsetting Charlie. I hadn't cared about anything except that I had a one-way ticket out of town and my parents were trying to tear it up. I hadn't thought about Charlie at *all* that summer, I'd been so determined to forge my own path. I'd been selfish. And this is the reason why my brother is gone.

"So is it important?" Ariel asks. "Something from college?"

"Yeah," I say. "I don't think I ever told you, but I almost went to Smith College."

"Really? You got into Smith?"

"I was third in my class, I'll have you know," I say.

"Wow," she says. "You never told me that."

I never told her that because there had been no point. Nothing that I had worked so hard for at her age ever came to fruition. If anything, I feel like a cautionary tale.

"Why didn't you go?" she asks. "Because of what happened to Charlie?"

I take a deep breath. "Yeah. I couldn't leave Grammy and Grampa here after he disappeared. It was just easier to stay home and go to State."

"That's sad, Mom."

"It's fine," I say. "A million years ago."

I put the letter back in the envelope and turn it over in my hand and see some smudgy handwriting on the back. I didn't notice it before. Blue ink, some letters, I think, but hard to decipher. An S maybe? An O?

"Hey, any idea what this could be?" I ask, pointing to the blurred ink.

"Sorry, no idea," Ariel says. "Henry really just wanted to make sure the letter inside was salvaged."

"Well, please tell him thanks," I say.

The rain is coming down so hard, the windshield wipers on my Subaru can barely keep up. I turn on my lights, honk a little honk, and cross the covered bridge, holding my breath and praying that I won't be greeted by the lights of an oncoming vehicle.

Safely on the other side, I take Route 42 westward along Lost River, which is so high now, you can see its surface from the road: frothy and brown, violent and ominous.

When I get to The Farm's mailbox, I stop the car and look up the drive. Parked by the house are two cruisers: the local police and the sheriff's department. This must have been what Nathan saw. There's yellow tape blocking the driveway entrance and circling the periphery.

I feel dizzy, my head spinning. I quickly back up, do a three-point turn to flip the car around, and head back toward the main road, pulling over at the turnout when the rain makes it too hard to see. I pound the palms of my hands against the steering wheel until they ache, trying to figure out what to do.

Suddenly, a van slows at the juncture, turning onto Lost River Road from Route 42. WCAX, a satellite affixed on top. How on earth did the media find out so fast?

On the passenger seat, my phone buzzes, and I flip it over. Ariel. Shoot. It's five until one. My mother's hair appointment.

"Hi, baby," I say. It feels like I've swallowed marbles.

"Mom, you need to come home. It's Grammy."

"What happened?"

"I'm so sorry," she says, her voice breaking. "I just went back to bed for a minute. I guess she wanted to take a shower before her hair appointment, and she slipped and hit her head. She says she's okay, but I don't know. The bump is getting bigger. I'm really scared, Mom. I'm sorry."

I take a deep breath, remind myself it is not Ariel's responsibility to keep my mother safe. "Should I call an ambulance?"

"I don't think so, but can you please come home?"

"I'm coming, hon," I say. "I'll be right there. Air?"

"Yeah?"

"This is not your fault."

June 1986

On graduation day, I found myself feeling oddly nostalgic. Despite the blow-up with my parents, the breakup with Nathan and its disastrous aftermath, despite wanting nothing more than to get the hell out of Dodge, I was strangely wistful.

I had called Smith on Friday and accepted their offer. They said they'd put me in touch with a financial aid officer who would help me navigate the logistics. My parents had reacted with a kind of stunned incredulity, though I wasn't sure whether it was at the audacity of my decision or that I was moving forward without their approval or help.

Charlie had overheard us talking and had come to me later as I was decorating my cap. I'd used a chalk pencil to draw the outline of the Smith College logo—an elaborate gate—on the other side of which I envisioned my bright future. I was carefully painting over the sketch with a skinny paintbrush; it felt important to get this right.

"Edie?" he said. He stood in my bedroom doorway in his *Ninja Turtles* pajamas, which were at least two sizes too small for him. This made me feel even more weepy.

"Hi, Charlie Brown," I said, and motioned for him to come in.

He plopped down on my bed, crisscross applesauce, and picked up my old sock monkey, swinging it by its arm.

"What's up?" I asked.

He'd been quiet ever since the fight at dinner. We were all acting like the floor was carpeted with eggshells.

"How far away is that college?" he asked. He'd just gotten out of the bath, and he smelled soapy.

"I told you. It's only a few hours' drive. I can come home all the time." What I didn't suggest was that he could come to me. I couldn't imagine my parents venturing down to Smith to visit me any more than I could imagine them packing up to take a trip to the moon.

"Who's going to take care of me?" he asked then set the monkey down and started picking at his toenails.

"Ew, Charlie! Don't do that on my bed," I said, and he folded his arms. Frowned.

"Like who's going to take me to school?"

I honestly hadn't thought about it. With Mickey gone, Mrs. Nichols would have to go out of her way to bring Charlie to school and to pick him up. I wouldn't be here to walk with him as I had been doing since Mickey passed.

"You'll probably take the bus," I said. He would be going into fourth grade that fall. He was old enough to take the bus alone.

"What about after school?"

"There's a bus after school too."

I thought about Charlie letting himself into the empty house after school. I tried to imagine him making frozen lasagna all by himself and felt sick with worry. Then it made me mad. Deeply mad. My parents had been banking on me going to State and staying at home, doing all the things I had been doing for them since I was not much older than Charlie was now. They had depended on me. I thought about what Trill had said: that I was my parents' daughter, not their nanny. Did they just want me to stay home for free childcare?

"It'll be okay, Charlie Brown. Mom will figure it out."

Charlie lay back, staring up at the ceiling. Hanging over my bed were some origami stars I'd made in sixth grade.

"Hey, Charlie," I said. "Did you know that our bodies are ninety-seven percent stardust?"

He popped up, intrigued.

"Yep. Before the Big Bang, all the atoms that make up our bodies were inside of stars. When the stars exploded, the earth and everything on it was made. So, basically, we're all made from that stardust."

His eyes widened and he picked up the monkey again. But this time, he held it close to him. He was quiet for a long time, and I turned back to my mortar board.

"So somebody will pick me up?" he asked.

"Yeah, buddy. Somebody will pick you up."

Normally, graduation was held outside, with the students walking from the high school entrance down the walkways on either side to the football field, boys in yellow robes on one side, girls in purple on the other. The lilacs and cherry blossoms would be blooming, the air fragrant with their sweet smell. It was always a spectacle, like Mother Nature herself was caught up in the pomp and circumstance. But today it was overcast, the sky ominous and the air thick with humidity. The forecast was for thunderstorms, and Principal Gilman reluctantly made a last-minute call to hold the ceremony in the auditorium. No need for a hundred families to be caught in a downpour or racing across an open field during a lightning storm. It was disappointing, but we were all in good spirits and excited to graduate whether it happened inside or outside.

Lisa was the first person I saw once we were all corralled inside the school, and she came to me and hugged me so hard I could feel her heart beating. After the initial shock of it, I returned her embrace and that swell of nostalgia overwhelmed me again.

"I can't believe it, Edie," she said. "It went so fast."

Lisa was one of those people for whom high school really had been the best years of her life. She was popular and had a boyfriend all four years (a boyfriend she actually liked). She wasn't being ironic when she showed up for pep rallies and football games, when she wore her boyfriend's football jersey and decorated floats for Homecoming parades. She was so earnest, and right now, for whatever reason, that made me feel teary. In a single meaningful glance, I felt that the rift that had grown between us was now complete, with Lisa's future here in Quimby. Marriage, babies, playgrounds, and the PTA. Sitting in the bleachers as her boys played Pop Warner football or at the public pool in the summer, slathering tiny shoulders with sunscreen. There might be affairs. There might be sickness. There might even be divorce. And one day, she would grow old. Her eldest child would bring her to the Walgreens to get her prescriptions. To the Miss Quimby Diner for breakfast after church, to the salon for a cut and color. Then one day she would die and be buried in the cemetery we could see from here.

My future, on the other hand, was completely yet marvelously unknown. I would go to Smith, of course. Trill and I both planned to study abroad our junior year. Italy for Trill and England for me. Sylvia had lived there, and she'd died there as well. Perhaps Trill could take a train to me, and we could make a Syl-grimage to her gravesite. When I thought of my life beyond college, I mostly imagined little desks at big windows—windows that looked out at city streets or lush gardens or snowy vistas. I wanted to be a poet. I wanted to write. And I wanted to live a large and wonderful life. I wanted to love and grieve and travel and write about *all* of it. I wanted to feel *everything*, whatever that looked like. I also knew that I could never, ever do that here. That there were rules in this place. Rules I was too afraid to break.

"Hey!" Effie said as she and Tess came up to us. "Gilman said we're supposed to go down to the auditorium and line up in alphabetical order."

"Awesome," Lisa said. "Ready?" she asked me.

I had never been readier for anything.

I turned to scan the crowd for Trill. She was often late, and so I half expected she'd come flying in just as the first few notes of the graduation march began. But then I spotted her over by the front doors. She was holding her mortarboard in her hand, and she was looking around, and I realized she was looking for me. But rather than waving my hand to get her attention, I lingered in this rare moment when someone was hoping to see me, knowing that when she did, her mouth would stretch into a wide grin. There were only two people on earth I could make smile that way: Trill and Charlie.

I waved. "Trill!" My voice was louder and shriller than I had intended, causing a couple girls near me to turn around, scowling.

But sure enough, when she caught my eye, her consternation turned to happy relief. Her long arm shot up, and she pushed through the crowd. When she got to me, she collapsed into my arms. She smelled sort of funky, and I noticed when she stepped back that her hair was damp with sweat.

"What happened to you?" I asked.

"Oh my God," she said. "I had to walk all the way from the bridge. Nico broke down, so I had to leave it. Nobody would pick me up. Seriously, how fucked up is that? I'm clearly not wearing this getup for my health. But about six cars drove right past me."

"That's horrible," I said. "Where are your mom and brother?"

"They're coming, but they had to pick up my dad at the airport in Burlington."

"Your dad is coming?"

"Yeah. He decided to fly up at the last minute. He's staying at The Farm with us, we're doing dinner there tonight. *So* weird. What are you doing after graduation?"

"We're going to the Good Luck."

My parents had tried to convince me to invite Nathan and his parents to dinner after, but I had just rolled my eyes, and so they'd made reservations for four. Of course, Nathan would probably be there anyway, but at least we wouldn't have to sit together.

Trill had painted flowers on her mortarboard: a circle of daisies and a bright plum-colored peony in the center. "It's so pretty," I said.

I was grateful the ceremony was being held inside, because even in the auditorium, we could hear the thunder. There were no windows, but the lights inside kept flickering.

"Well, this is auspicious," Trill said as thunder cracked.

The speeches were long and boring, except for Mr. Howard's impassioned send-off in which he urged us to embrace life, to experience everything it had to offer. It was as if he were reading my heart. He turned to look at all of us assembled on the stage and caught my eye.

"A very wise young poet once said, 'I am at the edge of tomorrow. At the beginning of now. At the precipice of forever. Holding my impatient breath.'" I felt my eyes well up. That was my poem. *My* words. Trill leaned forward, looked down our row of seats, and gave me a thumbs-up.

"You are all at this precipice. Do not be afraid to leap!" he said.

Then there we were, lined up to get our diplomas from Principal Gilman, then listening to the braying of the crowd, then tossing our caps up into the air and shielding ourselves as they rained down.

Out in the lobby, the Student Council had set up a table with sickly sweet purple and yellow frosted sugar cookies and electric-purple punch. My parents found me, and Trill scanned the crowd for her family.

"Congrats, kiddo," my father said and gave me a hug. My mother also hugged me, and I saw she was clutching a tissue in her hand. Charlie was playing with his Stretch Armstrong doll but hugged me around my waist.

"Congratulations, Trillium," my mother said stiffly. "Is your family here?"

Trill looked a little nervous. "I don't see them. Not sure what happened."

Nathan came over with his mom and dad and stared at his feet while Mrs. Nichols hugged me. Nathan gave me a stiff hug as well, and I noted that he was skinnier than usual; it felt like I was hugging a fence post.

"Well, we'll see you at the Good Luck. We forgot to get a reservation, though; I hope we can get a table," Mrs. Nichols said, and they slipped away.

As families started to depart, it became clear that Trill's family was not here.

"Maybe something happened on the way home. My brother's truck might have broken down? Or maybe there was an accident?" she asked, as though I had the answer.

"I bet his flight was just delayed," I said. "Because of the storm."

"Oh," she said. "I bet that's it."

"Well, you should come with us to dinner," my father said.

My mother glanced at him as if to protest, but he just reached into his pocket and pulled out a quarter, which he handed to Trill. "Call your house from the pay phone and leave a message so they know where you are."

"Oh, thanks, but we don't have an answering machine," she said.

For as much time as I had spent with Trill's family, she had spent hardly any time with mine. It felt odd for her to be sitting in our station wagon, sandwiched between me and Charlie, who kept trying to talk to her about the Galaxy Rangers. She was a good sport, though, and within minutes we were at the restaurant, along with half of the senior class.

We were seated at a table for four, and the waitress put a chair at the end to make room for Trill and added an extra set of silverware in front of her. The restaurant was packed. I saw Nathan and his parents walk in, look futilely for an empty table, and then walk out. With their departure, I felt my body relax.

We each ordered individual plates rather than sharing family-style, though I knew it was more expensive this way. I could practically see my mother doing the mental calculations.

"So, Edie says you're going to school in Massachusetts?" my mother asked Trill. Not "as well" or "near Edie."

"I am! Hampshire College. I'm going to study film."

"Well, we'll make sure to watch the red carpet for you in a few years," my dad said.

Trill smiled. "Edie probably told you already, but Hampshire is really close to Smith. Just a few miles away. I'll have my car. I can give her a ride home for holidays."

My mother stiffened, her mouth twitching. The tips of my ears started to burn. Why was she being so weird?

"Oh, speaking of holidays!" my father said. "I almost forgot! We have a gift for you."

I knew some kids got extravagant gifts for graduation: cars or fancy watches or diamond earrings. Lisa's mother had bought her a real pearl choker. But I honestly hadn't expected anything.

"Bonnie, did you bring it?" he asked.

She nodded and reached into her purse, pulling out a gift-wrapped package that she handed to me.

It was a narrow, rectangular box. A necklace? I didn't really wear jewelry, but maybe they hadn't noticed that.

I untied the ribbon and carefully unwrapped the paper. I was bracing myself, preparing for how to react to a necklace. But when I lifted the lid, it was a pen.

Of course, pens are the kind of thing that most people don't get excited about. They're the punchlines of jokes—the sort of impersonal gift somebody gets for retirement or that distant relatives send for birthdays. But I knew this pen: a Waterman fountain pen, the body a swirled pearly-copper color, with a delicate gold nib.

"Grampa's?" I asked my father. My grandfather had died before Charlie was born, but I had adored him. He read to me, and we played endless games of Chinese checkers.

"It is. I know it's not really practical, but I thought it might be special to you. That you could write some really great poems with that."

"Thanks, Dad," I said, truly touched. "This is really nice."

"Thank your mom too," he said.

"Thanks, Mom," I said, though I knew she had nothing to do with this.

"We're also opening a checking account for you," she said. "With three hundred dollars."

"Thanks, Mom," I said.

"I made you a card," Charlie said, reaching into his back pocket and pulling out a piece of yellow construction paper that had been folded over. In purple crayon, it said, "Hapy Grajuashon!" with a drawing of a Teenage Mutant Turtle holding a diploma.

"Thanks, Charlie Brown."

Trill said, "Oh! Wait, I have something for you too!"

I turned to her. "But I didn't . . . I don't . . ."

She flicked her hand like there was a mosquito buzzing around and reached into her big tote, pulling out a package wrapped in brown paper and tied with twine and two wilting daisies.

I looked at her apologetically, hoping to convey how badly I felt for not having a gift for her too. But she just shook her head and motioned for me to open it.

Inside was a faded red hardcover book. It looked old. I turned it over to look at the spine. Sylvia Plath's *Ariel.*

"It's a first UK edition," she said. "Second printing."

"Oh my God," I said as I opened the cover and studied the table of contents, which blurred through my lens of tears. "This is so nice of you. Where did you get it?"

"My dad found it at a used bookstore in the Village. I sent him on a mission."

"I love it," I said. "Thank you."

The waiter arrived with our entrées, and we ate until we were all stuffed, though I noted my mother only ate a bowl of wonton soup.

When the check came, we each grabbed a fortune cookie and ceremoniously cracked them open, dry cookie dust scattering across the placemats.

"You first," I said to Trill.

"Be untraditional, even visionary," she read dramatically.

"Mom?" I said.

"Do your job to the best of your ability," she read. "Now that's silly. Why wouldn't I do my job to the best of my ability?"

"Dad?" I prompted.

"Ha!" he said and laughed. "Be untraditional, even visionary."

"Lazy fortune writers," Trill said. "Do yours, Edie."

I pulled the slip of paper from the half and spread it out on the table.

"She lives the poetry she cannot write," I read. "That's crazy! But I'm not sure what it means."

"Mine, mine!" Charlie said and cracked his cookie open.

"What's it say?" I asked, leaning over to look at it.

"You can keep a secret," he said.

"No, you can't." I laughed.

It was true. Charlie couldn't keep a secret to save his life.

"Yes, I can!"

"How about the time I bought your mom that hibiscus plant?" my father said. "Remember? You went right up to her and said, 'Daddy bought you high-biscuits!'"

Trill laughed.

I chimed in, "Or what about the time you told me that our cousin Amy was coming to visit? It was supposed to be a surprise, and I had to pretend like I didn't know."

Charlie crossed his arms and scowled.

"Do you need a ride back home?" I asked Trill, though what I really wanted was to go to The Farm and hang out. We were done with school. Graduated. There was nothing in front of us except summer.

I had gotten a job working four nights a week at the drive-in movie theater's concession stand, and Trill had arranged her schedule at the Video-Q to work nights too. I didn't even have to babysit Charlie, since he would be attending a day camp held at the public pool. My mom had hoped it would help him make new friends before school started in the fall. All of this left the days wide open. Hours upon hours upon hours of freedom.

"I should call my mom," Trill said. "I also need to deal with my car. I hope it doesn't need to be towed."

"Oh my God," I said. Her not having a working car might really put a wrench in our summer plans. "I forgot about Nico."

"It's fine. I'm like ninety-nine percent sure she's just out of gas." Nico's gauge always said she had a full tank.

Trill slipped away from the table to use the pay phone as my dad settled the bill.

When she came back, she said, "If you could drop me off by the bridge, that would be awesome. Jericho is meeting me there with gas."

"Why weren't they at graduation?" I asked.

"You were right. My dad's flight was delayed by two hours," she said. "It's okay. He brought a cheesecake from Junior's. We'll celebrate tonight."

I longed for her to invite me to come along. I wanted to sit with her family around their table. I wanted to be a part of that. To hear their stories. I wanted to meet her dad, the man who had gone to a bookstore in search of Sylvia for me. What had she told him about me?

"I'd ask you to come over," she said, "but my mom and dad haven't seen each other in like ten years, and I'm sure it's going to be totally awkward. Let's hang out tomorrow. Okay?"

"Sure," I said.

Jericho was, as expected, waiting for Trill near the covered bridge, bright red gas can in hand. The storm had passed, and the sun was out.

Charlie rolled the window down and leaned out. "Hi, Mr. Jenkins!"

Jericho seemed startled, but then shielded his eyes from the sun, and said, "Oh, hi there, Charlie!" and waved. "Looking forward to summer?"

"Yeah! I'm going to camp!" he said, smiling.

But on the way home, Charlie was quiet again.

"What's up, Chuck?" I said, punching him lightly in the shoulder.

"How would you know?" Charlie said.

"Know about what?" I asked.

"If I can keep a secret or not. Aren't those what secrets are? Things you *don't* tell?""

July 2023

My mother's fall, like so many things, is my fault. I shouldn't have left Ariel and my mother alone; this isn't Ariel's job. My mom really needs to be somewhere with nurses who can care for her. My chest feels like someone is sitting on it as I race back home.

In the driveway, rain pounds the roof of the car and obscures my view of the house. I take three deep breaths, trying to put the image of the police tape, of the news van, in the back of my mind before going inside. *One disaster at a time.*

They're in the guest bathroom, Mom sitting on the toilet lid, Ariel kneeling next to her, pressing a bag of frozen raspberries against her head, speaking softly to her.

"Mom?" I say, and she looks up at me. But her eyes are unfocused; it's like she's looking through me. When Ariel lowers the bag of berries, I see a bump the size of half of a ping-pong ball near her temple. The skin around her eye is already mottled and turning blue.

"Mom, Ariel said you took a little spill?" I ask, squatting down and studying the bump.

"I'm fine," she says, but it sounds more like a question than a statement.

"Why don't you tell me what happened *before* you fell," I say and put a hand gently on her knee.

"I . . ." she starts, then grimaces. "I was just . . ."

"You were taking a shower?" I prompt, motioning to the bathrobe she's wearing.

"No," she says firmly. But then she sighs. "Maybe?"

"Listen, Mom. I think we should go to the hospital and get you checked out. Make sure it's not a concussion. Okay?"

When she looks up at me, I expect a fight. Despite an entire adult life spent administering care to her patients, she rarely went to the doctor herself. I can count my own childhood visits to the ER on one finger, though there were several times I should have gone, the scar on my chin a reminder of my mother's insistence that I didn't need stitches despite the bone being exposed after a pogo-stick accident.

"Okay," she says.

Ariel drives us to the regional hospital thirty minutes away in St. Johnsbury, but after four hours in the busy waiting room, she has to leave to get to her shift at Carmello's on time.

"We'll get a Lyft home. Or I can have Amanda come pick us up," I say, though I'd feel bad asking Amanda to come here when she's likely still reeling from her own mom's passing. Also, given how long we've been waiting to see a doctor already, I'm not confident we'll be getting home before morning, anyway.

Every time it quiets down and it looks like we'll be seen, a new patient arrives with a more pressing issue: broken bone, chest pains, even a severed finger. We've been here for nearly ten hours when the eleven o'clock news starts on the waiting room TV, and I panic. My mother isn't paying attention, seeming to drift in and out of sleep in her chair, but if they start talking about Charlie, her ears will prick right up. I search in vain for a remote control. I would stand up and turn it off manually, but I don't want to call attention to it. Thankfully, it's just more coverage of the flood's aftermath, cleanup and fundraising efforts, and another shooting in Burlington.

By the time the nurse finally calls us back, there's only a sick baby and another elderly woman with an egg on her head as well who has been waiting almost as long as we have.

The doctor examines my mother thoroughly, asking questions about her general health, and the accident. She still can't recall what happened exactly.

As I'm explaining that she's been diagnosed with Alzheimer's, trying hard not to upset her, my phone buzzes in my purse.

"I'm fine," my mother says, though she sounds skeptical.

The doctor listens patiently, and my mother fiddles with her wedding ring.

"Well, I'd like to do a CT scan, just to take a peek," he says.

"Thank you," I say.

A new nurse takes her to get the scan done, and as soon as they're gone, I reach into my bag and pull out my phone, which I haven't checked since we got here. Three missed calls.

The first is from Nathan. The transcription says that the mold guys will be back tomorrow to work on the rec room. That he expects the sump pump by Wednesday. *Also, wanted to see if you'd heard anything about whatever was going on out at the Jenkins property. Hope everything is okay.*

The second and third calls are both from the same unknown number, not in my contacts. Fingers trembling, I click on the first one. Transcription unavailable.

I press Play and hold the phone to my ear. There's not much but static and then silence. Quickly, I return to the voicemail and click on the second message, not bothering to read the transcription but clicking Play right away. "Hi, sorry, my last call got dropped. This is Barbara Huddle from WCAX, calling for Edith Marshall. Hoping to get a comment from you regarding the recent developments in Charlie's case."

How did they get my cell number?

My palms are so sweaty, I can barely hold onto the phone. I decide to try Trill one more time. Hopefully Paloma will let her answer.

I'm surprised when she picks up on the first ring.

"Edie," she says, her voice tremulous.

"What happened this morning?" I ask.

"Oh my God, so, Jericho called the police, like we planned. They came out to The Farm, and he gave them Charlie's backpack. But when they asked him where he found it, they had to call in the sheriff's department, because the tree where it was hidden is on unincorporated land, which is the county's jurisdiction."

That explains the two cruisers that Nathan saw flying up the road, likely the ones I saw parked at The Farm.

"Did you know that Jake Nichols is a fucking *sheriff*?" she asks.

"Undersheriff," I say. Sheriff is an elected position; there's no way he'd be *elected* to fill that position, at least not by the women in this town.

"Whatever. So, Jake shows up and starts threatening to get a search warrant, and Jericho is just saying, *Go ahead and look. I have nothing to hide.*"

My skin crawls thinking about Jake Nichols; once a bully always a bully.

"Where is Jericho now?"

"He's at the police station," she says. "They asked him to come in for questioning. Paloma went with him, and I moved our stuff to the Flannigans' place up the road at the old Playhouse. Ryan's letting us stay in the cottages. We can't be at The Farm while they're conducting the search."

"So, he's not in any sort of trouble, right?"

"Not that I know of. He's there voluntarily. Paloma said it should be open-and-shut, but it's been more than twelve hours already. I really need to see you," she says.

I squint against the glare of the fluorescent lights. The medicinal smell of the hospital is sickening.

"I'm actually at the hospital with my mom right now."

"Oh no, I'm so sorry. Is she okay?"

"Yeah, just a bump on her head. I'm not sure how long I'll be here, though. They're doing a CT scan right now."

"Okay," she says. "What about first thing in the morning? Can you meet me somewhere?"

"Of course," I say, unable to quash that forgotten shiver of happiness that Trill's invitations have always made me feel.

June 1986

TIME STILLED. WHEN summer began, the days became liquid, languid. Slow.

For the last six months, I had been living in a state of uncertainty, anxiety, *holding my impatient breath.* And while everything was happening exactly the way I had hoped (breaking up with Nathan without the world ending, getting into Smith), I still felt like I was on the edge of something, teetering. Though now it was just the delicious anticipation of whatever came next.

Each summer day began with the soft buttery light of the sun coming through my window. On the periphery of my consciousness were the sounds of my parents getting ready for work, Charlie's little boy noises, and then the *knock, knock* on my door, "Bye, Edie!" from Charlie, then the slamming of the front door and the sound of the car pulling out. Then silence. In that quiet, I lingered between waking and sleeping, listening to the steady hum of someone mowing a lawn somewhere and birdsong. Because I didn't have school, or a daytime job, or Charlie to worry about, I would pull my comforter over my head and slip back into a cozy state of semi-sleep. Those were dreamy hours.

I started drinking coffee that summer, which I sipped from a mug Trill had given me. Her mother used to make pottery, and it was one of her creations: chunky and rustic. Etched into the side was a hippie-looking sun with a face. The mug was a sandy gray, and the sun was glazed orange and yellow. After Nathan and his dad had left for work, I liked to take my coffee out onto the front porch—a place I never hung out when my family was home—with my notebook and my grandpa's pen. I would prop my feet up on the railing, balancing the notebook on my lap, and write. I was so full of words, it felt as if I had been waiting my whole life to be alone, with only my thoughts and my pen, a mug of coffee and the smell of freshly cut grass.

Afterward, I'd go for a long, slow run—taking the loop around town—the sun beating down on me, my muscles straining, my heart pounding, my feet beating against the pavement. At home, I'd take a cold shower, my hair squeaky and shiny and clean. I lived in a pair of denim cutoffs and Trill's cast-off T-shirts: R.E.M., The Strand Bookstore, I ♥ New York. Sometimes she'd give them to me without washing them first, apologizing for her BO, but they never smelled like anything but Trill, the earthy, musky scent of her.

Usually around eleven, the phone would ring, and I'd answer, "Hello?" though it was always Trill with the same greeting: "What kind of trouble should we stir up today?"

We didn't really stir up any trouble, of course. Instead, we spent hours driving around with the windows down, taking back roads and listening to music, the bass pounding, our voices soaring over the road noise. We went to The Farm. We grabbed bread from Jericho in The Bakery and put it in an old picnic basket along with big hunks of cheese from her mother's kitchen, fresh herbs, and her mother's homemade raspberry preserves. Some nights when neither of us had to work, we stole a bottle of dandelion wine from her mother's dusty stash. We hiked for miles along Lost River, catching polliwogs in glass jars, naming them after poets and filmmakers: Ginsberg and Fellini, Sexton and Bergman. We spread a ratty old patchwork quilt underneath the willow tree at the edge of the river and ate until our bellies were full. Every moment with Trill was pulsing with possibility. With promise. And oddly, for *this*, I was happy to wait.

I felt like a bee on those days: fat, sluggish, buzzing. I talked nonstop, flitting from one subject to the next. Daydreaming aloud, as Trill closed her eyes and listened.

On rainy days, we lounged in The Library, lying on the lumpy old couches. I read her my poems, and she showed me her ideas for movies. She sketched her stories out in her leather-covered journal, and I read her my poetry while she sat quietly, listening, chin in hand. When I finished, she'd nod or clutch her hands or say, "Holy shit, Eeds. You're amazing."

Still, even with entire days to ourselves, I wanted *more.* More time. More Trill. I wanted so much, things I couldn't name. That moment in the graveyard haunted me, taunted me. Had I only imagined it? My body and brain and heart and skin felt *thirsty.* At night I dreamed that I had just finished a run and was drinking but couldn't get enough. That I drank glass after glass after glass of water but still felt parched.

When the clock hands inevitably approached three o'clock, I would start to feel antsy. Irritated.

"Ugh," I'd say. "I wish I didn't have to work."

"Buck up, little camper," she said. "I'll be there at nine thirty."

I'd change at her house, while she also got ready for work. Then we'd drive out to the drive-in where she dropped me off, and she'd go back into town for her shift at Video-Q.

One perk of working at the drive-in was that I got free passes and as much popcorn as I could eat, which I gave to Trill. When she closed up shop at Video-Q, she'd drive over and park near the concession stand. I'd deliver her a bucket of popcorn and a box of

Junior Mints, and she'd watch whatever was showing. There were double features almost every night. Old movies and new movies. Kids' movies and R-rated. It was basically a mishmash, but Trill didn't care. During the week, the drive-in didn't get a lot of cars, and sometimes we'd sit on Nico's hood together, sharing the huge bucket of popcorn, fingers greasy and lips slick with salty butter.

"Oh my God," she said one night in late June. "That's that creepy van guy again."

She pointed toward the play area that was below the screen. Parents usually let their kids play there if the movie wasn't G-rated.

The red Ford Econoline van was parked in the row right in front of the playground. The windows were up, even the driver's side, which should have been rolled down to hold the speaker. But the speaker next to the van was hanging on its stand.

There were two kids playing on the playground, a boy and a girl. Siblings, I thought, though they looked about the same age. Maybe five or so. I started feeling really antsy, the way I felt on the rare occasions when I was home alone with Charlie at night: hypervigilant.

"We should figure out who those kids belong to," Trill said.

"Hey, Jerry?" I said, poking my head into the concession stand. "I have to run to the porta-potty. I'll be back in a few minutes."

"Okay," he said. "Be back before the credits on this one roll."

Trill and I walked quickly through the maze of cars, toward the front where the screen was perched on a hill above the playground. The kids were giggling as we approached, swinging higher and higher on the swings. The sound of the chains catching and clanking put me on edge.

We were careful to keep our distance from the van, though I did glance over to try and see who was in the driver seat. But the cab was dark.

"Hey," Trill said. "Can we use these swings?"

"*May* you?" the little girl said sassily.

"May I?" Trill said.

The girl said, "I don't care" and hopped off the swing, running to the monkey bars. She shimmied up one of the bars, and I turned to look for the boy. He was nowhere in sight.

"Hey. Where did your brother go?" I asked, feeling panic rising acidic in my throat.

"I don't know," she said, hanging upside down now, her hair dragging in the dirt below.

I looked toward the van, but he had put on his brights and was backing out of the space. Heart pounding, I said, "Where are your mom and dad?"

She pointed in the distance, but it was only a sea of darkness scattered with headlights.

"I'm going to take you back to your car and find your brother," I said. "Trill, can you read that guy's license plate?"

She squinted at the bright lights. "I can't see it," she said.

"I said come with me," I repeated to the girl, my voice cracking. "I work here. Kids aren't allowed on the playground alone."

"Fine," she said and ran down the small slope toward the cars. I ran after her, watching as the van disappeared down a row of cars and started making its way to the exit.

Suddenly, the sky was filled with light as the credits rolled against a white screen. I could see the little girl standing at a pickup truck that had backed into its spot. A lot of people did this, propping themselves up in their truck beds to face the screen.

I arrived at the truck, breathless. In the bed of the truck was a couple, the woman holding a toddler on her lap who was fast asleep. "Your little boy," I said, trying to catch my breath.

"Oh shit," she said. "What did he do now? *Anthony!*"

A head popped out of the passenger window. "What, Ma?" He was silhouetted by the light coming from the screen.

"That's him," Trill said to me. "Thank God."

"Nothing," I said to the woman. "I'm sorry."

"There's a creeper in his van who was watching him," Trill said. "You might want to keep a better eye out." With that, she grabbed my hand and yanked me along, and we ran all the way back to the concessions.

"Oh my God," I said. "That was so scary."

"So scary," she agreed.

"But he's okay," she said firmly. "Everything is okay."

"Who *is* that guy?" I asked stupidly. "I mean, what kind of weirdo watches little kids playing?"

"Pedo," she said. "So many sickos out there."

After everyone had left and we'd closed the concession stand, I still felt unsettled.

"What do you feel like doing tonight?" Trill asked.

"I don't know," I said. "Anything, I guess. Surprise me."

"Let's go swimming," she said.

"Swimming? It's like midnight."

"Why not?" she said.

Then we were barreling down the road back into town and past the turnoff to The Farm and eventually onto the road that would take us to Lake Gormlaith. The air was thick and warm, especially for a June night.

We pulled into the boat access area but left the headlights on so we could see.

"Nathan and his dad are building a house up here," I said. "This is where he brought me on prom night."

"He was going to let you walk all the way home from *here*?"

It seemed ludicrous now. How angry he'd been. How upset. It made me furious even thinking about it, that old rage mixed up with the awful memory of Nathan on Grad Night and Mickey's funeral and that little boy at the drive-in we thought had gotten nabbed, and I wanted nothing more than to be submerged in that cool, dark water.

The lights at all the camps around the lake were out. Nobody really came up here until the Fourth of July. So, I stripped down to my JogBra and underwear and ran into the water as fast as I could. It was shockingly, breathtakingly cold. It felt wonderful.

Trill was splashing into the water only moments later. "Holy fuckbuggers, that's cold!"

The headlights from Trill's car were blinding, and I was suddenly self-conscious. I was not someone who stripped down to my underwear and went swimming at midnight.

Quietly, I treaded water, and Trill dove under to stand on her hands, her long legs glowing in the beams of the headlights.

When she surfaced, I said, "There's an island out there."

"Really?" she asked. "Like Sylvia's?"

"Smaller," I said, remembering the sweet ham and sticky pineapples. The delicious sweetness of that day, then the bomb dropping that Mickey had passed away. I worried that every bit of goodness in my life would always be tempered by tragedy. "Yin and yang," Trill had explained. "The good is meaningless without the bad. No light without darkness."

"Do you think we could we swim out there?" she asked.

"No," I said sharply. Envisioning disaster. "It's too far."

"You okay?" she asked, swimming over to me. "You've been kind of quiet since we left the drive-in."

I leaned back, my hair dipping into the water. It felt heavy when I lifted my head.

"*All cool, all blue*," I said.

We treaded water next to each other, then I turned to face her. She was looking up at the sky. I followed her gaze.

"Are we about to get abducted by aliens?" she asked, gawking at the blue and green lights above.

"Oh, wow! That's the northern lights," I said. "Aurora borealis. It's super rare for this time of year."

She lowered her head to look at me now, and she paddled closer.

"How lucky," I marveled.

"How lucky," she repeated.

At first, I thought it was just pondweed, the tickle at my ankle. But as it lingered, I realized it was Trill's foot. The scoop of her arch, cupping my calf. My chest heaved, and I hoped she didn't notice.

I let my wet hair pull my head back, and I stared up at that miraculous display above.

When I looked at her again, she moved closer to me, rested her wrists on my shoulders as if we were slow dancing. She kissed me playfully first. Like it was a joke, lips only grazing mine. Unserious. But then, when I responded, with all that need and hunger that had been nearly driving me mad, it wasn't a game anymore.

July 2023

When the Lyft drops my mother and me off at home after the hospital, it is two AM, but Ariel is sitting in the kitchen with headphones on, sketching. A cup of coffee and an empty pizza box sit next to her, Daisy asleep on the lid. I'd thought Ariel might be in bed, so I hadn't called her to come get us.

"Oh my God, Air, you shouldn't be drinking coffee this late at night."

She looks up at me and pulls off her headphones. "What?"

"Nothing. Can you help me get Grammy to bed?" I ask as I help my mother peel off her wet coat.

It's two AM, but rather than admit her, the hospital sent her home with a handout about concussions: what to watch for and what to do if any troublesome symptoms appeared. Luckily, the CT scan showed nothing of concern. No bleeding on the brain. Her confusion is likely from dementia, not her fall, though who's to say?

"Mom," I say after I help her out of her clothes and into her favorite nightgown, then into her bed. "You need to let me know if you start feeling nauseous, okay? I'm putting your phone right here. Just hit this button to call me, okay?"

She looks at the phone like she's never seen one before.

"Actually, maybe I'll sleep in here with you tonight. Would that be okay?" I haven't slept in my parents' bed since I was a toddler.

Normally, she would balk at such a proposition, but tonight she shrugs.

Back in the kitchen, Ariel is making Toaster Strudel. The air smells like hot raspberry jam.

"Those are so bad for you," I say, but when I realize I haven't eaten in more than twelve hours, I ask, "Can I have one?"

She pulls two plates out of the cupboard, hands me a frosting packet.

We sit at the table, and I tear the packet with my teeth, squeezing the frosting across the hot strudel. Out of habit, I scrawl my initials: *EM*. Lisa and I used to have Toaster Strudels every Saturday morning when we did sleepovers at her house. We were weaned on Red Dye #2.

Ariel squeezes a blob of frosting on her plate, dips the strudel in it with her fingers, blows on it, and takes a bite.

"Listen," I say, wondering if Jericho is home yet, thinking of the news van, the call from WCAX. How to tell my mother what is going on with him. If I don't tell her, it's only a matter of time before she finds out. If they found my cell number, there's no doubt they've found the landline and her cell number as well, though she thankfully never answers unknown numbers. "I just want to give you a heads-up that things are about to get a little crazy here."

Ariel looks up from her sketch, eyebrow raised.

"How so?" she asks, flaky crumbs falling to her plate.

"There's some new evidence . . . in Charlie's disappearance."

Now her eyes are wide open, stunned.

"What *kind* of evidence?" she asks, setting down the strudel. When I don't answer, she put her hands to her mouth. "Oh my God, did they find him?"

"No, no," I said. "Oh God, I'm sorry. It's two in the morning, and I'm so tired. I should have waited until the morning. But I didn't want you to see it in the paper."

"I don't read the paper, Mom."

"I know, I know. You know what I mean, though. I wanted to tell you before it turns into what it's probably about to turn into."

I remember the self-portrait in Jericho's studio. His face, his body, all of him made of nothing more than the accusations against him. The newspaper articles. The letters to the editor. My heart feels completely tattered.

"Who found it?" she asks. "And where?"

"Jericho Jenkins," I say. "On his property."

"Wait—that dude who lives out by Sasha's mom? The one Grammy thinks did it?"

"He didn't do it," I say firmly.

"You told me he was your friend's brother, right?" she says, as if dredging her memory for the family story. The lore. What happened to my brother is only a legend to my child. A tall tale.

"Yes. Trill. She and her wife are here to help him."

"She was your best friend in high school, right? I remember you telling me about her," she says. "How long has it been since you've seen her?"

Sitting at the bar at Good Luck with Trill last night feels like a million years ago already.

"It's been a really, really long time," I say. "Not since that summer."

"Oh, Mom."

She reaches out for me, and takes my hand, and looks at me with such compassion and tenderness, I start to cry. It stuns me. I never cry around Ariel. I try never to cry around anyone. I stopped that foolishness ages ago, when my tears were met with nothing but my mother's frustration, and my father's tentative hand patting my back. But now here is my daughter, and here is my heart in her hands.

In the morning, I awake curled up on my father's side of the bed next to my mother. I look at her, still lost in sleep, her face relaxed in a way it never is when she's awake. Like a child's. I feel a strange tenderness toward her, a heartbreaking pity. She has no idea what's happening, and I wish I could protect this peaceful nescience.

I climb carefully out of bed and walk gingerly across the floor to the door. She mumbles and rolls over. The air in the room is musky and stale.

I'm filling the coffee filter when the kitchen phone rings.

"Hello, is this Mrs. Marshall?"

"This is her daughter," I say.

"This is Lieutenant Strickland with the Quimby Police Department."

It's six AM, I note, just early enough to head off us finding out about the discovery on our own.

"I'm calling to let you know that some new evidence has surfaced in your brother's disappearance."

I have rehearsed the shock and delight and anger and despair I would offer in exchange for this "news," but I am unable to speak.

"Ma'am?"

"I'm here," I say, but I am only thinking of Jericho now. "What is it?"

"It appears to be a child's backpack. It was discovered on the Jenkinses' property. The next step is to verify that it belonged to Charlie."

"Yes, of course," I say, sweat forming on my hairline. I swipe at it with the back of my wrist. "Mr. Jenkins, you said? You don't think he—?"

He pauses. "I'm sorry, ma'am," he says. "I know Mr. Jenkins was a person of interest at one point, but he's come forward voluntarily, and he's agreed to a search of his property. He's been fully cooperative. We don't have any reason to believe at this time that he had anything to do with the crime."

I feel myself relaxing. It's going to be okay.

"You may also hear from the sheriff's department," he says. "We're working in tandem with the county. They're the ones conducting the search."

"Okay," I say. "Thank you."

"And Ms. Marshall?"

"Yes?"

"We're going to do our best to figure out what happened to your brother. I know it may not seem like it, but this discovery is good news. We have physical evidence now. We can get the FBI involved, use their resources, get it tested for DNA."

I had no idea they'd be so willing to work with the FBI. Maybe I won't even need to make the plea Trill asked me to make.

"That's terrific," I say. "Thank you."

"Do you think you'd be able to come by the station today and verify that the backpack belonged to your brother?"

"Of course," I say.

I hang up feeling a million pounds lighter. It's going to be okay. The police really are just getting Jericho's statement. I'll go look at the backpack, and then they'll get the FBI involved to test the DNA.

The memories of the police, the FBI, from that summer are hazy. There were men in suits and men in uniforms. Their names all sounded the same: Officer this and Sergeant that. Detective So-and-So. They all looked the same to me, too, in their shiny shoes and tired eyes. Hairy wrists and rough hands. And though I couldn't tell them apart, they all acted so familiar with us after even only the first few weeks. They called my mother by her first name, and they patted my father on his back like a work buddy might. I know now that it was their way of making us trust them, ingratiating and placating. But to me, they remained faceless, nameless: men who were supposed to be heroes but wound up doing little more than making empty promises, ones impossible to keep. I am not sure why I trust them to do any different now.

I am shaking as I slip on my sneakers and search for my purse. My mother and Ariel are both asleep. I can run down to the police station and be back before they wake up. Then I can figure out how to meet Trill.

But as I'm headed out the door, the kitchen phone rings again. I sigh and come back in, pick up the phone.

"Is this Edith Marshall?" a man asks, and I cringe. My mother is the only person who ever calls me Edith anymore.

"Yes?"

"Hey. This is Jake Nichols," he says then pauses, seeming to wait for recognition. "From the sheriff's department."

His voice sets me on edge. Even after all these years.

"Hey, Jake," I say.

"Did you get a call from the local PD this morning?"

"I did."

"Great. So, you've heard Jenkins has been hiding a little something on his property."

"I was told he *found* a child's backpack," I say.

He snorts, and I close my eyes, picturing Jake's seventeen-year-old face. That square, dog-like face atop his thick, muscled neck.

"He certainly did. We're conducting a full search of the property now and expect we'll be able to bring charges against him by the end of the week."

"Wait, *what?*" I say. *Bring charges?* This makes no sense. "Jericho isn't the one who put the backpack in that tree."

There's silence on the other end of the line.

"I didn't say anything about a tree," Jake says. "Have you been in *contact* with Jenkins?"

My mind races. The last thing I want is to get Jericho in any more trouble than he's already in. "I spoke to him. Jericho just wanted me to know that he planned to turn it in, and that he had no idea how it got there. He could have disposed of it. He certainly wouldn't have reached out to my family if he put it there."

Jake laughs, but it sounds like a bark.

"Did Howard ever make you read that story about the heart beating under the floor?"

"Poe," I say. "'The Tell-Tale Heart.' I teach it to all my freshman. What does that have to do with anything?"

"I've been doing this a long time. Most people can't live with a secret like that their whole lives. It's torture. You know?"

Do I know? Of course, I know. I know better than anyone. Do I sense something in his tone? It feels like he's just touched me with a hot poker.

"Lieutenant Strickland said they just need me to confirm the backpack is Charlie's, and then they're going to get the FBI involved. To test it for DNA. To try to track down who really did this."

"That won't be necessary," he barks. "Listen. I know you had a—*complicated*—thing going on with Jenkins's sister. Probably making it hard to see what's right in front of your face. But we've got our guy, Edie."

July 1986

It was just a kiss, the water between us, below us, the aurora borealis above. Just a kiss under a spectacular sky. But something shifted after that night. I had been teetering at the edge, but now I was falling, at mercy to gravity. To Trill.

At The Farm, I would now lay my head in her lap and let her thread her fingers through the spirals of my curls. We clung to each other when we watched scary movies, projected on a sheet she hung between two trees behind the barn. We embraced every time we said hello and goodbye, and we took to saying, "Love you!"

I felt about Trill the way I had never felt about Nathan. I loved talking to her, I loved when we were silent. When she wasn't around, I counted the hours until I would see her again. I hoarded stories and jokes and anecdotes, so when we were reunited, I could make her laugh or slap my arm in astonishment at whatever tidbit I had shared. I loved that when she and I were together, we didn't need anybody else to have fun.

When Lisa and I had been best friends, I always felt like she was waiting for someone better to come along. A boy, usually. Sometimes a more popular girl. But with Trill, I *was* the someone better. She made me better.

I was so happy. I would have done anything for her.

Trill wanted to make a movie that summer, and I wanted to help her, but I had no idea how. Then I remembered my dad's video camera. It was pretty high-tech, a JVC, and not one of those big clunky ones everyone else's dads had. I had no idea if he'd let me use it, but a filmmaker without a camera, I thought, was like a poet without a pen.

"Hey Dad, would it be possible to borrow your video camera?" I asked after supper one night. "For the Fourth of July?"

He turned away from a rerun of *Who's the Boss.*

"It's a pretty expensive piece of equipment, Edie," he said. "I can't afford to replace it if anything happens to it."

"I know, Dad. If something happens, I promise I'll replace it. I have money from work. But it won't. I'll be super careful."

"You have to keep it in the case when you aren't using it," he said.

"Thanks, Dad," I said and went to him for a hug. It seemed to startle him, but he returned my embrace.

"*Super* careful," he said.

Neither Trill nor I had to work on the Fourth of July; even the drive-in closed for the night.

She had created a storyline for her movie and a skeletal script—a story about two girls lost in the woods, kind of based on an old movie called *Picnic at Hanging Rock.* She also had an aesthetic vision that required shooting during the golden hour before sunset. Despite my not having acted since my fifth-grade production of *The Wizard of Oz* in which I played a flying monkey, she insisted I would make a fine actress. I suggested she ask Piper Kinkaid from our class, who starred in almost every one of our high school productions, or Piper's best friend, Becca, who was also far more gifted than me. But Piper was visiting her brother in Colorado, and Becca was in New York at college orientation. Trill had managed to procure a tripod and planned to co-star.

The costumes were borrowed from the Lost River Playhouse, and the moment I put the dress on, Trill stepped back and said, "My God! Lucy Honeychurch has arrived!" It was true. With the turn-of-the-century dress, replete with petticoat and corset and bustle, with my hair down in loose curls, I could have stepped off the set of *A Room with a View.*

I followed Trill's direction, reciting the lines she fed me. I ran through the woods as the late afternoon sun streamed through the leaves and knew that what she was making would be beautiful. Seeing her focus and excitement was like watching myself when I was in the zone with my writing. I had never been able to explain that feeling to anyone before. But now I was watching it happen. We were *artists.* It was thrilling.

When the sun slipped behind Franklin Mountain, the air grew cold. It was midsummer, but the temperature still dropped down into the fifties most nights. I shivered and said, "Brrr" as we leaped across a narrow part of the river, my skirt dragging in the cold water.

Normally, the Fourth of July meant a barbeque with Nathan's family in his backyard. But even if Nathan and I hadn't split up, I was pretty sure the Nicholses would have opted out. It had always been fun, though: Charlie and Mickey running around with sparklers, our dads cooking hot dogs and burgers on the grill, our moms making red, white, and blue Jell-O parfaits. Nathan's father would get fireworks, which he set off from their back deck, while our mothers squealed in combined terror and delight.

Trill's family didn't have any traditions around the Fourth of July. No burgers or dogs on the grill. No bottle rockets or Roman candles. It felt strange to sort of ignore the holiday, but her mom did offer to make pasta primavera with veggies from the garden, said she'd leave it in a pot in the kitchen, and we could come and eat whenever we were done. Jericho had been working on a new sculpture, a woman made of willow branches—Mother Nature, holding the earth in her gnarled hands.

In period costumes, and with giant bowls of pasta in our hands, we sat and watched him work. We hung out until the sky was dark and Jericho said he was going to grab some supper, then read in his room.

There was the distant sound of fireworks going off, but we couldn't see anything at all. The sky had gotten overcast and dark, and the scent of a storm hung in the air.

The Mother Nature sculpture loomed over us, illuminated when lightning lit up the sky.

"Shit!" Trill said when the sky tore open, and rain poured down on us. "Let's go!"

She took my hand, and I ran after her up the little hill to the barn. The rain was insane: it pummeled us and pounded the ground. We were soaked and shivering as we ran inside the barn and up the stairs to The Library.

"Oh my God, I hope we didn't ruin the dresses," Trill said, looking down at her drenched gown. "We should hang them up."

"Do me," I said, turning my back to her. She carefully undid the laces of the corset, and I only then realized how compressed my breasts and waist had been.

"Now me," she said, and turned her back to me. I also carefully unwrapped her.

We both peeled off the dresses and hung them on a couple of nails sticking out of the wall, shivering in our damp underwear. She grabbed two blankets then handed one to me and wrapped the other around herself. We plopped onto the sofa, laughing, teeth chattering.

Above us the rain was pounding against the roof. The single light in The Library flickered, then went dark.

It didn't take much for the power to go out here, though it usually came back on pretty quickly. But tonight, we were plunged into darkness and stayed there. It was pitch-black in the barn. In the darkness, my other senses were now heightened. The rain's patter sounded thunderous. The scent of books was overwhelming: musty and nostalgic. When I felt Trill scootch close to me, the sides of our bodies separated by only our blankets, I held my breath.

I heard rustling and felt her hand touching my shoulder.

"Come here," she said, lifting her blanket up and inviting me inside her cocoon. I unwrapped myself from my blanket and joined her.

Her skin was cold, bumpy with goose pimples.

"Eeds?" she said, and I started to breathe so rapidly I was worried I might pass out.

"Yes?"

"Yes?"

Yes.

Then, the patchouli smell of her, the cherry blossom smell of her, the softness of her and the roughness of her, and the words, *the words* that went through my head—the poetry of all that want. And all the while, rain beating out its iambs on the roof above us.

For hours we kissed and touched in the darkness. Neither of us knew what we were doing; we hadn't seen any movies or read any books about girls like us to know if we were doing it right. We fumbled, and giggled, and fell gently into a rhythm. I thought of the first day I had met Trill, our bodies running up and down the bleachers. Our strides matching each other's. Our hearts racing at the same pace. Our breath, our breath, our breath.

Later, exhausted, we fell into a sort of half sleep. One blanket over us, like little girls playing inside a tent fort. I dreamed of the woods at twilight, of our long dresses and long hair and bare feet. I was inside Trill's movie. I was inside, inside, then I was *watching* the movie: from a distance, projected on a billowy screen. I saw Trill kiss me, the image projected on that soft white sheet suspended between the trees. Rain tapped at the sheet lightly, then harder, the makeshift screen getting wet, dark, the image of us melted like watercolors.

I bolted out of sleep and out of the fortress we'd made.

"Trill," I said, my heart banging, as I struggled to untangle myself from the blankets, from her arms and legs.

She came out of her slumber more slowly, mumbling, "What?"

"Trill, my dad's camera."

I could picture it, sitting on the tripod where we'd left it, thinking we'd grab it on our way back to Trill's house.

"We left it in the rain," I said, my voice ragged at the realization. My father was going to *kill* me, and every dime I had made this summer would have to go toward replacing it. Then the double whammy: Trill's movie. That dream, it was gone. And it was all my fault.

July 2023

I DRIVE TO THE police station in a daze. I wonder if Jericho will still be there. Will I have to face him? I had assured him that everything would be okay, but now it feels like I've betrayed him.

I park my car and search the lot for Paloma's SUV. I am glad to see it's not here. Maybe Jericho's been sent home?

I wait in the lobby of the station for about twenty minutes after speaking to the woman at the reception area. I try to drink a paper cup of weak coffee, but it makes me nauseous. I haven't eaten anything since the Toaster Strudel I had with Ariel a few hours ago.

"Ms. Marshall?" the woman says, and motions for me to come to her.

"I'm so sorry," she says, "but apparently the evidence has been transferred over to the county."

"What? I was told to come here to identify it."

"Looks like the sheriff's department is taking over the case," she says. "It was transferred over before I got in this morning. I'm sure you can give a call over there."

"Is Lieutenant Strickland here?" I ask.

"No ma'am," she says. "But I expect him soon. I can have him reach out when he gets here."

My phone buzzes, and I pull it from my pocket. A text from Trill.

> Can you please come up to the Playhouse? I don't have a car. I'm in the first cabin. It's urgent.

My heart is thrumming as I turn onto Lost River Road. I drive past The Farm's purple mailbox, and the news van is, thankfully, gone—for now, anyway—but the yellow police tape is like a strange velvet rope. *Keep out.*

At least it's not raining today, but as I continue toward the Playhouse, the road grows narrower and muddier, and I worry I might get stuck. Then the drive splits, one road leading to the main house and barn (formerly the Lost River Playhouse), the other going down toward the river where a string of cottages sit at the river's edge. I'm shocked they survived the floodwaters.

Trill is sitting on the porch steps of the first cottage, in a gauzy white dress and a fuzzy yellow cardigan. She stands up when I park the car and walks quickly toward me.

Her hair is in a sloppy bun on top of her head, her bangs so long they fall in her eyes. She looks almost as she had the day we made that lost film. Diaphanous and lovely. Though today she has a pair of reading glasses hanging from a beaded necklace.

I get out of the car and move toward her. All I want to do is to hold her. To apologize. To wind back the last thirty-seven years and do everything differently. She opens her arms, and I lean into her. Her body is shuddering. When we pull away, I hold onto her shoulders and brush her tears away with the pads of my thumbs.

"Where is Jericho?" I ask. "Paloma?"

She throws up her hands. "They came home late last night after I was texting you. And everything seemed to be okay. He said the police questioned him for a long time and took his statement. He said they seemed genuinely grateful that he came forward and that he was being so forthcoming. But then like an hour ago, the sheriff's department pulls up here and starts reading him his *rights*. They put him in handcuffs."

It feels like someone has punched me in the chest.

"They had a warrant for his arrest." She stifles a sob. "Paloma followed him. She's looking for local representation before they file the charges, so if you know anybody . . ."

"*Trill*," I say and reach for her.

"He can't go through this again. He won't survive this, Edie."

I think again of his self-portrait. How could I have been so naive? So stupid? So selfish. I'd convinced myself that it was over when the police had said he was no longer a person of interest. But I knew even then that labels matter. And labels stick.

I remember the first article about him that appeared in the paper that August; the entire front page of the *Quimby Record* had been dedicated to Charlie, with his class photo above the fold and the photo of Jericho below. Jericho's was also a school portrait, a faculty photo, from the previous year's yearbook. In the picture, Jericho was smiling, a big, happy smile. His beard was trimmed, his hair slicked back into a ponytail. His eyes looked kind, and he was wearing a button-down shirt and sweater vest. How could anyone look at that photo and see a man who would hurt a child? I was certain then that the whole theory would seem as ludicrous to everyone else as it did to me.

But I also recall Mrs. Nichols and my mother sitting at the kitchen table, whispering their theories, their fears like buzzing bees. "His mother," Mrs. Nichols hissed. "That witchy woman and her herbs and remedies." Together, they speculated about what was really going on out at The Farm. My mother had read an article, she said, about two separate daycare centers where children were abused and used for Satanic rituals. "I know it's crazy," she had said warily. "But what if . . ."

"I always knew there was something off with those people," Mrs. Nichols had said. "All that peace and love bologna was just a cover for what was really going on over there." My mother had nodded in agreement, desperate. Certain.

It was ridiculous. I knew that even back then. It wasn't until decades later that we were all able to look back at these delusions for what they were—mass hysteria. *Satanic Panic*, they called it. All the people who'd been convicted of conspiracy and child abuse had been exonerated. But my mother, a devout Catholic, took the longest to relinquish this conspiracy theory. Perhaps this explanation, while far-fetched, was less painful in the end than the one I knew scared her even more.

"Jericho wouldn't hurt Charlie," I had insisted one afternoon when she was railing against the local police for not doing more

"What is wrong with you?" she snapped. "It's like you're defending him."

I *was* defending him.

"Did you forget? *Your brother is gone!*" she had yelled, so loud that the veins at her temples had looked about to burst, and I had withdrawn into myself.

My father had come in at this point, reaching for her and steering her away from me, as she broke into a series of gut-wrenching sobs.

"What can I do to help?" I ask Trill now. "The lieutenant in charge—Strickland?—he said they'd get the FBI involved. But Jake totally trashed that idea."

"I can't believe Jake Nichols is a freaking cop," she said. "This is such a nightmare."

Trill sits back down on the porch steps and hugs her knees. I have only ever seen her like this one other time, though I shake that other image from my head; I can't allow myself to spiral down that particular sucking drain of memory.

I kneel on the ground next to her and reach for her hands, realizing I'm not the only one who has aged. Her beautiful hands look *old*: age spots and calluses, a map of fifty-five years on her flesh, though her slender wrists remain childlike, adorned with the same kind of jewelry she wore as a girl: silver bracelets circling her arms and heavy stone rings on her fingers. When I bring her hands to my face, they still smell like the cherry blossom hand cream her father used to buy her for her birthday. I hold her hands in mine, and trace one vein with the tip of my finger.

When I look up at her face, she is studying me. Trying to glean, I imagine, what is going through my mind. But while we had once been able to understand what the other was thinking with a simple smile or nod or roll of the eyes, I had shut that communication off thirty-seven years ago. In a single moment, I had lowered a dark curtain, shutting her out.

"I miss you," she says, framing my face in her hands.

My jaw tenses painfully, tears welling up in my eyes. Then her forehead is pressed against mine.

"I have spent my whole life missing you," I say.

Her eyes are sad.

"I'm going to fix this," I say. "I promise."

July 1986

AFTER. AFTER THAT night, on the Fourth of July as the rain came down and the sky exploded, as *I* exploded, everything was different yet strangely the same. It was like one of those dreams where you walk through a landscape that should be familiar but no longer is. Or the way it feels to come home after a trip, when your house feels slightly askew, the proportions off: ceilings higher, hallways narrower, windows letting in more light. The furniture of my life remained the same, but my perspective had shifted.

Every single moment was charged with possibility, and each stolen touch carried the memory of a thousand touches. My body felt on edge, the yearning to be alone with Trill almost unendurable. It was scary; it was thrilling. And in those honeyed hours, I realized: *I was in love with Trill.* I was in love for the first time in my life, but I couldn't tell anyone. What we had was dangerous. Consuming. My father's ruined camera was proof of this.

On the morning of the fifth, I had gone to my father with cash in hand, the money I had planned to use for spending money at college. My father, a man I had never disappointed before, looked at me as if disenchanted. As though I had betrayed him. I had presented myself as a careful person, a *trustworthy* person, and I had let him down.

"I'm so sorry, Dad. I don't have any excuse. I was just distracted," I stammered.

He had looked at me with something akin to pity. But also searching. What had distracted me? What had I been doing that was more important than taking care of this expensive camera that he had entrusted me with?

Trill had insisted I take the contents of her piggy bank as well, which I held out in my upturned palms.

"There's six hundred dollars here," I said. "I should be able to make up the rest by the time I leave for school. I'm so sorry, Dad."

"I don't want your money," he said and studied me with sad eyes. "You're about to go out into the world on your own. I worry that you're going to forget something important, or be careless, and next time the consequences will be bigger. This is just a camera. It can be replaced. But not everything can."

I had no idea what he was getting at, but his worry troubled me.

"Your friend. Trill," he said, and I caught my breath. "Your mother is concerned that you've changed since you started spending time with her."

Trill, I thought, and my body hummed.

"What do you mean?" I asked, though I didn't want to hear his answer. Nathan had accused me of the same thing.

"We used to be able to trust you. To count on you. But now, you're barely here. And when you are, it's like your brain is somewhere else. Your mom was worried you might be doing drugs, but I told her that's not it. That's not it, right?"

I almost laughed but shook my head firmly.

"Also," he said, "these are your last few months at home with your brother. He's going to be any only child soon, and I think he feels like you've abandoned him."

"Charlie?" I said. "He's at camp all day. He's making new friends. I'm not abandoning him. Jeez Louise. Did Mom say that too?"

My father smiled sadly. "I just don't want you to have any regrets later. This is time you can't get back."

I felt accused. My parents had been talking about me behind my back, talking about Trill. They'd decided that I was not only irresponsible but a *bad sister.* I didn't allow myself to speculate about what else they might have discussed.

"Fine. I'll just stay home and wait for Charlie every day," I snapped. I knew I was being petulant. Petty. So did my father.

"You know that's not what I meant, Edie."

With that, the conversation was over. I had come to apologize for the camera, to make amends by giving him my savings (and Trill's savings too), but now I somehow felt worse.

It was Saturday, so my mother was home too, working in the small garden plot behind our house. From my bedroom window I could see her on her knees, tearing up weeds like her life depended on it. I wanted to go outside and yell at her for turning my father against me. I wanted to tell her that I *was* different now. That Trill *had* changed me, and I finally felt like myself. That it was like I had been wrapped in a tight cocoon my whole life. Strangled by this town, the people here, by their expectations. By *hers.* But now my chrysalis had burst, and inside it I had been growing into exactly who I was meant to be. I might be unrecognizable to them, but this was my destiny.

Instead, I yanked my curtain shut, then slammed my door shut too. I put my headphones on, and popped The Velvet Underground into my Walkman, closed my eyes, and dreamed myself back into that barn with Trill.

Though there were still almost two months before move-in at Smith, I had started going through my things, deciding what would stay and what would come with me. The following Saturday night, Trill was working, but I had the night off, so I was sorting through my books when my mother knocked on the door.

"We're going to eight o'clock Mass tomorrow," she said. My mother liked the early Mass in summer because it was less crowded and not as hot in the church.

I had all the freedom in the world during the week, but Sunday Mass was nonnegotiable.

"I'm busy tomorrow morning," I said, bitterly thinking about her planting those thoughts about Trill in my father's head.

Trill and I had planned to hike up Mount Pisgah on Sunday. There was a lookout, she'd said, overlooking Willoughby Lake. The idea of being alone with her up there was thrilling. She had said she'd come pick me up right after church. She wanted to get to the top before it got too hot.

"You're leaving for college soon," my mother argued. "The least you can do is come to Mass with your family once a week."

I took a deep breath.

"We leave at 7:40," she said, her lips pursed, then she marched back down the stairs.

I had separated my small collection of books into the ones I couldn't live without and those I'd outgrown, which I planned to donate to the library. Of course, I would be coming home for holidays and summer vacations, but my mother had said that when I was away at school, my room would function as a guest room, which seemed ridiculous since we never had any guests, but I knew better than to argue.

At ten, I knew Trill would be home from work, so I picked up the phone to call her, but instead of a dial tone, I heard my mother's voice.

"I just don't know what to do," my mother said.

"That college, it's all girls?" Nathan's mom asked.

I pressed my hand against the mouthpiece.

My mother was quiet, then she sighed.

"Oh Bonnie, maybe you're wrong," Mrs. Nichols said. "You know how girls are at that age. Friendships are intense."

She was talking to Mrs. Nichols about me and Trill? I was furious. Mrs. Nichols was her best friend, but she was also my ex-boyfriend's mom. But my initial anger gave way to a sickening dread. Everything I knew my mother was alluding to, everything she feared, was *true*.

The next morning at seven thirty when she knocked at my door, I growled, "I'm *sick*."

I pictured her on the other side of the door, debating whether she was going to make me go to Mass. Instead, she just said, "*Fine*. Make sure you load the dishwasher when you get up."

The moment the car pulled out of the driveway, I called Trill.

"Can you come get me now?"

On the steep and narrow hiking trail, Trill lagged behind me, breathless and pleading.

"Edie," she wheezed. "You're killing me."

The path was straight up, practically vertical. It was hot out, the air humid and heavy, but I felt an urgency I couldn't begin to describe. I needed to ascend. It felt like I was a balloon, untethered, and I had no choice but to go up, up, up.

At last, we were at the summit. I bent over, exhausted, my muscles complaining, but below was the most beautiful view. So much green and the long blue ribbon of the lake. We had transcended the world.

It was early. We hadn't passed anyone on the trail coming up, and no one appeared to be behind us. Still, when Trill pulled me to her, my instinct was to resist, even alone at the top of the world.

She whispered into my hair, "It's okay."

"Is it?" I asked, a challenge. I thought of my mother's hushed whispers of concern to Mrs. Nichols and felt consumed by my sense of betrayal and rage.

"It is, it is, it is," she whispered into my ear, and I thought of Sylvia, the "old brag" of her heart: *I am, I am, I am.*

I didn't tell Trill what my mother had said to Nathan's mom. What my father insinuated to me. I didn't tell her anything except, "I love you." And I kissed her.

I'd planned to get back home before my family returned from church, but halfway back, Nico sputtered and stopped.

"Ugh," Trill said. "I totally thought there was at least a quarter of a tank."

"What are we going to do?" I asked, panicking. My parents would be home from church soon, even if they stayed after for donuts and coffee.

"We'll have to call Jericho," she said.

We were at least a mile away from Hudson's, which had a payphone. There was also gas there, but that would mean a two-mile hike to get there and back, and we had no gas can.

"My parents are going to totally freak out," I said.

"I'm sorry," Trill said. "It'll be okay."

"That's easy for you to say. Your mom doesn't care what you do."

At that, she gave me a strange look. Hurt.

"I'm sorry. I didn't mean that in a bad way. I wish my mom was like yours."

We walked to Hudson's. The sun was hot in the cloudless sky, and by the time we got to the convenience store, my head was pounding. At first, I thought it was because I had scaled a mountain without stopping followed by this long walk in the blistering heat, but now I was pretty sure it was the beginning of a summer cold. The worst. At least I hadn't lied to my parents about being sick.

She called her brother, and I called my parents. Thankfully, my father picked up. He didn't say much except, "Tell Mr. Jenkins thank you. I'm sure he has better things to do today."

"Dad?" I said. "Please tell Mom I'm sorry."

"I think maybe you should plan to do that yourself."

Trill and I rode in the back of Jericho's pickup, and I was grateful for the road noise and the din of the wind, so I didn't have to speak. We both knew I would be in a lot of trouble once we stopped.

I traced the edges of the peace sign decal on his window with my finger.

When we pulled up to the curb, I climbed out of the back. "Bye," I said to Trill. "Thank you!" I said to Jericho.

"Hi there, Charlie!" Jericho said, leaning out the open window to wave to Charlie, who was sitting on the porch with his Stretch Armstrong doll.

"Hi, Mr. Jenkins!" he said.

"Hey," I said to Charlie as Trill got into the cab of the truck and they drove off. "What's up, Chuck?"

He looked up at me, squinting into the sun behind me, which was bright and relentless.

"Mom is really mad at you," he said.

I nodded and glanced toward the door. I thought about my dad's admonishment about ignoring Charlie.

"You want to play *The Legend of Zelda* this afternoon?" I asked.

He had gotten a bunch of Nintendo games for his birthday. My parents did not give gifts like this, but since Mickey passed away, they'd been spoiling Charlie.

His face brightened. "Can we have Zotz too?"

"Totally," I said. The last time I had played Nintendo with him, I'd run to the store and bought a half dozen chains of Zotz. For whatever reason, that had stuck with him.

Inside, my mother took a deep breath, clearly trying to contain her rage, then launched into a tirade about the dirty dishes and where the heck had I gone, and I wasn't eighteen yet and didn't get to do whatever I wanted and didn't I have any respect for anyone anymore. "Doesn't that girl's mother have any rules for her at all?"

"I'm sorry, Mom. I know I shouldn't have gone, and then Trill's car ran out of gas, otherwise I would have been back, and it took forever for her brother to get us and now they have to go put gas in her car," I rambled and went toward her. "But I swear, I really *am* sick."

My mother was a nurse first. I knew this, and I also knew I was feverish, because my skin was prickling in that way it did whenever my temperature rose over a hundred.

She pressed the cool underside of her wrist to my forehead, skeptical, but her wrist as accurate as mercury, and she nodded tersely.

"Take an aspirin and go lie down. Drink at least eight ounces of water."

"I told Charlie I'd play Nintendo with him," I said.

She started to say no but must have realized this was my effort to be a better sister—and I was sure that my father had told her about our conversation—and so she said, "Fine. But don't get too close to him. He has camp tomorrow."

The aspirin didn't do much to lower my fever, so despite the stifling summer heat, I was chilly. I wrapped a blanket around myself and sat on the opposite side of the couch from Charlie.

I was trying to follow Charlie's explanations about the world of the game, the characters and the quest. But my head was swimmy and thick.

"Did you get candy?"

"I'll get Zotz next time," I said. "But I have some Starburst if you want." I'd found the candy in my nightstand.

He peeled the outer wrapper all the way off so he could get to the lemon ones, his favorite. Within minutes, yellow wrappers littered the coffee table, and he'd moved on to cherry.

We played until my headache was so bad, I could barely look at the screen without wincing. At one point I got up to pull the shades to keep the glare off the TV screen, and my legs had felt wobbly beneath me.

"I'm not feeling so great," I said. "I need to take a nap. That was fun though, right?"

Charlie sighed, disappointed, and tossed his controller down.

"I don't have anyone to play with anymore," he said.

"That's not true. I bet you've been making lots of friends at camp." I had no idea if this was true or not. I *hadn't* been home much lately, had no idea how camp was going.

"I hate camp," he said.

"Why?" I asked.

"It's dumb. We have to swim laps. And lunch is peanut butter and jelly every single day with plain chips. And the milk is warm. And everyone calls me a baby because I won't go to the ice cream truck if that weird guy's parked in the parking lot."

"What weird guy?" I asked.

"The one in the red van."

My heart stuttered as I remembered the incident at the drive-in.

"Has he said anything to you, Charlie?" I asked. "Done anything to you?"

"No," he said. "He just watches us."

"Don't talk to him," I said. "Ever. And don't go in that van. Also, you're not a baby for being scared. That guy's a creeper."

"What's a creeper?" he asked.

"Remember Stranger Danger?"

I needed to tell my parents about the guy in the van. It couldn't be a coincidence that he kept showing up in places where kids hung out.

"Do me a favor, Charlie?" I asked. "Can you remember to write down the number on that man's license plate?"

"Okay," he said. "I have my drawing pencils in my backpack."

I patted his cowlick down tenderly. I'd miss him too, when I went off to college.

I felt the headache behind my eyes now. I needed to lie down. I would tell my parents about the van later. Maybe they could talk to the camp director, have them reach out to the police. It wasn't illegal to park your car in public places, but if it was freaking kids out, then they should do something about it.

In my room, I moved a pile of books off my bed and, keeping the throw wrapped around me, lay on top of my comforter. I didn't even have the energy to get under the covers. The pounding in my head matched the fevered pounding of my heart, but I couldn't imagine making my way all the way back down the stairs for more aspirin.

I felt oddly panicked. I wanted to talk to Trill, to make sure she had gotten her car back and that it had just been out of gas. I picked up my phone and dialed her number, let it ring ten times and then hung up. The second I did, the phone rang, and I grabbed it.

"Trill?" I said.

"Hey, you sound weird. Like you're in a tunnel."

"I'm sick," I said. "My temperature is a hundred and two and I feel like I might be dying."

"Please don't die," she said.

"I'll do my best," I said, smiling despite the agony of my headache.

"Oh shit," she said. "I'm probably going to get sick too."

I thought about her lips at my ear. *It is, it is.* And her lips on my mouth. I closed my eyes.

"Or is it just mono you get from kissing?" she asked, giggling.

Then I heard something else: the sharp intake of breath.

"What was that?" Trill asked.

A loud click.

"Oh my God," I said, jolting upright, the pain in my head spreading down my arms, into my chest, my legs. Weakening. "My mom."

July 2023

I LEAVE TRILL AT the Playhouse, though I want nothing more than to stay with her in this cool, dark cabin along the river. To spend the rest of my life with her here. To *be* with her. It's true, what I told her. I have spent my entire life missing what could have been. What *should* have been between us.

But I made a terrible mistake back then. Then another and another. So, instead of staying with her now, instead of comforting her, I drive away from her again.

Trill is the only girl I've ever loved. Or let myself love, anyway. After that summer, I closed the door. Bolted it shut. When I met Michael, I convinced myself that his intellect and intelligence were enough. Sex was secondary, something I endured because the rest was so wonderful: the conversations, the words. It's not like the sex was terrible, after all, and it made him happy. This was what women did, I thought: relinquished their bodies in exchange for other kindnesses. Other joys. When things grew ugly—joy*less*—between us, I'll admit a small, cruel part of me wanted him to believe that the problem was with him and not with me.

There were moments, of course, when that door creaked open. The one time, during college, when I was wasted at a party and a friend dragged me, laughing into the shadows, and kissed me sweetly. But after only moments, my eyes burned, and I'd shaken my head, biting my lip, plump from her kisses. Then years and years later when Amanda first started working at the high school, we'd gone to a movie one weekend, and when she'd tried to kiss me in the car, I had pretended to be shocked. Pretended she'd been mistaken about who I was and what I wanted.

It's easy to let go of dangerous dreams. It just is.

As I pull up the driveway to our house, I catch my breath. There's a sheriff's cruiser parked in front of the garage. The light in the kitchen glows warmly. It is nine AM, but the sky is dark and rumbling.

Inside, my mother and Ariel are sitting at the kitchen table with a young, uniformed female deputy, a blond woman with white, white skin and icy blue eyes. Her partner, I presume, stands in the doorway to the family room, lanky and seemingly uncomfortable in his own skin.

My mother's eyes are red, and the egg on her head has turned a horrific shade of blue, circled in plum.

"Edith, they found Charlie's backpack!" she cries out. "His *things*."

I think about his room filled with his little boy stuff. Snakes, snails, puppy dog tails.

On the kitchen table is a fanned display of color 8 × 10 photos. They reveal what I saw at Jericho's a couple days ago: the worn, mud-stained, red backpack. A photo of each item inside: a Rubik's cube, a sketch pad, wet swim trunks in a moldy plastic bread bag.

My heart thunks as I recall the torn-up letter from Smith I pilfered.

Seeing the photos is a bigger blow than seeing the backpack itself. Presented this way—against a white backdrop, with numbered tags—turns Charlie's backpack into *evidence*: the clinical proof that Charlie was abducted, his possessions hidden.

"May I speak to you a moment?" I ask the male deputy and lead him onto the porch, the door shutting behind us. "I went to the police station this morning. I was supposed to identify the backpack there."

"Yeah, sorry, everything's been transferred to us at the county," he says.

"I hadn't told her yet," I scold. "My mom. She's eighty years old, and she spent most of last night at the hospital. She has a concussion. She's also in the early stages of Alzheimer's. I'd really hoped to share this with her before she spoke with you." I am trying to be polite. These people don't know us. Before yesterday, this guy probably hadn't even heard of Charlie. The more time that passes, the further Charlie is from the town's memory.

I take a deep breath and exhale through my nose.

"I understand that Jericho Jenkins has been arrested," I say, and his eyebrow shoots up. "And I really need to know what's going on."

He starts to speak, but then closes his mouth, giving me one of those condescending smirks that Michael used to give me. Withholding. My response to Michael when he used to pull this was to shut up. To force *him* to speak. I try that now; I cross my arms and wait.

"Ma'am, this is a major breakthrough. I am, honestly, not sure why you seem so combative. Your brother is the victim here, and we believe we've found the person responsible."

"But you haven't. You found his backpack because Jericho told you about it. He came to *you*. What kind of murderer brings evidence they've hidden to the police? It doesn't make sense."

The cop takes a breath and frowns.

"Ms. Marshall. I'm not at liberty to share any details, but the backpack isn't the only item found on Mr. Jenkins's property. I'm sure Chief Deputy Nichols will be in touch very soon."

"I'm sorry," I say. "What are you talking about?"

"The search yesterday turned up something else," he says.

"What do you mean?" I demand.

"I mean we've found, um, something pretty damning."

July 1986

"I HAVE TO GO," I said to Trill when we realized what had happened, what my mother had overheard us saying on the phone. About mono. About *kissing.* I hung up, lay back down on the bed, my head spinning.

A terrible feeling fell over me. A darkness. A poisonous rot starting in my roots and extending upward.

My mother's footsteps on the stairs were heavy and determined. She didn't knock; she simply turned the knob, pushed open the door, and stood in the doorway, palm pressed against the frame. Her face was ashen, her hands visibly shaking.

I was also trembling under my blanket from the fever, the fear. I tried to come up with an explanation, an excuse for what Trill had said on the phone. An inside joke. A line from one of Trill's favorite movies. Something innocuous. But I was feverish, my brain not working the way it should. My head was pounding. Words failing.

She stepped into my room and looked around like she had never been in there before. I was tidy for a teenager; she only came in once a week, pushing the vacuum in four or five precise rows that reminded me of grass after it had been mowed. I put my laundry in the bathroom hamper. I never left dishes in my room. But now, the room was in shambles. Books and clothes on the floor. My life divided into the objects of my past and the ones that would come with me into the future.

I was too afraid to speak.

She walked to the window that faced Nathan's house and spun back around.

"Is that why you broke up with Nathan?" she asked. "Because of . . ."

I flinched. "What? No," I said. "Nathan . . . on prom night . . . he wanted . . ." But I realized she wasn't listening to me at all.

"You're just confused," she said, shaking her head, but she wasn't speaking to me. She was talking to herself. "She's put ideas in your head. First this girls' college business—"

"No," I said. "I applied to Smith before Trill moved here. You can ask Mr. Howard. He helped me with my application. He wrote my letter of recommendation. Trill didn't have anything to do with that. She didn't even live here then."

My mother picked up one of my track trophies, third place in the 880, 1985 State Finals. The bronze statue on top was a female runner, golden hair forever blowing in the wind behind her. My mother clutched it like a weapon.

"I don't know what you're talking about or why you're so mad," I said. Trill was wrong; I was a terrible actress. "Trill is my best friend."

"What about Lisa?" she asked, her voice catching. "You two were such good friends. She's from a nice family. You dropped her, and you dropped Nathan. For what? Something someone is telling you is okay? It's not *okay*, Edie."

My mother looked at me, challenging me, but I only stared back at her.

"I think it would be best if you stayed home and went to State this fall," she said tersely.

"What are you talking about?"

"We need your help with Charlie, and we don't want to be swimming in debt forever."

I tried to stand up, but my headache was blinding.

"I am not going to State," I said. "I'm going to Smith. I already accepted the offer. It's too late for you to change your mind." I had no idea if this was true.

"If you want our help, then you need to stop seeing that girl. If you don't, you won't go to Smith."

"You're blackmailing me?" I asked.

She let out a sharp laugh. "It's not blackmail. It's an ultimatum," she said, mocking. "You plan to be an *English* major?"

I thought I might implode. My body was rocking with anger. The center of me was white hot, but I was shaking with chills. My head was congested, my head pounding.

"You can't stop me from going away to school," I said. "I'm almost eighteen."

"Well, you *aren't* eighteen yet, and you need us to co-sign the gap loan," she said, and her body calmed. She was the one in control now, and I was the one flailing, like someone drowning.

She started toward the door then turned back around.

"Edie," she said, and her expression softened just a little. "Someday you'll thank me for this. What you two are doing? It will only bring you heartache."

What did my mother know of heartache? What did she know about anything? About the world. About life? She'd never left Quimby. As far as I could tell, she'd never been deeply in love. My poor dad. Did he know he was married to someone completely soulless?

"I'm going to be an *adult* next month," I repeated, though I felt like a scolded child.

"Well, you still live in our home. And if you think you're going to sneak around behind our backs, you better think again," she said and marched over to where my phone plugged into the wall. She yanked the cord out and picked up the phone, holding it like a small dog in her arms. "Any calls you need to make from now on can be made in the kitchen."

Then she was gone, and I was desperate and sick. How would I get in touch with Trill? I was too ill to run away. And even if I could get to her, my mother would make sure I never set foot on Smith's campus. Never walked through those gates.

July 2023

BACK INSIDE THE house, the deputies speak to my mother about the next steps now that they have confirmed the backpack belonged to Charlie. Jericho is in custody, a search has been conducted on The Farm, and charges are expected to be brought against him. They say nothing about whatever it is they found during the search, and my mother, despite her recent experience as an armchair detective, doesn't ask. They say nothing about testing the backpack for DNA, but now it seems the only way to exonerate Jericho is to prove someone else's guilt.

As the female detective gathers the photos, two catch my eye. They are pictures of a torn envelope, or rather, *half* of one. But that doesn't make sense. The letter from Smith that Charlie had taken is upstairs in my underwear drawer. Is this a photo of the other half? Could this be what turned up in the search? But how would a letter from Smith implicate Jericho?

"Excuse me," I say, gesturing to the photos. "May I see these?"

The first photo is of the envelope's front, the blurred Smith logo on the upper lefthand side of the envelope. The left half of my name and our address. The second photo is of the back of the envelope. Something is handwritten in faded, smudged blue ink, the words severed by the tear.

"What is this?" I ask.

"It looks like some sort of letter. It was recovered from the tree where the backpack was hidden. Do you recognize it?"

"May I?" I ask and motion to my phone. "I can zoom in that way."

I take a photo of both the front and back. Then I pretend to read the return address.

"It's mine. It looks like a letter from a college I was accepted into back then. Charlie must have taken it."

"Great," she says. "I'll make sure to note that."

I need to put the two halves of the envelope together, try to decipher what that smudgy blue ink says. But Ariel has disappeared from the kitchen, and her absence worries me. It reminds me of when she was just old enough to play alone in one room while I was busy in another. I had become so attuned to her varying degrees of silence, somehow intuiting when *quiet* meant *danger*.

The cruiser backs out of the driveway, and my mother says she needs to lie down. I help her into her bed, then take the stairs two at a time to Ariel's room.

Inside Charlie's old room, Ariel is bent over, head between her knees as she tries to get her breath. Daisy is on the bed, looking at her with concern.

"Hey," I say, touching the knobby ridge of her spine. "Air?"

I sit next to her and rub her back in small circles. Her heart is racing. I can feel it in her back.

She sits upright, her eyes puffy and red. She's having a hard time breathing.

"Where is your inhaler?" I ask, trying not to panic.

She motions to her nightstand.

I reach into the messy drawer and grab it, shake it, before handing it to her. But her hands are trembling so hard she has difficulty pressing the lever.

Finally, she inhales, holds the medicine in, and exhales. Her heart still hammers against her spine under my fingers.

"It's okay," I say, trying to remain calm. "It's okay."

Her breathing has returned to normal, at least.

"What's going on, honey?" I ask.

She turns to me, her eyes sorrowful.

"It always just felt like a story before," she says. "Like, somehow, not really real? But seeing those pictures. Of his toys? I mean, I know his stuff is here too. But seeing them like that. Like evidence?" At this, she shudders with a hiccupy sob. "There are so many terrible people in the world. So many monsters. How can you ever trust anybody? How am I not supposed to be totally scared all the time?"

She is crying now. *Hard.* The way she only cried when she was a toddler, and her words couldn't capture the depth of her emotions.

"Listen," I say. "There *are* bad people in the world, but that can't keep you from living your life."

I think about her idling here, her life on hold. I think about the anxiety she holds at bay with tea and weed and sleep.

"But it kept you from doing that, didn't it? You stayed here. You never got to go to Smith. You didn't get to be with Trillium."

At this, I stiffen. I feel flayed. My heart splayed open. I am an open wound. Is this my legacy? Is this my *fault*?

"What do you mean?" I ask.

"Mom, you *loved* her," she says, those words that have been too dangerous to say. That I have been too afraid to acknowledge. Her gaze is pleading with me to admit the truth. "I mean, it would be no big deal now. But back then. With Grammy, and everything—you were too afraid? Right? You're telling me to be brave, but you're *still* afraid."

I am reeling. Somehow, she has seen through the walls I've built around my secret. My pain. The ones made of years and denial.

You loved her.

I think of my mother's hands—the transparent flesh rivered in blue veins. The first time I noticed this, it nearly took my breath away. Am I also becoming translucent? My body turning to glass, a window to everything I've boarded, *hoarded* inside?

But she's right. I'm asking her to be brave, when I have been nothing but cowardly nearly my whole life. With Trill, I had found courage: to make decisions on my own, to take chances, to pursue what I wanted. What happened to that girl? Where did she go?

After Ariel is breathing normally again, I go downstairs to check on my mother. Thankfully, she's sleeping, likely overwhelmed by the new information, by the morning spent with the police after a night in the ER. I hope she will sleep until suppertime. She lies flat on her back, arms crossed as though she has been laid to rest. The small *o* of her open mouth feels almost obscene. I close the door quietly and go to my own room.

I pull out my phone and am searching for the photo of the envelope I snapped when it buzzes, startling me.

One text notification after another begin to stack up on my lock screen, all linking to an article from WCAX. I click.

> New Evidence Unearthed in 1986 Disappearance of Charlie Marshall, Former Person of Interest Under Arrest

Charlie's face. Jericho's.

The article is basically a recap of everything that transpired in 1986 followed by the news of "evidence unearthed on former person of interest's property."

Unearthed. That makes it sound like Jericho buried the evidence himself.

I reread the short article, but it doesn't reveal anything I don't already know. It just spins the facts, like candy floss.

Despite every instinct telling me not to, I scroll down to the comments. There are twenty-six already: varying from "Finally," to "RIP Charlie," to "Sicko. I hope he pulls an Epstein."

I close the app and search the call log for Jake's call from earlier, click on the number.

"Nichols," he says.

"I need you to tell me what you found on Jericho's property," I say.

"Edie! I was just about to give you a call."

"Whatever it is, I assure you, it's not Charlie's," I say, sounding more certain than I feel.

He is quiet.

"What is it?" I demand, struggling to imagine what they could possibly have discovered. *Unearthed.*

"A kid's book."

"*What?*" I say.

"One of those *Choose Your Own Adventure* books," he says smugly. "*Space and Beyond.*"

My throat thickens. My vision vignettes.

"It was stuffed into a crevice in the wall of Jenkins's root cellar," he says. "Charlie's name and phone number are written inside."

July 1986

THIS IS THE day my brother disappeared.

In my memory, it is the drip from a popsicle stick, the click of the clock on the kitchen wall above the telephone. It is sheets stiff with the sweat that drenched me when my fever broke. It is a damp, musky-smelling washcloth I had laid across my forehead to bring the fever down. I was better, but the vestiges of my illness crowded the room: a bowl of Campbell's Chicken & Stars soup, congealed to a Corningware bowl, a thermometer resting on my nightstand, the puff from inside the bottle of aspirin, and a glass freckled with pulp.

I hadn't been that sick since I had the flu in first grade. But my parents still needed to work, and Charlie still had camp, so those hazy hours, those protracted days, were spent alone inside my fevered dreams.

In my delirium, there was something tickling my brain. Though *tickling* is too gentle. It felt like a knife playing with the edge of my thoughts. But no matter how hard I tried to remember or untangle or uncover it, I couldn't. I knew vaguely that it had to do with my mother. Then, remembrance. Reality.

She knew about me and Trill.

My mother had heard us on the phone. She had listened to us flirting, our hearts beating for each other. She *knew.* She had probably known for a while, and the call was simply confirmation. I had heard her on the phone with Mrs. Nichols, her concern. I had heard her words in my father's mouth, the poison on the tip of his tongue. Now, she was putting an end to it, the only way she knew how. By holding my singular wish hostage: Smith.

It was only the illness, I convinced myself, that made me feel so helpless, the flu that held me in its arms, compressed my chest with its embrace. Surely, when I emerged on the other side of this, reason would return. There would be a solution to this.

But when I awoke on Friday, drenched in sweat, as if I'd leaped with my pajamas on into the river, the dreamscape, the *nightmare,* lingered.

For days, my mother had been hardly more than a sigh on the other side of the door. The sound of a pot clanging on the stove. Hands clearing away the detritus of my illness. The tissues, plucked like poisonous white flowers from my bed. Then she was gone.

Only my father spoke to me during those endless hours. Checking to see how I felt and if he could get me anything. *Juice? Aspirin?* But he also kept his distance. He said nothing about my mother's "ultimatum," her threats.

My mother didn't want Charlie to get sick, so he didn't visit. I heard him skipping down the hallway outside my room, the rumble and roar he made with his lips when he played with his Matchbox cars. The splashing sounds of his baths. But that morning, he'd poked his head in.

"Hey! Dad says *Flight of the Navigator* is coming to the theater soon. Will you take me? If you're better?"

"Sure thing, Charlie Brown." I'd managed to sit up and look at him: backpack on his shoulders, cowlick defiant.

"Can I borrow your Walkman?" he asked. "We're allowed to listen to music at lunch."

"Sure," I said, my voice froggy, and motioned to it on my nightstand.

"Thanks! Bye, Edie!"

"Bye, Charlie," I'd said.

The flu had left my body in a deluge of sweat, my flesh now cool to the touch. The headache's pernicious drumbeat was absent; it was like when a plugged ear pops. The world was too loud, too bright.

I got out of bed and stretched. It felt as if I hadn't moved in decades. For a moment, I wondered if, like Rip Van Winkle, I had awoken from my slumber as an old person.

In the bathroom, I brushed my teeth and studied a new ripe zit on my forehead, and showered, the water steaming up the bathroom and filling my bruised lungs. Cleansing them.

No one was here. And, for a minute, I imagined I was in an episode of *The Twilight Zone*. A girl awakens to find herself alone on the planet. But when I looked out the window, I saw our neighbor mowing his lawn, a woman on the sidewalk pushing a stroller with one hand and holding a wriggling toddler on her hip with the other.

In the kitchen, my mother had left a note:

Hope you are feeling better.
Looks like your fever broke. But even if you're okay, you are not to go ANYWHERE today.
I will call you during lunch. PICK UP.

I didn't know if she meant to pick up the house or pick up the phone. Or maybe both.

I was alone in the house. The kitchen felt strange and still, the clock ticking next to the phone on the wall.

The phone! With nobody home, I could use the kitchen phone to call Trill.

Cradling the handset between my ear and shoulder, I grabbed a piece of bread and spread a glob of peanut butter across it. The phone rang and rang. I knew her room was stuffy; now that it was summer, she slept in the barn most nights, the window open to let in the cool breeze. She was probably in The Library.

I rolled the bread and peanut butter into a log and shoved half of it in my mouth. I had hardly eaten in days; I was starving.

My mother had threatened that if I saw Trill again, she would make it impossible for me to go to Smith. But once I was eighteen, once I had left her house, had left Quimby, she would have no control over me anymore. Though I worried that the other plans Trill and I had made—driving home together for Thanksgiving, spending the monthlong winter break here together at The Farm—would not be possible anymore. And what about next summer? I had dreamed of more midnight swims, more hikes to the tops of mountains, more lazy walks and picnics by the river. Poetry and movies—*together*. That could never happen now that my mother knew.

A wave of sadness, of desperation and longing overwhelmed me. I needed to run. I knew it would probably kill me, but my whole body felt antsy. If I didn't move, I thought I might scream, and so I gathered my running clothes from the dryer in the basement and slipped them on.

The clock in the kitchen seemed louder than usual, *tick-tock*, and I saw it was only nine thirty. I had two hours to go see Trill and then get back before my mom called to check in.

Outside, I noted that Nathan's truck was in the driveway. Normally he worked with his dad on Fridays. Maybe he'd somehow caught the bug I had and was home sick too. I felt an odd twang of nostalgia for the sick days we'd spent together as kids. My mother could never get out of work, but Mrs. Nichols would take care of us. Let us watch *The Price Is Right* and *As the World Turns*. Those were grilled cheese and tomato soup days. Coloring book and Luden's cough drop days. I wondered, after Grad Night, if his mom had set him up with a TV tray in the living room to convalesce. I wondered if he blamed me. I hadn't meant to hurt him; I'd only wanted to be free.

Then I remembered overhearing my mother tell my father that Mr. and Mrs. Nichols had gone to Myrtle Beach for the weekend, and that Nathan and Jake were going camping. He must not have left yet. I didn't want to have to make small talk if he came outside, so I didn't bother to stretch, just set off running, the muggy air filling my lungs. I coughed and hacked up a good-sized ball of mucous and spit it into the ditch alongside the road. By the time I got to the covered bridge, I felt lightheaded. I was probably dehydrated. I'd lost gallons of fluid when my fever broke, and the only thing I'd had to drink was a Dixie cup of water after brushing my teeth. I bent over, waiting for it to pass, before I picked up my pace and took a left onto Route 42.

Lost River Road, with its canopy of leaves, provided a cool respite from the relentless sun. I slowed my furious pace but kept moving forward, up the hill, to the purple mailbox and into Trill's driveway.

Her mom was in the city for the weekend. Nico was in the driveway, and Jericho's truck was parked up by The Bakery, though I didn't see him.

I went straight to the barn, the property feeling so much like home to me now, I didn't think twice about letting myself in. Inside the cool, dark barn, my heart rate slowed, and I climbed the stairs to The Library.

"Hello?" I said into the darkness. "Trill?"

I heard a soft moan. "Over here."

I moved around the dark room, touching things, but everything felt as if it could vanish: the woven mat at the center of the table, the milk-glass jar filled with wilting daisies and black-eyed Susans. I touched the stack of art books. My fingers grazed the stiff crinolines of the dresses we had worn in the film. My heart sank at the thought of my dad's camera, Trill's film. Both destroyed by my carelessness.

Trill was on the couch, where we had spent the night together just two weeks ago. That rainy night felt far away now, slipping.

I sat next to her. She moaned again.

"I'm so sick," she said.

"Oh no!" I touched her forehead, which was burning with fever.

"Can you hand me that cough syrup?" she asked, motioning to the coffee table, which was littered with crumpled tissues.

She sat up, and I unscrewed the cap before handing her the bottle, from which she drank directly. "Whoa," I said. "It's the sleepy kind. Don't take too much."

"Will you put some of this on my chest?" she asked and pointed to a small brown vial on the table. When I opened it, it smelled of cloves and eucalyptus.

She lifted her shirt, and I slowly rubbed the oil against her chest, her skin like fire under my fingers. I pressed my palm gently against the flesh between her small breasts, felt her heartbeat quicken under my palm, my own hastening as well.

"Thank you," she said and lay back down. "Lie here with me?"

I lay down next to Trill, my front to her back.

"What happened? After . . ." she asked. "What did your mom say?"

"She . . ." I started, trying to find the words in the shape of my heart. Finally, I told her what had happened—my mother's anger, her fear, her threats—but I promised her that it didn't matter, that it wouldn't change anything between us, wouldn't destroy what we had made. I would figure out a way to go to Smith, even if it meant lying to my mother about who I was, and what Trill and I had become to each other.

She was quiet, though her breath was ragged.

"You're really here?" she asked, delirious.

"I'm here," I whispered.

At this, her body shuddered, and when I touched her face in the darkness, I felt her tears.

Pressed against her, I could feel and hear the rattle of her chest with each breath. Outside, the windchimes keened in the breeze.

I must have drifted off to sleep, because I woke to the sounds of someone walking across the creaky barn floor below. Jericho. Some days he brought us little treats: a bowl of raspberries freshly picked from the bushes near The Bakery. Or warm bread spread with goat cheese and herbs. Once, he delivered two crooked carrots and two radishes freshly plucked from the garden. He never disturbed us, just left his offerings for us at the top of the steps. I heard him climbing up, pausing to drop off the goodies, then going back down.

Trill was pale, her hair plastered to her face.

"Are you hungry?" I asked, but she was asleep, her chest rattling.

Overwhelmed with tenderness, I whispered, "I love you." I wanted to protect her. I wanted to take care of her. I pressed my lips to her fevered head. "Trilly. I love you so much." But she was fast asleep.

The doors to the barn closed shut, and we were swallowed in darkness.

I looked at my watch. It was eleven forty-five already. I'd been asleep longer than I thought. I'd have to leave now and run fast to get home before my mother called at noon. I kissed Trill's forehead, then went to the steps, but there were no gifts waiting there. No berries or bread. That was weird, though maybe Jericho had just come in to check on Trill.

Outside, his truck was still parked up by The Bakery. I could see him now, hunched over something—*an oven?*—in the truck bed. On any other day, I would have hollered his name, offered him a smile and a wave, but it was eleven forty-five, and I only had fifteen minutes to get home. I also worried about what he might have seen or heard when he came to the barn. And so, I ran.

At home, the kitchen clock said 12:10, and the answering machine was blinking angrily. Breathless from my run, I hit Play. First message, 10:45 AM. "Edie? Edie, please pick up." Second message, 11:15 AM. "Edith, I need you to pick up the phone. Your brother's sick, and you need to go get him from camp."

Shit.

Third message, 11:45. "Edith, I am *furious* right now. Where *are* you? Listen, I am calling the counselors and giving him permission to walk home alone. I *need* you to go and meet him. And when I get home tonight, we're going to have a long talk about this. All of this."

Shit, shit, shit.

I'd have to ask Nathan to drive me to go pick him up. But next door, Nathan's truck was gone.

If Charlie had left the pool after my mom's last message, he probably hadn't made it very far. But which way had he gone? He didn't like the covered bridge, but if he was sick, he wouldn't have wanted to take the long way home. Yes. He would definitely have gone the short way, across the bridge.

At least I already had my running shoes on. I flew down the hill. At the high school I turned left, taking the loop over the bridge and then toward town. I kept running, expecting any minute to see Charlie, kicking rocks and swinging his wet towel, or wearing it like a cape around his neck. I pictured his backpack, weighing him down like a turtle. But nothing. No Charlie.

As I got closer to the pool, I realized he must have actually taken the long way—which meant I was *behind* him, both of us going in the same direction. If I ran, I'd be sure to catch up to him along the loop.

An old woman I didn't recognize was the only other person on the sidewalk as I approached the entrance to the pool.

I stopped to catch my breath.

"Excuse me, ma'am, you wouldn't have happened to see a little boy—nine years old?" I asked.

"Sorry, dear," she said and shook her head.

As I started to run past the entrance to the park, the red van—the creeper!—pulled out of the park's lot and turned right onto the road.

I'd told Charlie to keep an eye out for this guy. He was afraid of him; he'd never have left the park if that van was loitering there. Would he?

That's it! Charlie had probably seen the van, remembered what I'd told him, and decided to wait for me, knowing I would be there in a few minutes. I pictured him sitting at one of the picnic tables where the kids ate lunch, playing with Stretch Armstrong. Pushing his glasses back up on his sniffly nose.

The picnic tables were filled with kids. I looked at each one, searching for Charlie. But he wasn't there. I quickly scanned the playground, imagining him at the top of the fort or on one of the swings, but the playground was deserted. I ran to the pool's gate and found one of the counselors wearing a bright yellow shirt with the camp logo on it.

"Hi! I'm Charlie Marshall's sister. He got sick today and was going to walk home—my mom called and gave him permission—but he might have just waited for me?"

The teenage girl smiled a toothy smile. "Yeah, poor little guy. His temp was a hundred and one. We aren't allowed to let kids stay when they're that hot."

"Cool," I said. "Where is he? Do you have like an infirmary or something?"

"Oh no, he left already. Right about noon. I remember because the eleven forty-five whistle had just blown for lunch—she motioned to the kids eating their PB & Js, sucking on straws stuck into milk cartons. "I bought him a popsicle from the ice cream truck and sent him along after he changed into dry clothes."

My expression must have been one of horror, because she was suddenly on the defense: "His mom *said* to send him home."

"I know," I said. "Can you please just tell me which way he went?"

"I think that way?" she said, pointing to the right. The long way, just as I'd expected. The direction the van had gone.

"Okay," I said. "If for some reason you find him, please tell him to wait here. I'll come back for him."

"We really aren't allowed to let kids stay if they're sick," she said firmly.

"Seriously? Just have him sit at one of those picnic tables, please?"

It was twelve thirty now. If he'd left at noon like she said, there was plenty of time for him to have gotten home by now, even going the long way. I should never have stopped at the pool. I tried not to think about the van. My stomach lurched as I remembered the incident at the drive-in, that he wasn't even listening to the movie, just watching the kids play. I had told Charlie not to talk to him. To never talk to strangers.

But with panic rising, I ran until my lungs felt like they were on fire, then I dragged myself up the hill to the house, flinging the door open.

"Charlie?"

Silence. The house smelled sick. Stuffy and infected. I ran up the stairs to Charlie's room, but it was empty. No sign that he had been there. I looked in my own room, the bathrooms, the backyard.

Nobody was home at Nathan's, so I knocked on our other neighbor's door.

"Have you seen Charlie?" I asked.

But Mr. Elms shook his head. "Sorry, sweetheart. Maybe he went to a friend's?"

"Charlie doesn't *have* any friends," I said, choking on a sob.

Then I ran all the way back to the pool.

My legs were jelly, and Charlie was not there. I was going to kill him when I finally found him.

"Maybe somebody gave him a ride?" the head counselor said.

I thought of the van again. And I thought of Charlie, sweet Charlie, and my muscles stopped working. My legs collapsed. And I knew I'd made the biggest mistake of my life.

"Can you call the police?" I asked. "Please. I think somebody took my brother."

July 2023

My nerves are on fire when I hang up with Jake. One of Charlie's books? At Jericho's house? How can this possibly be? How did it get there? And suddenly, sickeningly, my certainty falters. What I have known to be true for nearly forty years shimmers like a heat mirage. Is it possible I was wrong about Jericho? Is there any possible way I had only imagined seeing him that day when I left Trill? Was it possible he hadn't been up at The Bakery when I left her? *No.* I'd seen him, his truck, the new oven sitting in the bed. And I'd heard him come into the barn; he was the one who shut the doors. And I see him in my mind's eye now, staring at me over the backpack between us on that little table. *I didn't hurt Charlie.*

I squeeze my eyes shut, sicken at my momentary willingness to believe, like so many others, like my mother, that Jericho had harmed my brother.

After revealing that they'd found Charlie's book hidden in Jericho's root cellar, Jake had gone on to tell me that the DA's office was preparing the indictment and that Jericho would be arraigned at eight AM Thursday morning, at which point bail would be set.

That's less than two full days from now.

There's no time to get the FBI involved. No time to find the culprit, the person who has managed to elude us for nearly forty years. The only way out of this is through. I need to do what I failed to do all those years ago. I need to tell the truth: I saw Jericho that day. I can corroborate his alibi. My selfish lie is the reason he is in this position, and I am the only one who can save him. Even if it means I lose everything. Again.

Gathering my courage, I call Trill's cell, but it just rings and rings.

"It's Trillium!" her message chirps. "Leave a message. Or don't. I'll still know you called . . .'cause, technology."

"The mailbox is full . . ."

I lie back on my bed, but nothing I do calms me. I am crawling out of my skin. Usually, I remedy this feeling by going for a run. As if I can simply run away from the fretful thoughts. But really, it's only the illusion of escape, because, inevitably, when I stop, whatever has been chasing me will still be chasing me.

My heart has finally stilled when Ariel knocks gently on my door, then pokes her head in.

"Hey, Mom. Siena is bringing me to work. She can probably give me a ride home too, so I don't need the car."

"Sounds good," I manage. "Are you okay? Bring your puffer to work."

She leans into me for a hug. She smells so sweet, like maple candy, which sends my heart whirling. I remember when she was first born, the first time her unfocused eyes locked on mine. A love so powerful, I knew it would be enough. That I didn't need anything else. Anyone else. What will happen when she learns that her mother allowed a man's life to be ruined in order to protect a stupid secret? When she realizes I am one of those monsters she fears? Can I really do this to my own daughter?

"I love you, Air," I say.

After Ariel's coworker Siena pulls into the driveway and I hear the car door slam shut, I call Trill again and am startled when she picks up.

"Edie," she says, breathless.

"Where are you?"

"I went back down to The Farm to get some of our stuff, but they aren't letting me in. There are news vans everywhere. Reporters. Neighbors. People from town."

I don't know what to say.

"Are you still there?" Trill asks.

"I'm here," I say. Though I feel like I'm floating. I am here, now, but I am also in the past.

"Jake told me what they found in the cellar," I say. "Charlie's book?"

She goes silent, and I worry for a moment that we have been cut off.

"I'm sorry," I say. "That someone is doing this to him."

The release of her held breath is audible but choked with tears.

"I need to see you," I say. "I need to tell you something. To help Jericho."

"What is it?" she asks, despair tinged with hope.

"Not over the phone," I say.

My mother cannot be left alone, and Ariel will be at Carmello's until ten. I could call Nathan, I suppose, to come over and watch her. But I'm sure he's heard about Jericho by now, and that is a conversation I do not want to have.

We have just shy of thirty-six hours before Jericho is arraigned.

"Can you meet me at the track tonight? Around ten fifteen?" I ask. I know it's late. Paloma will likely be back by then. She may refuse to let Trill go.

Trill is quiet for a moment, then says, "I'll be there."

July 1986

AT THE PARK, after the camp counselor called the police, I used their phone to call my father at work. Before I broke down, I managed to explain that I couldn't find Charlie but that I was sure he must have just wandered off. That he couldn't be far.

"Please tell Mom I'm sorry," I said. I thought of the messages on the machine. One after another. I thought of my body curled around Trill's fevered one, my hand pressed to her heart. "I must have slept through her calls."

The first lie. It seemed innocuous. A little white one to keep the focus on Charlie.

Still, once we all got home, my mother wailed, railing at me. "You were supposed to pick him up! I called three times. I left messages!"

But, I explained—the lie having already to spread its toxic fingers—I had missed the calls because I was still sick, asleep. How could I have known?

At this, my mother had collapsed. She'd finally completely broken, and I realized what a mistake I had made.

It wasn't her fault Charlie was gone. It was *mine.*

"I'm sorry, Mom. I'm so sorry," I said, but she wouldn't touch me, and she wouldn't look at me. "We'll find him," I insisted.

The police arrived at our house at around three o'clock, and I retraced every step I had taken in searching for my brother, the circles, looping endlessly from home to the park and back home again. I told them everything I could remember: the lady on the sidewalk, the counselor at the park, the van.

The van.

At this, the lead detective, Detective Dwyer's, eyes widened, and I told him about the guy in the van, that everybody thought he was a creeper. I'd seen him near the elementary school, at the drive-in, and today at the pool.

Dwyer called the description of the van into the station right after he finished taking my statement. As terrified as I was of what that man might be doing to Charlie, I felt like I was being helpful, giving them the clue they would need to find my brother.

They'd catch that man. Charlie would come home; my mother would forgive me.

The police questioned my parents, checked their alibis. Both of them had been at work the entire time. "Apologies, it's protocol," they explained. "When a child goes missing."

"And where did you say you were you again when your brother left the pool?" Dwyer asked me.

My eyes burned, as if I could still smell the scent of clove oil I'd rubbed across Trill's chest. I did not tell him I wasn't at home when my mother called. I did not tell him I was at The Farm, with the girl my mother had forbidden me to see. I did not tell him that I'd snuck past her brother, running all the way back home but still missing the call that would have changed everything.

"I was in my room. Asleep. I'm getting over the flu."

Seeing Jericho had seemed irrelevant then. But I would learn soon enough that when a little boy vanishes into thin air, nothing is irrelevant.

When the sun went down that night, and as the sky darkened, I felt like I was plummeting into a black hole. I sat alone in the living room as the police kept talking to my parents in the kitchen. I stared at the dark TV screen, thinking of that movie *Poltergeist*, where the little girl was trapped in another dimension—communicating through the staticky screen. I willed Charlie to reach out, to somehow transmit to me where he was. But I only saw my own reflection in the glass.

That night, no one slept.

My mother sat in the kitchen drinking cup after cup of coffee, and my father drove all over town. Mrs. Nichols called from South Carolina after she got my mother's message. She and Mr. Nichols would change their flight home. Nathan and Jake were camping, and she had no way to reach them, but she promised that as soon as she did, she would send them all out to look for Charlie. In the meantime, was there anything she could do for us? From afar?

My mother said, "I just want my son to come home."

The moment the words left her lips, I saw a look of shame and regret cross her face.

"I'm so sorry, Judy," she said. "I didn't mean . . ."

But Mrs. Nichols must have understood. Better than anyone could.

At around five AM, I finally fell asleep for about an hour, waking to sunlight streaming through the curtains in my room. I was still wearing my running clothes.

Downstairs, Detective Dwyer was drinking coffee at the kitchen table with my mother. My eyes darted around the room, thinking he must have found Charlie and brought him home, but Charlie was still gone.

Despite my worries about that man in the van, I prayed that Charlie was only lost.

The rural stretch of road heading east between downtown Quimby and the high school, the long way home, is bordered on both sides by grassy fields leading to thick woods. I *knew* Charlie, he was like a puppy: at the sight of some shiny object, he'd take off. I imagined him chasing a monarch, a chipmunk, some glittery thing in a treetop.

Indeed, later that morning an elderly man out for his morning walk spied that trail of items, which had seemed to him like breadcrumbs, hopefully leading to the boy who had lost them: Charlie's towel, a Walkman, the tape from my Velvet Underground cassette curling through the grass, a popsicle stick (stained cherry, which the counselor later confirmed was the flavor he requested from the ice cream truck), but also: his broken glasses.

He would not have wandered into the woods without his glasses. He could barely see at all without them. If anything, he would have been terrified that our parents would be upset they were broken and would have carefully picked them up before making his way home.

A more careful inspection revealed blood on the grass.

He was not lost. Something had happened to him.

The police had cordoned off the field, the road, which did bear some odd skid marks, though teenagers often raced that stretch of road, peeling out and making spontaneous U-turns.

We were not allowed there until after they'd completed their processing of the crime scene. We arrived just as the sun was starting to sink behind the mountain, the trees and grass gilded in golden light. Had an entire day passed already? It felt impossible.

We got out of the station wagon, the doors thunking shut behind us.

The police radio crackled at the officer's hip as fireflies began to flicker and tease in the grass. I pictured Charlie chasing them, his little hands gently cradling his catch. *Look, Edie! I got him!*

We stood there, staring into the field where my brother had disappeared, until the sun fell behind Franklin Mountain, and my mother fell to her knees.

July 2023

TRILL IS SITTING at the top of the bleachers when I arrive at the track at ten fifteen. She's wearing running clothes: leggings and a ratty Hampshire sweatshirt. Her hair is up in a ponytail, which trails down her narrow back.

I climb the bleachers to her in the darkness, the sound of my steps on the aluminum risers echoing loudly.

From here, in the weak glow of the moon, we can see the school up on the hill, the graveyard beyond. I think of our bodies, only stardust.

"Should we run?" she asks.

"Yeah," I say. This way, I figure, we'll look like any other couple of middle-aged women running laps around the track. Just a late-night run. Maybe it will also release the nervous energy in my legs.

I need to tell her what really happened the day Charlie disappeared. That I had lied to my mother. That I had lied to the police, and it was my lie that had ruined her brother's life. What a coward

I had been, what a selfish fool. My teenage myopia had made it impossible for me to see beyond my own worries, to understand the repercussions of protecting myself. But I am an adult now; what excuse do I have?

I consider what Jake had said about the tell-tale heart beating beneath the floorboards. But he was wrong. It wasn't Jericho who heard it beating; it was *me*. That steady drum had deafened me for thirty-seven years.

I run next to Trill, our strides synching the way they had that first day we'd run the bleachers together. Silently, we circle the track once, then twice. I can see she is out of breath, struggling. She is still a sprinter, and I am still the plodding, long distance runner.

When we get back to the bleachers, she bends over, hands on her knees. I see her chest is heaving and quickly realize it's not just from the run. She's sobbing.

I reach out tentatively to touch her, and when she doesn't flinch at my touch, I gently stroke her back. When she stands up, I lead her to the bleachers, where we sit down. I put my arm around her slender shoulders. It feels like embracing a ghost. This woman is somehow both a stranger and someone I once knew better than I knew myself.

She smells like summer rain. Like earth.

She wipes furiously at her eyes.

I worry that telling her the truth will be like taking a hammer to an already broken glass. I think of shards, of the shattered pieces. There will be no putting her back together. *Us*, back together.

Trill looks me in the eyes. I imagine she can see the inner workings of my mind.

"You said on the phone you can help? How?" she asks. In her question, I can hear her fear. It's as though she knows that whatever I have come to share with her might change everything.

But I have no choice. If I don't speak up, on Thursday morning Jericho will be indicted.

I look down, feeling like I can't get enough air.

"Edie," she insists, taking my hands in hers, forcing me to look at her.

I think of the mold growing in the walls of our home, poison. Secrets will slowly kill us if we ignore them.

Trill puts her hands on the side of my face, as she did yesterday. Searching, searching.

"Lucy," she says softly, smiling, hoping to lighten things. To bring me back to her.

"I saw Jericho. The day Charlie disappeared." My words feel like bullets.

"What?" she asks, smile fading to a puzzled scowl.

I close my eyes, allow the rest of the words to gather.

"That morning? After you took the cough medicine and fell back asleep . . . when I left, I saw him at his truck up by The Bakery, but he didn't see me."

She tilts her head as the fractured pieces of what I'm saying begin to reassemble.

"I thought you were a dream," she says, shaking her head in disbelief. "You were there?"

"It's my fault," I say. "I was with you when I should have been picking up my brother. I wasn't supposed to be with you. If my mother found out that Charlie went missing because you and I were . . . together . . . she would never have forgiven me."

"I don't understand," she says, but I can see that she does. That everything is starting to make sense.

"I was at The Farm, and I saw Jericho when I left you. I could have corroborated his alibi. I saw him, but I never told anyone," I say, my voice weakened with grief and shame. "I lied."

She shakes her head sharply, once, as if trying to negate what I have just said. Like those bullets hadn't lodged themselves into her heart.

She covers her mouth with her hands, a cry stifled behind her fingers.

"I would have said something, if he'd been arrested. I swear. But then they cleared him, and I thought it was over. That they'd leave him alone. I didn't know how bad things were for him."

"He had to leave his job, Edie. People vandalized The Bakery. Did you know that? They broke out the windows. People stopped buying my mother's medicine. He's a *pariah*."

I knew he'd quit his teaching job, but I had no idea about the rest.

"Why did he stay here?" I ask.

She looks at me, astonished. "This is his *home*. Our home."

"I'm sorry," I say, shaking my head. "I'll make it right. I promise."

"It's been almost forty years," she says, cold now. "You had all this time. To make things right."

Trill is standing now.

"I was scared, Trill. I was so scared of what people would say about me. About us. My mother? How could I explain that my brother disappeared because I'd gone to you?"

Then, with a look of pure horror, she flies down the bleachers. The metal clanging. I can feel her flight in my jaws. And she disappears into the dark night.

July/August 1986

THAT WEEK AFTER Charlie disappeared, I did not see Trill, though she tried to call me. The first time, my mother answered but abruptly hung up. The second time, the machine picked up, and Trill left a message, pleading with me to let her know I was okay. The third time, my father and mother had gone to the police station together, leaving me home alone, and I answered.

"I need to see you," she said. "I need to know you're okay."

"I'm sorry," I said. "I can't." The truth.

Alone in my room, I wrote. I had a notebook left from school, three-quarters of the pages empty, which I filled, stanzas like incantations aimed at bringing my brother back. In ink, I conjured him: his breath, his knobby spine, the heart-shaped birthmark on his chest. And yet—the words didn't relieve me. Instead of release, I felt burdened. The weight of ink, the weight of my guilt, the weight of my mother's grief and my father's hope leaking from my pen. I was steeped in it.

During that first week after Charlie disappeared, the people from town rallied, of course. But, for me, their acts of kindness felt oddly performative, like people feigning sympathy, following a script: *We're praying for you. You are in our thoughts. God is watching over him.* The neighbors came, as expected, with their casseroles and compassion. The food piled up in the freezer. One morning, I caught my mother dumping three aluminum pans of lasagna into the trash can behind the house.

"I can't eat another bite of this," she said, as if she needed to explain anything to me.

I couldn't eat either, this comfort food providing not comfort but a glimpse into the kitchens of these families whose lives were intact. Whose seats were filled.

Of course, those casseroles also made me think of Nathan, about how insensitive I had been after Mickey passed. This was karma. Yet, I also felt enraged by the injustice of it. What had Charlie done to deserve this? What had my mother and father done?

Lisa came by, and we'd sat uncomfortably in my room, talking about Charlie. About our friendship, which felt far away. Out of focus.

"You should come over sometime," she said. "We just got a new kitten. Her name's Fluffernutter."

I smiled, remembering making peanut butter and Marshmallow Fluff sandwiches with her when we were little.

"I'm here if you need me. Just call," she said, though we both knew I wouldn't.

In late July, about ten days after Charlie disappeared, the police came by the house.

"We found the owner of the van," Dwyer said.

At this, my mother winced and covered her mouth with her hand. Still, her eyes sparked with hope.

"His name is Linwood McAfee. He's a Quimby local."

At this, she drew in a breath that sounded like she was drowning, fighting for air.

"Mrs. Marshall, he's a Vietnam vet. No criminal record. We brought him in, and he admitted to parking near the school and at the park. Says he enjoys watching the children play."

"Oh my God," she said, her eyes wild with terror. "Did he take Charlie?"

"Oh, no, I'm sorry. I didn't mean to suggest . . ." He went on to explain that when McAfee returned from Vietnam, and after being at Walter Reed for three months, he had come home to an empty house. His wife had left with their two young sons. He explained that watching the children gave him joy.

My mother waited, not satisfied.

The detective continued. "He was injured in the war. He lost his left leg. He uses a wheelchair. There's no way he could have abducted a nine-year-old boy."

Besides, while he had, indeed, been at the pool when Charlie left for home, he had gone straight from the park to the Miss Quimby Diner for lunch, where three waitresses corroborated his alibi. He'd had the Blue Plate Special. Meatloaf and mashed potatoes. A side of wax beans.

He wasn't the man who took my brother.

The next day my father installed the tip line phone in the family room. Just a simple black rotary dial phone, utilitarian and nondescript. Answering the house phone was such a crapshoot. We never knew if we were going to get personal calls or something related to Charlie. This way, he explained, there would be a special number just for tips. The police would share it, and we would advertise it as well.

The installation of the tip line enervated my mother. She acted as though droves of people had simply been waiting for a means to reach us with their tips and clues. Their sightings and suspicions. The night after he installed the phone, she collapsed in her bed, sleeping for almost twelve hours after not having slept for more than an hour or two at a time for over a week.

After the first ad went into the paper, it started to ring. And ring. Early on, even I started to think that maybe my mother was right. Someone knew something, and now they had a way to tell us.

"People are afraid to call the police," she said sagely. "This allows them to speak openly without worrying about getting in trouble."

My father was also running on empty, but like a soldier, he sat sentinel by that phone.

After about a week, however, I had already grown jaded, weary of the speculations and so-called tips. My days had become fluid, one running into the next, each day both the same as the previous yet, somehow, worse. The desperation of the search was escalating; we all knew that the more time that passed, the less likely it was that Charlie was alive.

When the phone rang that first week of August, my first thought was that it was Trill again, but it wasn't our kitchen phone; it was the tip line.

After my father hung up with the caller, I listened to the sound of my mother's raised voice, and the low rumble of my father's, muffled by my closed door.

Something was happening.

I shut my notebook and walked quietly to the door, which I cracked open, and it was like the sky splitting open with rain.

"He said he saw a pickup truck," my father said. "Speeding away from the spot where Charlie's things were found just after noon that day."

"Whose truck?" my mother demanded.

My father paused.

"Burt? Whose truck?"

"He said it was that Jenkins boy's, a '72 red Ford pickup, a peace sign decal in the back window."

In the doorway, my body stiffened. *What?*

"I don't understand," my mother cried. "That man took Charlie?"

"Bonnie," my father's voice lowered. "It was just a call. And the guy wouldn't even give me his name, said he wanted to remain anonymous. There have been hundreds of calls. People want to help. It's probably nothing."

"Did he call the police?"

"I don't know."

"You have to go out there," she said. "To the Whittaker farm."

At this, there was nothing but stillness. My mother's mandate and my father's silence.

"You have to go find Charlie," my mother said, her words liquid, gurgling in her throat. An order. A plea.

"Bonnie," my father said. "We need to let the police know. There's a procedure to this. There's a protocol."

At this my mother's voice reached a pitch I had never heard before.

"You're a coward!" she cried. "A fucking coward."

My mother had never sworn—at least not that I'd heard—in my life. There was poison in her words. There were knives. She meant to slice him open. She meant to wound.

After this, I heard nothing but some scuffling and then the slamming of a door.

I ran to the window and looked down at my father climbing into the station wagon. His face was red, and shoulders stooped.

Someone thought Jericho had taken Charlie? Why? My heart skittered at the implication of this accusation. Then, the stone sinking. Jericho, and his truck, had been at The Farm that entire morning. He was there when I left Trill to go home. I'd *seen* him. There was an oven in the back of his truck. The caller hadn't said anything about that. There was no way he could have taken it out of the truck by himself. No way he could have taken my brother.

I ran down the stairs, intent on telling my mother what I knew. To warn her she was making a terrible mistake. But when I reached the bottom of the stairs, she turned to me, her eyes narrowed and chest heaving. The skin of her neck was splotchy, a virulent rash.

"This is because of *you*," she said evenly. "That girl. Those *people*. What is wrong with you? Do you realize what you've done?"

I felt the way I did when I fell off the monkey bars onto my back once in third grade. The air completely knocked out of me, my words and breath trapped inside my chest.

"What are you talking about?" I asked, though I knew exactly what she was talking about. "I didn't do anything! I'm sorry I didn't hear the phone."

I sobbed as I thought about running to The Farm that morning, praying I'd find Trill so I could hold her. Tell her that nothing would keep me away from her. I thought about how I'd been clinging to her as someone stole my brother.

"You're *sick*," she said, shaking her head.

"Not anymore, Mom," I said, but as I said it, I knew she didn't mean the flu I'd just gotten over. She meant what I felt for Trill.

Vomit crept up the back of my throat.

"You took my phone," I said angrily, defiantly.

"What?" she said.

"You took my phone away. That's why I didn't hear it. Because of *you*."

The slap startled me, and for a strange, painless moment, I thought I'd imagined it, except that she was staring at me in horror. Her lips were parted, but no sounds were coming out. Then, the pain arrived: an anguished sting that enveloped the entire left side of my face.

"Edith," she said, starting to crumble.

"Oh my God," I said, stunned. "Oh my *God*."

When the doorbell rang, for a confused moment, I thought it was only the ringing in my head.

But then the knob twisted, and Mrs. Nichols poked her head in, carrying another aluminum casserole dish, steam escaping into the kitchen air like a ghost.

I didn't know what my father planned to do to Jericho. And as much as I wanted to, I couldn't call Trill to warn her that he was coming. My phone was gone, the kitchen phone hanging right where the three of us stood for several awkward moments before Mrs. Nichols handed me the casserole to put in the freezer and ushered my mother to the kitchen table, where she helped lower her into her chair, as if she were elderly instead of forty-three years old. Mrs. Nichols looked at me, as though I had answers for what she had interrupted. My mother offered nothing; she seemed catatonic, her eyes glassy and vacant.

I retreated to my room, and my father didn't return for hours. Mrs. Nichols had long since gone home, and the sounds of kids playing Kick the Can in the street must have sent my mother into her room. I heard the door shut from upstairs. I heard her cries traveling through the walls.

I turned on the TV to distract myself, but when the nightly PSA came on with Cyndi Lauper demanding, accusing, *It's ten* PM, *do you know where your children are?* I shut it off.

When the station wagon pulled into the driveway, I felt a deep ache in my bowels, forcing me to clutch my knees to my chest. I listened to him downstairs. The opening of a cupboard. The clatter of ice and the glug of Scotch. The scraping of a chair across the linoleum.

I quietly walked downstairs and wordlessly stood in the stairwell door, staring at him.

My father looked defeated. He was alone at the kitchen table, slumped over, his head hung low. Through his thinning hair, I could see the top of his scalp, freckled and pale, and his vulnerability made my throat close.

"Did you go to The Farm?" I asked.

He looked up at me. His eyes were ringed red. His shirt wrinkled. It was the same shirt he was wearing the day before. None of the rules—of grooming, of eating, of living seemed to apply to our lives anymore.

"Did you talk to Jericho?" I asked.

He closed his eyes, nodding.

"What did you say?" I asked, and he opened his eyes.

"I told him someone saw his truck speeding along the loop where Charlie disappeared, and I needed to know if he took him."

"And?" I asked.

My father grimaced, then shrugged. "He wept like a child."

"Jericho would never do anything to Charlie," I said firmly in case my father thought his breaking down might support the ridiculous claim.

My father nodded. "I still need to let the police know. They'll question him. Get an alibi. He said he was at The Farm the whole morning, that he didn't go anywhere that day. So, if anyone can corroborate that, he'll be okay."

But Phyllis had been gone, and Trill had been in a fevered sleep. Even if she had been awake, she wouldn't have been able to see his truck; it was parked way up by The Bakery, which wasn't visible from the barn window. I was the only one who knew he was there. But just as I was about to tell my father this, to confess that I had gone to see Trill, that I could vouch for Jericho, I remembered the sting of my mother's slap, the burn of her words. The slice of her accusations. "You're *sick*."

"He says he'll let them search his property, that he has nothing to hide. He wants to help."

"You believe him, right?"

"I do," he said.

"What about Mom?" I asked.

"I'll worry about your mom," he said and examined me with kind eyes. "Edie? She just wants answers. This is the wrong answer, but she just wants to know what happened to your brother."

"Where did you go, after?"

His chin quivered, and he looked down. "I just drove around, looking for him."

"Daddy?" I hadn't called him this since I was a little girl.

"Yeah, honey?"

"I'm sorry," I said. "I'm so sorry about Charlie."

At this, he beckoned me to him, and I collapsed onto his lap, wishing myself small. Imagining time rewinding, reversing, spinning backward from eighteen to seventeen to sixteen, all the way back to six. I pressed my face into my father's chest and listened to his heart. *I am, I am, I am.*

In the morning the police descended on The Farm, though I wouldn't learn about this until the next day, when the newspaper the paperboy hurled at our door offered the details. And I wouldn't speak to Trill again until the night before she left for college.

July 2023

THE MOLD REMEDIATION team shows up at seven on Wednesday morning, and I haven't slept. Nathan pulls up in his work truck behind them, both vehicles blocking in my car, which makes me feel anxious.

"Hey," Nathan says as I open the door, his brow furrowed. "I read the news about the arrest. Are you okay? Your mom?"

He seems to be waiting to see if I might need a hug, but I just shake my head.

"We're fine," I say.

"They found new evidence?" he asks, his voice cracking. "On the Jenkinses' property?"

"Jericho Jenkins didn't hurt Charlie," I say firmly, though the thought of Charlie's book shoved into their root cellar wall is sickening. Unexplainable. "We're getting the FBI involved. See if they can test for DNA. Trill is here too. With a lawyer for Jericho."

At Trill's name, Nathan tenses.

I can't help but feel exasperated. Really, an innocent man's life is at stake, and here he is with his ancient, petty grievances. He never liked Trill. He'd been jealous. I know he—like my mother—must have associated my breaking up with him, my wanting to go away to college, with her. But even without Trill, I'd have left him eventually. At least I think I would have. Though, honestly, I had been so cowardly before her. So worried about pleasing everyone but myself.

"How long is all this going to take?" I ask, motioning to the mold guys outside.

"Probably just another day or two. It depends on what we find when we pull the drywall down in the rec room. Worst case, probably four or five more days. After, I'll come by to seal things up. The sump pump should be here today, and I'll put it in this week. That won't take long."

He takes his baseball cap off and rubs his hand across the top of his head. An old, nervous habit, for when he's at a loss for words.

"I hope that . . . all of this . . . brings some closure," he says.

"There won't be any closure until we find Charlie," I say.

In the basement, the men tear down the walls, exposing the toxins growing there. The noise has woken my mother, and she comes to the kitchen, looking a hundred years old. It's as if the tragedy has returned and she is reliving it, all these decades later. But beneath the anguish, there is an expression I have seen only a few times in my life. It's a smugness, a sort of satisfaction. She believes that justice will finally be served. This is the expression of *I Told You So*, the visage of someone who, once doubted, is now vindicated. Her suspicions and speculations are now *fact*. And she doesn't even know about Charlie's book.

I know I need to call the police and tell them what I know about Jericho's whereabouts at the time of my brother's abduction. It is too little, of course, and far too late. But it's the only way to put an end to this. I promised Trill. The image of her running away from me makes my heart ache.

My confession will also destroy my mother. I think of those games of Chutes and Ladders I used to play with Charlie. About how you could get almost all the way to the top of the board, then with the flick of a spinner, be sent tumbling down the chute and back to the beginning. My mother has been waiting for justice for our family for thirty-seven years. What I am about to do will steal this from her. But what was stolen from *me*? My brother. My future. *Trill.*

"Mom," I say and sit down across from her at the table. "I need you to know something."

She looks up, as if just realizing I'm here. She throws her shoulders back defiantly, like she knows I am about to challenge her. Still, that self-satisfied smirk.

"He'll die in prison," she says. "For what he did to Charlie."

I take a deep breath. "Jericho didn't hurt Charlie."

She flicks her wrist at me angrily, dismissively.

"I *saw* him, Mom," I snap. "That day. I wasn't at home sick. I went out to The Farm to see Trill, and Jericho was there. He was there the whole time, when Charlie disappeared."

"That's not true," she says.

"It is true. I went there to be with Trill," I say and then softly, "I loved her, Mom."

At this my mother, like a child, puts her hands to her ears and shakes her head.

"We were together that morning. She was sick, and I took care of her. She fell asleep, and when I left, I saw Jericho. He was at home all day. He wasn't anywhere near Charlie."

"You're lying!" my mother says, her face pale and her voice crackling. "You always lie to me."

"Mom. I'm going to the police. Jericho didn't do anything to anyone, and we need to figure out who did. The FBI will get involved and test the backpack for DNA. We can find out who *really* took him, Mom. Isn't that what you want? To know what really happened to Charlie?"

"Charlie's backpack was on *his* property," she says, shaking. "How do you explain that?"

Again, I think about Charlie's paperback book, his name and our family's phone number printed inside. I have no explanation for this, and something about it niggles at me. A sliver lodged under tender skin.

"I don't know, Mom. I only know that I saw him at the exact same time Charlie was walking home. And whoever said they saw his truck, it's just not possible. His truck was at The Farm. I saw it."

Her body is quaking now, the veins in the bump on her head are pulsing. "I need you to leave," she says. "You're confusing me."

"Mom," I plead, reaching for her hand.

"Where is your father?" she asks. "I need to tell him that I was right about that awful man."

August 1986

DESPITE HAVING ZEROED in on Jericho as a person of interest, by late August, the police had hit a wall. There was nothing at all except for that anonymous tip, the supposed sighting of Jericho's truck, to tie him to Charlie's disappearance. His property and truck had been searched. He'd passed three lie detector tests.

I didn't come forward, because I didn't need to. He was cleared by the police. *No longer a person of interest.* I told myself that if there had been any danger of him going to jail, I would have gone straight to the police.

Of course, I did know that despite the dearth of evidence, many people in town still believed he was responsible, that the police had been negligent in exonerating him, including my mother and Mrs. Nichols. I watched them at the kitchen table, wringing their hands, heard their whispered speculations. My mother was thrilled when she heard that he had decided not to return to his teaching job that fall after a letter to the editor came out suggesting that someone suspected of such a crime had no place teaching children. And when Mrs. Nichols, who still worked as a teller, offered my mother the private details of his precarious financials—his depleted account, how much he had paid a lawyer, the overdraft fees—my mother seemed appeased by what she saw as a small bit of justice. But despite all this, I kept silent. Shamefully and cowardly silent.

My mother took a leave of absence from her job; the agony of caring for other people's children was too much for her. My father, however, had to return to work. He had a mortgage, bills, and a daughter going off to college.

But I didn't go anywhere.

I was supposed to start Smith after Labor Day, but a week before move-in, I told my parents that I wouldn't be going away to school. I would take the semester off, and as soon as Charlie came home, I would start at Smith. There was no contingency for if Charlie did not come home.

My father made the call to the registrar. As I stood biting my nails in the doorway to the kitchen, he explained our family's situation, and I pictured the horror of the woman on the other end of the line. I imagined her later, at her lunch break with the other staff, recounting the atrocity that had happened to one of their incoming freshmen. The clucking and nodding of the women in my imagination filled me with anger.

"They said you can defer acceptance due to family hardship. Up to a year." Then, as if he knew he had to convince me, he said, "You'll get there, honey. You will."

My eyes stung with tears of gratitude, but I knew even then that I would never go to Smith. The same way that I knew Charlie would never come home.

I hadn't seen Trill since the day Charlie went missing, and when Jericho came under suspicion, I had no idea if I would ever see her again. We were forbidden. She was forbidden. She was supposed to leave for Hampshire the last weekend of August, classes at Hampshire also starting after Labor Day. In a week, she would be gone, and I would remain here. This was my punishment, I thought, the penance for losing my brother. And for failing hers.

The phone rang all the time back then. The tip line was a relentless, clanging harbinger, and our regular landline was constantly jangling with calls from the police, the neighbors, the media. So, when the kitchen phone rang that Friday after my mother and I had eaten lunch, I grabbed it, readying myself for whatever might be on the other end of the line. I had scripts I'd memorized depending on who was calling. But I had no script for this.

"I need to see you," Trill said firmly.

I looked at my mother, whose face was expectant. Every call elicited the same hopeful response from her. I shook my head, and, disappointed, she returned to whatever she'd been doing.

I took the phone down the hall as far as the curling cord would allow and sat down with my back against the wall for support.

"I don't know how," I said.

"I'll pick you up at school. Say you're going for a run."

I could do this. I could put on my running clothes, lace up my sneakers, run to the high school and wait for Trill to pull up. I envisioned the way my lungs would feel breathing in the thick summer air, the mosquitos biting the soft pink of my bare arms. I imagined the sound of the car door as it closed us inside.

"Okay," I said. Just one last time before she left.

I hung up the phone, waiting for my mother's inevitable, "Who was that?"

"It was Smith," I said. "They had a couple questions. About my deferral."

Talking about Smith always silenced my mother.

"I'm going for a run," I said. "I need to move my legs."

She looked at me skeptically, and I thought she must know. My shame was a worn T-shirt I never changed out of. Filthy and comfortable at the same time.

"Do *not* go to that house," she hissed.

My chest tightened.

"I'm going to Lisa's. I told her I would come see her new kitten," I said, then added, "Her name is Fluffernutter."

She studied me, wary.

"Which way are you going?" she asked.

At first, I thought she might follow me, then I realized she was asking this in case I disappeared too. Was she worried I might simply walk out the door and vanish as well?

Feeling like I might vomit the meager lunch I'd managed to eat, I ran as fast as I could to the high school. I hadn't run since the day Charlie disappeared. I had hardly eaten; I was thin and weak. By the time I got to the school parking lot, it felt like my legs were on fire. I bent over, trying to catch my breath, feeling the acidic juices of my empty stomach creeping up my throat.

Trill was there only moments later. I glanced around then opened Nico's door and slinked down into the passenger seat like a criminal.

Trill looked even more feral than usual in a wrinkled white sundress and red high-top sneakers. I could see she hadn't shaved her legs, and there were pale yellow bruises on her shins, dark circles under her eyes. No makeup, and her hair was a tangled mess.

Without speaking, she pulled out of the parking lot and headed over the bridge and out toward The Farm.

"I can't," I said. "I can't go there."

Trill's jaw tightened and she gripped the wheel tighter, smashing the turn signal down. She was angry.

"I'm sorry," I said.

"Then where do we go?" she asked, her voice shrill.

This question felt impossible to answer. There was nowhere for us here.

I shook my head. "I don't know."

She took a deep breath and pressed the gas pedal harder, Nico shuddering.

We passed the turnoff to The Farm and to the mountain toll road. When she eventually signaled, I realized we were driving to Lake Gormlaith.

She parked at the boat access area, which was only about a quarter mile before the turnoff to the construction site where Nathan and his dad were building their house. The place Nathan had taken me after prom. The idea that these two moments—the one with Trill, and the one with Nathan—could occupy the same physical space felt jarring. Cognitively dissonant.

It was a weekday, and so the lake was quiet: just one little boy wrestling with a tangled fishing line, sitting on the jetty that jutted out into the placid water.

"We can't hang out here," I said, nervously looking toward the road.

Everyone in town knew Trill's brother had been suspected of abducting Charlie. News of me being with Jericho Jenkins's sister would get back to my mother by the time I got home.

"Effie's grandparents have a place up here. I heard her say they keep a flat-bottom boat tied up to their dock," I offered, eager to get out of sight. "We can borrow it."

We walked quickly to Effie's family's camp, the gambrel-roofed cottage with the treehouse. Sure enough, there was a blue flat-bottomed boat, tied but not locked, to the dock. I glanced at the camp, worried that someone might come out and see us, but the shades were drawn. They weren't there.

"Come," I said, and we scurried down the embankment to the dock, where I freed the boat from the mooring and motioned for her to get in. The oars were in the bottom of the boat.

"Let me," she said and sat down on the bench in the center of the boat, gripping the oars, which clattered and clanged in the oar locks.

I'd just wanted to get off the road, but now I felt like a sitting duck out here on the lake. It was cooler on the water, though, and my skin, hot from the run, was grateful. I dipped my fingers into the water, which was warm and silky.

"Let's go to the island," she said, jerking her chin over her shoulder.

"Like Sylvia and Marcia," I said, remembering that trip, our Syl-grimage. I recalled the sweetness of pineapple and ham, the sunset behind us as we looked off in the distance at Children's Island.

We didn't speak the rest of the way. The sun was overhead now; Trill was sweating with the effort. In the pale white sundress, she looked ghostly, and—I realized—thinner than when I last saw her. I wanted to touch her. Her skin had that effect on me,. like seeing a soft kitten or the smooth surface of a lake. I wanted to drag my fingers across the silky shallows of her.

When we approached the island, I could see it was maybe only thirty feet in diameter. Rocky and thickly populated by evergreens.

I followed her out of the boat, and together we pulled it up onto the shore, using the rope to secure it to the trunk of a spruce.

Despite the island being uninhabited, it was not untouched. A narrow trail led from where we got off the boat into the woodsy and rocky terrain.

When we had gotten to the dark center of the island, Trill stopped and turned to me. Then she fell into my arms.

I had wanted her to comfort *me*. To tell me everything would be okay. I had wanted to lean into her, have her coo her assurances into my ear, but instead she was trembling, full of need. I felt useless.

"Sit," I said, trying to take charge.

There was a small clearing, with soft pine needles creating a natural blanket.

Trill dropped down, hugging her knees to her chest. I sat across from her and reached for her hands.

"I leave Sunday for Hampshire," she said.

"The day after *tomorrow*?" I said, quickly sifting through the calendar in my brain. There was still over week left before Labor Day.

"Orientation week," she said. "For freshmen."

"Oh," I said.

"And I wanted to talk to you before I go. I need you to know some things."

"Okay," I said.

"My brother didn't hurt Charlie," she said firmly.

"I know," I said, my chest aching. "The police cleared him."

"But your mom will never believe that. And she'll never let me see you."

I felt a sob rise like a bobber in my chest.

"The second thing is that you need to leave here."

"What?" I said. "I can't leave. My brother is still missing. My parents need me. I . . ."

"Listen to me," she said. "You need to leave here because this place will destroy you."

"What do you mean?" I asked, even though I knew exactly what she meant.

I thought about the lies I'd told to protect this secret, and not only the one about being with Trill when I should have been protecting my brother. I had been lying for years. To Nathan. To my parents. To myself. I was not who any of them wanted me to be.

"I have a deferral," I said, mustering positivity. "To Smith. When Charlie comes home, I'll go."

But she and I both knew Charlie wasn't coming back. Her brother had not taken him, the man in the van had not taken him, but someone else had.

"Okay," she said, her face crumpling. She wanted to believe this lie as much as I did. But tears were running down her cheeks now, and she was trembling.

All around us, the island was quiet and green. Small waves beat softly against the shore, and we held on for the last time.

That Sunday morning, I went to Mass with my parents. But as hard as I tried to focus on the sermon, as much as I wanted to believe I could say the right thing to God to make whoever held Charlie captive relinquish him, I could only think about Trill. I imagined her loading up Nico with her old suitcase, her books, and her VHS tapes. I pictured the back seat full of records and milk crates, her clothes pulled off their hangers and tossed into garbage bags. I pictured her hugging her mom and Jericho goodbye before getting into the car and blasting "American Tune" as she pulled out onto the road toward her new life.

"Where's Nathan?" my mother whispered.

Mr. and Mrs. Nichols sat in their usual pew three rows up. But Nathan, who should have been doing his thurifer duties, had been replaced by a pockmarked kid who looked about twelve.

"No idea," I said.

When Father Tavares got to the prayers of the faithful, his usual intentions—for the sick, for the elderly, for the youth—were followed, as they had been for a month now, with a special prayer to deliver my brother from harm. To keep him safe and protected until he was able to come home. At this, my mother broke down. As she had every Sunday since Charlie disappeared. As she would every Sunday for the next thirty-seven years.

July 2023

MY MOTHER SHUTS herself in her room after our fight about Jericho. She has a TV in there, and I can hear her streaming an old episode of *Dateline*. Loudly. Taking comfort with all those victims' families, with the liars in their own lives. In her confusion, I wonder if she ever loses the details of our own tragedy, conflating her grief with the grief of so many other mothers.

My head is pounding in time with my heart. There it is. The secret I've kept beneath those floorboards for decades. I have torn up the boards, told my mother. I have told Trill. Now, I need to call law enforcement. But who? *Jake Nichols?* That feels ludicrous.

I think of him, seventeen-year-old him, anyway. His lewd comments about me and Trill. I try to imagine what he'll say if I tell him that he was right about us. Right about me. I feel like a girl again: ashamed, terrified. He is not the person I want to confess this to: that I failed my brother, that I failed my family. That I failed Jericho and Trill.

And what if they don't believe me? My own mother refuses to. I wonder again what the legal ramifications of lying about my own whereabouts that day might be. The only consequences that mattered back then were what my mother would say if she found out I'd snuck out to be with Trill. I feel like the earth has shattered into slivers, each piercing a different place in my heart.

I can hear the men below us working, doing whatever it is they need to do to kill the toxins growing inside our walls. Before Nathan left, he said he would come back when they were done to install the new sump pump. What will *he* think when the truth comes out?

My body feels like it weighs a thousand pounds as I climb the stairs to my room, where I shut the door. I am still wearing the clothes I wore to the track last night. I need a shower. I pull clean clothes from my drawer: jeans and a T-shirt. I open the underwear drawer and see the letter from Smith I stashed there.

Poor Charlie. He must have thought he could stop me from leaving him by simply hiding this letter, by tucking it away. Pretending it did not exist.

I turn the envelope over. There it is, the faint blue handwriting, blurred into an inky Rorschach butterfly. I grab my reading glasses from my nightstand and study that strange blue, winged creature:

SOS

Following this, almost completely faded, is another ghostly word:

Lost

Lost? Did Charlie write this? Was he trying to get help? But why would he write a note like this and then put it in his backpack? I have the illogical thought that Charlie was the one who hid the backpack in the tree. And this was his message for help?

SOS Lost.

Could he possibly have been lost in the woods like we first thought? Could he have stashed the backpack in the tree before setting off to try to get home? He couldn't see much without his glasses. Had he stumbled into the river?

None of that makes any sense. The Farm is miles from where his glasses were found. The woods were searched. The river was dragged. He had stayed missing. And none of this explains his book being found in Jericho's house.

I grab my phone and search for the police photo of the other half of the envelope.

ver Rd

I zoom in and hold the phone next to the envelope in my hand.

SOS Lost ver Rd

Maybe they aren't letters at all. Perhaps they are *numbers.*

I picture the purple mailbox at the entrance to The Farm.

505 Lost River Rd.

The Farm.

Lost River Rd.

Why would Charlie have written the address to The Farm on this envelope? Then my stomach lurches. This is not Charlie's handwriting.

I recognize that *Lo*—the loopy, sloppy script I've seen a zillion times:

Love, Nathan. Love you, Nathan.

I feel a sickening thud in my chest.

Nathan?

September 1986

Fall came to Vermont. Trill was gone. Effie and Tess were gone. Of course, not everyone went to college. Lisa had gotten a job at the Walgreens, and I suspected she'd be engaged by Christmas. I imagined Bobby on his knee, presenting her with a ring. With a future. Though I had never wanted that, I envied her. I envied the normalcy, the certainty, the promise and predictability of what would come next.

Days passed, each one comprised of hills and valleys, like being stuck on the same roller coaster ride, ascending on the rickety tracks of hope followed by the inevitable plummeting of disappointment, with only a breath before the cars chugged forward again. It was torturous.

My father returned to work, though my mother did not, eventually typing her resignation on my father's electric typewriter. Now she spent her days focused solely on Charlie. She truly believed that Jericho was responsible for his disappearance, and until someone could prove otherwise, she was convinced of his guilt, committed to it. She collected bits of information like a magpie: the speculations about Jericho's mother's involvement in the occult (*she reads tea leaves, you know*), the statistics about child abuse perpetrated by members of Satanic cults. She'd seen a whole episode on *Phil Donahue* about this. *What if, what if* . . . She had a notebook where she assembled these bits together, creating a nest of culpability. She spun these tales for reporters: her heartache and ludicrous, desperate theories splayed in black and white.

I tried to write, but my creativity had withered. Poetry had lost its power; what I had thought were incantations were nothing more than silly spells. No different from prayers in the end: feathery syllables sent up into the ethers.

Without writing, without Trill, I didn't know what else to do with my time, and so I ran. I got up in the morning, pulled on my workout clothes, and ran until I couldn't feel my legs. I ran through the fallen leaves, the crush of ice when the temperature plunged, then through the first layer of snow. I ran even as the air cut with its bitter blades.

Some days, I saw Nathan; he and his father were often leaving together for work as I exited my house. We didn't speak. Really, what was there to say in a situation like this? We just nodded at each other—an acknowledgment: *We are both still here.*

My mother said the house on Lake Gormlaith was almost complete. The walls were up, there was a roof. Floors. A front porch. The accounting of the house's progress felt like a personal attack when she relayed it to me.

"They've put in wall-to-wall carpeting," she said. "There are four bedrooms. The master has its own bathroom. Judy says that from the porch, you can see the lake."

I ignored her, and I ran.

On my most desperate days, I wondered, was it possible to run all the way to Hampshire College to find Trill? How many miles had I traveled on the endless loop around town? Probably more than the 175 miles that stretched between us now.

This was what I imagined as I ran through the fallen leaves, then the bitter mist: running to her. Arriving at her dorm room, breathless. Muscles burning and bathed in sweat. Knocking on her door and falling into her room, into her arms, into her bed. Trill was my destination, my destiny. But, somewhere around the halfway point of the loop—at the stretch of road where my brother disappeared—the dream of Trill would slip away. It was absurd to think there was any possible future in which Trill and I were together. And devastated, I would run home, so hard and so fast I thought my heart might simply explode with the effort.

Alone in my room, I tried to read, though the words only swam across the page. This had also happened to Esther Greenwood, the protagonist of *The Bell Jar*, when she first started losing her mind. First, she lost the ability to read—the words becoming unrecognizable. I worried I, too, might be going crazy, which would send me into a panic. However, while Esther's (and Sylvia's) mothers were keenly aware of their respective descents into madness, my own mother seemed oblivious to mine.

"I'm having Nathan take care of the gutters today," she'd said. "It would be nice if you two could at least be friends again."

But oddly, I sensed that Nathan didn't want anything to do with me either.

He had changed. He had stopped being an altar boy at church, stopped attending Mass altogether. His face looked tired. Older than the eighteen-year-old boy he was. He didn't appear to have much of a social life. Not even Jake came around anymore. He didn't date, as far as I could tell, and spent almost as much time with his parents as I did with mine. Both of us were in the unique situation of being the only surviving child. That should have brought us together. I suspect my mother hoped it would. There was so much hope in the house, that old thing with feathers.

But my mother's friendship with Mrs. Nichols didn't survive the loss of their sons either. About a year after Charlie disappeared, Mrs. Nichols abruptly stopped coming by. Stopped calling. Maybe the shared grief proved too much. Like two people suffering through drug addiction, their respective misery only exacerbated the other's. Rather than supporting each other, they were simply drowning in the same body of water. Then, just over a year after Charlie disappeared, a For Sale sign went up in the Nicholses' yard.

Mrs. Nichols hadn't said anything about their family moving. She'd been busy with work, but she hadn't even bothered to call. When my mother finally called *her*, the conversation was short, my mother simply listening, nodding, then saying, "I understand."

"With Nathan moving out soon, they don't need the space. And the memories . . ." my mother explained that night over dinner. "With Mickey gone. Charlie too. It's too much."

Even I had felt awash in pity for my mother. Mrs. Nichols had been her lifeline. Her best friend. She no longer had anyone to spin her stories or field her theories with. And my mother, bewildered and feeling abandoned, became even more sullen.

By New Year's Eve, Nathan had moved into the house by the lake, and Mr. and Mrs. Nichols were gone. They'd left to go to Myrtle Beach, where they'd bought a condo. His father took an early retirement, and Nathan took over the business.

A family with three children moved in next door.

"Charlie will love having a boy his age next door," my mother said. "When he comes home."

But Charlie never came home.

July 2023

505 Lost River Rd., written in Nathan's handwriting on the back of the envelope from Smith. A letter, torn in half, that was found in Charlie's backpack, stuffed into the hollow of a tree on Jericho's property. My mind reels, trying to figure out what this means.

Had *Nathan* somehow intercepted the letter? If so, how? I rack my brain, and then I remember the night of the prom. That bumbling encounter Nathan had with the mailman. Had he seen the letter from Smith addressed to me and picked it up? But I hadn't even told him about Smith then. Though that certainly would explain his anger after prom, and the way he'd behaved at the construction site. I remember the way he'd almost closed my fingers in the glovebox when it fell open. Had the letter been inside?

But why would he have written Trill's address on the envelope? And how had the letter gotten into Charlie's backpack? None of it makes any sense.

Unless. Unless he had something to do with Charlie's disappearance. But how? That doesn't make any sense either.

I have relived that day so many times; what could I have missed?

I'd been sick with the flu, my body wrecked. Though that morning, I had woken feeling like the heavy cloud of illness had lifted. But then, I'd remembered my mother eavesdropping on me and Trill, the sinking feeling that she knew about us. Her mandate that I do not leave the house, as though she could simply keep me prisoner there.

I had seen Nathan's truck in the driveway that morning as I set out for Trill's. I remember because it was a Friday, and he usually drove to work with his dad on Fridays. But his mom and dad had gone out of town for the weekend. He didn't have to work, so he and Jake were going camping.

I hadn't bothered to stretch—I didn't want to risk running into Nathan—and so I had set off running to Trill's—furious, defiant, desperate.

I remember arriving at the barn, seeing Jericho's truck parked up by The Bakery.

I recall the feel of Trill's feverish skin pressed against mine, the salty tears running from her eyes into my mouth. I remember promising her that I wouldn't let my mother ruin my life. I was going to Smith. We would be together in September. Until then, we just needed to bide our time. I remember her long fingers, the bony steps of her spine. I remember kissing her feverish skin. She'd looked pallid in the dusky light of The Library, and I'd felt selfish for wanting her when she felt so terrible. I'd given her the cough syrup and stayed with her until she fell asleep, stroking her hair and listening to her rattly chest as she breathed.

I remember hearing the footsteps on the stairs to the loft: Jericho coming to leave us plates with warm bread and strawberry jam.

"Are you hungry?" I had asked her, but she was deep asleep. Then, overwhelmed with affection, I had said, "Trilly. I love you so much."

I recall hearing the barn doors close and going to the top of the steps to retrieve the snacks but finding nothing there.

Oh my God.

I turn the envelope over and over in my hands, and it is as if I have been plunged into an ice bath: the shock of it profound, my body quaking in the aftermath.

I run down the stairs and without checking on my mother, go outside and get in my car, grateful Siena gave Ariel a ride to work. My leg is shaking too much to hold the brake pedal down, and I lurch out of the driveway.

It's raining again. Nathan will likely be at his house at Gormlaith; it's too wet for the project he's working on at the Masons'.

I fly all the way to the lake, tears streaming down my cheeks as the pieces click together, assembling into the shape of the day my brother disappeared.

I pull into the driveway; Nathan is working in his open two-car garage. On one side is his table saw, on the other is his old truck; I'm surprised to see he's held onto it all these years.

I get out of my car and slam the door shut. But he has his back to me, working at the table saw with noise canceling headphones on and can't hear me as I march up the driveway to him.

As I approach, he whips around, startled. At the sight of me, his eyes grow wide, and he turns off the saw.

"Edie, you scared the crap out of me," he says, pulling the headphones down around his neck. "But I'm glad you're here. I meant to call you earlier. There's been a delay on the sump pump. It's supposed to come by Friday now, and as soon as it comes, I'll get it installed. The sooner the better," he says, motioning to the rain.

The earth feels tilted. How can he be talking about sump pumps, about weather?

"Did you take my letter from Smith?" I ask, pulling the half of the letter from my pocket and holding it under his nose as if to make him smell something rotten.

"What?" he says, his face flushing red.

"My acceptance letter from Smith. This."

"I have no idea what you're talking about," he says, but he refuses to look at it.

I peer at him, at this face I have known my whole life. At this child inside a fifty-five-year-old man. At this teenaged boy wearing a middle-aged man's clothes. Time feels nebulous.

I remember prom night. When he'd talked about marrying me, about living here. When he'd tried to get me to sleep with him, then attacked Trill. His jealousy had been terrifying. He'd slammed his fist, and I had been afraid of him. I had been *afraid* of him.

"You saw me leave my house that morning and knew I was going to Trill's."

He grips the edge of the worktable.

"This is Trill's address, written on this piece of mail you *stole* from me."

He knew about The Farm, but he wouldn't have known how to get there. He couldn't follow me, or I would have seen him. He had to wait. I picture him searching for *Jenkins* in the phone book, reciting the address as he went to his truck, where he grabbed this envelope from the glovebox and a pen to write it down before it slipped away. He kept a map in the glovebox too.

He hangs his head, closes his eyes.

He must have parked his truck down by the turnoff and then walked up to The Farm.

I get close to his face and say, "Did you *spy* on us?"

Nathan was the one who came into the barn, then shut the doors behind him after he saw Trill and me together. Or heard us. "I love you," I had said to her. My chest feels the heat of those words, that ember that has continued burning all these years at the very center of me.

His eyes blink against tears.

"*Nathan?*" I insist.

He sits down on the sawhorse and rubs his beard with both hands.

"I loved you," he says. "I loved you so much. What you were doing—with Trill—it terrified me. And it pissed me off. You *betrayed* me, Edie."

"We were broken up," I say. "You didn't have any right. You stalked me."

He frowns and scratches his eyebrow. There is sawdust in his hair, and for a moment, I glimpse the old man he might one day become.

I try to keep my breath even, but my heart is beating like a gong. What does any of this have to do with Charlie?

"This was in Charlie's backpack," I say, shaking the letter at him.

The red at his neck drains away, his face blanching, and I feel dizzy.

"Do you know what happened to my brother?" I ask in disbelief.

Nathan presses both hands to his head, as if the memories are trying to escape and he is holding them inside.

"It was an accident," he says softly.

The tilted world underneath me begins to quake. I need to hold onto something, but there is nothing to grasp but air.

"You have to believe me," he says, looking at me now. Imploring. "I would never have done anything to hurt him on purpose. I loved Charlie like a little brother."

"What did you do?" My hands clench into fists.

"As soon as I realized what was going on in that barn, I left," he says. "I just wanted to get home. I couldn't unsee what I'd seen, and I knew I'd completely lost you. That maybe I never had you to begin with."

He looks at me, his eyes red.

"I took the long way home. I needed to clear my head before I picked Jake up to go camping. He'd tried to tell me—about you and Trill—and I hadn't believed him. I was such a fool. I was upset, and I was driving too fast. I crested the hill, and it was too late. Charlie was on the wrong side of the road, with headphones on. He knew he wasn't supposed to walk on that side of the road."

His words are like an electric jolt.

I think of those items strewn in the field. He must have hit him so hard—his towel, the Walkman, his popsicle stick flung.

My body is buzzing, my ears ringing.

"I was so scared, Edie. I was just a kid. It was an accident."

"What did you *do* with him?" I demand, my voice raw.

"I thought he might be okay if I could just get him to the hospital. There was hardly any blood, even. I put him in the cab of the truck with me, but by the time I got back to the house, he wasn't breathing, and I panicked."

My legs begin to collapse beneath me, and so I move to sit on the porch steps, staring at the driveway that leads to the house that Nathan built for me.

"Why didn't you just leave him there? Why couldn't you at least let us discover what happened to him? We had no body. We thought he might still come home." I picture my mother, waiting for the phone to ring. Waiting for Charlie to walk in the door. "For *decades*, you let us hope."

Nathan is crying now. He is seven years old. Seventeen.

"Where is he, Nathan?"

Nathan shakes his head.

"I didn't know what to do, so I went to get Jake, and we drove up here."

"*Jake?*" I say in disbelief, though everything is starting to make sense now.

No wonder Jake didn't want the FBI involved. *This* was why he insisted on the county taking over the investigation. I feel sick.

"Where *is* he?" I ask, but I already know. I remember the excavating equipment I'd seen on prom night. The backhoe that had been used to dig the foundation.

"Oh my God," I cry. My brother has been here the whole time? "*You're* the one who called into the tip line about Jericho's truck?"

"No," he says, eyes wide. "I didn't. I swear."

"Oh my God," I say. "*Jake?*" Of course. He'd been the one from the start. "You let an innocent man take the fall. You were mad at Trill, so you destroyed her brother's life."

"*You* destroyed his life," Nathan says, his voice rising angrily. "You must have seen Jenkins there that day too. Why didn't *you* say anything?"

A knife in my heart. He's right. We are both guilty.

"But you took Charlie's backpack and hid it on Jericho's property to pin this on him!"

"*No,*" he says, his eyes wide. He shakes his head, adamant. "When I got home, the backpack was still in my truck. And that stupid letter. I tore it in half and put it in the backpack. Jake told me to dump it, but I couldn't bring myself to get rid of it. I put it in my closet."

His hands begin to shake even as he presses them against his knees. He's telling the truth. He has nothing left to lose.

"Who knew you still had the backpack, then?" I ask. "Jake?"

His face is in his hands now, but I can see he is still shaking his head. *No, no.*

I feel a spark in my chest as I remember the way Mrs. Nichols wouldn't look at my mother the day the U-Haul pulled away from their house. The way she had hugged her, but her arms had looked limp. "Oh my God. Your *mother*?"

He hangs his head.

"*Judy* hid it?"

I remember her sitting at the table with my mother, helping her fabricate the monster. Like Dr. Frankenstein, she created a picture of Jericho from bits and pieces. I thought of the collage in his barn. The fragments making up the image of his kind and gentle face.

"You have to believe me. I had no idea she put it on his property," he says, looking up at me at last. "I swear. She found it about a year after the accident. I guess maybe I was hoping she would. The guilt was awful. I was just a kid, Edie."

The horror of what he is telling me begins to settle in my chest. I can barely breathe.

"When she confronted me, I told her everything. I thought she would tell your family. That it would finally be over. But she just took the backpack. That was the last time we spoke of it."

My head feels both leaden and as if it might float off my shoulders.

Mrs. Nichols had lost one son already. She couldn't bear to lose another one.

January 1988

AT FIRST, I lied to myself that I would still leave Quimby. That no matter what happened, I would eventually pack up my belongings and my parents would drop me off at Smith. That I would sit on the porch at Haven House with my notebook, into which I would write all the words that had been bottled up inside me since my brother disappeared. I imagined a life beyond this town. Beyond this house. Beyond the rules.

But seasons passed, then another year, and I stayed. If Trill came home for breaks from school, I didn't see her. She didn't call—she was waiting for me, I knew—but I didn't reach out. I was too afraid of my feelings. Of hers. College changed people. I had been banking on that for myself. But my hopes of leaving Quimby, like the hope that Charlie would come home, were slowly but certainly fading.

My mother, however, clung to the certainty that we would find my brother. Searching for him became her full-time job. She posted fliers, procured funding to put up billboards. She spent days at a time at the library, where she searched the databases of missing children, reaching out to other mothers. Our home was her command center, and the tip line was her lifeline. And regardless of the lack of it, she insisted that concrete evidence connecting Charlie to Jericho would surface. That someone *knew* something.

But when the call came that night, right after our second Christmas without him, she was not home. She had flown to Chicago to speak at a conference. The mothers of missing children had become her coven, and I pictured her learning their spells.

My father had gone to bed. He'd started getting migraines, and the only solution was solitude and darkness. I sensed he was glad my mother was gone.

"Hello?" I said, waiting for the nut job or do-gooder or wannabe hero that would inevitably offer up their "tip" like so much cotton candy fluff. It seemed substantial but was made of little but hot air.

The voice on the other end of the line was female. Muffled. Like she was holding a handkerchief over the phone.

"The police need to go back to the Jenkins property."

I took a deep breath. Since Jericho had been cleared, we'd had at least half a dozen calls insisting he was to blame. That they had proof of occultism, rituals, of human sacrifices. But *Jericho* had been that human sacrifice.

"I had a dream," the voice said. "About a tree, near the river."

I rolled my eyes. At least once a week, there was a so-called psychic who called in with their visions.

"Thank you," I said, and started to hang up.

But the woman insisted. "Edie," she said, and I bristled. Of course, everyone knew my name by then. But the familiarity with which she said it unnerved me.

I slammed the phone down.

I looked at my father's notebook with all the latest tips etched in his careful script. I even picked up the pencil and started to scratch it down. But then I thought of my mother. How she would react—that she would insist the police do another search of The Farm. That I hadn't stopped the first ambush. But I could stop it from happening again. So, I set the pencil aside and never told anyone. If the caller reached out to the police as well, they never told us.

July 2023

"WHY WOULD YOUR mother do this? If she was trying to protect you, why wouldn't she just get rid of the backpack? Throw it away? Why would she do this to an innocent man?"

The sky looks like a bruise above us. Nathan has curled into himself now, head between his knees. Oddly, I recall the way he and the other altar boys would prostrate themselves at the altar during Mass.

He looks up at me. "I guess she thought if someone else was in prison for this, they would never come after me."

"She was my mom's *best friend.* How could she let her think her son was alive, all these years?"

"I don't know," he says.

Then I remember Charlie's *Choose Your Own Adventure* book. It hadn't been on the list of items on the Missing flyer. But then again, my mother had been wrong about Stretch Armstrong too.

"They found Charlie's book in Jericho's basement. Did she hide the book on his property too?" I ask. "How did she get into his house?"

Nathan jerks his head sharply. *No.*

And then it hits me.

Jake was the one in charge of the search, the one with access to the root cellar. The one with a motive to send Jericho away for good.

"How did *Jake* get Charlie's book?" I ask.

At this, Nathan's head falls to his chest, and his shoulders begin to tremble.

"I didn't want to do this," Nathan says, tears streaming down his cheeks. "I told him no."

"Tell me," I insist, my jaw aching.

"He came up here, on Monday night. To tell me what was going on. To make sure I kept my mouth shut."

I'm confused.

"I hadn't dropped the boxes from your basement off at the Masons' dumpster yet. They were still in my truck. He saw the one marked as Charlie's."

I remember the tiny jeans, the small T-shirts. His catcher's mitt and the waterlogged books. *Space and Beyond.*

"Why didn't you *stop* him?" I ask. I can barely breathe.

"I tried," he says, sobbing now. "He said it was the only way. That if I said anything, he'd come forward and tell everyone what I did."

"What about what *he* did?" I said. "Jesus Christ, Nathan."

"What proof do I have?" he says miserably. "My DNA and maybe my mom's would be the only DNA on that backpack besides Charlie's. Jake's a *cop*, Edie. And honestly, I couldn't do this to your mom. What my mother did was awful. But if your mom knew I was the one who . . ." He is crying now. "The one who killed her son?"

"You need to fix this," I say firmly. "You owe that much to Charlie. To my *mother.*"

Nathan looks up at me, and now, if only for a moment, I see the boy he once was.

"I want you to go inside and call the Quimby PD. Ask for Lieutenant Strickland. You need to tell them everything you just told me," I say. I recall the times I'd bossed him around when we were kids. His compliance. His eagerness to please. But he doesn't move. He just looks at me, his eyes filled with sorrow.

"Why couldn't you just love me?" he asks.

I ache.

"I don't know," I say. "I tried."

I get in the car. He doesn't move as I back down the long driveway and turn onto the road that will take me away from the lake and back into town. My whole body is trembling as I keep checking my phone, waiting for cell service.

I have to pull over at Hudson's, the gas station, on the way back, because I feel like I might faint.

I locate Trill's cell number. I imagine telling her what Nathan told me. Of offering it up like a gift. But somehow, I know it won't be enough. That simply finding the people responsible for all this means nothing if I don't own up to my mistake as well.

So instead of calling Trill, I dial Lieutenant Strickland myself.

July 2023

WHILE I'M PARKED at Hudson's, telling the police everything Nathan just told me, back at his house, Nathan climbs into the passenger seat of his old truck, the one he's held onto for all these years, the one that killed my brother. He grabs a piece of paper from the glovebox, just like he had that afternoon, and writes out his confession on the back of an old invoice. He draws a map of his property, and he marks an X where my brother is buried. Then he folds the paper into thirds and puts it under his windshield wiper. While I am shaking so badly I can't even turn the key in the ignition, Nathan closes the garage door and starts the old truck's engine.

Within hours after they discover Nathan slumped over the steering wheel, they begin the excavation, based on that grim treasure map. And when the bones emerge, they don't even need to wait for the identification to confirm it's Charlie. Because buried with him is the missing Stretch Armstrong doll. Nathan had made sure Charlie had it when he was laid to rest.

Despite everything, this pulls at my broken heart.

That night, I return to the police station and give my official statement to the police. I explain that I had been involved romantically with Jericho's sister and had been with her on the morning of July 18, 1986 in the barn on the Jenkinses' property. I tell them that my mother had found out about us and had forbidden me from seeing her. That she'd threatened to keep me from going away to college if I didn't end things with Trill. If my mother had known I was there, I explain, she would never have forgiven me. But I *was* there. I had seen Jericho. He was at The Farm at the exact moment Charlie disappeared.

I confirm that Nathan had been my ex-boyfriend and that he'd been devastated by my relationship with Trill. I give them my half of the letter from Smith with Trill's address and explain that I heard him enter the barn that day but I had mistakenly thought it was Jericho.

I tell them what Nathan told me about the accident, and Jake's insistence that they bury Charlie's body. And I confirm that Nathan had taken the box of Charlie's clothes and books from our house, and that Jake Nichols would have had access to them.

I tell them Nathan's mother was the one who hid the backpack, and about the call to the tip line I had ignored, the call that was likely Mrs. Nichols trying to implicate Jericho.

"But I need to ask you a favor," I say, when the detective sets down his pen. "Judy Nichols was my mother's best friend. I am not going to tell her this part. It would kill her."

He doesn't speak.

"Is this something you can maybe withhold from the media?" I ask.

He gives a curt nod.

After Charlie's remains are recovered, Jericho is released and Jake is taken in for questioning, though when confronted, he denies everything, claiming he had been camping solo the weekend Charlie disappeared.

Though, of course, there is no one to corroborate his alibi.

July 2023

It's raining the day of Charlie's funeral. Years ago, my father had tried and failed to get my mother to have a service for Charlie when it was clear to everyone but her that he was not coming home. She had balked and then not spoken to my father for nearly a week. But now we have found him, it's time for all of us to grieve.

The plot is at the top of the hill in the cemetery by the high school, not far from where Trill and I had gone to look at the stars on Grad Night. Ariel and I help my mother navigate the steep drive, the slippery grass.

The funeral Mass had been packed. Five hundred people at least, with a broadcast outside for those who had come too late for seats. Jericho did not attend. Trill was absent too.

"You okay, Grammy?" Ariel asks as my mother lets out a haunting cry at the site of the empty grave, the small coffin suspended above it.

We sit together in the folding chairs assembled at the gravesite under a makeshift tent that shudders beneath the rain. It's just us here: the only family Charlie has left.

Father Tavares is ancient now, but he sees Charlie into his final resting place and offers my mother the same kindness and gentleness he has for decades.

When the service is over, I linger for a moment before touching my hand to the cold casket

"Bye, Charlie Brown," I say.

My mother didn't want a reception. She didn't want the house crawling with looky-loos and media. The news vans outside the church had sent her spiraling. I managed to keep her from watching the various press conferences, from reading the paper with Nathan and Jake's photos on the front page.

"I just want to go to bed," she says when we get home.

"Okay, Mom," I say and help her change out of her black dress, unzipping it and watching it fall like a dark puddle at her feet.

She turns to me, and the sight of her—old, fragile, broken—nearly brings me to my knees.

"Did they check?" she asks. "To see if he had the birthmark, the one shaped like a heart, right where his heart is?"

I swallow the sob forming like a bubble in my throat.

"They did, Mom."

"You're sure? They're sure it's Charlie?"

"They are."

"It was an accident?" she asks.

"Yes," I say. "Just a terrible accident."

I have explained at least three times that it was only an accident. That Nathan had been scared. That he had made a horrible mistake. She doesn't know that Nathan is gone now, though. There was no funeral, and I have blocked the news on her iPad. I am not sure I will ever be able to tell her.

My grief over Nathan's suicide is complicated. I am still filled with anger toward him when I think of all he stole from us with his decisions. But then, I sometimes find myself awash in sorrowful compassion when I remember: he was just a teenager then. And like me, he made a dreadful mistake, panicked and told a lie, one that would hold him in its grips for decades. We weren't so different, Nathan and I.

As much as Sylvia meant to me, as much as her poems felt like mirrors held up to my own life, I had never understood her suicide. I never wanted to believe it was possible to go from wanting something so much, to wanting nothing at all anymore. I could never forgive Sylvia for taking her life. But maybe I can forgive Nathan.

In the family room, Ariel has changed into her pajamas and is curled up on the couch with Daisy, rain pounding against the glass. I worry about the basement flooding again. The insidious mold coming back. I realize that we need to sell this house. Maybe not this summer, but soon. My mother needs memory care. Ariel needs to go back to college. And I need—what?

"This is so sad," Ariel says, gently stroking Daisy's fur. "All of it."

I nod.

"Have you talked to your friend?" she asks.

At first, I assume she means Lisa or Amanda. Lisa has called twice and left messages asking what she can do for us. She has brought six different casseroles so we wouldn't have to cook for at least a week. Amanda has checked in every evening; she knows that nighttime is the hardest with my mother. *Sundowning*, it's called.

But Ariel doesn't mean Lisa or Amanda; she means Trill.

"I'm sure she's back home in New York," I say.

"Maybe you should go there," Ariel says.

"Where?"

"To New York."

"And do what?" I ask, laughing. But her suggestion sticks like a barb in my chest.

"Find her?"

Would it be that easy? Could I just get in the car or hop on a train and leave this place? Go find Trill? Go find my life?

I think of Charlie's *Choose Your Own Adventure* stories. *Stay in Quimby, turn the page. Go to New York, turn to page 12.*

"I can't leave Grammy," I say, the excuse I have been using for a lifetime.

"Yes, you can. I can take care of her while you're gone. It's summer. You should go." Ariel's eyes were wet and pleading. "You love her, Mom."

After Ariel disappears into her room, I find *Flight of the Navigator* on streaming and curl up on the couch. It's the story of a boy who falls into a ravine and wakes up eight years into the future. But while his brother and parents have aged, the boy remains exactly the same.

Charlie would have loved this movie. And even though it's campy, Trill might have too.

I can't sleep, not even after two cups of Ariel's sleepy tea, and so I get up and go to the desk in the family room and grab a piece of my mother's stationery. I try to recall the last time I wrote a letter and can't. But as my pen begins to move across the paper, something shifts inside me. My thoughts assemble like clouds, the storm in my chest gathering until there is no option but release. The music of the words is like rain on an old barn roof, underneath which two girls hold onto each other for dear life.

Dear, dear life. *Dear Trillium*, I begin. *I'm sorry.*

Spring 2024

SHE WRITES BACK. Longhand, in that lovely script of hers. We become old-fashioned pen pals. No email or Facebook Messenger, no FaceTime or Zoom. Just words on a page. Permanent and real.

She tells me that her father is failing, in hospice; it won't be long before he passes. She says she will miss him dearly, but she won't miss listening to Rachel Maddow on full volume or the deviled ham and mustard sandwiches he eats for lunch every day.

I tell her about my mother's latest fall, this time breaking her hip. An accident that puts her in the hospital for a week and rehab for six more. I tell her that it is with a heavy heart and great relief that I put her name on the waitlist for the local memory care center. I tell her that since we found Charlie, she seems to have slipped into a new realm. One where my father is still alive. Where Charlie is still a boy. And while it breaks my heart when she speaks of them, she also appears to be happy. All her sharp edges have dulled into a softness I barely recognize.

Trill tells me she is taking a couple film classes at NYU, getting back to the basics. And do I remember that movie we made?

I remember, I write. *Of course, I remember.* I tell her that Ariel is also enrolled in two courses at the college for the fall semester: Art History and Ceramics. She's still working at Carmello's and volunteering at the library. For the spring semester she plans to take a full course load and, maybe, transfer back to UVM for the fall. "I'm going to be the oldest sophomore on the planet," she moaned. "You're going to be brilliant," I said.

And what will you do then? Trill asks. *In your empty little nest?*

But I don't know how to answer, and so instead of plans, I send her poems. And it feels again like I am offering up delicate slivers of my heart.

Our nest. The nest that none of us has been able to leave. My mother, because she was waiting for Charlie. Me, because of my mother. And Ariel because of what the world outside has become. But now, everything has changed. It is time for our respective flights. Hope is the thing with feathers, after all.

Ariel and I start fixing up the house. It's still a seller's market, and there's no mortgage. We could probably walk away with enough to pay not only for her college, but for my mother's care, and then some. Next summer, maybe.

We start with the family room; the shag carpeting and paneling need to go. But first, I pull the tip line from the wall and toss it in the dumpster I've rented, the one parked in the driveway.

We remove wallpaper and paint. We pull up carpet and sand the beautiful oak floors that have been hiding underneath. We buy new appliances, which come to our doorstep swaddled in soft white wrappings. New fixtures and faucets and finials.

When spring arrives, I will tackle the landscaping, planting a perennial garden replete with red tulips.

Someone will love this home, I write to Trill. *Maybe a family. Maybe someone with children.*

One Sunday afternoon in April my cell phone buzzes in my pocket as I am coming inside with groceries. Probably the memory care center. My mother has had some setbacks in the last week. A bout with Covid, then a UTI. But when I pull the phone out of my pocket, my breath catches, and I answer.

On the other end of the line, I hear windchimes. She's *here.*

"Hi!" I say. As if no time has passed at all.

"Can you ditch school early tomorrow?" she asks, like we're seventeen still.

"It's the eclipse tomorrow," I say.

"I know, that's why I'm here!"

"We have a whole thing planned at school. Why don't you come?" I ask.

"To school?"

"Yes! Last period. You can talk to my AP kids about your work. We could even show one of your films. It'll be great."

"Really?" she asks.

"*Come,*" I insist.

That night I can barely sleep. It feels like I imagined the entire thing. But when I check my phone, Trill's number does, indeed, appear in the list of recent calls.

The next day drags, just as the days had dragged back when I was in high school. I watch the clock, listen to the hammering *tick-tock* and roll my head to get the kinks out of my neck. The students are restless too. School ends at two o'clock, but we're hoping they will stick around for the eclipse. The science teachers have everything set up down on the football field, including cardboard eclipse glasses and telescopes with solar filters. The Family and Consumer Sciences teacher had her students make black-and-white cookies and Moon Pies. Amanda will recite a poem before the eclipse, and I have something planned for the moments of totality.

At lunch, I am sitting with Amanda when Trill steps tentatively through the cafeteria doors, looking anxious. She's wearing a long red floral dress and an oversized cardigan. Her hair is down. She looks beautiful.

My arm shoots up in the air, waving her over.

"That's her?" Amanda asks, squeezing my arm. She knows Trill is coming today. Over wine during Christmas Break, I had told her everything that happened the summer we lost Charlie. It felt so good to share this with someone who didn't judge me for my secrecy. She hadn't come out to her family until she was in her forties. "It's never too late," she had said.

"Trill," I say, feeling an ancient flutter of wings in my belly.

I stand up and give her a hug.

"I have a surprise for you!" I say. "You brought a DVD of your film, right?"

She nods.

"Awesome."

My AP Lit kids, my seniors, are excited for Trill's visit. Two of them have plans to study film in college. I'd been trying to get Ryan Flannigan to come to talk about her experience as an actress, but she has, so far, politely declined. She's a private person; I don't blame her. But the kids are thrilled to meet someone who works in film, even if it's behind the scenes.

When the bell rings, Trill follows me from the cafeteria to Mr. Howard's old classroom, mine now, where the kids are waiting. Kelsey, the class artist, somehow procured a roll of bright red paper and has made a makeshift red carpet leading halfway down the hall and into the classroom.

The kids are peeking out at us from inside, and I whisper, "You've got the fancy-ass dress on. Now, you just need to slip off your shoes."

She grins and wrinkles her nose, then takes off her boots and socks before walking the runway, barefoot, to her waiting audience.

We walk down to the football field after the last bell rings. The hill is steep, and we descend slowly.

"My knees are shot," I explain. "I'm fine on flat ground, but hills kill me."

"I'm thinking about moving back to The Farm," she says.

Stunned, I try to stop, but gravity and momentum are having their way with me.

"Here?" I say. Trill is coming home? Flutter. "I didn't think anyone moved *to* Quimby," I tease.

She grins. "Jericho's here. When my dad is gone, it will just be the two of us. We need each other."

"How is he?" I ask, chest heavy. "Jericho?"

"He's good," she says. "He had a showing at a gallery in the city last fall. A little place in Soho. *The Museum of Innocents* pieces? He sold three of them to a collector from China. He donated the proceeds to the Innocence Project."

"That's wonderful," I say.

"He's also starting to sculpt again. He's been making these beautiful birds out of willow branches. They're so stunning. You should go see them sometime. Go see *him*." This is not a suggestion but a plea.

My eyes sting. "I will," I promise.

When we get to the football field, I grab two pairs of eclipse glasses and hand her one.

A few kids from my class come up and nervously ask Trill the questions they didn't get to before the bell rang.

For a half hour or so, we mingle on the field, eating Moon Pies and drinking Capri-Suns. We got a spring snowstorm a week ago, and there are still patches of snow on the football field. It will be a couple weeks before they bring out the pole vault pit and start track practice.

"It's starting," Amanda says to us excitedly and makes her way to the podium.

"Everybody put on your glasses," she says into the microphone, and the students dutifully obey. She recites the poem "A Solar Eclipse" by Ella Wheeler Wilcox, and when she finishes, everyone is quiet. In this strange silence, as the sky goes from bright blue to a strange dusk, as the air cools and the birds cease their singing, I remember watching the *Challenger* launch into space. And when this odd twilight becomes total darkness, the sun swallowed whole, fear rises in my chest, and I reach for Trill's hand.

"You can look now!" Amanda says.

The kids chatter nervously, then quiet in hushed wonder.

We take off our glasses and look at the black hole that was the sun, and I feel oddly unsettled.

"Don't worry," Trill says, sensing my unease. "It'll come back!"

Sure enough, when the shadow begins to pass, the sun shines bright again.

All cool, all blue, I think.

"Trill?"

"Yes, Lucy?" she says, the lines at her eyes deep as she smiles.

But I don't speak. Instead, I smile and squeeze her hand before letting it go and making my way to the podium.

"Is everybody ready?" I ask, looking out at my students' expectant faces. At Trill's expectant face. They all know exactly what to do. "Three, two, one . . ."

And we open our mouths wide and howl.

ACKNOWLEDGMENTS

FROM THE TIME I first put pen to paper, I have had teachers assuring me that writing is my superpower. Thank you all for giving me that cape and making me believe I could fly. You are all in this book (disguised as a farmer's daughter, a hairstylist, a detective, and even a priest), but truly, you are in *every* book I write.

This novel, like so many, would not exist in its current form without my first readers. Amy Hatvany and Jillian Cantor, your fingerprints are all over these pages. I am so grateful to you both for your unflagging generosity, kindness, and sage advice.

Neal Griffin, you are my go-to guy whenever the police show up on the page. As someone who (thankfully) has no firsthand experience with law enforcement from which to draw, I would be at a loss without your expertise.

Molly McCloy, it has been such a delight to reengage with you after all these years. You are a stellar writer and reader, and I appreciate your making sure I got the love story between Trill and Edie right.

Miranda Beverly-Whittemore, I can always count on you to show up with your moral support and delicious snacks. There's no one I'd rather be eating TJ's pumpkin pastries with in these mucky trenches.

Toni Donk, I can always rely on you to make me laugh (and let me cry). Thank you for the memes and TikToks and for always being one of the first people to read whatever it is that I write.

Janet Dunphy-Brown, thank you for being a friend for fifty years now. Writing about being a teenager in the NEK conjured the best memories, and you are a part of them all.

Carlene Riccelli, thanks for supporting my writing and teaching. Don Howard was breathed to life at your behest. (And sorry about the food in these pages: it'll be a tough choice between American Chop Suey and tuna noodle casserole for my book event fare.) And Angie Vorhies, you'll find (finally) all three of your daughters' names in these pages. Thank you for supporting SDWI!

David Forrer, you held my hand through the entire process with this one: from the moment the tip line rang. Thank you for believing in my writing and sticking with me, even when things are tough.

To my new team at Crooked Lane Books: thank you to Matthew Martz and Marcia Markland for loving this story and these characters, to Thai Fantauzzi Perez, Julia Abbott, Shannon O'Neill, Dulce Botello, Mikaela Bender, and Beata Garrett for helping share Edie and Trill's story with the world. To Rebecca Nelson for the stunning cover, and to Elizabeth Oliver for your fine-tuning. Thank you.

To my family, please know I still write mainly to make you proud.

Patrick Stewart, you've been with me on this trek from the start. Sixteen books later, and you're still here? How lucky am I?

Lastly, to Kick and Maims, please know it is you two who give me a reason to keep making art, even when the world is on fire. Because, as you both know so well, that is what artists do. I love you.